Unseen Riches

Book Two

THE CHRONICLES OF THE GOLDEN FRONTIER

UNSEEN RICHES

~

GILBERT MORRIS

and

J. LANDON FERGUSON

CROSSWAY BOOKS • WHEATON, ILLINOIS

A DIVISION OF GOOD NEWS PUBLISHERS

Unseen Riches

Published by Crossway Books
A division of Good News Publishers
1300 Crescent Street
Wheaton, Illinois 60187

Cover illustration: Tony Meers

Cover design: Cindy Kiple

First printing, 1999

Printed in the United States of America

ISBN 1-58134-022-2

Library of Congress Cataloging-in-Publication Data

Morris, Gilbert.
Unseen riches / Gilbert Morris and J. Landon Ferguson.
p. cm. — (Chronicles of the golden frontier ; bk. #2)
ISBN 1-58134-022-2 (alk. paper)
I. Ferguson, J. Landon, 1952- . II. Title. III. Series: Morris, Gilbert. Chronicles of the golden frontier ; bk. #2.
PS3563.08742U57 1999
813'.54—dc21 98-51867
CIP

15 14 13 12 11 10 09 08 07 06 05 04 03 02 01 00 99
15 14 13 12 11 10 9 8 7 6 5 4 3 2 1

For my father

J. L. "Buddy" Ferguson,

who encouraged me through some very difficult times

and taught me that hope is a mighty powerful thing.

J. Landon Ferguson

Contents

PART ONE

~

A Journey of Faith

CHAPTER

1

Good-bye to Virginia City

The late summer sunset left the sky over Virginia City, Nevada, awash in a blur of layered violet. The heat of the day lingered in the dead air as Jennifer DeSpain, tired and exhausted from packing, readied herself for a hot bath. Abe Washington had been kind enough to fill the tub by bringing buckets of hot water. Abe, a muscular black man in his fifties who'd grown close to the family, had worked all day without complaint, packing and preparing for the move.

Abby, Jennifer's ten-year-old daughter, came shuffling in, sloshing another bucket of water to top off the tub. "Thank you, Abby," Jennifer said tiredly as she pinned her hair up over her head.

"You're welcome, Mama." Abby smiled. Her long and dark and wavy hair bordered her young face with bright blue eyes as she gave her mother a final glance before she left, pulling the door closed behind her.

Taking a deep breath, Jennifer glanced around at the flowered wallpaper. The small room with a tub adjacent to her bedroom was almost barren, everything having been packed. *This has been a good house—it seems so long ago since we came here—almost like another lifetime back in New Orleans*. But that was ten years ago now; she'd reached thirty. Her 5'7" figure was full and robust, though her waist had not thickened. The thick, auburn hair still had the shine of youth; a widow's peak accented her oval face, and a small mole flecked her left cheek. She had a straight, English nose and fair skin; her green eyes with long lashes had the shine of emeralds. Her generous mouth faintly smiled, turning up the corners of full lips with well-defined edges. No doubt, she was still an attractive woman.

So much has happened since New Orleans, she thought as she disrobed and prepared to step into the sudsy hot water. She had inherited a newspaper in Virginia City and had come west to run it. Her experience at the *Picayune*, a prominent New Orleans newspaper, had given her a good background in journalism. She had left all security and arrived in Virginia City to find the newspaper defunct and her editor, Jason Stone, a drunkard. The years in Virginia City had seen rivalries with the other newspaper and corruption and fires and the discovery of the Big Bonanza.

"Ohhh! That's good!" Jennifer sighed, settling down into the hot, soapy water. She lay there, her eyes closed, thinking suddenly of her abortive engagement with a lawyer, Charles Fitzgerald. She had discovered his ambitions were selfish and had broken off the engagement. *I wonder why I always fall for the wrong kind of men*, she thought. *Is it bad luck or is it my own blindness? God kept me from making the worst mistake a woman can make*, she thought, and, picking up a soft, white cloth, soaped it and began washing her face. The memory of Charles faded, and she turned her thoughts to Jason Stone. With a warm glow of satisfaction, she thought of how he had defeated his alcoholism and turned his life over to God. Quick images flowed as she remembered how he'd summoned up enough courage to single-handedly challenge the town tough, a brute who'd threatened Jennifer's welfare.

"How *do* I feel about Jason?" Jennifer paused and sat in the tub, startled by the echoes of her voice. A troubling thought came to her, for ever since Jason had told her that he loved her, she had fallen into a state of confusion and uncertainty. Although she cared for Jason, she didn't trust herself after the miserably failed romance with Charles. *I wonder how I get myself into such situations? Do other women do things like this?*

Deliberately setting the problem of Jason Stone aside, Jennifer soaked for fifteen minutes. The relaxing tingle of the hot water soothed her tired muscles as she relaxed in the tub. *I can't wait to get to the cool mountain air,* she thought as she rinsed off the grit from a hot day.

She had just sold her successful newspaper, *The Miner's News*, and now she thought of her new destination—the boomtowns in the Colorado Territory, a region she'd passed through on her train ride to the West. She had loved the steep gorges and green valleys of the Rocky Mountains and had whispered, "Someday I'll live here and have a newspaper—the best in the country."

But her thoughts were interrupted as something slimy wiggled under the water against her!

Scrambling from the tub in horror, Jennifer stared at the water and saw a large, green head appear. The two big eyes blinked at her, and a bullfrog quickly disappeared under the water.

"Abby!" Jennifer screamed at the top of her lungs. "Abby! You get in here right now!" She grabbed a towel and wrapped it around her while she waited impatiently.

The bathroom door eased open and Abby stuck her head in, an innocent smile on her pretty young face. "Yes, Mama? What is it?"

"Abby! Get that awful frog out of my tub right now!" Jennifer shouted angrily. "I should punish you for this!"

Her smile disappearing, Abby went and thrust a hand in the water. "I was just funnin', Mother!" she said defensively. "You don't have to get so upset!" In a moment she had the long-legged frog and pulled him from the water. Holding the frog close to her chest, she stroked his flat, green head gently. "Did that mean woman scare you?" she asked the frog in a sweet voice.

"Get out!" Jennifer said pointing at the door. "I'll deal with you later."

Abby scooted out of the bathroom, laughing and amused by her mother's lack of a sense of humor.

Staring at the water, Jennifer thought, *A frog has been in my bath-water—oh well, I'm too tired to worry about it.* A frown brought faint wrinkles to her brow. She worried about this headstrong young daughter of hers. *Grant would never have done that*, she thought. Grant, her eleven-year-old son, was very mature and responsible for his age. He'd done his best to be a man and look after his mother through hard times. He resembled Jennifer, having the same green eyes and thick, auburn hair. But Abby, with her dark and wavy hair and piercing blue eyes, resembled her father, Drake DeSpain. She was like him in other ways, unfortunately, demanding and stubborn and scheming.

As Jennifer dried with a large, white fluffy towel, memories flashed through her mind—especially of how Drake had swept her off her feet when she was only seventeen. He'd been so romantic and affectionate then, and after a brief courtship they had married. Grant was born the first year and Abby the second, but Drake had wandered away, most of the time pursuing ambitious dreams, leaving her with the children and little with which to get by. Then Drake got in a scuffle over a card game on a riverboat and shot a prominent man. His sentence in a horrible Louisiana prison became too much for him, and he was shot in the back in an escape attempt. Then Jennifer remembered her last touching moments with him on his deathbed. *He seemed so absolutely helpless and pitiful*, she remembered. But she recalled the light she saw in his eyes after she told him the story of Jesus and, as if by a miracle, he accepted Christ as his Savior. *At least he's in heaven*, she thought. The other memories deeply saddened her, but that thought provided her with some comfort. She may have made a mistake as a young girl, falling for a rogue, but the Lord meant for the ultimate good to come out of it—the salvation of Drake. And if *he* could be saved, then grace truly was amazing, and there is hope for everyone.

Jennifer was almost dressed as Lita banged on the door. "Miss Jenny, supper almost ready! Our last supper in Virginia City."

"I'm coming," Jennifer said as she perked up. She smiled gently, thinking of Lita's round and smiling black face. Lita had been her faithful servant and nanny to the children since Jennifer's mother died back in New Orleans. She was a pillar of strength in the family, and as Jennifer left the bathroom, a surge of warm gratitude came to her. *Thank You, Lord, for sending Lita and Abe—and Jason!*

~

At the office of *The Miner's News*, Jason Stone packed his personal belongings. His room in the back of the building was small, but he still shook his head at the number of items left to pack. "Hard to believe how much junk a man can collect in such a short time," he said disgustedly.

Grant DeSpain stood watching him with interest. Jason had become his best friend—and even somewhat of a hero. In the past few years, Jason had taught Grant how to write and print newspaper articles. But most of all, Grant admired Jason's courage for standing up to the town bully; something nobody else would do. Grant smiled at Jason's dilemma, his green eyes forming slits. "How did you collect so much? It hasn't been that long since you lost everything in the fire."

"Don't know," Jason murmured, scratching his head. Jason was no more than 5' 10", but he had big shoulders and an angular frame. His jaw was set square below striking blue eyes. There was a scar on his left cheek from the fight with Big Ned, the town thug, but it was a battle scar he wore proudly. He pushed his straight blond hair out of his face and grinned at the boy. "Well, are you packed?"

"Sure I am," Grant shrugged. "Been packed since yesterday. " He was efficient for a boy his age and sharp as a new knife. He watched Jason remove newspaper articles and pictures from the cluttered, board wall. When Jason came to the calendar, he found a pencil and circled the date, August 28, 1875.

"Tomorrow morning, Colorado, here we come," Jason said. He paused for a moment with a faraway look in his eyes, the kind of look a man has when he's remembering important scenes in his mind. "There's too many bad memories here. I'm ready to leave."

Nodding in agreement, Grant asked, "What do you reckon it's like in Black Hawk?"

Shrugging his shoulders, Jason swung around to Grant. "According to your mother, it's some kind of beautiful mountain town—some kind of gold boomtown. We're newspaper people, and we have to follow the news—go where things are happening, Grant." Jason bent over and stacked items neatly in a huge trunk.

"It could be rough country. I know winters in the Rockies can be tough, plus being in a mining town—you know how that can be from living right here."

Grant could only imagine. He'd passed through Colorado on a train and enjoyed the high country scenery most of all. About all he could remember was rock walls and huge, green mountains covered with fir and spruce trees. "Do you reckon we can get a paper going there?"

"Why not? We've already survived some of the toughest times a mining town could ever see." Jason smiled; he knew Grant was a worrier. "No need to fret, Grant. Think of all the new people and the wild outdoors—no more desert, sand, and grit!"

Giving in, Grant smiled. It was true—he could be worrying about nothing. "I wish we were already there," he said, eagerness in his eyes. "I'll bet we—"

The front door banged open and Abe entered, his huge arms bulging from the short sleeves of his white cotton shirt. He came through the office and to the back where Jason and Grant stood. Glancing at the two, he said, "Lita say supper ready—y'all come on now."

"Good, I'm hungry enough to eat a stick of stove wood." Jason nodded. "All this moving and packing is too much work. What's Lita got fixed for supper, Abe?"

Abe shook his gray-haired head and frowned. "I don't rightly know, Mr. Jason. All she told me was to come and fetch y'all."

Grant knew these were two men who had great respect for each other—for each had proven himself in trying times where most men would've failed. "Everything Lita fixes is good! C'mon, let's go, Jason!" Grant said, hurrying his friend. "We don't wanna make her mad!"

"Sure don't!" Abe agreed. "Don't let dat woman get on no rampage!"

Grant smiled. *Abe's sweet on Lita!* he thought, *and he sure doesn't want to make her upset!*

The three left the office and stepped into the dark and noisy streets of Virginia City. The saloons jingled with glass and music and coarse miner's talk, while their dim lights shone through hazy windows. The smell of the day had been dry dust and smoke and sun-bleached wood, but the town continued to busily reap the profits of the mills processing gold and silver taken from hundreds of feet below.

~

Lita had taken great pride in laying out one of the finest suppers she'd ever prepared. By scooting two tables together and covering them with oil cloth, she'd made a display of delights fit for royalty. A pile of golden, steaming fried chicken and plump biscuits sat next to a dish of browned chicken gravy sprinkled with black pepper. A drift of fluffy mashed potatoes rose high above the edges of a heavy, glass bowl. Stacked like firewood, the boiled, bright yellow corn on the cob glistened with melted butter. Beside that, a pot of greens sat simmering in the juices of onions and salt pork. A heaping pile of butter beans supported a huge serving spoon, and a blackened, smoked ham rested heavily on a carving board next to the carving knife. Of course, there was Abe's favorite, a black skillet of fresh and tender corn bread. Dessert sat on the stove, two apple pies cooling and filling the room with their sweet, aromatic fragrance.

"Dat should do it," Lita said, giving the table a thorough inspection. Moving a huge pitcher of ice water to the table, the big dinner reminded her of cooking down South, where she'd been a slave in her early years. Now in her fifties, Lita held no animosity for the hardships in life but praised the Lord for each and every day. Noting that she had forgotten to set the knives and forks beside the plates, her round face distorted. "Reckon I'm gettin' too old if I can't remember to put the silverware on!"

Admiring her work, Lita's pleasant face lit up approvingly with a self-conscious smile. Perspiration glistened on her forehead underneath the red scarf she wore over her head. There had been little romance in her long life until she met Abe, the big man that would soon be coming through the door. Although Lita had put on a show of discontent and impatience with Abe, it soon became obvious that she would never let him escape. "If dis don't fill dat big man up

I don't know what will!" She'd gone to great trouble to find butter beans and greens, some southern delights she knew the big Georgian would love.

When Jennifer entered the dining room, she was astonished with the fine dinner ready and waiting on the table. "Why, Lita! This looks like a celebration!"

"It is, Miss Jenny," Lita said as she set napkins beside the plates. "I'm ready to get out of the likes of this town."

"Is there anything I can help you with?" Jennifer asked, straightening the collar on her blue and white gingham dress.

"No, ma'am. You just round up Abby—the men should be comin' any minute now."

That reminded Jennifer and her face changed. "Do you know what she did, Lita? She put a frog in my bathwater!"

Shaking her head, Lita sighed. "I tell you Miss Jenny—dat child gonna be trouble when she grows up!"

"When she grows up? No, she's trouble *now*!" Shortly after Jennifer left to search for Abby, the men stepped through the front door discussing moving the trunks in the morning by using a freighter Abe had borrowed. When they came into the dining and kitchen area, they all stopped and fell silent, staring at the table. Jason spoke first. "This looks like a feast! Do I smell apple pie?"

"You sure do!" Lita confirmed. "Before y'all sit down, wash up under the pump. Go on now!"

Following orders, Jason, Abe, and Grant moved to the pump mounted in the kitchen. Jason worked the pump handle while Grant washed up and Abe stood in line.

Jennifer returned with Abby in tow. Abby had grown irritated since she couldn't bring her frog to dinner. The men were cleaned up and everybody took their seats. Making sure all was in order, Lita sat down at her end of the table opposite Jennifer.

Lita rolled her big brown eyes to Jennifer. "Miss Jenny, this here being our last supper in Virginia City, I'd like to ask you to say a special grace over this meal."

"I think that's a wonderful idea," Jennifer responded. Her bath had refreshed her and she felt good. Bowing her head with a pleasant smile, she said a blessing. "Dear Lord, we'd like to return a special thanks for looking out for all of us through trying times—for bringing us all to You in one way or another—for leading us in the right direction. We are about to depart for a new adventure in life, and I pray You'll continue to show us Your grace and mercy. You have blessed us and we thank You for this fine meal in the name of Jesus."

"Pass the chicken!" Grant said almost before she had finished. "I'm so hungry my stomach thinks my throat's been cut!"

Lita picked up the plate of hot fried chicken and held it over for Grant to select a piece "Eat all you want," Lita nodded vigorously. "We got plenty." Grant took a piece of crispy breast and set it on his plate. He had always been a little bashful but had gained confidence in his maturing experiences with hardship. Although establishing a new life in some strange town troubled him to some degree, he was ready for the adventure.

"I haven't seen a meal this good since I can remember," Jason said as he heaped a pile of mashed potatoes on his plate. "Someone pass me some of that gravy." Happily, he enjoyed the company of the small band that had grown so close together through their trials in Virginia City. Being a Harvard graduate, he had a good mind and had been able to make the jump to journalism better than most. But his weakness had been alcohol, which had left him in ruins. After years of failure, Jennifer had finally convinced him that there was a Higher Power in the form of a loving and caring God and that God could help him defeat his troubled life. When Jason hit bottom, he accepted the Lord and found strength and courage that had before been unknown; he became the man he'd always wished he could be. Yet uncertainty remained to some degree, considering he'd seen his share of trouble. Wearing a simple smile as he enjoyed Lita's cooking, he was willing to venture to Colorado as he eyed Jennifer—the woman he was madly in love with.

"Tell us about this new place—Black Hawk," Jason said around bites. "You say you've already purchased a building there?"

Touching a napkin to her mouth, Jennifer couldn't hold back a smile, revealing her anticipation. "I know it sounds stupid—to buy a building I've never seen—especially since you'd think I'd have learned my lesson here the first time I did it, but, yes, I have. It's an office building in the business district and has a stone front. It's not very old and has a good stove for heat and windows facing out front. Best of all, it's a big office divided into three rooms."

"Sounds nice," Jason agreed. "How'd you come by something like that?"

"I saw it advertised in a Denver paper," Jennifer continued, eager to tell of her good fortune. "When I contacted them, they sent me a description, and it sounds like it will work out perfectly for us." Her face showed the satisfaction of rewarding research. "I've already contacted another company in Denver, and we'll have a new and modern press—everything will be new!"

"I can't wait!" Grant said enthusiastically, speaking with his mouth full. "I wanna learn how to run a new press!"

Glancing at Grant, Jason had a great deal of respect for him, a young boy who'd set his mind to learning the newspaper business. "Sure you will, and I'll have to learn how to work it, too," Jason reminded Grant.

"I hope wherever we stay has a big kitchen and a big stove!" Lita said, getting her own wishes into the gay conversation. The kitchen was Lita's domain, for she loved to cook and spent most of her time there. A devout Christian, she'd spent her early life as a house slave on a plantation outside of New Orleans. She'd learned to cook at an early age, but life as a slave had been hard and cruel, especially after the war when she was freed with no money and nowhere to go. Her prayers had been answered when Jennifer showed up at her front door seeking domestic help.

"You get some of this ham!" Lita ordered Abe as she placed a thick slice of the pink meat on his plate. Abe mumbled in response, his mouth full. Lita, a stern realist, felt it was her job on earth to see to it that folks remained fed and healthy, the first criterion for a good life.

"What about Black Hawk?" Jason asked, his mind overflowing with questions. "You have any idea what it's like?"

Rolling her green eyes as if remembering, Jennifer replied, "It's said to be the richest square mile on earth—of course, they're referring to the mining of gold and silver. Actually, from what I'm told, Black Hawk is the center of the community of several small towns, and Central City is right next to it. It's not far from Denver, almost thirty miles west up into the mountains. We'll be taking a train from Denver right up to Black Hawk."

"I take it this is no tent-roofed mining camp," Jason figured.

"Not at all," Jennifer said. "Black Hawk was incorporated in 1864 and is a well-established town."

"I can't wait to see it," Jason said. He had been reluctant to make the move. To make the decision more acceptable, he fantasized an alpine town nestled in the conifers of massive mountains.

"I can't wait to leave! No place could be worse than this old place!" Abby said impatiently between bites. Having been constantly in trouble, Abby blamed her surroundings, the town of Virginia City, a boring place with nothing for a girl her age to do.

"I wonder if they got any fish in dem mountains," Lita mumbled as she gnawed on a chicken bone. "I sure miss my fishin'!" She rose from the table to bring over a cooling apple pie and waved it under Abe's nose.

"Dat smells mighty good," Abe said, rather reserved. It was then that Lita noticed Abe had eaten without a word. Although he was usually a quiet man, all had been allowed to put in their feelings about the trip and their soon-to-be home—yet Abe hadn't said a thing. Everyone knew he was going along because he was crazy about Lita and would go anywhere she did. "What's wrong with you? Ain't you excited to be moving out of dis hot and dusty place?"

Abe raised his eyes to Lita as she stood over him dishing out hot apple pie. He had been a superstitious man all his life and still was. Having been raised in slavery in Georgia, he'd learned a trade of shoeing mules. Once freed and eager to leave the South, he had ventured west, where he had heard the miners worked countless mules, and eventually found his way to Virginia City. He'd kept to himself, a lone black man that nobody bothered, because Abe was a huge and muscular man. One day he spotted Lita and, like a hungry puppy, he'd stayed at her heels ever since. They'd been through a lot together, facing fears and uncertainty. Lita was bent on leading Abe to the Lord and felt she'd made great strides. He paused before he answered Lita's question. He knew his response would get him into trouble, but then again, he was a man of truth.

"A bird flew in my window," Abe intoned gloomily, his voice deep and heavy. "Ain't no good gonna come from it."

Lita swatted the back of Abe's head with a cotton towel she held. "Shame on you! You know about the Lord now, and you know there ain't no call to be superstitious!"

Abe knew he'd angered Lita, something he hated, but he knew what he saw. Although he was trying his best to believe in God and read the Bible, he wasn't fully acquainted with Christian ways. Sitting like a stump, he quietly savored the helping of apple pie, his brow knitted and his dark eyes troubled.

After Lita's outstanding supper, the group wandered their own ways. Jennifer put the children to bed and then helped Lita with the kitchen, where they not only had to wash dishes but also had to pack them. Abe and Jason readied the big freighter in front of the house, loading some of the trunks in the dark. The night air was still and thick, and the mining machinery works could be heard in the distance. "I guess we're off first thing in the morning," Jason said.

"Yes, sir, I reckon so," Abe responded as he shifted a heavy trunk up in the wagon where he stood.

"Say, Abe—" Jason said as he leaned on the wagon and swung his eyes up to the big man.

"Yes, sir?"

"You don't *really* believe that bird is bad luck, do you?"

Abe shook his head in dismay. "It's a bad sign," Abe said with certainty.

"Humph!" Jason grunted, not liking anything that indicated ill fortune. "Well, I guess I'll see you in the morning," and he strolled off into the night, heading back to the office where he slept.

Abe turned his gaze upward, a sky frothy with stars. He wondered about the heavens, if indeed there was really somebody up there looking down on him. Finally, he said, "Well, Lord, You know all 'bout dat bird flyin' in my window. I guess if You can walk on water, You can take care of us anyhow!"

CHAPTER

2

Excitement on the Train

The shrill clarion call of a rooster broke the silence of the early dawn, awaking Jennifer. Rising slowly, she sat on the edge of her bed, gathering her thoughts. A quick glance out the window revealed the orange hue of daylight trembling over the mountaintop. *So much to remember,* she thought as she jumped to her feet. A faint tickle of excitement stirred her—a long trip to a new home and a new business in a new land. *I hardly know what to do first,* she thought as she took off her nightgown and found the dress she'd laid out to wear on her trip. It was a green and white calico dress, one that made her eyes shine with color. Quickly checking, she saw her handbag and travel bag sitting next to each other on the floor. *I'll have to keep my handbag with me all the time,* she reminded herself. *It's got all the important goods in it.*

Jennifer had sold most of the furniture with the house, since it wasn't worth the cost of moving. She sat at her bureau for the last time and brushed her long hair thinking, *This has been a good old house. I'm going to miss it.* Glancing around at her bedroom furniture, the thought came that leaving it was like losing some dear old friends. Suddenly, a faint sadness touched her as she realized she was leaving something she had established on her own—a home and a good business. *It's like leaving part of myself behind!* Sitting silently, her face expressionless, she again recalled the memories of Virginia City—Mark Twain, Miner Tom, the struggles and the victories, such precious memories. It wasn't the first time a doubt crossed her mind, weakening her will.

But I felt the same way when I left the Picayune *and New Orleans*, she remembered. *And it was the boldness of seeking adventure that brought all of this!* She shook off her doubts, saying aloud, "Well, Lord, You'll have to guide me all the way!" This encouraged Jennifer's spirits as the waves of the amber sun peeked through her window. *We have a lot to look forward to and a lot of work to do. I'd better get with it!*

Downstairs, Lita was already hard at work making sure the boxes were in order and that everything, except for the coffeepot and coffee cups, was packed. Always thinking ahead about meals, she had leftovers from the night before safely tucked away in a large bag she carried. A gentle knock came from the kitchen door.

"It's open," Lita called.

Abe stepped in, closing the door silently behind him, his hat in his hand. He was dressed in his usual blue overalls and white cotton, short-sleeved shirt. "What you wants me to load, Lita?" Abe asked politely.

"You sit down here and don't give me no talk about loadin'!" Lita ordered. "I can't have no man of mine working on no empty stomach!"

As Abe took his seat, Lita poured him a fresh cup of hot coffee. She groaned as she bent over to pick up the lunch sack and set it on the table. After digging for a minute, she came out with two large squares of corn bread and set them in front of him. "That ought to hold you a spell," she mumbled.

"Yes, ma'am," Abe muttered as he sipped the strong coffee and munched on the corn bread.

Lita stopped and glared at Abe, as if she dared him to doubt what she was about to say. "You ain't thinkin' of no birds flyin' through windows, are you?"

Pausing, Abe raised his big face to Lita. He had a few days' growth on his salt-and-pepper beard. "I don't like it none," he admitted.

"Let me tell you somethin'," Lita warned, shaking a finger at him. "A man gets to believin' in somethin' bad, and he make it happen his own self—and it ain't got nothin' to do with no bird or superstition! The same with good. A man believe in good, and it will follow him like his shadow. The Lord knows what I'm talkin' about! Now you get them funny notions out of your old, gray head!" She heaved a final sigh, content with her statement.

Staring at her, Abe wanted to believe Lita, because he liked her way of thinking. He even liked her ideas of having a good God, one that didn't mess with superstitions since, after all, it was a nuisance to remember all the signs and what, if anything, a man might do about them. "You is plumb right, Lita. I get tired of worrying with all this stuff." He resumed eating, feeling better about having admitted his feelings. "You got to explain some of this Bible you gave me. I know I ain't the best at readin', but I still have a hard time makin' any sense of it."

Coming over to Abe, Lita put her strong arms around his head and gave him a hug. "You are a *good* man, Abe Washington, and I know the Lord is lookin' for you to work for Him."

Abe delighted in Lita's affection, and he wanted to please her. He reasoned that maybe her prediction was right, maybe he could work for the Lord someday.

The front door swung open and Jason came strolling in, the new day showing its light in his cheerful face. He saw Lita holding the big man close. "I'm not interrupting something, am I?" Jason asked jokingly.

"No!" Lita and Abe said at the same time, half-embarrassed, as Lita quickly pushed away from Abe.

"That coffee sure smells good, Lita," Jason said as he grabbed a tin cup and poured it full. "We better get rolling, Abe. The train leaves at ten."

Quickly, Abe came to his feet, found his hat, and placed it on his head. "I got the wagon out back."

"Y'all can start by taking them kitchen things," Lita said, pointing to a heavy crate. "And be careful. It's full of glass and I don't want none broken."

Jennifer came down with Abby and Grant, the children still wiping sleep from their eyes. "All of our bags are ready," she said to Lita. "Have the men load them last. We'll need to be able to get at them on the trip."

"Yes, ma'am, Miss Jenny. They out back now, fixin' things in the wagon."

Once loaded, and having scouted the house for any loose or forgotten items, the crew piled onto the wagon, Jennifer and Jason riding up front on the buck-board with Abe, who held the reins. Two blue-nosed mules wiggled their long ears and snorted at Abe, ready to follow his commands. Taking one last look, Jennifer studied the big saltbox house, a house some miner had built with loving care for his family, a miner with a head full of dreams. And she would always remember the years she and her family had spent there—good years.

"Good-bye, old house!" Jennifer lifted her voice, then waved, anxious to get moving. The children called good-bye to the house as the wagon lumbered down the street until they turned the corner and their former home was out of sight.

~

The steam engine breathed a plume of hissing steam into the dry morning air, and the bell clanged harshly, urging the passengers to climb aboard. Abe pulled the big wagon up by the loading dock, where a freight car waited with its side doors open.

"All that stuff going in here?" a young railroad worker asked as he approached the wagon. He sucked briskly on a corncob pipe, his alert, freckled young face imprinted with a smile. "My name's Joshua. I'll help you get loaded." He winked at Abby, who grew tickled with his flirting. "You ladies can go on up and find your car—just go over to the ticket agent's window right there," he said, pointing the stem of his pipe.

While the men loaded the freight, Jennifer and Abby picked up their reserved tickets and found their way to their seats. The conductor, a kind old man with a silver handlebar mustache who wore a sharp, black uniform, was more than happy to show the two pretty ladies to their seats. "Do you drive the train?" Abby asked the gentleman.

"No, miss, I don't. I'm the conductor."

Frowning, Abby asked, "What does a conductor do?"

The old man smiled, pleased that someone cared. "I collect tickets and make sure everyone is seated," he said proudly.

"Then what do you do after that?"

"I ride the train, just like you, except I make sure everyone is comfortable and that there are no problems," the twinkly-eyed man added delightfully.

Thinking a minute, Abby responded, "That's easy—and you get to ride the train free I bet!"

The old man's smile squinted his eyes. "I'm the one that gets to call 'All Aboard!'" he informed Abby.

Now satisfied that the man was worthy after all, Abby took her seat, anxious to be by the window. After the conductor left, she said, "Mother, he's important after all—'cause the train couldn't leave if he didn't call 'all aboard.'"

"I'm sure they wouldn't have him working here if they didn't need him," Jennifer said, shoving her handbag neatly by her leg.

The morning sun was growing hot when the whistle sounded and the train jerked into motion with the chugging of steam and heavy soot filling the air. Lita and Jason sat across from Jennifer and Abby and Grant.

"I've been in Virginia City for so long I forgot there was another world out there," Jason said, half-surprised at his own assumption. "I guess it's going to be a warm ride for a while—getting through the desert and all."

Jennifer nodded, recalling her last trip through the desert and salt flats and tremendous heat. "We can get refreshed in Reno. We have to change trains there. Then we're in for the long haul."

Lita remembered their last venture across the desert as well. She'd just as soon have forgotten it. "I wish there was some way to sleep through this and wake up where we are goin'," she said. "Where's Abe?"

"He's riding with our cargo, back in the freight car with Joshua.

Said he'd rather ride back there than try to fit into one of these little seats," Jason said.

Lita acknowledged with a blink of her eyes, slightly disgusted. The truth was, she'd rather be riding in a big, roomy freight car herself.

The train twisted and turned until it broke into the open and then settled down to what the travelers thought was a long journey. Just about the time the passengers began to get settled in for traveling, the train whistled to a stop in Reno. "Here we are!" Jason said, swinging to his feet. "I'll go and help Abe make sure all of our things get handled."

Jennifer nodded and got to her feet and grabbed her handbag. "Come on, children. Let's go see if we can find something cool to drink. Our other train will be along soon."

Noon came and went before the engine bearing the title Union Pacific rolled into the station, ready to load up with people and freight, and wood and water. At least this train had Pullman cars, a place to sleep, which pleased Lita, who had worried about having to sit in the same seat all night long.

Jason and Abe had seen to it that their freight was properly loaded. A black man named Boots was the freighter for the Union Pacific train and had helped them with their things. He was a tall, skinny black man with hollow cheeks and a bald head; his eyes danced when he talked. "Looks like you movin'—done brought all your things."

"Too many things!" Jason added, sweating from his exertion.

"Dat's why I don't own much," Abe grinned. "I don't have to worry with too many things."

"How right you are, brother!" Boots said as he slapped Abe on the back. "But you try and tell these womenfolk that!" He howled with laughter.

Abe showed his teeth as he laughed out loud with Boots. "Say, it be all right if I ride back here with you? Them travelin' cars gets a bit small for me."

"Tell you what," Boots said. "If you don't mind my preachin', you are welcome to ride back here all the way!"

"Preachin'?" Abe asked.

"From the Holy Gospel!" Boots said, suddenly serious.

"I been meanin' to learn more from the Good Book," Abe admitted. "It's hard for me to understand."

"You are in the right place, then," Boots said amiably, taking Abe by the arm and pulling him on over to where he had a comfortable place fixed up. Boots waved over his shoulder to Jason, who watched.

Turning, Jason found the women and Grant relaxing in the cool shadows of a small restaurant. "I think the train is going to be pulling out before long," he said, addressing Jennifer.

"Why don't you sit down and have something cool to drink," Jennifer offered. "I don't think the train will escape us. Is everything loaded?"

"Yep," Jason nodded. "And Abe's got him some good company. Some preacher is the freight man, wants to preach to him."

"Well, he plumb needs it!" Lita said. "Get dem fool thoughts out of his old head!"

Jennifer couldn't help but laugh at Lita. "Don't you think you're a little too hard on Abe?" she asked.

"Land no! He's thick-skulled as an old bull and sometimes as stubborn as them old mules he takes care of!"

Shaking her head at Lita, Jennifer called the waiter to bring Jason some cool water.

"You have any idea how long it will take us to get to Denver?" Jason asked.

"The train is fast. We'll get into Denver by tomorrow night."

"Whew!" he said, his eyes opening wide with surprise. "They're a lot faster than they used to be. And if I remember, you could always count on more than one breakdown to delay the trip."

Jennifer smiled, thinking that this was exactly like Jason. He was worried but then again showed the excitement of a little boy. The anxiety revealed the inner man. He was curious and clearly nervous. Being out of his element was unsettling, and he worried he might make a mistake and somehow disappoint her. He'd made every effort to let her know how he felt about her—yet she had remained noncommittal, still leery of any romance thanks to her flagrant failure with Charles. "I think we'll have a pleasant trip," she said with assurance. "Salt Lake City is something to see, and from there we'll head straight for those beautiful mountains, and that should be a lovely ride."

Jennifer's words raised enthusiasm in the children. "When are we going, Mother?" Grant asked. "The train's been sitting here for an hour."

"I'm ready, children. Is everyone else?"

"Let's go then," Jason said, helping Jennifer up from her chair.

As they left the restaurant and started down the boardwalk, Jennifer suddenly wrenched in despair. "Oh my! I forgot my handbag!"

Jason soothed her. "Hey, don't worry. I'll get it for you." He jogged back to the restaurant and found her bag beside the table, picked it up, and quickly brought it to her. "It was right where you left it," he said, winded but happy to be of assistance.

"Thank you so much!" Jennifer said, relieved.

After they boarded the train and found their seats, the train chugged clear of the station, then quickly picked up speed—its wheels a steady drumming rhythm that lulled them to sleep in spite of the uncomfortably warm and dry air.

From a distance, a copper-skinned Indian studied the train as it crawled along the floor of the desert. To him it appeared to be a black and shiny streak that left a trail of tumbling black smoke, a dark line on the horizon dividing the white desert sands and pale blue desert sky. He sat on his pony as still as a statue, then grunted and turned the horse's head aside with a cruel jerk, thinking of how good it would be to take a scalp from those inside the white man's machine.

~

By the time the train rolled into Salt Lake City, the travelers had grown weary, the heat and hours having drained their energy. "I'm exhausted," Jennifer complained. "Let's find somewhere to freshen up and get something to eat. We've got a little while."

"I'm with you!" Lita agreed, fanning herself with a newspaper. "It's too hot for me!"

Jason mopped his forehead with a handkerchief and pushed his straw-colored hair back from his face. "I think if we just walk a little and get some fresh air, we'll be better," he suggested. "I'm too hot to be hungry."

Abby stared around at the mean-looking building that constituted the station, discontent in her eyes. "You mean this isn't it? We're not there yet?" She held her long and wavy hair back and took a deep breath and spewed it out in disgust.

"We're going to big mountains, Abby," Grant told her. "You won't have to ask when we get there." He was determined to handle the testy trip with a man's patience.

The steel wheels groaned to a halt, and the cinders settled as Jennifer stood and took Abby's hand. "Let's go find a cool place and rest a little," she said, taking up her handbag. The group slowly followed the other passengers, who had similar ideas, and stepped from the coach into the scorching daylight.

Back in the freight car, Boots rolled open the huge door. Abe sat mesmerized, studying a tattered Bible. He had come to some conclusions after hearing Boots tell the amazing Bible stories of the Old Testament. "If God can do all of that, then He's everywhere and He knows everything."

"Why, of course He does," Boots confirmed as he took in the sights of Salt Lake City from the train depot.

"Then I reckon we just do the best we can and trust God, 'cause He's the one dat has all the power," Abe said, closing the book.

"Something like that," Boots confirmed. "We can't control the weather, can we? Or tell a river where to run? We just pray for the best and take what we get, 'cause if we are in a godly way, then everything turns out just fine. It's the results in our hearts that are important, not what happens."

Slowly, Abe was forming his own judgment as he worked this new concept in his mind. He was already a man well aware of the spiritual world, but he'd depended on superstitions before and hadn't had much knowledge of the Bible. Standing, he came over to the door and stood by Boots. "A man has got to have something to believe in," the man muttered, "and God says we got Him to believe in 'cause we can trust Him. As long as we got the Lord Jesus, we got the thing right. God says we got a life with Him in heaven after we die—and that we never really die."

This was even more for Abe to think on, and as far as he was concerned, it just sounded better and better. He already knew about a hard life on earth and was old enough to realize that he'd already lived most of his own. "This sure is somethin'! Why didn't nobody tell me about it before?"

"Why, they should have told you," Boots answered. "We supposed to spread the Word of God, which is that book you are holdin'. That's part of being a good Christian." Thinking a moment, he added, "Many a poor man don't believe in the spiritual world, neither good or bad, and that's the kind of man evil preys on. No matter how much money a man can collect in this life, if he don't recognize the spiritual world, he's a poor man." He swung a look at Abe and sharpened his glance. "There's more to it than just the eye can see."

Nodding his gray head, Abe took this in. He was impressed by this world that existed around him that he'd never even been aware of. About that time, a truck of freight rolled up to the open door. "Let me give you a hand with that," Abe offered, more than happy to be helpful.

~

After Salt Lake City the scenery was forever changing, almost making them believe they were in a foreign land. "Are those mountains?" Abby asked as she studied the countryside from her window.

"I'm not sure," Jennifer answered as she glanced at the wind- and rain-carved landscape. "But it sure is pretty."

The day turned to dusk, and the sun crushed against the ragged horizon in a mix of orange reflections from the bottom of a string of wispy clouds. Night came quickly as the mountains swallowed the light, leaving the rail coach in dim lantern light.

"I'm ready for bed!" Lita said as soon as it was good and dark outside. "Ain't no sense in sittin' up in here."

Jennifer had passed her time in a book, but the rocking of the train had made her eyes heavy and tired. "It's early, but I don't think I'd have any trouble falling asleep."

"Me either," Jason drawled. He couldn't believe how the journey had taken the energy out of him. Abby was already nodding as Grant giggled at her.

"Why don't we go to our compartments?" Jennifer suggested. "Grant, you and Jason can go to yours."

Nobody argued as the group slowly got up to prepare for bed.

Things in the freight car were much the same with Boots and Abe as they played dominoes on a crate top by lantern light. "You look tired, my friend," Boots said, watching Abe lose his concentration. "Throw that blanket over them boxes there and get some rest. Me? I think I'm going to read the Good Book for a little bit." He placed a small pair of spectacles on his nose and flipped open the book. Abe was used to going to bed early and did as his new brother suggested. It wasn't long before he was dreaming pleasant dreams to the staccato rhythm of the noisy iron beneath the floor.

~

The travelers woke up refreshed and hungry, and pleased at the beautiful view from the windows. Peaks stretched upward in a variety of colors, while wide valleys stretched below in a soft green. "Look at that!" Jason said, the first to wake. He reached over and shook Grant. "Wake up!"

Slowly coming to life, Grant wiped his eyes and stared out the window into the morning dawn. He sat motionless in total disbelief. "This is so different from anything I ever saw! I can't wait to live here!"

Abby awoke and showed the same astonishment at the sight outside, her blue eyes fixed on the scenery. There were no words in her little head that could describe how she felt. The air seemed somehow sweet and delicious and cool, and the vast and clear depths seemed to swallow her along with her imagination—it was like a scene from a fairy tale.

"Oh look!" Jennifer said, her hopes rising. Of course, Abby paid no attention to her mother, not wanting to be disturbed from her daydream.

Lita glanced out the window and then recoiled as if she'd been shocked. "My goodness! I can see all the way to heaven!" Easing closer to the window as if she were afraid of falling, she viewed down into the passing canyon below where she could see a small stream sparkling in the morning sunlight. "Woo-wee! I bet there's some fish in dat water!"

Smiling, Jennifer got out of bed, her faith renewed, her anticipation high. "We're in Colorado," she said happily. Eagerly, the women got dressed and left their compartment, ready for breakfast.

Grant and Jason had already gone to get something to eat from the dining car, and when they saw the women, they expressed their excitement. "Can you believe it?" Jason asked, waving his hand at the window. "I don't remember seeing this before. It's beautiful."

"And we're going to be living right in the middle of it," Jennifer said happily as she sat down beside Jason, which pleased him very much. She gave him a look that said more than words, the corners of her lips slightly turned up into a faint smile, her eyes alive with joy. For a moment, Jason felt like some invisible barrier between them had fallen. She looked as lovely as the view, even more so.

"I guess we should be arriving in Denver this evening," Jason said, sipping on a cup of coffee.

"We won't actually be going into Denver," Jennifer corrected. "The Colorado Central we want to be taking goes up to Black Hawk from Golden, just outside of Denver. We'll change trains there."

"Oh well," Jason said, smiling. "I'm not particular."

Jennifer smiled back, a pleasing smile, the kind of smile Jason was sure meant more than just "good morning." His chest swelled and his confidence rose—he was beginning to see real possibilities with her in their new adventures.

The day went quickly with the forever-changing panorama and pageantry of the Colorado Rocky Mountains. The air was crisp and cool and comfortable while the Union Pacific labored to higher altitudes. Spruce and aspen waved in the breeze as the train sped by, while Jennifer and Jason tentatively planned their business ideas of operating a newspaper in Black Hawk. The afternoon quickly turned into evening, with the mountains hiding the sun quickly. The train stretched through rocky gorges and valleys and skirted the edge of mountain walls.

"Next stop—Golden!" the conductor called out in a loud voice.

Feeling her heart beat faster, Jennifer tried to calm the anxious excitement she found difficult to hide. Suddenly, the train lurched and the steel wheels squealed in the darkening light.

"Nothing like skidding into the station!" Jason complained. "Kind of abrupt, don't you think?"

Lita had almost been thrown from her seat and wrestled to right herself. "Somebody need to teach dat man driving this train how to drive!"

Glancing out the window, Jennifer could see the train had stopped in the middle of nowhere, a small valley where no lights could be seen. "I don't think we're in Golden," she mumbled, curious as to what might be happening.

Just then, the door at the end of the car swung open and three men rushed in. They were wearing scarves over their faces and had their hats pulled down low—and they held pistols pointed at the passengers.

"This is a holdup!" The speaker was a tall, well-built man with dark eyes that glowed. His voice was muffled as he announced in a loud and rough voice, "I don't want to see any dead heroes! Just remove your jewelry, watches, and moneybags, and we'll pick them up and be on our way!" The three men slowly moved down the aisle, nudging passengers with the barrels of their pistols. "Give it up, old man!" one of the gunmen grunted, "or I'll blow a hole in you wide enough to drive this train through!" The gray-haired man quickly removed his wallet from his vest pocket and handed it over. "The watch!" prodded the gunman as the old man nervously removed his watch chain and unclasped it from his vest.

Watching in horror, Jennifer clutched her handbag to her chest. Jason threw her a glance and then looked back at the approaching gunmen. "Just give them what they want!" Jason whispered to her. "Everything will be all right!"

"N-no!" Jennifer stammered. "You don't understand—everything we own is in my handbag!"

"What?!" Jason whispered, his eyes hard and cold as he looked at Jennifer in disbelief.

"All the money I sold the business and the house for—it's in my bag!"

Totally shocked, Jason said, "Quick! Stuff it under your seat!"

A cold gun barrel touched the side of Jason's head. "I'll take the bag," came a smooth and clear voice from the outlaw. He was tall and angular and wore a scarf below his dark eyes. The brim of his hat shadowed his face.

"No! You don't understand! This is everything—it's our future, the only thing we have!" Jennifer pleaded.

The man snatched the bag and turned it over. A variety of items fell out, but he quickly noticed the thick envelope bound with string and picked it up. Ripping it open, he revealed the heavy wad of currency. "This will do nicely," he said happily, his cocky arrogance offensive. Without warning, he leaned over and kissed a horrified Jennifer on the lips through his scarf. "Thank you, darling."

"You no good—!" Jason grunted as he jumped to his feet. But the alert highwayman quickly flicked his gun barrel, batting Jason across the head and sending him sprawling to the floor, out cold.

Lita sat deep in her seat quietly watching the man over her holding the gun, her eyes big as saucers. When he grabbed her bag and looked in, he gave a slight laugh. "Chicken and corn bread?"

"Good evening, ladies," he said as he tipped his hat to Jennifer and moved down the aisle to rob the next passenger. At the end of the car, a robber stood over the passengers with a rifle aimed at them. It became obvious that there would be no rescue attempts. As quick as the bandits had come, they were gone, leaving a terrorized and dismayed group of disgruntled travelers.

Quickly, Jennifer fell to the floor over Jason and lifted his head. He was a mess, the cut in his scalp leaking blood all over his face. "Somebody get me a towel!" she called while Lita scrambled and quickly found something. Wrapping his head, Lita and Jennifer pulled him up into his seat. He was groaning.

"What hit me?" he murmured, dazed and confused.

"Hold this towel," Jennifer ordered Jason, trying to remain brave. "Try and relax so we can get this blood stopped."

Grant was definitely afraid. He sat motionless and silent by the window watching everything that happened as if it were not real. He'd withdrawn into his private world, frozen by fear, unable to move or speak. He had watched his mother get robbed and his friend and hero get swatted out like a fly, and it had all happened too fast for him to understand.

Abby held a different view. She was stunned by the most exciting and devastating moment of her entire life, and her heart was still banging inside her chest. She wondered who this highwayman really was. The money and robbery meant little, but the thrill and daring captivated her.

Soon the car buzzed with the heated conversations of protesting passengers. Lita began to shake uncontrollably, and Jason remained dizzy and in pain. For the moment, Jennifer was able to remain strong, seeing to it that Jason was tended to and Lita comforted.

The conductor broke through the door and announced, "Everybody remain calm. We'll be in Golden in twenty minutes."

The train lurched forward and highballed into the night. Relaxing, Jennifer sat back in her seat, her face dark and haunted. She knew about loss and had dealt with it before, but what had happened began to sink in. She felt personally violated, as if she'd been taken against her will. The sickening feeling sapped her very strength, making her weak, weary, and helpless. *Oh, God!* she prayed *We've lost everything—all we have left is You!*"

And then, as clearly as spoken words, an inner voice came to her—*If you have Me, you have everything!*

CHAPTER

3

Welcome to Black Hawk

When the train reached the Union Pacific Station in Golden, news spread quickly of the robbery. A crowd gathered to get the newsworthy story, while the local sheriff had his hands full trying to subdue the complaints from the train's passengers.

"Everyone just calm down!" he demanded, holding his hands up in the air. The sheriff was a big man, in his early thirties, strapped with muscle and huge shoulders. "There's no way I can go after them tonight. We'll have to form a posse and see what we can find tomorrow. As for you people getting off the train here, the Union Pacific will be glad to put you up for the night until matters can be settled. I'm sorry this happened—that's all I got to say!"

Jennifer turned to Jason as he pulled her to his chest. He wore a white bandage around his head and had a forlorn look of desperation. "We'll manage," he said, trying to encourage Jennifer. Grant stood close by, holding Abby by the hand. Abe held Lita, who'd had the wits scared out of her. Abe hadn't found out about the robbery until the train stopped in Golden.

"Why don't we find the hotel," Jason recommended. "We haven't much choice."

Jennifer lifted her face to Jason. He could see she was lost in the way of a person suffering from shock. "What are we going to do?" she mumbled. The only thing that gave her any hope was the inner voice she'd heard. Somehow the memory of that moment gave her strength, and she managed to smile at Jason.

"There's nothing we can do tonight," Jason shrugged. "We'll get some rest and continue in the morning as we planned. We'll get by."

Hearing Jason, Abe looked down at Lita, who was unusually quiet. "He's right," Abe said. "We'll get by—we got to."

Lita nodded as Abe picked up the luggage. Talking to herself, she said, "The good Lord—He ain't never let me down—and I don't reckon He's about to start!"

~

When morning came, Jennifer had just fallen into a deep sleep, having stayed up most of the night tossing and turning and worrying about the uncertain future. "Mother! Wake up!" Abby said as she pushed on her mother's limp form. "They're waiting for us."

"What?" Jennifer moaned as she rolled over to see her daughter standing beside the bed dressed and ready to go. It took Jennifer a moment to realize where she was—then it all came back to her. Here they were in a strange town and broke, and she wasn't sure where their next meal would come from. Slowly, she rolled to her side and sat up in the bed, an expectant Abby staring her in the face. "C'mon, Mother!" the girl demanded.

"Hold on," Jennifer groaned, tired from not having slept well. The empty feeling of being robbed swept over her, followed by the hundreds of questions, all asking the same thing, *What will we do?*

With Abby overseeing her every move, Jennifer got dressed, her face expressionless, her eyes sad with despair. "Where's Lita?" Jennifer asked.

"She's downstairs with Abe and Jason and Grant. They're waiting—hurry up!"

"That's enough!" Jennifer griped. "I'm going as fast as I can. Why don't you go tell them I'm on my way."

Cocking her head to one side with the idea, Abby dashed out of the room, slamming the door behind her. *I'm not feeling so well,*

Jennifer thought, dejection ruling her emotions. *What must I have been thinking? Carrying the money was a foolish thing to do. I should have*—Then she stopped, realizing all of the *ifs* would account for nothing.

Glancing at the mirror, she saw herself as a different person than the one she'd viewed just days before in a more hopeful reflection at their home in Virginia City. Now she looked worn and tired, stripped of dignity and hope. She still couldn't get over the feeling of being violated and how it disturbed her so deeply and personally. It was at this moment that she understood the events were more than she could handle and bowed her head in prayer. "Dear Father, I don't know why all of this has happened, but it has dampened my spirits. I pray for strength through these trying times and pray for Your guidance. I know You haven't let me come this far just to fall into ruins." Pausing a moment, she went on to pray, "Don't let me lose sight of the faith that has brought me so far—I need something to cling to right now. In Jesus' name I pray—Amen."

As she lifted her head, Jennifer felt better, her spirit renewed. *Somehow,* she thought, *today the Lord will show me His grace!* Quickly she dressed, then hurried downstairs to meet the others.

There were several people in the restaurant, but Jennifer didn't see anyone she knew. As she searched, she heard unmistakable laughter coming from the kitchen. She stuck her head in and saw a crowd of people gathered around the table where Jason, Abe, Grant, and Abby sat eating pancakes. Lita had taken her natural position in the smoky, little kitchen, helping with the cooking and serving while another cook and other strangers gathered around the table asking questions about the robbery. "Did he stick the gun in your face?" asked a woman wearing an apron and her hair up in a bun. Her withered face was animated with excitement.

"Right in my face," Jason said, "right before he knocked me out with it."

Abby bragged, "He kissed my mother!"

Grant didn't seem so thrilled with the story, but he eagerly paid attention to make sure no exaggerations changed the facts.

"He kissed your mother?" the homely cook asked Abby. "Why,

he must have been the Kissing Bandit. There's an outlaw that robs stagecoaches around this area—and he always kisses the pretty women." The lady rolled her eyes, thinking the event a romantic one.

"He didn't try to kiss me!" Lita protested, angered by any such thought, "or I would have slapped his face!"

Everyone laughed heartily except Lita, who maintained her firm belief in what she would've done.

Abe listened as he filled up with tasty flapjacks. He'd been angry that he'd been in the rail coach when the robbery took place, but he knew that he would have been shot trying to prevent the crime. And for the first time, it crossed his mind that maybe he should thank God for not having been in the passenger car. Then he remembered the teachings he'd learned from Boots and decided that all things, good and bad, happen for a reason. He'd be interested in seeing how this one worked out, although he wasn't really worried, he knew they'd get by—he'd seen worse times.

Jason had laughed so hard at Lita that he was holding the bandage on his head, which throbbed when he laughed. Glancing up, he saw Jennifer in the door. Swiftly standing, he came to her. "Jennifer, come in, sit down, eat something. Get her a cup of coffee, Lita." Turning back to Jennifer, he said, "I hope you're feeling better this morning. Last night was a little rough. What a welcome to Colorado!"

Jennifer forced a smile. "What's going on here? Looks like a little party."

"We have some people interested in the details of the robbery—say they don't have many dramatic things like that happen around here. Too bad we don't have a paper to print; we could write the account as eyewitnesses."

Dropping her head, Jennifer realized it might be a long time before they would have a newspaper to write. But then she gathered herself, reminded herself of a word called *hope*, and said, "Well, the outlaw robbed us of our newspaper. That might make a good story. Maybe we can sell it when we get to Black Hawk." Lita set a cup of coffee in front of Jennifer, and she took a sip. "That reminds me, how are we going to get to Black Hawk? We don't have any money."

Jason smiled and almost laughed; his eyes were alive with excitement. "Maybe it was a good thing that brute knocked me out—he forgot to grab my wallet!" Jason flung his wallet from his vest pocket and opened it. It was crammed with bills.

"Where'd you get that?" Jennifer asked, astonished.

"What do you think I did with all my money back in Virginia City?" Jason demanded, but he was pleased with himself. "Spent it at the dance hall? I can pay our way for a while."

Abe leaned back and removed a wallet from his overalls. He handed it to Lita who opened it and inspected the contents—another fat wad of bills. As her eyes grew big, Abe said, "I got money. You're welcome to it."

Lita smiled, amazed at Abe for saving so large an amount. But when she thought about it, he never bought anything except food that he brought her. He had always said he didn't need much. When she handed him back the money, Abe said to Lita, "No, you look out for dat for me. Never know, we might get robbed again."

Proudly, Lita stuck the wallet away, impressed that Abe would trust her to watch his money.

"I'm overwhelmed," Jennifer said, a true relief filling her features and bringing color to her face.

"Was you the one that robber kissed?" asked the regular cook, a more than curious woman, who obviously thought that was the most important fact of the robbery.

"Yes," Jennifer admitted, not sure whether this was a point to dwell on.

"Well, you's a perty one!" the woman said enviously. "I hear tell he's a handsome man, sweeps women off their feet when he ain't robbing them."

Raising her eyebrows, Jennifer said, "Thank you, but I don't care to ever meet a man like that, and I hope I never see him again."

"Amen to that!" Lita agreed. "I sure don't want nothin' to do with no outlaw!"

"I'd like to see him at least *one* more time," Jason remarked, a determined light glinting in his eyes. "I'd like to see the bottom of his boots when they string him up!"

~

When the Colorado Central engine stoked its firebox and clanged the bell, passengers boarded, still talking of the train robbery the night before. It was the biggest news in a while and had everybody's attention. The sheriff had left earlier with a posse in tow to search for clues and a trail. Jason and Abe had seen to the freight and the luggage, and this time Abe rode up front with the rest of the gang. He didn't approve of any man threatening Lita and would stay near to make sure it didn't happen again.

"Scoot over, you big ox!" Lita said to Abe. "Give me some room!"

"I'm scooted all I can scoot," Abe apologized.

Jennifer held her hand in front of her mouth to stifle a laugh; Lita had a way about her that came across humorously.

"Would you look at that!" Jason said, pointing outside. The scenery was like a textured painting, almost beyond belief.

Then all of a sudden the lights went out, and it was pitch-black where it had been daytime just a second before.

"What's happening?" Grant yelled, frightened by the unexpected.

In an instant, the light was back, and they realized they had traveled through a tunnel.

"Wow!" Grant said in amazement, once he realized what had happened.

"You were scared!" Abby taunted.

"No, I wasn't," Grant protested. "I was just—curious."

Abby turned her nose up at Grant—she didn't believe him. *He's all right, for a brother,* she thought. *But he doesn't have to act so grown-up. I wish that sometime he'd just turn loose and go crazy!*

The train followed Clear Creek up the gorge, and the view was fantastic and incredible, mountains rising on each side as the engine climbed the steady grade.

"What are those?" Abby asked, looking out the window.

Everyone turned to look at once, but nobody was sure what the group of brown animals with horns that curled around the side of their heads were. "They're beautiful!" Abby said as she watched the animals effortlessly scamper up a rock wall.

"Those are bighorn sheep," a man said from behind a newspaper. "They live in these parts."

Abby turned to the informative stranger. He dropped the paper to reveal his eyes. "How do you know? Do you live around here?" Abby asked.

The man dropped the paper to reveal his face. "Yes, I do, young lady. And what might your name be?"

"My name is Abby. What's yours?"

"I'm Jake Sandelowski," he announced proudly with a slight British accent—a sharply dressed young man in his twenties. He had the kind of youthful smile of a man well contented with his station in life. Wearing his derby hat smartly tilted, his light brown eyes twinkled.

"This is our first trip to Black Hawk," Jennifer said. "Our plans were to open a newspaper there, but we were robbed last night. I'm not sure what we're going to do now—at least we still have our building on Gregory Street."

"The train robbery? I heard about that!" Jake said, now interested and setting his newspaper down. "That must have been quite shocking—to be robbed!"

"To say the least!" Jennifer confirmed, a playful smile in her eyes cloaking her remorse.

Jason noticed the way the handsome young man was eyeing Jennifer—the way Jennifer responded. "What do you do, Jake?" he asked evenly, suddenly conscious of his own faded blue jeans and worn, brown coat.

"I own a clothier store, and it's on Gregory Street also. I think I know which building you own—it's vacant now. There's been talk of a newspaper moving in there. Some people from out West bought it, I believe. Might that be you?"

"Yes," Jennifer answered. "Only now, we're not sure how we're going to get it started."

Smiling, Jake tilted his hat. "Perhaps I can help. I know everyone in Black Hawk and Central City, and they're a jolly lot. Maybe we can make some arrangements."

"That would be most gracious of you, Mr. Sandelowski," Jennifer said, smiling pleasantly.

Jake smiled and returned to his newspaper.

The group enjoyed the breathtaking view as the steam engine chugged higher and higher, laboring to make the slight but constant grade. The gulch was incredible and fantastic, a spectacular view that kept the faces of the newcomers to the windows.

After a two-hour climb the whistle blew, announcing the train's arrival as it puffed into a covered building that more resembled a stamp mill than a train depot.

"We're here!" Jennifer announced, a tinge of excitement stirring her.

Abby bounced to her feet, followed by Grant. "We're here!" the children mimicked, excited to finally arrive at their new home and be done with train rides.

Inside the dark station, the group disembarked from the coach and made arrangements to have the freight held until they called for it. Carrying only a few things, they walked into the light outside. Suddenly, the entire group grew silent, each beholding the sight simultaneously. "Oh dear!" Jennifer mumbled. Disappointment wavered across her fine features as her eyes adjusted to the light and took in the sights.

"This is Black Hawk?" Jason asked, his eyes following the bald mountains stripped of vegetation and pockmarked with mines and unsightly yellow tailings.

Lita was astounded also as she let her eyes roam in her new surroundings. There were few words in her vocabulary to express her disapproval of the city's appearance. "So, dis is it," she uttered.

"Just another mining town," Abe mumbled as he picked up the luggage. "Which way, Miss Jenny?"

Withdrawn, Jennifer barely heard Abe. What she saw was a dismal sight, a town of pounding stamp mills, rutted streets of mud and manure, and an uncommon stench that sickened her—all dashing her hopes about arriving in any beautiful, mountain town. She felt an emptiness in the pit of her stomach as an expression of dismay fell over her face.

"This place stinks!" Abby protested. "This isn't where we're going to live, is it?"

Calmly, Jennifer silently took Abby's hand, not sure which way to turn. Grant watched his mother, disheartened that she'd made such a tragic mistake. He was curious as to what she'd do next.

Jason was no better. To him, they'd left a tolerable mining town only to descend to the depths of a town protesting with discomforts. He wasn't sure if he smelled sewage or rotten eggs, but the smell heightened his first impression, one of grave dissatisfaction. "Maybe we could check around," he said wearily, unsuccessfully trying to add a little hope to the situation. "Maybe there are some nicer places around—surely there *must* be!"

The air was thick with a yellow haze and smoke from the mills, a sort of dingy, thick cloud that hung over the town. Steam engines whirred with their unmistakable hissing and thumping, while the mills pounded loudly out of cadence. It was enough to wreck the nerves, an unpleasant rumble of industry that staggered any thoughts of undisturbed living.

"Well, what do you think of our fine town?" Jake asked as he stepped up to the group. "This is the center of gold production—from all these mills," he boasted, waving his arm at the hillside. "This area is sometimes referred to as the richest square mile on earth." He smiled brightly and turned to Jennifer. "Well? What do you think?"

Trying to be polite, Jennifer forced a smile. "It isn't exactly as we pictured it," she said truthfully, concealing her shock at the washed-out and stripped appearance of the mountainsides.

"Would you like for me to show you to Gregory Street?" Jake asked, eager to be helpful. His good-natured mood seemed unsinkable.

"Yes, of course," Jennifer answered, slightly hesitant, unsure of anything else to do at the moment.

"Is it like this all the time?" Jason asked, knowing what the answer would be.

"Certainly!" Jake bragged. "The sweet sound of those mills churns out more gold than anywhere. What was your name, sir?"

"Jason, Jason Stone."

"My pleasure, Jason," Jake said, extending his hand and taking Jason's in a formal shake. "Lots of money here—lots of money."

"Is that what smells?" Abby asked.

Jake let out a good laugh. "No, Abby. What you smell are the sulfides from the mills where they separate the rock from the gold. Quite a bit of sulfur in the rock, you see."

The group began to stroll along, following Jake as he showed off the town. Abe and Lita followed behind, listening carefully.

Jake explained, "Back in the early days, around 1860, Denver and Auraria were a huge disappointment to the gold-seeking settlers there, and the place almost dried up. Then John Gregory made a strike up here, and the rush was up Clear Creek. It's come a long way since then, wouldn't you say?"

"Oh definitely!" Jason agreed, sarcasm in his voice.

"Yes, well, Gregory Street is right up here," Jake said, a high step in his walk. "There are so many things to tell you about Black Hawk I hardly know where to begin."

As they moved along, the midday sun was high and bright, the temperature pleasant, and the streets busy with people of all sorts.

"How'd it get the name of Black Hawk?" Jennifer asked. "That's an Indian name, isn't it?"

"Yes," Jake said. "But if you took a walk through the mills and looked at the name on the heavy equipment, you'd mostly see Black Hawk, the name of the company back East that produces that heavy machinery. When this became the hub of the gold towns with it's mills, they quit calling it Gregory Gulch and called it Black Hawk, a name that stuck." He held out his hand and helped Jennifer and Abby over a mud puddle as they crossed the street. "This is Gregory Street headed up the hill here, and it goes to Central City, right up there," he said, pointing. "That big sign you see hanging over the boardwalk—that's my store. Two doors down, that nice brick building, that's yours!"

Curious and inquisitive, Jennifer and Jason hurried, Abby and

Grant rushing along behind them. Abe and Lita took their time, falling behind, as Abe lugged some of their suitcases. Quickly approaching, Jennifer could see immediately that she'd made a fine investment; at least the building was new and had a pleasant appearance from the front.

"It's lovely," Jennifer said, her eyes rising up the brick facade to the two upstairs windows.

"Do you have a key?" Jake asked politely.

"Oh, I almost forgot," Jennifer said, digging through her things. Shortly, she produced a brass key and shoved it into the lock. As they entered, the sunlight shone through the front windows revealing a roomy front office richly trimmed in wood. "This is beautiful!" Jennifer said, a vague regret in her voice.

"You sound disappointed," Jake said surprisingly.

"There's no way we can keep it and buy the things we'll need to run a newspaper," Jennifer said, almost heartbroken. *We were so close*, she thought. *We could have had this!*

Quickly looking around, Jason felt the same despondency he had heard in Jennifer's voice. The building was truly magnificent—ideal for a newspaper office, with ample room upstairs for living quarters or whatever suited their needs. "It's a shame," he muttered. "But maybe we can figure out something."

Turning, Jennifer saw Lita and Abe enter, their brown eyes rolling as they inspected the interior of the building. Lita came closer. "Where we gonna stay, Miss Jenny? Are we stayin' here?"

A worried sense of indecision swept Jennifer's face. "I don't see how. I have to contact the man I bought it from. Maybe he can sell it for me. We'll have to find a room somewhere for tonight."

Overhearing Jennifer's dilemma, Jake spoke up. "I was trying to buy this building when you purchased it awhile back. I'm still interested," he said, his tone changing from the jolly young man to a serious businessman. "I'll give you a fair price for it."

Sorrow straining her face, Jennifer turned to Jason. She was drained from the long trip and the robbery and the worry of making new and quick decisions. "What should I do?" she asked, confronting him.

For the first time in a long time Jason felt needed, felt worthy enough to be consulted about major problems. But foremost, he felt glad that Jennifer trusted him—she was asking for help. Abruptly, he placed his arms around her and pulled her to him. As he looked her closely in the face, he advised, "Let's get settled into a hotel and get some rest. There's no need to rush anything today. We've seen the place. We know what we've got. Tomorrow we can make up our minds as to what we're going to do."

Jennifer sighed, relieved that such a simple answer could comfort her. Turning to Jake, she agreed with Jason. "Can we get together tomorrow? We're awfully tired and need to get our heads clear before we decide what to do."

"Absolutely!" Jake amiably rendered his hand to her for a gentlemanly shake. "Have you made arrangements for a room?"

"Well, no, not yet. Are there any reasonable hotels around here?"

"Allow me," Jake offered. "I'll be glad to assist you back to the Gilpin Hotel. We passed it on the way in. I'll personally see to it that you're well taken care of—you and your servants!"

Withered from disappointment and exhaustion, Jennifer's face suddenly changed, showing some hope. *Jason's right*, she thought. *We shouldn't make any decisions until we're well rested and have had a chance to think things over. He knows how to take control of things*. Deep within, Jennifer harbored emotions in the form of affection for Jason, and at times like these she saw something in him she was strongly attracted to. In many ways, she'd come to rely on him. "Let's go to the hotel and get settled in."

~

The next morning brought with it rolling, dark clouds and the threat of a thunderstorm. Jason was up and viewed the sky from his second-floor window with slight remorse. *It's funny how a man adjusts his mood to the weather*, he thought, vaguely troubled. *We have to sell the building, otherwise there won't be enough money to buy a press and establish a paper. Maybe we should just leave this God-forsaken place and go somewhere else*. But then again, he didn't know anywhere else to go to. They were hopelessly stuck.

Quickly getting dressed, Jason glanced at his stubbled face in the mirror's reflection. The scar on his left cheek was slightly puckered, and his eyes showed the puffiness from heavy sleep. *Jennifer's relying on me*, he remembered. *I've got to be strong—to show her I'm really made of something*. With that, he combed his hair but decided shaving would take too much time. His money, he recalled, would last them for a while. Danger was not immediate; they could get by, but he'd have to support Jennifer and her children, a thought that gave him a strange satisfaction as he left the room.

Knocking on Jennifer's door, Jason found her up and dressed. "Sleep all right?" he asked,

To Jason's surprise, Jennifer welcomed him with a warm smile. "I slept hard," she said sleepily. Then she did something Jason found unusual. She pulled him into the room and continued holding his hand. She held a look of regret as her eyes roamed over his rugged face. "Jason, I'm sorry I got you into all of this. It's all my fault. If I hadn't brought the money in my bag—if I'd known what this town was like . . ."

Jason squeezed her hand and brought her a little closer. He could see the sincerity in her eyes, the depth of concern in her face. "I think I once told you, Jennifer, that I'm in with you all the way—no matter what."

She dropped her eyes and let them slip away. "I feel so stupid! I'm not sure what to do."

"We'll do the best we can," Jason assured her, pulling her even closer. He touched her chin with his finger and moved her face up to meet his. Slowly, he kissed her gently on the lips.

For Jennifer, this was a moment that grasped her. Having a man she cared for hold her and comfort her when things had gone so terribly wrong gave her a satisfying warmth. She knew deep down that she needed a good man, and Jason's kiss stirred many old memories and deep emotions. She didn't pull away but let the moment dissolve in its own sweet time. She looked into Jason's sharp, blue eyes—

there was nothing like having someone to be close to in difficult and demanding times.

Caught off guard, Jason suddenly saw no devastating circumstances, only the possibility of his future with Jennifer. Nothing seemed better. "I'll love you always," he promised.

There seemed to be a light in Jennifer's eyes that glowed with complete understanding. She was not excited or scared or indifferent, only passive and relaxed. "It's nice to know that somebody feels good about me," she said calmly. "I've made some big mistakes. Got any ideas?"

There seemed to be something easy and soft between them, no refusals or commitments, just basic affection. "If we stay, and I don't see that we have much choice," Jason said, confident in his thoughts, "then we must sell the building, rent a place, and buy some used equipment to start a paper with. It's either that or move away to the same situation somewhere else."

Jennifer turned away and looked out her tall window into the gray clouds in the sky above. It was a little depressing, having to sell the building, but then again it could serve as their means to a livelihood. "Yes, I guess you're right," she mumbled calmly. A long moment of silence passed as they both stood there, Jason staring at her back as she stood looking out the window. He wanted to tell her so much more, to make her believe that they were meant to be together forever. But the simple trust she had displayed made the moment much too delicate and prevented him from saying a word.

Jennifer finally picked up her shawl, saying, "Let's find the others and have some breakfast. We'll tell them what we're going to do."

Jennifer stepped outside and pulled the door closed behind her. What had passed between them gave Jason confidence and a strong will to make things in Black Hawk work out, for this was a woman like no other, one he'd love for the rest of his life.

~

Later in the day, Jake Sandelowski made good on his word and was kind enough to make a deal with Jennifer, giving her exactly what she'd paid for her building. It was enough money for a feeble start, providing they were careful. The only other building available to rent was somewhat rundown, a long and thin affair located on a small back street, a building that had once been a saloon. Above it were rooms that had once served other less noble purposes.

Jason and Abe opened the front two doors to let light in as Jennifer and Lita and the children stepped in to see what a saloon looked like. Long and dark and thin, the main room looked more like a corridor with a huge stove at the back. A stack of chairs and rickety old tables were piled against the wall opposite the bar, the wall having kerosene lamps every few feet. The giant mirror behind the bar showed a long crack and two spiderweb holes, apparently gunshots. Glancing over the dirty floors and dusty bar, Jennifer tried to sound hopeful. "It's going to take a lot of work just to clean this place up. I'm not real fond of its history of being a saloon and dance hall."

"Since we got this place—let's forget the newspaper business and open a bar!" Jason grinned.

"That's not funny!" Jennifer warned Jason. "You know the nightmares drinking caused you."

Jason's smile fell from his face. "I was only joking," he apologized.

"We can have dis place cleaned up in no time!" Lita said out loud, certain to be heard. "If we all work on it, we can have it clean as a new shirt!"

Jennifer marveled at Lita and how she never cringed in the confrontation of any kind of despair. Her strong will remained unscathed by their unpleasant circumstances.

"Miss Jenny," Abe said, speaking up in his deep voice, "dis bar is made of walnut wood—I know what I see. Enough of dis wood to build somethin' out of."

Coming closer, Jennifer wiped the dust from the top of the bar with her hand to expose the dark wood. "The man said we could do whatever we wanted with it. I wouldn't know the first thing about building something else out of it."

"We could make some desks out of the bar top," Jason suggested.

"Look, Mother!" Abby shouted from the other end of the room where she stood on top of the bar. She kicked a leg in the air and said, "I'm going to be a dance hall girl!"

"Child! You get down from there before you break your neck!" Lita cried, rushing over to help Abby down.

"Abby! You'll not talk like that!" Jennifer scolded. "That's sinful!"

"She doesn't even know what a dance hall girl is," Grant said, disgusted with his sister.

Briefly, the entire group enjoyed the security of the trust they placed in each other. The possibilities of opening a newspaper no longer seemed remote, and now their vision was clearer than when they'd arrived in Black Hawk.

"Better get started on the bedrooms," Lita said. "We got to sleep in them."

"Abe, I guess we can go get all of our belongings down at the train station," Jason said.

"We'll need lots of hot water and some soap," Lita said.

"This should be interesting," Jennifer commented, gingerly smiling. She lifted her head, and even in the dismal surroundings felt a burst of sudden confidence. "We've got the Lord—and if we have Him—why, we have everything!"

CHAPTER

4

A Start

September brought the most pleasant days Jennifer could remember, and outside of the milling area the shimmering mountain aspens had painted the countryside in a variety of brilliant yellows and golds. The air was delicious to breathe, neither too sedative nor too exciting, but had that pure and sweet flexible quality that seemed to support all of one's happiest and healthiest moods. After a day of hard work in renovating the old building, Jennifer found in this exquisite atmosphere the lightest and most restorative slumber she ever knew.

"It's looking like something," Jennifer remarked to Jason one sun-filled morning, turning her attention to the front room that would serve as the newspaper office. A wall had been erected, separating the long room into front and back rooms. The old bar was disassembled and served to make several roomy tables, now covered with tools and paperwork.

"Yes," Jason said, his eyes roaming over their efforts. "It's time we find a press and the rest of the things we'll need. I've been checking around—there's nothing for sale up here. I hear that I might find something in Denver. I suppose we'd better go and have a look."

Thinking for a moment, Jennifer wondered exactly how they'd approach Denver in search of the necessities for starting a newspaper. "I'm not sure I'd know where to begin—it's not like they'd have a store with used presses for sale." She stepped out of the front door into the morning sun, her smooth face showing fine lines of worry.

Admiring her soft complexion in the golden sunlight as he followed, Jason stroked his chin, his face darkened by a short beard. "I'll go and see what I can find, you don't have to go," he volunteered, knowing Jennifer wasn't fond of the idea of making a trip into Denver.

Turning to him, Jennifer glanced up into his beholding eyes. Jason somehow looked different, more mature, more certain of himself, his bright blue eyes set off even more by his short and dark beard. His blond hair now longer, his rugged appearance seemed to fit well into the comfortable mountain atmosphere. There was something attractive about his new look, but she returned her thoughts to business. "You know more about those things than I do," she admitted, letting her eyes follow the streets that ran above and parallel to the gulch, one on top of the other in stair-step fashion. The little houses clung to the mountainside in a death grip. "I've made an allotment for equipment and materials, and we'll somehow have to buy something for that small amount of money. The rest of the money I got for selling the building—I think I'd better stick that back for rent and something to live on. We haven't much."

Jason nodded. It was true. Remodeling the old bar into living quarters and a business office had strained their funds, because lumber, along with everything else, was expensive. He cast his view down through the powdery air to the spewing smokestacks of the countless mills and squinted in the glare. "I think I've found a horse. I'm going to see the man this morning." Glancing at Jennifer, he made sure of her approval. "A horse seems like a good idea in this spread-out area—all these little towns around here. A man's got to get around somehow. I'll ride into Denver and see what I can find in the way of what we need."

Absorbing the news, Jennifer stared at Jason in disbelief. *He has changed,* she thought, but she liked the change. "I want you to take the money with you in case you find something—buy it. Have it shipped up here."

Jason scuffed his boot on the boardwalk, knocking off a stubborn clump of mud. "I could be gone for several days—but I won't let you down." He let his eyes wander to meet hers. They reassured her of his intentions.

Her hand gently touched his arm. She stood motionless for a second and then turned and walked back inside. Jason remained on the boardwalk in the sunshine, his sharp shadow unmoving beneath him. He dared to think, *Things are looking better between us*. Accepting the newfound confidence this gave him, his chest swelled as he took a deep breath.

~

Later in the morning, Jason wandered up Gregory Street to Central City, noting it was difficult to determine where the boundary lay between Black Hawk and Central City. However, Central City supported a different attitude up above the many mills of Black Hawk. It was a well-settled establishment of fine buildings and well-planned streets of lucrative businesses. Unlike Black Hawk, it seemed to brim with finer establishments like the dominant Teller House, a hostelry where often the famous performers of the day could be found.

When Jason found the stable, he walked on through to the back, where several horses stood on their feet munching, their heads down. A group of long-eared mules absorbed the warmth of the day in another small pen. One horse in particular had caught his eye, a spirited paint that stood off to the side with its head up sniffing the air.

Sirus Rhodes appeared, an old man well tuned to horses, owner of the livery. He was a short, fat man with a face full of long, yellow and gray whiskers. His hat was as worn-looking as he was, his leathered face showing wrinkles upon wrinkles around his cheerful eyes. "Still eyein' that paint, are yeh?" He glanced at Jason and, while waiting for an answer, he spit.

"Maybe," Jason said, not wanting Sirus to know that he wasn't a knowledged horseman.

"He's a mite spirited," Sirus boasted, "but he's young."

Jason nodded and, not looking at Sirus, put his boot up on a crossbar of the fence and rested his elbows on the top runner. "So you think he's got the wind to get around these mountains?" he asked, meaning that a young horse should.

Immediately Sirus thought he'd been exposed, since it took an expert to recognize that a horse was or wasn't a mountain horse. "Well . . ." Sirus said, laughing some. "No, he wasn't raised up here in the high country." He reflected a moment and said, "You know, I've brought horses up here from the flatlands and had them as long as ten years—they never develop the lungs for these mountains. That paint come from a man out of Kansas."

Glancing at the old man, who held his fat thumbs in his suspenders, Jason let him do the talking.

Pausing, Sirus glanced through slits for eyes, appraising Jason. He thought Jason had the look of a man who knew his business and he figured there wasn't any sense in wasting time with the haggling he reserved for amateurs. "Tell you what—you see that heavy roan over there? She's got muscles, was raised up here—now that's a tough mountain horse. She'll hold up to about anything, 'cept a mule. She's only seven years old. That'd be the horse fer yeh."

The animal does look sturdy, Jason thought, studying the horse that shone a deep, red chestnut color sprinkled with white in the clear sunlight. "She even-tempered?"

"Like no other. Say, you looking fer a saddle?"

"That's right," Jason said. "I came by train from Nevada, have to re-outfit." Jason thought this might sound good, a westerner who knew what he was talking about.

Sirus detected no false substance in Jason, only sincerity. He was a man who prided himself in not only knowing horses but being able to see men for what they were as well. This was a necessity for any seasoned poker player, and Sirus had never been known to walk past a poker table. "She's freshly shoed," he added.

Jason threw a stern look at Old Sirus. "Make me a deal."

Sirus smiled a toothless grin. "C'mon inside, let me show you this saddle. We can bicker over the price—depending on how much money you got."

No longer able to stay serious, Jason laughed at the old man.

"Makes no difference how much I got!" he said, provoking a laugh from Sirus.

A half-hour later, Jason trotted out onto the street, proudly sitting high on the handsome mare. He was amazed at how much better things looked from high up on a solid horse. She seemed quick to respond to his request, eager to be rode. Slowing her to a walk, Jason noticed the many stares he attracted from busy boardwalks, and he couldn't remember a single person noticing him when he'd walked up the street earlier. *This is a good day,* Jason thought as he rocked slowly in the squeaking saddle. The smell of saddle leather and the heavy horse scent filled his nostrils. He was eager to ride back to the office and show off his prize.

Jennifer heard a horse snort and glanced up to see a rider through the front window. She rushed outside to find Jason proudly leaning on the saddle horn, a big smile sweeping his bearded face. "How do you like her?" he asked, obviously well pleased with himself.

It was sort of deceptive, seeing Jason on a fine horse, for Jennifer saw something different in him. He had a natural look on a horse, something that enhanced her view of the man. "She's beautiful," Jennifer said, finally noticing the stocky and muscular build of Jason's mount.

From behind Jennifer, Abby came running, her eyes wide open with excitement, her heavy curls bouncing. For a second she just stood with her mouth open, then blurted out, "Is that yours, Jason? I love it—it's so pretty. Will you take me for a ride?"

Leaning over and offering her his hand, Jason gladly pulled little Abby up into the saddle in front of him. Grant soon appeared, curious as to what Abby was screaming about. "Ladies first," Jason said to Grant as he turned the mare and trotted off with a giggling Abby sitting in front of him.

"Where'd he get that, Mother?" Grant asked, surprised to see Jason on a horse.

"He decided he needed one," Jennifer said in simple and defensive praise.

Grant noticed the change in his mother. She hadn't always been this way toward Jason. He sifted through his emotions and came up with one plain answer—and it made him feel good.

When Jason returned, Lita and Abe were waiting, eager to see the new horse. Things had changed—nobody in the group could make any kind of decision without the others being involved. When Jason dismounted, Abe took the reins and held the horse steady, soothing her. He inspected her teeth and then dropped down to inspect her legs and hooves. Having been a mule expert most of his life, he figured he knew a little about horses as well. Lita watched, wiping her hands with a towel, waiting to hear Abe's appraisal. When he rose, he spoke to Jason. "She a strong horse," he said. "This horse used to pulling a heavy load. She glad to be out from under the harness."

Jason smiled, thinking, *Maybe that's why I get along with her. I'm glad to be out from under a harness, too.* Although they had a challenging survival in front of them, Jason did feel relieved of the burdens that had previously plagued him. It seemed life was finally opening up, and he credited this to his newly found spirituality, his faith in God, something he thanked Jennifer for.

~

Lita had her way with the backroom of the newspaper office, and it slowly became transformed into a homey kitchen, with pots dangling over the huge, black cook stove that replaced the old wood heater. Abe had footed the bill to suit her and did the work under her watchful eye. A large, weathered table surrounded by a conglomerate of different chairs served as the general hangout. She'd fixed Jason a bag of corn dodgers and jerky to keep him well fed on his trip. He'd left the next day at sunup, giving Jennifer a brief goodbye at the front door. Now she sat at the rectangular table with Lita, below a hanging kerosene lamp that burned with an oily scent.

"I hope he can find his way all right," Jennifer mumbled, referring to Jason. "There's a lot of people in the gulch, lots of people everywhere."

"Oh, he'll be all right," Lita said, impatient with any kind of nonsense. "He's a good man."

"Yeah," Jennifer sighed over a cup of coffee. "I just hate to see him take off on an unfamiliar horse like that into places he doesn't know."

Lita caught the glimpse Jennifer gave her and recognized the look a woman has for a man she truly cares about. It was no secret that Jennifer was developing feelings for the changing man, Jason Stone.

The back door rattled and Abe stumbled in, his big feet tracking mud.

"Wipe your feet!" Lita ordered, quick to catch Abe before he took another step.

Patiently, Abe stepped back and tried to knock the sticky mud from his boots. He held a hammer in his hand. "I got the step fixed," he said, trying to divert her attention to something more promising.

"Good. Now you can go around front and fix dem loose boards."

"Yes, ma'am. I get right to it." Abe crossed the board floor and poured himself a cup of Lita's coffee and swigged it down. "Dat taste good," he said and smiled a little, then left the room through the backdoor.

"I don't know what we'd do without Abe," Jennifer said, watching the big man's shadow disappear as he closed the door.

Lita turned, her mind on Abe. "He a good man, too. They both lucky men—they got good women."

Suddenly catching her intent, Jennifer straightened her shoulders. She'd didn't realize that Lita now associated her with Jason in that kind of way. *Is it obvious?* she wondered. *Is it true?*

The day seemed long for Jennifer as she tried to concentrate on arranging the front office with the little bit of junk they'd already collected. She kept wondering about Jason's whereabouts and if he was doing all right. By evening, she'd grown tired. Keeping an eye on the children and planning the business and worrying about Jason had worn her out. After seeing that the children were safely tucked in, she went to bed, a lamp burning at her bedside.

It was dark outside. Jennifer's room being a front room on the second floor, her window overlooked the street. A group of miners wailed drunkenly in a cheerful song as they passed below. *Those*

Cornish men, she thought. *They always seem so happy, and I know they have such hard lives in the mines*. But she'd learned quickly that Black Hawk and Central City were peaceful towns, rarely suffering the rowdy misfortunes she'd seen in Virginia City. *Things seem in order now—and planned out as best we can plan them*, she reasoned, yet something tugged at her inside. The fact that Jason wasn't there disturbed her. Blowing out the lamp, she laid back on her pillow, the distant night filled with the irregular pounding of the mills. For the first time, she addressed her real feelings for Jason. *I can't be falling in love. It just isn't rational, not right now*. Rolling over, she pulled the covers up against the crisp night air. *But when has love in my life ever been rational?* she asked herself. For a long time she lay there before she finally fell into a dream-filled sleep.

~

Jason took off out of Black Hawk filled with hope, happily guiding his new bay down Clear Creek toward Denver. Passing the persistent placer miners, he rode deep in the saddle with his legs pushed against the stirrups and his rein hand lifted and ready to swing the horse. He was swallowed by the gulch surrounded by steep mountains, rough and old and massively somber from their many years of survival. In all of this, there was a serenity that stopped him and sent its thready feelings into those places where a man keeps his ancient instincts. The pressure of the mountain country, its secrecy, its hint of dark, hidden glens, its massive indifference, was upon him. But he pressed onward, the day's light growing, the sun's warmth finally beckoning him out of his coat.

Relaxed, he did some soul searching, pondering how all things are somehow tied together. It was like he'd been awakened to a new enlightenment—ever since he'd read the Bible and tried to comprehend the thousands of years that it covered. A few things he knew—he knew he loved Jennifer and wanted her, but there was more. He had a need to be somebody, yet this somebody slightly eluded him, for he wasn't sure who this somebody was.

Spurring his horse, the mare grunted to the other side of the road to let a mule team and freighter by. Jason tipped his hat to the two men riding on the buckboard. One waved a callused hand.

Only a day's ride, Denver showed itself from the buttes out of Golden late in the afternoon as Jason picked up his horse's gait. He'd learned much in a short time about Denver and Black Hawk. It seemed the gold rush had brought thousands to Denver, only to be led to disappointment. Denver wasn't even in the mountains but out in the plains, and it soon became a desperate tent town, until the gold strike up Clear Creek encouraged the Denver fortune seekers to take to the hills. Back in the 1860s, people in Black Hawk and Central City outnumbered the people in Denver—the heyday of a gold boomtown. But then the surface ore petered out, and the sulfide rock from the deeper depths was much more difficult to separate from the gold, so much so that Black Hawk dwindled to small numbers of people. But thanks to Nathaniel P. Hill's smelter, built in 1867, called the Boston and Colorado Smelting Works, a smelter that had a process for obtaining the gold from the stubborn ores, the towns were renewed to their now-flowering status.

But Denver! Look at this! Jason thought as he rode into the city at dusk. *I never would have believed it!* It was a brick metropolis, well-lit in the late afternoon and thriving with people. Flat and expanding, it enclosed around him as he rode in, taken by the sights. He had heard that people still arrived by the hundreds every day to the city that was now known as the Gateway to the West.

Entering on the long east-by-west avenue that stretched across the town, Jason found a livery to retire his worn-out steed. In his search for a room, he unknowingly ran into a saloon district buzzing with nightlife. Pianos jangled their tunes into the streets, while a singing chorus of women's voices came from another high-spirited saloon.

"Hey, handsome, need a date?"

Turning, Jason saw a lovely young girl dressed in a scarlet, low-cut dress. He immediately saw Molly in her—the resemblance was astounding. A sadness touched him; he'd been close to the unfortunate Molly back in Virginia City, who'd given her life to save his.

"No thanks," Jason said, moving on, but his eyes stuck to the attractive young girl.

Tired from a full day's ride, Jason had a hot meal and checked into a cheap hotel—a bed was all he needed. Collapsing on his bunk in the darkness of a small room, he again found his mind searching for more answers to those things unknown, the lack of knowledge that drives a man forward. And then his thoughts drifted to Jennifer and the fact that she seemed so far away. A disturbing doubt rose in him about her. *What if she doesn't come around?* He felt a sickening pulse rise in his stomach and knew he definitely couldn't accept that. In reality, things were looking better than they ever had.

~

The next morning the sights and sounds of Denver were astonishing, but Jason turned his efforts into a search for a press and printing materials. Questioning the shop owners all morning finally led him to a miserable dump near the market area, where he found a weasel of a man sitting on a fortune in junk. The man introduced himself as Horace Fornby. It was easy to assess the situation. This man was a speculator, like most others who had come west, only he speculated in the misfortunes of others. When the fortune seekers arrived to find their destiny one of despair, they were forced to sell what little holdings they might have in order to survive or to return to where they'd come from. Hence, the scandalous parasite appeared—Horace Fornby—offering a dime on the dollar to those too desperate not to accept.

"I'm looking for a press," Jason said, a little disgusted at having to deal with the man.

Horace Fornby was short, thin, and weak-looking, with close-set eyes and thick glasses; his hair was greased to a shiny sharpness. He looked like a shrew. "I have a few good presses," he said, leading Jason to a back room over-stuffed with everything imaginable. Mr. Fornby removed some boxes to expose a dusty press.

"That's for printing handbills," Jason said, growing impatient. "I need the things for a newspaper—a press, letters, woodcuts, printer's drawers, ink and paper. I was told you had these things!"

"Yes," Mr. Fornby sighed with a hiss of pleasure. "And what was your name, young man?"

"Stone! Jason Stone."

"Yes, of course. Are you a chronicler, Mr. Stone?"

"Yes, I am," Jason said.

"Well, why didn't you say so, Mr. Stone? Follow me."

Jason followed the little, hunched-over man to a door he unlocked and stepped into the dark, where he lit a huge kerosene lamp. When the glow filled the room, Jason almost fainted. The room was crammed with several presses and every kind of newspaper item one could think of. "Whew!" Jason said. "What's all of this?"

"There were many people who had the idea of starting a newspaper." Mr. Fornby obviously took great pleasure in their failure.

Rushing over, Jason inspected the presses. "How much for this Washington Press?"

Mr. Fornby smiled, his tender nose sniffing money. "Three hundred dollars."

"Are you crazy?" Jason protested. "I could buy a new one for that."

"If you were back East, you could," corrected Mr. Fornby.

"What about this?" Jason said, pointing at an old roller press.

"Two hundred dollars," Mr. Fornby said greedily.

"I'm wasting my time here!" Jason said, pushing the weasel aside so he could leave.

"Wait!" cried Mr. Fornby, his voice high-pitched, almost squealing. "There's this," he said, pointing to a partial press. "If you know a blacksmith, this can be repaired."

Turning around, Jason saw a large, complex press with a sliding table. It wasn't a Washington Press but something like it. "What kind of press is that?" Jason asked, having never seen anything like it. "I can't read that writing on the side."

"It's German, brought here by some German immigrants. Like I said, if you know a blacksmith, you can have these busted legs repaired and be in business."

Well, Jason knew a very good blacksmith, Abe Washington. The only problem was, Abe would need access to a blacksmith shop.

"How much?" Jason asked, afraid of what the slippery little man might say.

"Only fifty dollars."

"Hmmm," Jason answered, bringing his hand up to his mouth. "How about all of the other things I'll need?"

And so it began, a day's worth of bickering over every little thing as Mr. Fornby tirelessly haggled over every penny, until the money Jason had was almost thoroughly exhausted. Satisfied he had all he would need, Jason assisted Mr. Fornby in crating up his purchase. "I'll have a freighter over here to pick this up right away," Jason said.

"Of course," answered a happy Mr. Fornby. "I'll have it ready."

Jason couldn't help but suspect that the little man had a sixth sense in determining how much money a person had in his wallet. Glad to leave and taking in some fresh air, he had the feeling he'd been fleeced—but the problem was blatant—there just wasn't enough money to buy anything worthwhile. Within twenty minutes, Jason had made a deal with a freighter to haul the stuff up to Black Hawk. It felt good for a change to do business with a hardworking and honest man, a man who smelled of sweat rather than swindle.

"This was a tougher day than I imagined it would be," Jason said, mounting his horse. Heading back to his room, he passed some of the grandest saloons he'd ever seen. "Be nice to go in and have a drink," he thought, almost entertaining the idea. "But I know I can't just have a drink—I always have too many. And that would displease God." Disgusted with his lack of discipline in that area, he spurred his mount onward.

~

The trip back up the mountain seemed shorter now that Jason was familiar with it. The wagon should only be a day behind him, but he was glad he'd found the deal, because the prices in Denver were far too high to have bought anything else. Although the machine was foreign, he felt sure they'd figure it out; a press was a press.

When he arrived in Black Hawk late in the afternoon, a smiling and curious Jennifer greeted him, her excitement weakly suppressed. "What did you find, Jason? Tell me about it. Something good, I hope."

Jason hadn't tied the reins of his horse yet. Lita was right behind Jennifer. "Miss Jenny! Give the man time to breathe—he just rode up the mountain all day. Get on in here!" she ordered Jason. "I got supper ready—we all want to hear about your trip."

"Oh, you're right, Lita," Jennifer said. "Come on in, Jason, and wash up for supper—we all want to hear about it."

Jason smiled, happy to be the center of attention, happy to see Jennifer happy, and happy to be back with her. Over a succulent antelope roast and stewed potatoes, Jason told his story to his eager listeners. "Then I told that little guy he'd have to give me a better price, either that or throw in another box of woodcuts!"

"I can't wait to see it," Jennifer said, happily pleased.

"I don't know nothin' about newspapers, but that man sound scandalous!" Lita said.

Abe grunted, laughing to himself as he bent over his plate. When it was polite for him to speak, he said, "I'd sure be glad to look at dat machine—if I can fix it, I will."

"I'm counting on you, Abe," Jason said, certain Abe would have no problem.

"Maybe we can have a paper out by the end of the week," Jennifer said hopefully. It was clear the vigor and excitement that inspired her to come to Black Hawk had returned.

From early the next morning and into the day, Jennifer and Jason expectantly watched for a freighter to turn up Merchant Street. When a mule protested the muleskinner's whip, they both ran to the front to see a wagon rambling up the long, dirt avenue.

Waving his hat, Jason recognized the freighter he'd hired. "Over here!" he shouted. "Over here!"

Once unloaded and scattered in the front office, Jennifer surveyed the purchase. "Looks like we've got everything we need."

Abe was bent over the heavy press, removing the stubs of broken legs. "I can have this fixed in no time," he said, proud that his skills were needed.

"You know a blacksmith that'll let you use his shop?" Jason asked.

"Yes, sir," Abe said. "I already been shoeing mules for him, Mr. Blake is his name."

"Well," Jason said, leaning over Jennifer, who was on the floor picking through the boxes. He gently placed his arm around her, and her smell was sweet. "Looks like we're about to be back in business."

Jennifer turned her face up to Jason's; they were very close. She smiled a smile of enthusiasm, almost a young girl's smile. "Yes, we are, thanks to you."

CHAPTER

5

New Faces

Grant and Abby were enrolled in school, the public school up on Church Street next to the Presbyterian church. For Grant it merely meant more dreary classes and boring studies; however, he felt compelled to make a good effort and get good marks so as not to disappoint his mother. He felt his real learning came from working with the newspaper, the center of local news.

But it was Saturday, and Grant wandered about Black Hawk, discovering his new surroundings. He moved along the west side of Gregory Street through the little pools of odors thrown out by adjacent shops—liquor and leather and bread and the dry fragrance of cotton goods and pungent odors of livestock. Liveries and counting houses and saloons and hotels crowded side by side, brick and wood and false fronts and board awnings tethered together made for a continuous statement of a prosperous town's industry. A dense jam of drays stood hub to hub, and brawling teamsters crowded Gregory Street in their fight to negotiate the hill up to nearby Central City.

For Grant, it had been immediately obvious that some sort of rivalry existed between Central City and Black Hawk, yet the people got along perfectly fine; their differences lay on a community level, each trying to outdo the other. Central City seemed to support the more social affairs, while the mining district depended on Black Hawk mills. Wide-eyed and amazed at the mountain cities, he rambled on, taking in the sights, the hard shadows a reminder of the warm noonday sun.

A loud commotion caught Grant's attention as he turned to see a man tumble down the steps and land facefirst in the muddy street. The swinging doors of the Toll Gate Saloon slapped behind him until a man appeared and steadied them, then stepped out on the boardwalk. The man in the street slowly came to his knees and shook his head, then found his footing and got to his feet. Covered with mud, he turned to the big man behind him on the boardwalk. "Let that be a lesson to you, McClary," warned the heavy man from the saloon doors. "Next time you get caught cheating in here, we'll ride you out of town!" His voice was deep and rough and had the texture of a voice that meant business.

The man in the street wiped the mud off his long face and swayed on his feet, drunk, then turned, his back hunched like a scolded dog, and swaggered away. The beefy man on the boardwalk stepped back into the saloon.

"Typical greenhorn," came a young man's voice. Grant turned to see who was speaking and saw a smiling young face, much like his own, a boy who had stood behind him and observed the scene. "Any gambler knows you don't play when you're too drunk to cheat," the boy said.

"Yeah," Grant agreed, staring at the boy. He was Grant's size and looked to be almost Grant's age. Straw-like hair hung across his forehead and a likable smile widened his square jaw. His blue eyes were lively and a little crazy. "Do you go to school here?" Grant asked, not remembering seeing his face before.

"I'm a result of the school of hard knocks," the boy boasted. "Nothing like experience for a teacher—at least that's what my Uncle Mike always says."

Grant studied this interesting boy. He seemed so immediately likable, a friendly sort of fellow who knew the ropes of a town like Black Hawk. "What's your name?"

"Robert Parker," the boy said, offering his hand for a manly shake.

"I'm Grant DeSpain," Grant said, taking the boy's hand and noticing his firm grip.

They were dressed similarly, two young men in woolen pants and cotton shirts, and both mature for their young years. "You talk funny—you ain't from around here, are you?" Robert asked.

"We just got here several weeks ago," Grant said. "Came here from Virginia City."

"Oh. Your dad a miner?"

"My father died a long time ago," Grant mumbled. "My mother's a newspaper woman."

Robert laughed out loud. "I didn't take you for no miner's son—you don't got the look. My Uncle Mike says these miners is for fleecing, just like sheep."

All of a sudden, Grant found himself liking this new acquaintance more and more. "What does your Uncle Mike do?"

"He's a gambler mostly, but he teaches me other things, the kind of things a fellow needs to know to get along in this world." Robert let his eyes turn to the street as he reflected on his well-traveled knowledge. "I ride with him."

"My father was a gambler," Grant said, proud to brag on something about his father for the first time in his life.

"I knew it!" Robert said, throwing his arm around Grant's neck. "We come from the same stock, I tell you. It's hard to find a man you can trust nowadays."

Well-mannered Grant couldn't stop the smile that came easily to his face. "I was born in New Orleans. My father was a riverboat gambler."

His eyes lighting up, Robert removed his arm and reached in a pocket to produce a small bag. He quickly grabbed a paper from a shirt pocket and professionally built a smoke. "I wish I was from somewhere great like New Orleans," Robert said as his hands worked with the tobacco.

"Where you from?" Grant questioned.

Rolling his eyes in disgust, Robert replied, "Beaver, Utah."

Grant shrugged his shoulders. "So what! What's wrong with that?"

"It's a strange place," Robert informed him. "All they talk about is religion."

"I'm a Christian," Grant said, admitting that his faith was a part of his life.

"Well, the folks there aren't exactly Christians like you're used to," Robert said. "I was proud to take off out of there with my Uncle Mike, only he really ain't my uncle. We spend time in the boom-towns—he gambles and I take care of everything else."

This seemed to be the most interesting fellow Grant had ever met who was around his own age. "Exactly what do you do?" Grant asked, kicking at a knothole in the boardwalk.

"I'm a runner when we're in a town. I run and get them meals while they're gambling, or I get our clothes washed at a laundry. I see that the horses are taken care of, and I watch our hotel room—make sure no unhappy loser tries to come rob us." He smiled and stuck the cigarette in his mouth. "I'm invaluable, at least that's what Uncle Mike says."

Amazed, Grant couldn't imagine such an exciting and loose life. *No wonder Robert is so smart*, he thought. *He's been around!*

"Tell you what!" Robert said, striking a match and lighting the newly rolled cigarette. "My close friends call me Butch—that's a nickname my Uncle Mike gave me from one time when I tried to cut up some meat from a cow—thought I was a butcher. But that's a long story; anyway, from now on you just call me Butch!"

"Sure," said Grant, proud to have a friend, since he'd never really had any close friends his age. "How old are you, Butch? Aren't you too young to be smoking?"

"I'm near eleven, but Uncle Mike says I act a lot older, and he says I can smoke if I want to."

"I'm eleven," Grant said. "How come you're not working now?"

Butch took a light draft on his cigarette, and the smoke scurried away in the pleasant fall breeze. "He's sleeping now, gambled all night."

Nodding, Grant realized he'd need to be getting back before long. "Well," he said hesitantly. "I've got to go now. Why don't you come by sometime—I'm over on Merchant Street, the old bar there turned into a newspaper office."

"You bet!" Butch said, happy to know Grant. "I'll be by."

~

Abe had done a professional job on the press, forging new, iron legs and riveting them sturdily into place so that the black, iron press sat squarely and proudly in the front office of the remodeled building. But the machine persisted in being a puzzle to both Jason and Jennifer.

"Do you have any idea what these adjustments are for?" Jennifer asked quietly, about out of ideas as to how to operate the press. The first five attempts at printing a page had come out smudgy and illegible.

Scratching his head, Jason sighed, "Could be something to do with holding the table steady. It's hard to tell." He was at a loss, having tried the many knobs and levers unsuccessfully. "I never dreamed a press could get the best of me. This thing looked like our old one, but I didn't notice that it had so many adjustable parts."

Again they tried to run their new first edition, a page introducing the paper to the town and what the paper's intentions were, but this time the press smashed the text into a motley double print. The large print with the name of the paper, *The Black Hawk Advertiser*, was the only part legible.

A long strand of wavy auburn hair hung across Jennifer's face as she struggled with a large lever under the table. Standing, her white teeth biting her bottom lip, a look of dismay engulfed her face. Jason noticed her concentrating on the workings of the machine, her determined enthusiasm now waning. Yet to him, her disheveled appearance and red cheeks struck him as something special, her good looks brazened by the turmoil. He had a deep sense of responsibility in that he'd been trusted to buy the equipment to get them into business, and now he felt accountable.

"It's all my fault," he offered apologetically. "I thought I knew what I was doing." She raised her eyes to him, clearly sorrowful. "Jennifer, there's only so many adjustments on this thing—I'll keep trying until it works, even if it takes all night."

Forcing a smile, Jennifer wiped her forehead with the back of her arm. "I'm sorry. I'm so tired."

"Why don't you go see if Lita needs some help with serving supper—take a break from this thing."

Glancing at the complex machine, Jennifer nodded her head.

She wasn't one to give up but, for the moment, she had grown tired of guessing. "I do need to take a break. We've been at this for hours."

About that time Grant came blowing in through the front door, slamming it behind him. "Mother—I found a friend! He's near my age, and he's been around, knows all about this town!"

"That's good, Grant," Jennifer said, trying to show some enthusiasm. She suddenly realized that her exasperation had drained her.

Grant turned to Jason. "My new friend—he's real friendly."

Understanding, Jason took advantage of the situation in using it as an excuse to forget the press. "Say! That *is* good news. Why don't we go wash up, and you can tell us about it over supper."

Rushing away, Grant disappeared to the back to prepare for supper. Jason smiled at Jennifer. "Well? It is good news. I don't remember Grant having any close friends before."

Jennifer had a hard time changing her line of thought. She was stuck on the worries of the press. She glanced at Jason with something between reserve and doubt, but then she realized that by dwelling on the immediate problem she had closed out everything else. "Yes, you're right. It's a good day for Grant—maybe things won't be so bad here—maybe I'm just impatient."

"Let's eat," Jason said, leading her to the back. "I've worked up an appetite."

~

In the days to come, Jason made the press work by using a series of wedge-shaped wooden blocks, each neatly fitted to a certain crevice to hold things steady or act as a jam for moving metal parts. Finally, the first edition came out with amazing clarity, the artistic title print an eye-catching work of art. Pleased with his labor, Jason was up first early the next morning and ready to make some deliveries. He took a bundle of papers and went behind the office, to an open area where he and Abe had previously fashioned a shed to make a stall for his horse.

The crisp morning chill whispered of winter coming, but Jason didn't notice, eager to get going. The mare neighed at his approach, now used to Jason, her head bouncing as he came closer.

"Good girl," Jason said softly as he stroked the horse's head. "How are you this morning, Dolly?" This was a name Jason had chosen carefully for the chestnut mare, and she seemed to already answer to it. The name came from memories back in his childhood, his large family and their plush farm, the horse he'd had when he was a child. The dream-like fantasy of his wonderful childhood abruptly ended with the war and the loss of their farm. *I ought to write a book about it someday*, he thought, remembering the tragedy. *Then tell of the adventures out west.*

Once saddled up, Jason took off for Nevadaville, a town up above Central City. *I'll see to it that just about every business has a copy of this*, he thought cheerfully. *First, we'll start off as advertisers, work in a few newsworthy stories—and see where it goes*. He knew it would take most of the day to make all the rounds and get back down through Central City and, at last, Black Hawk. The fine fall weather was at its peak and so was Jason, feeling better than he ever had.

Not far behind Jason, Abe had awakened to the smoky smell of sausage. He quickly got out of his bunk and threw on his dungarees and rushed downstairs. Early breakfast was a high point of his day, a moment to spend alone with Lita before the others got up, because he had to be at work early.

"Wash up before you sit at my table," Lita ordered when she saw Abe come through the kitchen door. She hadn't turned to him to speak. "How's your job?"

Abe smiled, his features heavy with sleep. He walked onto the back porch, hung up his hat and his worn jacket, and rolled back his sleeves. "Best I ever had," he said, and brought the wash basin to her. She filled it from a kettle on the stove and gave him her first moment of undivided attention in the morning light. Her eyes were as brown as his, and they held for him a certain interest, an interest she'd never held for any other man.

Taking the basin to the rear porch, he straddled his legs and washed in a noisy, thorough way. He brushed back his gray hair and had a look at himself in the cloudy porch mirror and stepped back into the kitchen. He stood by the stove while Lita lifted a pan of fresh biscuits from the oven. The heat from the stove gave comfortable, homey warmth.

"Dat man you work for—he a good man?" Lita asked.

"Yes, ma'am. I don't just shoe mules no more. I do all the blacksmithin'." Abe felt good about his work. He liked to forge things with big hammers and watch the hot embers turn the metal cherry-red. A sturdy wagon wheel rim or a pile of sharpened miner's bits left him filled with satisfaction.

After piling a heap of greasy sausages and flaky steaming biscuits on Abe's plate, Lita filled his metal cup with hot coffee, then sat before him and watched him eat. It wasn't necessary to say much; they knew how they felt about each other.

When Abe finished, he rose from the table, as did Lita, and he placed his huge hand on her round shoulder. "Nobody do better than you," he said in his deep and solemn voice. Then he turned and left through the back door for another day's work. He was a happy man.

~

Grant found Butch loitering near the same place he'd met him the first time, except it was late one afternoon after school. The days were getting shorter, and the pink sun sank behind the mountains. "Hey! Butch!" Grant called as he approached.

"If it ain't my good friend!" exclaimed Butch, happy to see Grant. "I was going to come see you but got tied up with business—you know how it is."

Tightening his lips, Grant nodded in a manly way, pretending he understood. He had his hands stuffed in his coat pockets; the afternoons were getting cooler. "Are you working?"

"Sort of," smiled Butch. "They just started a game. Won't be needing nothing out of me for a while. Say, do you want to have a peek at what's going on?"

Quizzically, Grant inspected Butch for seriousness, wondering if maybe he was joking since it was widely known that no children were allowed in bars and saloons. "Yeah, sure, but how can we get in a place like that and watch?"

"Not a problem," said Butch. "Follow me."

The two sneaked around the side of an old saloon, and Butch jumped up on a low-slung roof. He turned around and pulled Grant up. Once up, they made their way around to the back where there was an opening into a sort of attic. Butch removed some loose boards and crept in, Grant following closely behind. Through the darkness Butch led Grant until they came to a wall where Butch crouched down and peaked through a long crack in the boards. Grant squatted beside him and looked. Below them, through the heavy smoke, sat a group of men at a felt-covered table playing poker.

"Don't make any noise," Butch whispered.

Grant nodded, shaking a little with fear. *What if we're caught?*

"That man sitting away from us—that's Uncle Mike," whispered Butch. "I have to come back up here tonight where I can see the other player's hands from here. We have signals worked out where I can let Uncle Mike know when they're bluffing."

Swallowing hard, Grant looked through the crack in the board and sure enough, he could see the other players' hands.

"C'mon," Butch said, tugging gently at Grant's sleeve. It was a little scary, so Grant was relieved to be leaving.

Once back out on the street, Grant asked, "Don't you have to know how to play poker to do what you're doing?"

"Of course," Butch answered. "I'm a good poker player."

Amazed, Grant felt a little envious of Butch and his clever ways.

"Would you look at that!" Butch said, jutting his chin toward the street.

Following Butch's eyes, Grant saw a man riding down the street, but this was no ordinary man. He stood out like a gem among barren rock, tall in the saddle of his fine, black stallion. His clothes were as sharp as the horse, a black trim on the lapels of his pewter-colored waistcoat, his boots black and finely polished, the black top hat cocked forward. He wore the constant smile of a true gentleman, his thin mustache curling slightly up at the ends, his eyes alive with the kind of fire a man has who is filled with great self-confidence.

"Wow!" Grant said, highly impressed with this man and his ride.

"That ain't nothin' but money!" Butch said knowingly. "I'll bet you anything you want that he has an engraved pearl-handled Colt under that fancy coat and maybe another couple of pistols hid besides that!"

The boys, easily impressed by such as this man, watched him ride slowly out of sight down the street. "I wonder who he is?" asked Grant.

"I'll tell you who he is," Butch said. "He's somebody real important."

Grant agreed. "I better get home before it gets dark," he said. "I'll see you later, Butch."

"Anytime," Butch yelled after Grant.

~

Grant was shocked to see the fine, black stallion reined to a post right outside of the newspaper office. He stopped in his tracks, swallowed hard, then pressed through the front door. There before him stood a tall and angular man talking to his mother. He eased the front door closed and slipped around the perimeter of the room, his big eyes on this very different man.

"Yes, Mr. Rivers," Jennifer was saying. "We can run all of the advertisements you want. I don't care how many horses you have."

The man smiled, his sharp blue eyes catching Grant as the boy tried to slip by unnoticed.

Noticing, Jennifer said, "Come here, Grant. I want you to meet somebody."

Nervously, Grant approached.

"This is Mr. Lance Rivers. He owns the biggest horse ranch in the territory of Colorado—or so he says," Jennifer said, jokingly casting Mr. Rivers a knowing wink of an eye. "This is my son Grant, Mr. Rivers."

"He's a fine-looking boy!" Rivers said firmly, his face an expression of complete approval. "Do you like horses, Grant?"

"Yes, sir, I do," Grant muttered.

"Then you'll have to come to my ranch some time. I've got the finest string this side of the Mississippi. Do you ride, Grant?"

"Well, sir, I haven't had much of a chance to," Grant said almost apologetically.

Quickly, Rivers threw a disapproving glance at Jennifer. He was a dominant man, a full six feet tall, with raven hair and deep, black eyes. His thin mustache and hair were finely groomed, his clothes exclusively tailored. His prominence was due to more than wealth, for he spoke like a man well educated, a man quite sure of himself. "Mrs. DeSpain, we'll have to cure that right away! A fine young man like this can't live in these parts and not be a horseman."

"Well—" Jennifer said, placing her hand to her throat, almost stuttering. She couldn't help but be a little put out in this man's commanding presence.

"Winter is coming and I have plenty of fine horses that must go. Now, the *Register*, your competition in Central City, says I clog up their advertising section with too many horse deals. I need a paper that will run the advertisements I ask them to run. I only raise the very finest horses, Mrs. DeSpain," Rivers said, staring long and hard into Jennifer's eyes to drive home his point. "I was born and raised in Kentucky, and I know horses!" He glared at her again, but the pleasant smile remained on his mouth. "I'm sure there's some way we can manage to get this young man on a good horse, don't you think?"

Almost flabbergasted, Jennifer gulped a breath of air. "Well, I don't know, Mr. Rivers. We're not exactly solvent right now—we had a bit of bad luck a while back."

Rivers winked at Jennifer and glanced back at Grant. "Don't worry, son, where there's a will, there's a way." Changing his tone, he removed a group of papers from his vest pocket. "Here's a list of the horses I want you to run in your next edition and the asking prices. Also, I'll be holding an auction I want you to advertise, and here are the details on that." He spread the papers on the desk and looked at Jennifer politely for her response.

A quick glance at the papers and Jennifer could see the information would take up a lot of room in the paper. "Certainly, Mr. Rivers, but I'm afraid this will take up most of a full page—a rather expensive advertisement."

Quickly, Rivers removed a fat billfold from inside his vest and opened it. It bulged with so many bills that it looked like he had stuffed a newspaper in it. "Name your price, Mrs. DeSpain."

After some quick figuring, Jennifer rounded the price high and the gentleman laid down the money on the table. "Thank you very much, Mrs. DeSpain," he said in a friendly tone.

"All of the pleasure has been mine, I assure you."

He then gave her a glance, the kind of desirable glance a man gives a woman when he has strong feelings for her.

Jennifer hadn't seen an intense wanting in a man's gaze like that since Drake, her late husband, had first looked at her—she knew the look, and she didn't entirely dislike the attention. "We certainly appreciate your business, Mr. Rivers. We need all the advertisements we can get."

Lance Rivers turned to the door and then turned back to Jennifer. "I'll see how much business I can send your way," he said, smiling, his teeth perfectly straight and white. "I'll be in town next week to get a copy of your paper. I'll stop by to see you."

"Please do," Jennifer replied before she realized her answer sounded like an invitation.

Stepping out, Lance Rivers left, leaving Grant and his mother awestruck from his dominant presence.

"Wow!" Grant said. "I never saw anyone like him before!"

"'Wow' is right," Jennifer said. She was almost afraid of men like that—they were the kind she seemed to always get mixed up with and then would discover the bad news later. But this man was no stranger to money, power, and self-esteem. He had a sparkle about him, a graciousness found in Southern gentlemen, and obviously knew the right things to do around a woman. In him she saw a power that she'd seen in no other man before—the ability to make people like him, to make people want to see things his way, a leadership quality based on an illusive persuasion. *I'd better be careful around this character,* she thought, still staring at the door that this very unusual man had disappeared through. Then she thought, *What in the world am I thinking?*

CHAPTER

~ 6 ~

The Accident

Early the next morning, Jennifer, Jason, and the children sat cozily around the homey breakfast table while Lita stirred a number ten skillet full of scrambled eggs. A smoky haze hung in the air from the leaky stove while Jason sipped hot coffee.

"You must've gotten in late last night," Jennifer remarked, not having heard Jason's return.

Nodding, Jason skimmed over another newspaper he'd picked up during his ride, the *Register*. "Yes, I rode all over, gave everyone a copy of our first edition. This is some beautiful country once you get outside of the milling district, and Central City—it's something to see! I'll have to take you up there soon."

Smiling pleasantly, Jennifer thought of an outing with Jason, the new Jason, a man who was much more sure of himself. His different look with a short beard added to his appeal. "I had a little luck myself. A horse rancher came in, a fellow by the name of Lance Rivers, and ran a huge ad with us to sell some of his herd. He said he has a horse ranch in a valley below here."

"That *is* good news!"

"You should see the horse he rides!" chimed in Grant. "It's the most beautiful horse I've ever seen! He said he wants to get me a horse, too!"

"What?" Jason said, alerted to the strange proposition. "Why would a stranger want to get you a horse?"

"He's quite a character," Jennifer added cheerfully. "Reminds me of a gentleman from one of the wealthy plantations back down South."

Perplexed, Jason's curiosity swelled. "Is he an old southern aristocrat?"

"Not at all," Jennifer went on to say. "He appears to be quite wealthy—somewhere in his thirties—a nice-looking man, from Kentucky, so he says."

Jason caught Grant hiding a mischievous smile and suspected something was up. He felt a vague ripple of jealousy.

"He was making eyes at Mother," Grant blurted out.

"Grant!" Jennifer scolded. She set her coffee cup down. "He did no such thing! That's—that's just how Southern gentlemen are."

"I'm hungry, Lita!" Abby protested, bored with the talk.

"It's ready, child," Lita said as she circled the table and dished out a pile of steaming scrambled eggs on the plates she'd set out. "The biscuits is just about ready. Abe done ate the first batch an hour ago before he left."

Digging into breakfast, Jason didn't care to hear any more about this Lance Rivers. After a few bites, he said, "You know, Dolly is a good horse. She's strong, goes over these hills like it was nothing. The long rides don't seem to bother her at all."

"Do you plan on distributing this next edition the same way? Riding all over?" Jennifer questioned, her hair up and her eyes soft.

"Why not?" Jason replied. "Until we get established, I'll be glad to spread our paper around. "Looks like the *Register* here doesn't do as much advertising as we plan on doing. Plus, it looks like they're more determined to cover Central City social affairs than actual news. There may be a place for us here. Getting out and moving these papers gives me a chance to pick up on some of the things going on. Why, I heard of a bar fight yesterday."

"A bar fight! We don't want to cover bar fights in our newspaper," Jennifer warned.

"We might if the bar fight was between two city councilmen," Jason said, smiling. "I got the scoop right here," he added, proudly patting his coat pocket.

"Well," Jennifer said, a worried frown on her face, "we have to be careful. I don't want the *Advertiser* to get the reputation of being a gossip rag."

"Don't worry," Jason replied. "I'll write it with great scrutiny. It is a rather humorous story. Plus, I picked up another story that's somewhat interesting. There's more churches around here than you'd ever guess, and the competition is fierce. Not only is this the richest square mile on earth, but maybe has the most churches too. I think it'd make a good human-interest story—so many churches so close together, yet, ironically, the church memberships are very small."

Jennifer smiled. These kinds of stories pleased her, as well as the fact that Jason had taken an interest in noticing something like that. In the past he wouldn't have cared. "Off to school, children," she said evenly as she noticed them lingering at the table to hear any gossip-worthy news.

Grant got up from the table and went to help Abby, but she pushed him away and got out of her chair with a snide remark. "I don't like this school either. They treat me like I was a little baby or something. I wish I was older, like twenty, then I'd do what I want and nobody could tell me what to do!"

"You'll grow up soon enough," Jennifer said mildly, always careful with Abby's quick temper.

After the children had left the kitchen, Jason let his eyes swing to meet Jennifer's. He made sure Lita had her back to them as his blue eyes clearly expressed his overwhelming fondness for her.

Certain of what Jason said without the use of words, Jennifer gave a little smile back. The look in her eyes was the kind of look a woman gives a man when she approves of him, that certain look that makes a man feel worthy.

"What do you say we get to work? Print a paper?" Jason asked, eager to spend the day with the paper and Jennifer.

"Sounds delightful, Mr. Stone," Jennifer replied playfully.

~

The day went well, a pleasant autumn day of calm breezes and golden sunshine, until it came time to print the copies. The German press stubbornly refused to keep the print square on the page. Again and again Jason made adjustments, but the machine remained incapable of complying. "This looks terrible," he complained, running out of patience. "Maybe we would've been better off to have kept our old press and had it shipped out here."

Closing her eyes and rubbing her temples, Jennifer felt the discomfort of a dull headache. "I wonder if we'll have to go through this every single time we want to print," she said discouragingly. "Seems like this thing doesn't ever want to stay set—like it has a mind of its own."

Wadding up the copy and throwing it on the floor with several other failed attempts scattered about, Jason took a small hammer and tapped on the wooden blocks he had wedged in the loose mechanical workings of the press. Again he tried to print a copy, but the type had run off the page. "Looks like I'm in for a long afternoon!" he said wearily. "I can't understand why the table keeps moving. Maybe it's supposed to."

Jennifer shrugged hopelessly, not understanding mechanical equipment very well. "We made it work last time. We should be able to do it again."

About that time Grant came in the front door, his new friend rambling right behind him. "Hi, Mother. Hi, Jason. This is my friend, Butch." Grant turned, indicating his friend with a sweep of his hand.

"Well, pleased to meet you, Butch," Jason said friendly-like. There was no indication of his present disgust with the press.

"Good to meet you," Butch said in a manly fashion as he extended his hand to Jason for a firm shake. Then turning to Jennifer, he smiled and said, "The pleasure is mine, ma'am."

"It's nice to meet you too, Butch," Jennifer said, a little surprised at the boy's manners.

"We're going up to my room," Grant said as he pulled Butch along. "I want to show Butch those newspaper articles from Virginia City."

After the boys had left, Jason glanced at Jennifer. "It's good to see Grant has made such a close friend. Too bad Abby can't find someone to play with."

Shaking her head, Jennifer muttered, "Abby's got a tough shell—hard to break through. I often pray for her, that she can find some happiness. I'm not sure what else I can do—she seems so intent on being vengeful and stubborn."

Jason had a wrench and was turning a large worm screw underneath the table of the press. "She's going to be a heartbreaker, I can see it now. If she keeps getting prettier, I feel sorry for the fellows that give chase to her. And she is getting pretty—like her mother."

A slight color came to Jennifer's cheeks. It had been a long time since anyone had referred to her as being pretty, and in the dusty filth in a windy, rented building between rumbling quartz mills, it was hard to feel pretty. She glanced down at her boots and worn dress, her boots caked with dry mud, her dress dusty. "Thank you, Jason," she said, trying to put some heart in it. "This is a hard place for a woman to be attractive. It's the only place I've ever seen where a person can stand ankle deep in the mud and choke on dust at the same time."

Swinging the big lever on the press, Jason tried another copy. "Mud, dust, it doesn't matter," he said matter-of-factly. "Beauty is beauty." He lifted the arm and inspected the copy. "Got it!" he said happily. "Look at this."

Taking the copy, Jennifer inspected it. "When this machine works right, it really puts out some nice-looking print, nicer than anything our old press put out."

"Yeah! Now if it will just stay set, I'll run as many copies as I can for tomorrow," Jason said, freshly inspired.

"Maybe your story on the bar fight will make a little splash—get us known," Jennifer said hopefully.

"It is kind of funny—two councilmen rolling in the mud out in front of a bar, both drunk, and all the feuding over a dance hall girl. Makes you wonder, doesn't it?" Jason said.

"Wonder? Not at all! Whiskey and women and too many men is a potent mixture."

Smiling, Jason admitted, "I guess it is."

~

Up in his room Grant had a spread of newspaper articles and pictures, his collection from Virginia City. "This was our edition on news of the Big Bonanza. Everyone went crazy!"

Reading the newsprint, Butch, more than impressed, was literally intrigued by the wild gold town. "Wow! You mean you were actually there! I ain't never seen nothin' like this. I heard stories of Virginia City from Uncle Mike—he said it was one wild place!"

"It was," Grant confirmed. "I've seen gunfights and drunken brawls. I watched Jason fight the town bully, a big mean guy that was twice as big as him."

"You mean that man I just met downstairs? He don't look so tough," Butch replied, having observed a mild man in Jason Stone.

"That's not all," Grant bragged. "I saw Jason strap on a gun once and get in a gunfight."

Butch couldn't believe it. "I guess he won. He's still alive. He must be good with a gun." Letting his eyes roll upward, he let Grant in on one of his dreams. "I wish I was good with guns and good at fighting—so good that nobody would ever challenge me."

"It doesn't always turn out like you think," Grant warned. "A girl got killed instead—here's the story on it."

Taking the copy, Butch read the disheartening story of Molly, a dance hall girl, being killed by some fellow named Big Ned. "Well," he mumbled. "That Jason fellow must be mighty brave. I hope I got guts like that when I grow up."

Grant revealed some of his own dreams. "Yeah, I'd like to be like Lance Rivers."

"Lance Rivers? Who's that?" Butch asked.

"He's that fellow we saw riding a black stallion through town. He came here, ran some ads to sell some of his horses. He's rich, too—says he has a big horse ranch, even promised he'd get me a horse."

"You met that guy!" Butch said, jealous and amazed. "I wish I'd been here!"

"He had a diamond stickpin, and it was the biggest diamond I ever saw," Grant said, enthused by such unimaginable riches. "I'd like to be like that, own a big horse ranch. He's a nice fellow too. I think everybody likes him."

"I might not like him!" came a girl's voice from the door.

The boys turned to see Abby standing in Grant's door. "Oh, Abby!" Grant said, a little offended by her relentless persistence to be a hard case. "You never met him—you don't know!"

"Who's this?" Butch said, surprised as he came to his feet.

"It's just my sister, Abby," Grant muttered.

"I'm Butch. Nice to meet you, Abby."

Biting her lip, Abby let her eyes drop down to her feet, where she turned her foot in and drug the toe of her shoe on the well-worn wooden floor.

"C'mon in, Abby," Butch said, then looked at Grant for approval.

"It's all right, Abby. You can come in," Grant said. "I was showing Butch my collection of articles on Virginia City."

Suddenly, Abby came alive and pounced over onto Grant's bed beside the newspaper clippings. She laughed at accidentally disturbing the articles. "Did you tell Butch that I got kicked out of school?"

"No, Abby," Grant said, slightly embarrassed. "That's not something you brag about!"

"For me it is!" Abby protested good-naturedly, her deep-blue eyes sparkling.

Butch was instantly taken in by Abby and her rebellious attitude. "Your sister is pretty," Butch said to Grant, as if by addressing Grant it wouldn't offend Abby.

But Abby wasn't offended. She saw something in Butch, something special that she couldn't put her finger on. He was the kind of boy that went to extra trouble to be nice to people, the kind of boy that had a fire in his eyes, something like her own. She knew right then that they would be friends. "Do you live around here?" she asked.

"Sure," Butch said. "Me and my Uncle Mike live in a room over at the Pacific House. I ride with Uncle Mike—he's teaching me how to get by, you know, how to skin miners and such."

Abby found Butch fascinating. She'd be sure to keep him in sight as much as possible.

Grant and Abby told Butch some wild stories of Virginia City. Not to be outdone, Butch had his own wild stories, mostly of narrow escapes with vigilantes or the law.

Downstairs, Jason was steadily wringing newspapers out of the busy press while Jennifer put them in order on a desk and bundled them for the next day's ride. The front door opened and in stepped a gracious young man, his cowboy hat in his hand. "Pardon me, ma'am. Is this here the newspaper office?"

"Yes, it is," Jennifer answered politely. "How can I help you?"

The man's eyes smiled, since it was hard to see his smile through the heavy walrus mustache. His hair was long but not unkempt, and his clothes were worn but clean. "I'm lookin' fer a young'n, boy about this tall with blond hair," he drawled, holding his hand out to indicate the boy's height.

"You must mean Butch," Jason said, leaving the press.

"That'd be him," the cowboy said. "I'm his Uncle Mike."

"Jason Stone—and this is Jennifer DeSpain."

"Mike Cassidy," the man said, nodding politely.

"The boys are upstairs. I'll go get them," Jennifer said, leaving the room.

"I hear tell this here is the new paper in town," Cassidy said, trying to drum up some conversation with Jason.

"Sure is. We're off to a rugged start," Jason explained. "This old press is about to get the best of us."

"Everything's rugged in these parts," Cassidy said, trying to make Jason feel better. "I don't know where folks get the idea that it's easy riches."

"We just follow the news," Jason continued. "This seemed like the place for that."

"Yep, you got that right. News of this place has brought people all the way from the East Coast and further, even from across the ocean."

"What do you do, Mike?" Jason asked, overly inquisitive. The man's appearance made him look out of place. He looked more like he belonged on a horse, chasing cattle.

"I'm a gambler," Cassidy said, almost apologetically. "Just a small-timer, you know. I can't afford the big stakes."

"Uncle Mike!" Butch shouted as he came in with Grant and Abby. "These folks come here from Virginia City! Remember us reading about the Big Bonanza?"

"Sure do, Butch. You mean to say you folks is all the way from Virginia City? Why would you want to leave there? I hear tell the riches there are beyond belief."

"Beyond belief they were," Jennifer said, slightly tickled at Mike Cassidy. He seemed innocently comical. "We'd had enough of that and were ready to see Colorado."

"Yep. This here is some pretty country. Well, I reckon me and Butch better get goin'." Cassidy put his hat on his head and opened the front door. "Nice meetin' you folks," he said as he left.

Jason and Jennifer were both smiling and turned their attention to each other. "Seems sort of harmless for a gambler," Jason said.

"He's a gambler? Could have fooled me," Jennifer commented.

"He's a very good gambler," Grant said. "He just doesn't let on—told Butch that a man that shows off his money has a harder time hanging on to it."

"I wish he was pursuing a different line of work," Jennifer agreed. "But I do like your new friend, and his Uncle Mike seems nice, too."

"He's my friend, too!" Abby shouted, ready to quarrel with anyone who wanted to argue.

"Good," said Jennifer. "Now both of you have a new friend."

~

The next morning Jason was proudly riding Dolly in the nipping mountain chill before first light. Dolly snorted fog from her nostrils as the newspaperman made his way up the gulch toward Central City. He had two bundles of newspapers secured saddlebag fashion behind his saddle. *Going to be a great day*, he thought, spotting the first pink of light over the mountaintop. Like Virginia City, the saloons still bristled with miners and girls, the music and loud talk echoing down the street. He crossed through small pools of yellow light thrown out by the saloons where the liquor still flowed.

From somewhere came the roaring laughter of a miner, a laughter so contagious that it brought a smile to Jason's face. He shook his head and pressed onward up Gregory Street, a mountain downdraft bringing the sweet smell of spruce trees in its wake.

By midmorning, Jason had delivered newspapers to all of his stops in Central City and spurred Dolly on up the hill toward Nevadaville. Noticing a shortcut across a huge pile of yellow tailings, Jason reined Dolly on over to make the crossing. The mare suddenly nickered, alarmed by something Jason couldn't see. "What's the matter, girl? C'mon," he said and shook her reins.

Nervously, Dolly stepped out onto the massive, cone-shaped pile of yellow rock. Before Jason realized it, the horse's hooves sank into the rubble and started sliding downward. Dolly fought with all her massive strength, but the slide had started, and there was no way she could stay on her feet. Fighting to stay mounted, Jason pawed and stretched his legs in the stirrups, but it was no help. Horse and man went tumbling down the grade of fine tailings.

At the bottom of a thirty-foot incline, Dolly fought and came to her feet. She snorted and looked at Jason, waiting for him to get up. He wasn't sure what had happened, a stupid mistake on his part. Slowly standing, Jason did a physical survey to see if he was all right, noting any signals of pain. *How stupid! My own horse is smarter than me!* he thought with disgust. He wasn't sure, but he thought that Dolly had rolled over him at one point—it all had happened so fast.

Mounting up, Jason felt a tinge of pain in his lower back, something different, but it didn't seem critical. *Must've pulled a muscle*, he thought. Glancing around, he was glad to see that nobody had seen his stupid trick as he rode Dolly on back up to where he'd been before and took the regular road on up to Nevadaville.

Mid-afternoon came and Jason was growing increasingly uncomfortable in the saddle, and a burning pain in his lower back slowly began demanding all of his attention. By the time he rode down from Nevadaville and began distributing his newspapers around Black Hawk, he could barely climb back into the saddle once he'd crawled out of it. Finally, his legs began to grow numb, and Jason skipped his last stops to ride on back to the office, his face grimacing with pain.

Lita saw Jason first as she was out back hanging some wash. When Jason rode up, he bent forward and slid from his horse and fell to the ground. Lita rushed over.

"Mr. Jason! What wrong?"

"Lita—help me up, I—I can't stand," Jason groaned.

Grunting, Lita helped Jason to his feet and into the kitchen where she sat him down at the kitchen table. By now, the pain had produced beads of heavy sweat on his forehead. "What happened, Mr. Jason?"

"I had a little fall with my horse," Jason mumbled, his mind growing disarrayed.

Lita rushed from the kitchen to find Jennifer. When she returned, she had Jennifer with her, who hurried to Jason's side and squatted down beside him, his head on the table, his eyes closed. "Jason! Jason! Are you all right? Can you hear me?"

Slowly opening his eyes, Jason mumbled, "No. I'm not all right. Can you get me up to my bed?"

"C'mon, Lita!" Jennifer said with a sense of urgency. Lita had told her that Jason had fallen from his horse. The two women struggled to get their friend up the stairs, and it took every bit of the strength Jason could muster to make each step. Finally in his bed, sopping with sweat, he passed out.

Lita quickly fetched some damp towels to mop Jason's forehead. Horror-stricken, Jennifer quickly rushed to the door. "I'm going to find a doctor, Lita. You stay with him." Her voice trembled with despair.

"I ain't goin' nowhere," Lita said, her attention on Jason, who was breathing heavily in his fitful sleep.

~

After asking around, Jennifer found a doctor by the name of Moss. He was sitting in a card game in a smoky little bar on Chase Street. When Jennifer entered, panic-stricken, the talk in the saloon grew silent. "Is there a Dr. Moss here?" she asked feverishly.

A tall man glancing over his beer motioned with his eyes toward the doctor, who sat at a table with his cards held closely to his face. There was a fresh beer with a sudsy head sitting in front of him.

"Dr. Moss!" Jennifer shouted, coming to his side. "You must come quickly—a man's been hurt."

Slowly, Dr. Moss turned to Jennifer, glancing at her through his thick spectacles. He held his cards open for her to see—three kings. "Madam, as you can see, I need to play this one out."

Jennifer was racked with anxiety and impatience. "You don't understand! You must come now!"

The doctor slapped his cards on the table and made a face of disgust to his playing partners. "I'll be back," he said as he slowly came to his feet. He was a short and stocky man with a head full of curly, short gray hair that matched his thick gray beard. "I delivered twins this morning, and I thought I was through for the day," he mumbled, obtaining some laughter from his poker-playing friends. Jennifer saw no humor in his comment as she absentmindedly tugged at his coat sleeve. Dressed in a dark, baggy, dusty suit, he was led out by a hysterical woman while a hushed laughter swept through the bar.

Once outside, he asked Jennifer. "Where's the patient?"

"Over where we live—over on Merchant Street!"

"Let's take my buggy," he suggested, pointing over toward a small, barn-like structure. "My horse is still hitched up."

Rushing, they made it to the newspaper office in no time, and Jennifer escorted Dr. Moss upstairs to Jason's room, where Lita was bent over him, swabbing his forehead with a cool towel. Jennifer had explained the accident as best she could on the way.

"Help me get his shirt off," the doctor ordered Lita as they sat Jason up and got him unbuttoned. Jason groaned, out of his mind with pain. With nimble fingers, Dr. Moss felt around Jason's spine and shook his head. "I can't tell much. The muscles are so tight they're like iron. He'll need to be awake so I can talk to him, but for now, he needs to relax. I'm going to give him some laudanum, and that will knock him out, kill the pain too."

The doctor measured out some of the thick liquid and forced Jason to swallow it, similar to the way he might give a dog a pill. Jennifer and Lita watched helplessly, wanting to be of some assistance. "There's not much we can do right now. Let him rest." Dr. Moss said.

Jennifer protested, "But, Dr. Moss—"

"Everybody around here just calls me Doc!" he interrupted, a little impatient with Jennifer. "There's no emergency right now, I said. I'll be back in the morning."

Irritated, Jennifer glanced at Jason and then at Lita as Doc quickly left. "Some doctor he is!" she said scornfully. "He just wants to get back to his poker game!"

Lita shrugged her round shoulders, her face holding no expression. "He the doctor," she mumbled.

~

The next morning Jason woke up in severe pain, a back pain that made his legs totally numb. Jennifer was asleep in a chair next to him. "Jennifer!" Jason whispered harshly. She woke up quickly and stared wide-eyed at him. "I need some water," he pleaded.

Swiftly, Jennifer poured some water into a glass from the pitcher on the nightstand. "How do you feel?"

Gritting his teeth, Jason grunted. "Feels like my back is broken!"

Standing and leaning over him, Jennifer took his face in her hands, her face very close to Jason's. "The doctor will be back soon—we'll get you fixed up, I promise."

Tears filled Jason's eyes as he fought the pain. "Jennifer, I can't feel my legs."

Stunned, Jennifer leaned back, her face an expression of sorrow and helplessness. She took Jason's hand and squeezed it tightly, her eyes searching his face. She wanted to say something but couldn't find the right words.

When Doc Moss showed up, he went to work quickly, running Jennifer out of the room. He did a series of tests, working Jason's legs and bending his back this way and that, all to Jason's great discomfort. Soon, he'd reached a conclusion and called Jennifer back into the room. His demeanor had softened from the day before, his voice now one of a convincing professional. He was a man who'd seen it all, even his own failure back in Boston where his drunkenness had needlessly cost a life. Now he did the best he could, delivering babies and seeing to ailing miners, nothing too hard. He cleared his throat and placed his utensils back in his black bag.

"You may very well have a broken back," he said, addressing Jason, then letting his small, squinted eyes roam over to Jennifer. "Then again, it might be one of the discs has slipped. Either way, it's got the nerves shut off going to your legs. You'll need to stay in bed for several weeks—try not to move too much. It might get better; it might not—backs are a tricky business." He was solemn, but blunt with the truth.

"Will I always be paralyzed?" Jason asked, his voice weak.

Doc shook his head. "It's hard to say. You may get some of it back, maybe not. Then again, you might get it all back—like I said, backs are a tricky business. The best I can do is leave you something for the pain. All you can do is try not to move around too much in that bed. In a few weeks, we should be able to tell more." He picked up his bag, his eyes sad. "I'll come by to check on you from time to time." He paused and took a deep breath. "I'm sorry," he said, and eased slowly out of the room, closing the door quietly behind him.

Completely devastated, Jennifer stood there speechless, staring at Jason. He had the forlorn look of a man who had just been told that he only had days left to live. He turned his head toward the window, away from her.

Suddenly, she came to her senses and knelt down by him. She took his face in her hands again and turned it back toward her. She had never been more sincere. "Jason, you will get better—I just know you will." He blinked, his eyes watery. Then she said, "Jason, I love you."

It was like Jason had reached the highest plateau of his life, then been swept off and was falling to his death, only to learn that he'd found what had led him to such heights. But the pain told him something was very wrong. *How could a beautiful woman like her love an invalid—a man that can't walk?* he wondered. *Maybe her love is nothing but pity*. He turned his head back to the window and the light outside. All that had seemed so good was now so far away.

PART TWO

FAITH TESTED

CHAPTER

7

A Turn for the Worse

Overnight, autumn disappeared and, like a ravenous beast, the icy winds of a norther ripped through the towns of Black Hawk and Central City. Miners and storekeepers boarded up windows and brought what they could indoors and covered the rest with nailed-down canvas. Water buckets froze, windows iced, and the mud grew hard; the clouds, dark and heavy, lowered to the earth, unloading their burden of thick, white snow. Wind whistled through cracks and rattled shutters, while snow whipped sideways and gusted up abandoned streets. The temperature dropped forty degrees in six hours; winter had come.

Jason watched the white, heavy flakes float softly past his window, only to be instantly caught in a gust and whipped and churned into streaks of white. His room was cold and uncomfortable, a small bedroom with a bed, dressing table, and sagging wallpaper. Behind a lonesome little bentwood chair stood his swaybacked clothes rack. His bed was a simple wooden structure with a straw-stuffed mattress and heavy, worn quilts piled on top of him. Beside the bed stood a table with a kerosene lantern, a pitcher of water with a drinking glass, and a half-empty bottle of laudanum. Next to these items sat an undisturbed copy of the Bible, his copy, which Jennifer had placed beside the bed for him. No pictures adorned the tattered walls, and no curtains bordered the icy window. It was a room of gray and dark gloom.

I might as well be in my coffin! Jason thought miserably. The pain in his back was so severe it prevented him from moving or even wanting to move. The laudanum didn't seem to help the agony much—it only succeeded in putting him in a crazy trance or a dream world of the absurd. *I should be dead!* he wished silently. *It would be a lot easier.*

Doc Moss had finally reached a diagnosis after several visits. "It would be my guess that you've cracked some vertebrae and something has either placed great pressure on your spinal cord or has partially severed it. Either way, the nerves to your legs have been blocked." He shook his gray head in pity. "I'm sorry, young man. This is very unfortunate, and I hope that I'm wrong, but I don't believe so."

Closing his eyes, Jason couldn't imagine such severe and lasting damage, and all from a silly little fall. "But, Doc, it didn't even hurt at first. I rode for several hours before I even felt any pain. You must be wrong!" he had argued.

"Shock," Doc had said. "Sometimes after a bad injury you're in shock and might not even realize you're hurt. I had a miner walk into my office with his hand blown off from a dynamite blast. He held a rag tight around the bloody stub, acted like it was nothing. After I sewed him up, he left, then fainted in the street later when he realized what had happened. The human body and mind are capable of some far-fetched things." Doc had come across as a cold and indifferent man, but Jason could tell he was tender underneath—something about the sad look in his old eyes—something disturbed the old man.

"What am I supposed to do?" Jason had asked.

Doc had gotten up from the small chair beside his patient's bed and moved slowly over to the window. He spoke to the glass. "You'll have to wait. Maybe some of the feeling will come back, maybe you'll be able to walk again—but you'll have to wait and see. It's in the Lord's hands, not mine."

"Some God I've trusted in!" Jason said bitterly. "I turn my life over to God—and now I'm an invalid. I should have stayed a drunk!"

Doc knew about Jason's spiritual suffering. He too had once been a strong Christian. But after losing his family and practice, he came west to live a secluded life and never prayed again. As he was leaving, he said, "You'll have to find a preacher for spiritual problems, Jason, a doctor of the soul. I'm merely a doctor of the body." He paused at the door, studying the frightened man like he wanted to tell him something, but then he said, "Good day," and left.

Being paralyzed was a helpless feeling for Jason, but not being able to do anything about it made him feel worthless. *If I could just move around—even if I had to crawl!* Jason thought, wishing with all of his heart. *This is unfair—just as my life was finally turning around—just as Jennifer was coming around—it isn't fair!*

~

When the norther had blown itself out, the mountainsides were solid white, with drifts of up to six feet leaning heavily against straining buildings. Gray clouds still clung closely to the mountaintops, holding Black Hawk captive under its dark silence. The thick white blanket had temporarily halted all travelers, at least until the town could dig out. Abe had spent most of the previous day shoveling behind the building and the next morning shoveling the front. When he came up on the back porch, Lita called to him, "Get yourself in here and get some hot coffee!"

When Abe glanced up, his eyes showed big and white from underneath his worn hat. Before he could say anything, Lita shouted, "I don't mean tomorrow! I mean right *now*!" She slammed the flimsy kitchen door to save the heat.

Abe's eyes squinted as he held back a muffled laughter. *How could anyone not love that woman?* he thought cheerfully as he cleaned the ice and snow from his thick-soled boots.

Waiting on the table sat a steaming cup of coffee and hot corn dodgers. Abe took a few minutes to unwrap from all the garb he wore, while Lita shook a poker in the coals, sending a shower of popping sparks up the stovepipe. The big man took his seat at the table and carefully sucked a sip from the hot metal cup. "When it comes winter here, it don't mess around!" Abe said, amazed at the abrupt change he'd seen in the weather. "It's so cold out yonder, I couldn't draw no water—reckon we'll have to melt snow."

"You let me worry 'bout kitchen things," Lita informed him as she came around the table to be closer to Abe. She placed her hand on his muscular shoulder and let it rest there for a moment as she watched him from behind. She gave a slight squeeze, then removed her hand and sat in the chair next to him, something obviously on her mind. "I'm worried," she said, addressing Abe in a direct fashion unusual for her.

Knowing Lita was about to say something important, Abe let his eyes move over to hers to let her know he was paying attention. "What you worried 'bout?" he asked.

"It's Miss Jenny and Mr. Jason, and I don't know what to do," Lita said almost apologetically. "Dat woman—she don't know what to do about Jason and she sure can't run that miserable machine by herself. I'm 'fraid all this mess might get the best of the both of dem. She's handled some tough things in the past, but somethin' different this time."

Abe gave Lita's comments some serious thought, then turned his eyes away and took a sip of coffee to wash down a corn dodger. "Ain't no use in worryin'," he said in his low and heavy voice. "What happens, happens. Only God controls that."

Lita looked perplexed. "What? Says who?"

"Boots," answered Abe. "He knows more 'bout the Bible than any man I ever met. He told me everythin' happens 'cause God wants it that way—we can't do nothin' to change that. All we can do is the best we can, no matter what."

"We can sometimes make things happen, or we can change things," Lita argued. "God gives us the power to make a difference if we choose to."

"Only if He wants it dat way," Abe said, strong in his beliefs.

"We'll have to see what's in all this for God, then, won't we?" Lita said stubbornly, placing her wide hands on the table and taking a deep breath. She'd heard of Christian faith like Abe's before, only she couldn't remember what they called it. "You been around mules too long," she said. "Grown just as stubborn as dem long ears."

Abe smiled without looking at Lita; he'd been told that many times before. But then his heavy features suddenly turned serious. "I was up to see Mr. Jason—told him I'd take care of Dolly. He told me to keep her—I could have her 'cause he wouldn't be needin' no horse." He shook his head sadly.

A troubled and saddened look held Lita's face, her mouth turned down at the corners. "He won't even talk to me," she responded. "I take him his meals and help him, but he don't say nothin'. I told him he need to read his Bible. 'You ain't got nothin' else to do,' I said. But he turned the other way. Dat man in bad shape."

"These folks," Abe reflected, "ain't seen no hard times, not like us. We'll have to give 'em help."

Lita stood and came around behind Abe. She put her hands on his shoulders and leaned over and placed her round face against the side of his in a moment of tenderness.

~

The front office was cold and uncomfortable as Jennifer struggled with the press, her fingers almost numb. Little light came from the gray skies outside, while two kerosene lamps battled the darkness. The office seemed so quiet and empty without Jason, and the job seemed impossible for her to accomplish alone. *What am I going to do?* she wondered, pulling a heavy shawl up tighter around her shoulders. Then her thoughts shifted to Jason. *He seems so defeated, like he's given up. Every time I go up to see him, he acts like I'm intruding into his private world of despair. He's shut me out of his life completely. I never appreciated how important Jason was to this business*—she paused, realizing even more—*or how much his company meant to me.*

Suddenly the front door burst open, letting in a cold rush of air and Lance Rivers with it. "Good morning, Mrs. DeSpain," he announced boldly, touching his fine hat. He came closer, a wide smile on his face. "My advertisement with your paper was so successful that I want to run another one." He pulled off his heavy topcoat and draped it over the back of an old chair while Jennifer watched, her pretty face showing astonishment at his audacious and charming character. He turned back to her and then cast a glance outside. "Some weather we're having, but don't worry—the sun comes back out quickly and it's nice again." He laughed heartily and let his dark eyes come back to hers. "They say if you don't like the weather here—just wait a few minutes."

Forcing a smile, Jennifer picked up a pencil and paper. "It's the wind that's unpleasant," she said. "You say you want to run another ad?"

Having remarkable perception, Lance Rivers noticed the tone of Jennifer's voice, the troubled look in her eyes. Quickly, his jolly temperament disappeared as he took on a concerned disposition. "Is something wrong?"

Turning away, Jennifer sighed. "Yes, I'm afraid so. My editor, Jason Stone, has had a fall from his horse. The doctor seems to think he may have broken his back, and now he's lying upstairs—his legs are paralyzed." She then threw a glance at the old press. "I can't seem to make the press work without Jason's help—we've had trouble with it." There was more, but she didn't dare express her inner feelings to a man she considered a stranger—albeit a concerned and handsome stranger.

Rivers glanced around at the office, a sad affair of makeshift tables, desks, and dilapidated chairs, with a strange-looking machine Jennifer called a press. The place screamed of destitution. Standing tall and erect, Rivers removed a fine cigar from a pocket inside his fancy jacket and carefully lit it, then strolled about the front office contemplating. Jennifer watched curiously, for he obviously was thinking. "Tell you what, Mrs. DeSpain," he said, pivoting on his heels and addressing her from across the office. "Let me help!" He took a thoughtful pull from his cigar and blew the smoke into a plume. "Let's make this into a real newspaper office, get a new press, anything you need. I'm sure I can find an editor for you as well." He gave her a most sincere glance, his eyes dark and penetrating.

Reluctant, Jennifer tossed her hand in the air as if shooing away a fly. "Mr. Rivers, I can't accept charity like that. I hardly know you."

"Charity!" Rivers laughed. "This isn't an offer of charity, Mrs. DeSpain. I'm making you a business proposition!"

"What?" Jennifer questioned. "If you expect a profit for your investment, you might be sadly disappointed. We're new and off to a terrible start. Who's to say we will make it?"

"I'm not interested in the money," Rivers replied, cool but dominant. "What if I was a silent partner? Part owner? If the paper makes a good profit somewhere down the line, then we can talk money."

Jennifer stood holding her shawl tight against her, shocked and surprised. It was too much to consider all at once. But Rivers held his pleasant smile, giving her a hard looking over. A most likable man, she feared he might just be another opportunist, yet she faced a bleak future without some sort of help.

"What do you say, Mrs. DeSpain?" Rivers persisted. "We can make a grand effort with this newspaper."

Just then, a group of riders stampeded by outside, their horses worked to a frenzy. Rivers and Jennifer both watched through the front window. The riders were yelling. Some of the men dismounted, while others tore a path down the street. The front door flew open, and the town marshal rushed in with two men behind him.

"What is it, Marshal?" Rivers barked.

"Mr. Rivers," the marshal said excitedly, his eyes darting around. "The bank's been robbed! There were three men—and now they seem to have disappeared."

Rivers ground his cigar underneath his black boot and grabbed his heavy coat. "Did you get a description? Which bank?"

"The Thatcher Brothers' Bank! Three masked men, probably miners!"

"I have money in that bank!" Rivers snapped. "What makes you think it was miners?"

"They were dressed like miners, dirty—had the smell of the earth about them and spoke with a Cornish accent!" The marshal was beside himself with uncertainty, his hat far back on his head to reveal a stiff shock of black hair that refused to lie flat.

"Let's get going!" Rivers demanded

The men stomped out the door, Rivers being the last out, but as he closed the door behind him, he turned to Jennifer. "Think about my offer," he said.

Once the men were gone, Jennifer got ahold of herself—so much had happened in the past few minutes. Her journalistic instinct took hold as she rushed back to the kitchen to tell Lita she was leaving. "Lita, there's been a bank robbery—I have to go get the story!"

"Oh my!" Lita mumbled as she watched Jennifer bundle up to go out.

"Watch the front. If anyone comes in, tell them I'll be back in a little while."

"Yes, ma'am," Lita replied.

Hurrying, Jennifer dashed out into the bitter cold. There was nothing like a sensational story to help out a struggling newspaper.

~

By that afternoon, news of the daring robbery had quickly spread. Butch caught Grant and Abby as they walked home from school. "Did you hear? There was a bank robbery! The robbers got away with over thirty thousand dollars!"

"Wow!" Abby stated. "That's a lot of money!"

"Those robbers were slicker than anyone around here. Outsmarted everybody! Nobody saw them ride out of town—now they think they are hiding somewhere. The marshal and Lance Rivers are leading search parties, looking everywhere."

"Lance Rivers?" said Grant. "Why is he leading a search party?"

"Said he had a lot of money in that bank!" Butch continued. "Said he'll string 'em up if he catches 'em."

"How exciting!" Abby said, clapping her mittens together. "What are they doing now?"

"Look," Butch said, pointing to the street down below. "See all them horses? That's Lance Rivers and his group. They're combing Gregory Street—going into every place."

"Let's get closer," Grant said, his curiosity rising.

"Yeah, I want to see too!" Abby added quickly.

"C'mon," Butch said, taking off into a run through a snowbank. Grant and Abby hurried behind him.

Down on Gregory Street, the children watched from a distance as Lance Rivers barked out orders to more than a dozen men. He sat high on his stallion like a cavalry commander, waving his hand to men who rushed about on foot. A large group of onlookers huddled in the cold, watching the spectacle, the children among them.

"Take that shed over there!" Lance ordered, waving to two men who held pistols. "You men!" he barked, pointing to another group of four. "Search the upstairs of that hardware company. I don't want a square inch missed!"

"He's really something!" Butch said, his eyes sparkling with excitement.

"He sure is," Grant agreed, admiring Lance Rivers and his ability to take charge.

"Yes, he certainly is!" came a familiar voice from behind the children, a voice they instantly recognized as they turned around and saw their mother.

Grant spoke first. "Mother, what are you doing here?"

"I might ask you the same question," she said, her eyes glaring at Grant and Abby. "This isn't the way home from school."

"But we had to see what was happening!" Abby offered as an excuse. "Do you think they'll catch the robbers?"

Jennifer could hardly blame the children for wanting to see all the excitement. "If I had to guess, I'd say that if Lance Rivers can't catch them, then they can't be caught."

"What are you doing down here, Mother?" Grant asked again.

"I'm a newspaperwoman, remember? I had to get the story."

"Did you get it?" Grant questioned.

"Got it all right here, two eyewitness accounts," Jennifer said proudly. "We need to go now children. We'll just be in the way." She took Abby's hand and led the way.

"See ya later," Butch said, waving to Grant and Abby.

~

Anxiety tore at Jason. He had asked Lita what all the commotion was about, and she told him there'd been a bank robbery. A sensational, newsworthy story had taken place, and he lay motionless in his bed, his legs paralyzed. He was sickened, his spirit of adventure dashed to pieces. *What's the use?* he thought disgustedly. *I'll never be able to get out of this bed!* A group of horses thundered past on the snow-packed street below. Disheartened, he took Lita's advice and picked up his Bible. He thumbed through it, looking for something comforting, something to help his frustration. He finally turned to the book of Revelation and began reading by the small light of his lamp on the stand next to his bed.

Hours later, Lita returned with a tray of hot food. "I got you somethin' to eat," she said, shuffling in with the tray. "You need to eat, keep your strength."

Closing his Bible, Jason looked sternly at Lita. "I've been reading the Book of Revelation," he said coldly. "I'll be glad when Jesus comes back for us—I've heard preachers call it the the Rapture—maybe it will be tomorrow!"

Taking this in, Lita set the tray down on the spindly, little bentwood chair. "The Rapture!" she remarked, disgruntled. "What you readin' 'bout dat for?"

"I'm supposed to have faith, right?" Jason questioned, his mood a dark one. "I believe in Christ, and I'm ready to see the Rapture—be taken out of all of this!"

A fury seemed to rise in Lita, her eyes glaring at Jason. "Let me tell you somethin', Mr. Jason! People who dwell on the Rapture and read about it, wishin' it to happen—that ain't right! The Lord ain't gonna have no Rapture just to bail you out of your misery! The Good Book says we should live our lives to the fullest. The Rapture will come when we least expect it! Shame on you!" She picked up a napkin and shook it out and laid it across Jason's chest. He was propped against the headboard, surprised at Lita's outrage. She took the Bible and set it on the table, then set his tray across his lap, her movements quick and certain.

Dismayed, Jason spoke in a hushed tone. "Are you disputing the Bible?" Jason quipped.

"No, I'm not!" Lita said, now angry. "But I know what you are thinkin'. You should pray to get well, not to be taken to heaven—not just yet! The Lord has work for us to do, and we should try and do it, and that includes you! Now, you eat up!" She turned and stormed out of the room, her heavy weight shaking the floor.

Whew! Jason thought. He'd never seen such wrath in Lita before, and her scorn left a burning sting. *Boy, does she have a temper! And a whip-like tongue!* He played miserably with his food and took a few bites, not really hungry. *Maybe she's right. I'm thinking selfishly. How stupid. Surely there must be something I can do, but I don't know what that would be.* Then he thought long and hard and realized that he hadn't prayed at all. *Maybe I should humble myself and pray.* Fighting self-pity, Jason closed his eyes and prayed long and hard, not just to be healed, but for God to guide him—for simple wisdom.

CHAPTER

8

The Benefactor

The morning after the robbery, Jennifer struggled with the press in the ice-cold front office. She'd written a fine story based on witness accounts the night before, but now, her hands numb, she struggled uselessly with a machine that was determined not to work. "This is ridiculous!" she mumbled, pulling at a cold, iron lever. *Every copy is smudged and smeared. The table just won't stay still!* Again she tapped on the wooden blocks lodged in between the works to tighten them more securely, but the press seemed to force them loose every time she tried to print a copy. Her hands frozen, she went to the kitchen seeking warmth.

"Lita, it's so cold in the front that I can't get anything done, and that press—I can't figure the silly thing out!"

Lita had been sitting in a chair near the stove mending socks for the children. She glanced up from her work, listening to Jennifer's frustration.

"Oh, Lita!" Jennifer said in a shaky voice, her eyes growing wet. "I've got a great story, and I can't even get it printed!" She paused a moment, wiping her cold nose, and gathered her emotions. Giving Lita a blatant look of hopelessness, she said, "I'm about out of money, and I don't know where the next rent payment is going to come from if I can't sell any newspapers. Jason can't help. We don't even have enough money to pack up and leave."

"Miss Jenny!" Lita scolded. "You just feeling down. Things will get better."

"How can you say that?" Jennifer lashed out in a sudden state of fury. "Nothing's going right! Jason is paralyzed and can't help me, and I can't even print a paper on that stupid machine!" She threw her hands up in the air and rushed over near the stove for warmth. "And this place! The kitchen is the only warm place in this entire building. We'll all starve and freeze to death before it's over with—I just don't know how much more I can stand!" Her lower lip quivered, and her face twisted in turmoil.

Patiently, Lita set her knitting down and got out of her chair. She moved over to the cupboard where she found a coffee cup and took it to the stove where she calmly filled it with hot coffee. Gently setting the cup on the old kitchen table, she turned to Jennifer. "Sit down, Miss Jenny."

The sternness in Lita's voice caught Jennifer by surprise as she found herself following orders. Taking a seat at the table, she took the cup and took a light sip. Lita planted herself across the table from Jennifer in a chair, her arms folded in front of her. "Honey, you don't know what tough times is."

Astonished, Jennifer stared at Lita in amazement. "How can you say that? We're out on a limb, Lita! I'm trying to tell you—I'm out of money and out of resources. I know Abe has been buying the groceries, but what about the rent that's coming up? What about staying warm—why, we can't even afford to pay someone to go chop us some firewood! The next thing you know, we'll wind up in the streets," she snapped testily, her patience short.

"Listen to me," Lita said forcefully, her round face taking on a grave expression. "Dis ain't nothin'! We got to have faith in the Lord. Don't it say in the Bible that the Lord takes care of everything? It say the lilies in the field, they neither spin nor toil, but they are beautiful. And you think the Lord won't take care of us?"

"I've tried praying—again and again," Jennifer argued. "Things keep getting worse. It's like I'm being punished." She put her hands over her face, distressed and pitiful.

"Now, let me tell you what hard times is," Lita said, her brown eyes settled solidly on Jennifer. "You think of a mother holding her baby girl—can you see that?"

Nodding, Jennifer pictured such, unaware of where Lita was going with this.

"I want you to think of that baby being torn from her mother's arms. The baby girl is screaming for her mother and her mother is tryin' to take hold of that child, but cruel men take the baby girl away, and they never see each other again. *Dat's tough times, Miss Jenny!*"

Pondering, Jennifer figured Lita was telling her old wives' tales just to cheer her up. "Of course that's terrible, Lita," she agreed. "But I don't see how that affects us."

"Sure it does!" Lita proclaimed. "I'm tryin' to tell you that we'll get by—this ain't nothin'!"

"I can't see how we're going to make it, and I feel like it's my responsibility," Jennifer said sorrowfully. "It was stupid to come here—not knowing what we were getting in to. I can't see how we're going to get by."

"We'll manage," Lita said with certainty.

"How do you know, Lita?" Jennifer sighed with disgust, deeply disturbed by the circumstances.

"I know, Miss Jenny!" Lita lashed back. "I know tough times. I was that little girl."

Suddenly, Jennifer felt a hot flush in her face—it was like she had been slapped with rare truth. Her eyes on the black woman that sat before her, she could only imagine such a nightmare as Lita had told. Yet Lita's faith remained like a rock, solid and immovable. "I'm sorry," Jennifer uttered. Standing slowly, she came around the table to Lita, bent over, and hugged her neck. "I'm so sorry! You're right. I guess I'm just beside myself with worry. There must be something I can do." She straightened herself and wiped a sleeve across her moist eyes.

Lita turned to Jennifer. "Don't forget your prayers, Miss Jenny," Lita offered. "Maybe for right now you can go up and talk to Mr. Jason. He probably needs encouragin'. He might be able to tell you how to make that old press work."

As if struck by reality, Jennifer felt a renewal of courage. "Yes, that's a good idea, Lita. I should be thankful that I'm healthy and able to do something. I'll take him some hot coffee."

"Dat's the Miss Jenny I know," Lita said proudly.

~

Jennifer discovered Jason asleep when she entered the drab, little room. Through the window she could see clear blue skies, but the temperature had fallen to a bitter cold, and the cold had invaded the room. "Jason," she said lightly. "Jason, wake up."

Stirring, Jason slowly opened his eyes. He stared at her a moment as if trying to recollect where he was and who she was. His eyes were glassy. "Oh, hello."

"I brought you some coffee," Jennifer said softly as she pulled the small chair up near his bed and handed him the hot cup. She sat down, close to him.

Taking the cup, Jason sipped at the coffee hungrily. "That's good," he said hoarsely. He was in a haze from the laudanum and felt uncomfortable in Jennifer's presence. He wanted to see her but didn't like her seeing him in his condition. "What can I do for you?" he asked.

Jennifer didn't like the way Jason's face looked—it was unnatural. The dark circles under his sunken eyes looked like death. "Jason, how much of that medicine are you taking?" she asked, her voice soft.

"Oh, enough to keep me knocked out," he croaked.

"Maybe you should take less. You aren't looking too good."

"And lose my mind?" Jason retorted. "Jennifer, all I've got to look at is these four little miserable walls and out a window I can't even walk over to. There are five quartz mills nearby with their constant hammering driving me crazy, and there's nothing I can do about it. What am I supposed to do?"

Thinking about it, Jennifer realized Jason was bored to tears. "How's the pain?" she questioned.

"Not much pain anymore," Jason admitted. "I just lie here, thinking, wishing I could do something."

Suddenly Jennifer was enlightened with what she thought was a wonderful idea. "Jason, why don't you use this time to write the book you always talked about writing. Maybe it will keep you occupied—keep your mind busy until you're better."

The idea seemed to catch Jason. He didn't say anything for several minutes as his mind raced over the subject he'd often planned to write about, his life and family as a child, which was torn apart by the war, which led to his adventures west. "Maybe I could do that," he admitted weakly. "Guess it's better than nothing."

Smiling, Jennifer felt like she'd made progress with the depressed man who lay in the bed. "I'll get you paper and pencils—whatever you need."

"Good," Jason said, sort of smiling. "How's the newspaper coming? Are you doing a story on the bank robbery?"

The sweet smile that held Jennifer's face quickly disappeared, and her gaze fell to the floor. "I can't get the press to operate," she mumbled. "It's so cold down there in the office that I can't even think."

"Great," Jason said sarcastically. His helplessness seemed to magnify in his own thoughts. "If I could only get downstairs—maybe I could show you how to make that thing work."

"But Doc says you shouldn't be moved yet. You know that."

"Try running it through slowly and watch the table closely," Jason suggested. "You can see it move up against those blocks I put in there. When there's the most slack in it, jam those blocks on the end—jam them in tight."

"I'll try," Jennifer said half-heartedly. "It's so complicated. I don't understand all of those adjustments and knobs."

"I don't either," Jason said truthfully. He felt a wave of euphoria from the laudanum he'd been taking and closed his eyes.

Watching closely, Jennifer could see that he was in a drug-induced state, his voice hoarse and his words slurred. She took his hand, which lay on top of the quilt. "Jason, you've got to get better. Don't give up—you can beat this."

A gentle snore rose from Jason; he was asleep. Jennifer sat and watched him; his beard and hair had grown longer. The passion she'd felt for him had slowly turned to pity. A vigorous and ambitious, hearty man had been reduced to a bedridden cripple. Closing her eyes, she silently whispered a prayer.

From downstairs came heavy rumbling as Jennifer jerked her head up from prayer. *What in the world is Lita doing?* she wondered. She sat patiently by Jason, holding his cold hand. The door rattled and Lita's face appeared. "Miss Jenny, you better get downstairs. There's some men down here."

Quickly, Jennifer stood and left the room, taking one last look at Jason, who slept soundly.

~

What Jennifer found downstairs was a group of men grunting and groaning over a heavy wood-burning stove they were dragging across the room. A large wagon was backed up to the front door. "What's going on here?" Jennifer demanded.

"This here is the *Advertiser* newspaper, ain't it?" a bearded man asked, removing a piece of paper from the front pocket of his overalls. He studied the paper, then looked up. "Says here we're to deliver this stove and install it. Where do you want it?"

"I didn't order a stove," Jennifer said, Lita standing behind her.

"Don't matter, ma'am," the impatient man announced. "This here order says to deliver and install it here."

"But I can't pay you," Jennifer insisted.

"Don't need to," the man said, tugging at his beard. "It's done been paid fer."

Jennifer's face filled with surprise. She turned to Lita, then back to the man. "Then who paid for it?"

"Don't know," the man replied. "Just says fer me to bring it out and install it."

"I'd better check into this before you do," Jennifer said. "I can't be accepting charity."

Lita poked a sharp elbow in Jennifer's side. "Let the man put it in," she said, glaring. "If somebody want to help—let him! We sho' can't afford to be proud. Lord knows we need some heat."

Biting her lip, somewhat uncertain, Jennifer eyed the big, black square stove, an upright model of heavy cast iron. "I suppose you could put it over there," she said, pointing to an empty corner.

"Yes, ma'am," the man acknowledged as he turned to the homely two boys helping him. "Jed, you get the saw and bring in that stovepipe. Levi, you help me scoot this thing over to the corner."

Jennifer and Lita watched the men in amazement as they did their work quickly and efficiently, banging around and sawing a hole in the wall for the pipe. Before they were finished, a rumble came from the front porch. Jennifer went to the window to look out and saw another man unloading a wagonload of cut wood. She quickly stepped out into the brisk, cold wind and asked the man, "Who told you to unload this wood here?"

"Didn't get his name, lady," the man said. He was a man that seemed to keep to himself, tall and limber and thin, a man who preferred to handle wood rather than talk.

"Did he pay you?"

"Shore did," the fellow said without looking up.

Frustrated, Jennifer scurried back inside out of the cold.

I have a feeling that Lance Rivers might know something about this, she thought. *He's up to something*.

~

Later that afternoon, with the woodstove heavily stoked and blazing until the sides glowed a soft red, the front office grew cozy and warm. Jennifer found that even the press seemed more manageable, as if its temperament had been improved by a more comfortable atmosphere. Taking Jason's advice, she worked each copy carefully through the stubborn machine until she'd produced fifty editions. *At least it's something,* she thought as she held one of the copies and read it over. *I need more copies than this, but then again, I still have to get out and sell them as well.*

The late afternoon was clear and crisp as the temperature dropped steadily. A deep blue sky was turning pale with a crimson hue when the front office door swung open and Lance Rivers stepped in. He noticed Jennifer; she had the air of having roused herself from being half asleep as she stood across the room—she was plainly tired.

Her eyes were large and her face expressive enough, but loose in repose. She apparently thought him safe, since she said, "Please close the door. It's cold out."

He smiled, giving him an entirely grateful appearance. Removing his long overcoat, he approached the roaring fire in the new stove and warmed his hands. "Now that's nice," Rivers said, indicating the glowing stove and the comforting heat it put out.

Showing an amusing smile, Jennifer said, "That's a compliment, isn't it?" She was polite and idly curious, but in watching him, she acquired some amount of interest. "Is this stove part of your business interest?"

"Not really," Rivers said, turning to see Jennifer staring at him. "I can't stand by and watch you freeze to death. Do you blame me?"

Rivers appeared genuine and sincere enough, his dark eyes holding the kind of gaze that said he had a keen interest in her well-being. "You're nice and seem honest enough," Jennifer observed. "But do you understand that this puts me in a strange position? I feel somehow . . . liable. It makes me beholden to you, and that's not right. I can't accept that."

"I realize what kind of woman you are," Rivers obliged. "I would think less of you if you acted any differently. I know it's hard right now."

"Hard?" Jennifer asked, and then he saw her interest grow.

"Getting by," Rivers affirmed. "It's a matter of considerable work—and some wits." He stood tall by the stove, his shaved face appearing like smooth granite."

"Well, Mr. Rivers, I know about work and wits, too." Jennifer's face lifted from its weariness and became somewhat lively. "If you don't overassert yourself, perhaps we can get along."

The effect of what she said and her anxious expression came across the room at him. He felt it and it stirred him while a new smile eased across his face. "I'm sorry if I seem forward; sometimes I'm like that. Loneliness—you may not know the extent of it."

"We're all lonely, Mr. Rivers," Jennifer said, ceasing to smile, but the expression on her face carried silent overtones, something that he understood entirely. She had her head tilted, and her lips were pleasantly formed. "Is this visit business or pleasure?"

"Both," Rivers replied, stepping away from the stove, now warmed. "I brought something for Grant, but it's a pleasure to be in your company—as always."

Avoiding the comment, Jennifer stepped closer to her benefactor and the stove nearby. "I thought maybe you just stopped in to warm beside your new stove since it's a cold day."

"Every day from now on will be a cold day," Rivers assured her. "If you're waiting for warmer weather, you'll be waiting until next summer."

The two seemed to find the remark amusing as Jennifer lowered her guard to this bold and handsome man. "So, you say you have something for Grant?"

"Oh that," Rivers answered. "Yes, I thought he might like to take a ride through town on a thoroughbred. The horse is tied outside."

Moving over to the window, Jennifer pulled back the shade and studied the fine animal just outside, a tall horse with sleek lines. It wore a new saddle, the stirrups already shortened for Grant. "My goodness," she said, recognizing instantly the beauty of such an animal. "I trust you don't plan on making a gift of this horse—that's not business."

"Oh no," Rivers admitted. "I just thought that Grant might like to ride a thoroughbred—no hidden motives, I promise. You see, I'm a man of my word, and I promised Grant I would bring him a horse like that to ride. Often, one thing leads to another, but still, we never know what the future may bring. At least I try."

Jennifer stiffened at Rivers's remark, but before she could respond, Lita popped in. "Miss Jenny, tell dem children not to run off when they get in—I got supper all ready." Then Lita glanced up, and her eyes caught Lance Rivers and stayed deliberately on him.

"Who's this?" Rivers asked, approaching with a wide smile.

Turning, Jennifer said, "This is Lita. She's been with me for years."

Not only was Lance Rivers quick, but he was smoothly shrewd as he came up to Lita and took her firm hand. "The pleasure is mine," he announced graciously. "I'm Lance Rivers." He continued holding her hand.

"How do, Mr. Rivers?" Lita said stiffly, surprised by his bold actions.

In time, Rivers released Lita's hand, and she quickly escaped back into the kitchen. "Back in Kentucky, when I was a child, there was a black woman much like her who practically raised me," he boasted proudly. "I adored her."

Rivers had shifted the subject, making it easier for Jennifer. "She's been a backbone in this family, helping me raise the children, taking care of house and cooking. But she's much more—with her spiritual encouragement."

"We all need that," Rivers agreed, now standing much closer to Jennifer. His eyes seemed to be drinking her in, his determination strong, but his manners foremost. "Will Grant be arriving soon?"

"I should hope so," Jennifer said. "But I don't want him out riding too long. You heard Lita—she has supper ready."

Rivers picked up a fresh copy of the newspaper Jennifer had recently finished printing and read the bank robbery article. She watched his eyes dart back and forth as he read and soon he laid the paper down. "That's very good," he said. "Where did you get your information?"

"Eyewitness accounts are always the best," Jennifer said.

"But you concluded in the article that you thought these robbers weren't really miners but highwaymen dressed as miners. You went on to say that you thought the leader might be the same robber as the Kissing Bandit. How do you come to those conclusions?"

"I made it clear that these are assumptions," Jennifer said testily. "I was an eyewitness to the Kissing Bandit in a train robbery—some of the things the witnesses said of the bank robbery seemed similar."

"Now you have to get out and sell these papers?" Rivers asked.

"Yes," Jennifer admitted timidly.

"Why don't you let me take this bundle with me?" Rivers asked, insisting. "I'm going over to Idaho Springs tomorrow. Undoubtedly, this will be the first written news of the robbery to reach that town, and I'll be able to sell them all easily. Whatever you think you can sell here you can print, but I'm sure that the *Register* already has the story out."

Jennifer thought for a moment—what Rivers said was true. "Well, take those. I'll print more tonight to sell locally."

The front door swung open and the children bounded in, Grant in front of Abby. "Mother! Did you see that horse out there?" he said out loud before he stopped in his tracks in front of Rivers. "Oh, hello, Mr. Rivers."

Turning his attention to Grant, Rivers said, "Grant, I brought that horse over for you to ride. Are you ready?"

Grant threw his eyes to his mother, his look already begging for approval. "Can I, Mother? Please?"

Nodding, Jennifer said, "Lita doesn't like people to be late for supper, and she has it ready. But I'll explain it to her. Don't you be gone too long." She smiled, pleased with Grant's excitement.

The gentleman horse rancher put on his long coat and swung around to look at Grant, who was still in his coat and eager to go. Rivers opened the front door and let Grant out under his extended arm. He turned to Jennifer and winked before he closed the door.

"I wish I was a boy!" Abby said, disgusted. She had observed the entire scene closely. "Why did Mr. Rivers wink at you, Mother?"

"I think he must have had something in his eye," Jennifer said, a little amused.

"No, he didn't!" Abby said angrily. "He was flirting with you."

~

Grant rode on the tall, prancing horse as Rivers rode along beside him, Grant grinning like a freed slave. They went through the main streets in Black Hawk and then rode on up to Central City, a place Grant wasn't nearly as familiar with. "That's the Teller House," Rivers said, pointing out a huge brick structure. "Not a finer hotel around. Did you know that many famous men come to stay here?"

"No," Grant said. Rivers was making a tour of showing him all around, the best places to eat, to buy clothes, to gamble, to drink; and while they made their way around, both towns readied for another wild night in the saloons and dance halls. There was no finer way to get about than on a show horse, and Grant felt the tingle of excitement every minute, the spirited animal under him shaking its shimmering coat and throwing its head, deliberately drawing attention. As if that weren't enough, Grant was proud to be seen with Lance Rivers, for almost everybody touched their hat as he passed, and he touched his like a salute in return.

"Do you know everybody in these towns?" Grant asked, not noticing the increasing cold at all.

"Not only in these towns, but in a few others as well," Rivers said. "Being in the horse business, I get around."

It wasn't long before Grant felt a closeness to the man. No one else had taken such an effort in showing Grant great personal attention. Jason used to, but that was before the accident made him a virtual ghost. Rivers spoke to Grant as if they'd known each other forever, and the boy felt his chest swell.

Rivers pulled his stallion to a stop and fished in his vest pocket to produce a fine gold watch. He flipped it open, then shut it, and carefully placed it back in his pocket. "Can't disappoint your mother," he said. "We'd better swing on back before she gets worried."

"Yes, sir," Grant said, minding his manners in front of the courteous gentleman. Riding back, he felt overwhelmed with Rivers, the kindest and most decent man he'd ever met. *He has the best manners in the world, and I bet he could shoot the clothespins off a wire at twenty feet*. The impression made a mental brand on Grant, yet he was smart; he knew Rivers could use his help to get closer to his mother—and he thought Rivers was doing a professional job of it, seeing as Grant delighted in the attention.

When they returned, they found Jennifer in the front office worrying over the reluctant press. "How was the ride?" Jennifer asked Grant, noticing his cheeks were bright red from the chill.

"That's the best horse I ever got close to, much less got to ride on!" Grant said enthusiastically. He approached the stove and warmed by it, as if it had been there forever.

"He's a fine rider," Rivers bragged. "I was curious to see how he handled a thoroughbred."

"I'm glad to hear it," Jennifer said, proud of Grant and happy for him as well. Her tension had eased with Rivers. His motives seemed obvious enough, and he made no pretensions.

"Let me get those newspapers and be on," Rivers said, not removing his coat. "Don't want to wear my welcome out."

Handing him the papers, Jennifer looked closely at him. He was almost too good to be true, a real benefactor and a gentleman. Turning to go, he announced, "Good night, everybody." Reaching for the door, he pulled it open.

"Mr. Rivers," Jennifer said, catching his attention. "Thank you," she said softly.

Rivers gave her that kind of look a man has when he knows he's on the right track. "Think nothing of it," he said as he gently closed the door.

"He's the nicest man I ever met. Don't you think so, Mother?" Grant asked, encouraging her to agree.

Glancing at Grant, a sly look in her eyes and her lips held tight to hide a smile, Jennifer let a thought pass and then said, "Oh, yes, he's *very* nice."

CHAPTER

9

Preacher Man

The metallic blast of church bells rocked the town's self-conscious stillness. Down at Scoby's Saloon, the drinks still poured freely and the piano music clambered on. Dance hall girls laughed and frolicked in the arms of lusty miners. The Saturday night crowd had left before dawn and been replaced by another shift of miners just getting off. Rarely was there a lull in business, as crowds swamped the saloon seven days a week, twenty-four hours a day.

Unnoticed, a tall man in black walked into the smoke-filled bar past the busy poker tables and up to the long, hardwood bar. He had a stature like a straight black fence post. The smell of stale whiskey, women's perfume, and men's sweat weighed heavy in the air. Above the lengthy mirror behind the bar hung a large painting of a nude woman lying on a red sofa. Kerosene lamps swung from the ceiling, and the noise of the place rattled the glasses lined up behind the bar. The stranger in black approached the bar and leaned on it heavily. He was a tall, big-framed man, his face weathered to a leathery sheen, his blue eyes piercing, and his voice heavy and clear as a bell.

"What can I get for you, friend?" asked the bartender, a shadowy man with a fake smile and slick, gray hair plastered to his skull. His white sideburns bristled—he was like an old mouse, cautious and slow, his movements deliberate and careful.

"Are you the proprietor?" the stranger asked.

The bartender's face lost its fake smile. "No, but I'm in charge—what's the problem?"

"I'm called 'Preacher,'" stated the stranger. "I'd like an hour with your crowd here."

The bartender reared his head back and let out a hearty laugh, then said, "Well, you're a mite confused. You're in the wrong place, Preacher. There's a big church just up on the hill. This here's a saloon, in case you haven't noticed."

"The church is full of God-fearing people," the preacher said sternly. "I prefer to go to the devil's den where the sinners are, where there's people in need of my preachin' the most!"

Rolling his eyes, the bartender showed impatience and disgust. "I don't think the clientele here would appreciate it," came his snide remark.

"Why don't we ask them and see," said the preacher boldly. He grabbed a heavy mug and banged it on the bar loudly as he turned to the crowded room. The music stopped abruptly, and everyone looked up to see what the disturbance was. "I bring the word of the Lord!" he called out loudly, his voice carrying a resonance of melody. "How many of you sinners need to hear a good preachin' on this fine Sunday morning?"

A raucous laughter rose from the boisterous crowd as rough men swigged at their frothy beers and rolled their jolly eyes at each other. "He's a wantin' to preach in here!" came the mocking voice of a drunken miner, and more laughter followed.

"Awe, let'm preach!" another Cornish miner yelled. "We be a needin' the fire and the brimstone!"

"Yeah, let'm preach!" came the consensus as the gamblers turned their chairs toward the preacher. Girls took a seat, as did their dance partners, and the piano player gladly closed the lid on the upright piano.

Turning to the bartender, the preacher gave him a scolding glare. The bartender meekly shrunk his head in his shoulders and slunk away.

"I come to the devil's kitchen to bring you the Word!" announced the preacher with a captivating smile. His voice filled every crack in the smoky room. "I have good news for you sinners. God can save you! He already has—now it's up to you to receive His gift. The punishment for sin, my friends, is death—everlasting and eternal death, a misery God wants no man to suffer. For you adulterers, fornicators, gamblers, and wine bibbers—yes, you are all present right here before me," he said clearly, waving his arm over the attentive crowd. "You!" he called, suddenly pointing to a big miner with a dance hall girl sitting in his lap. "Do you not have a wife and children waiting for you at home?"

Quickly, the embarrassed girl jumped up and moved away from the miner, a miner who suddenly lost his cheerfulness. There was a hushed laughter, but then the preacher pointed out another miner sitting at a poker table piled heavy with money and cards and drink. "And you!" he said, pointing to this miner who had laughed. "Is your money on the table the money that is to pay for food and rent for your family, the family that loves you and looks to you for support?" The miner dropped his head in shame.

"We are *all* sinners!" the preacher said even louder. Passersby had gathered at the door, for the preacher's voice carried through the walls. They slowly piled inside, curious as to what would gain the attention of a crowd in a saloon. "But the good news is the Lord loves you enough that He has given His only Son! *Jesus has died on the cross for YOUR sins*!" The preacher paused to let his words sink in, words that were still ringing in the air. He walked slowly down the long and vacant wooden bar, dragging his hand on the bar top. His piercing eyes searched those that stared at him, and each set of eyes that looked into his feared that he might announce their sins.

"Listen to me!" he called so loudly that most jumped. Then he calmed his voice. "God loves you so much that He's made it easy for you. All you have to do, my friends, is accept Jesus Christ into your life. Say it with your mouth so God can hear you. That is all you have to do—and you are forgiven by the Almighty!" He quickly turned and walked slowly back up the long bar, staring again deeply into the many eyes that searched his. There was no question in this unlikely congregation that this speaker was a man of captivating power.

"How many of you here are without sin?" the preacher called loudly. "Raise your hands, let me see."

No hands were raised—the haze-filled room remained totally silent, until, from the staircase, a saloon woman with an enormous bosom and a low-cut dress spoke up. "This man's a fraud! He doesn't tell the truth!"

Eyes quickly turned back to the preacher to see how he'd handle this contemptuous woman. Yet he stayed calm as he moved closer to the stairwell where he looked up at her painted face—his eyes locked into hers. "Truth?" he asked quietly. "But what do you know about truth? The truth is, you probably don't live under your real name. Is that because you stole your husband's money and ran off, leaving him? Or was it your own children you left behind? Chances are you're running from something. And you and God know what that something is."

The woman gasped. She threw her hands over her face and rushed up the stairs out of sight. The group listening to the preacher, mouths gaping open under wide eyes, now gave their complete attention.

Treating the disturbance as if it were nothing, the preacher continued his sermon for some time and finally wound it up by concluding, "For those of you who don't think you need the Lord's forgiveness, or His mercy, or His grace, then you must be happy. Answer truthfully when you ask yourself if you are happy with your life on earth." He waited a long moment, then removed his tall black hat and passed it to a man in the front row who had crowded in front of him. The pressure of silence increased until someone started clapping, and then another, and another, until the entire saloon stood, giving the preacher a standing ovation. By the time his hat came back, it was filled with money.

Smiling, the preacher turned around to the bar and sorted the money. "Don't worry," he said to those smiling faces near him. "The money will go for the work of the Lord."

"That was some show, preacher!" a burly, snaggled-tooth miner said as he leaned over toward the preacher. "Let me buy you a drink!"

"Thanks, my good man, but I don't partake in those kinds of spirits." Shoulders held back, the preacher gazed about the room and announced to the now noisy group, "Thank you, my friends. May the Lord show you His mercy. Good day." He then walked out of the saloon, his heavy footsteps the only sound.

The preacher left Scoby's Saloon in a whirlwind of mystery and talk. They had never seen anything like the performance they witnessed on that Sunday morning in the fall of 1875.

~

Quite satisfied with his morning's work, the preacher walked on down Gregory Street in the morning sun, which warmed his bones in the mountain chill. He often kept his travels to an itinerary that stated when and where he would appear in certain mining towns and camps, but it was time for him to have a new one printed up. He removed a tattered piece of paper from his coat pocket and studied it, a list of all the places he intended on stopping at during the coming winter. *I need to have copies of this printed*, he thought, *so that I can post them at all of my stops*.

Stopping a gentleman dressed in a finely tailored suit, he asked him, "Pardon me, sir. I'm in need of a print shop that can make up some copies of my itinerary. Would you happen to know where I might find a place nearby?"

"Certainly," the dapper young man answered. "Go on down until you hit Main Street, but cross on over to Merchant. There's a newspaper called the *Advertiser*. I'm sure Mrs. DeSpain could use the extra work. Tell her Jake sent you."

"Thank you, Jake," the preacher said and stepped back into his long-legged stride.

It was nearing noon when the preacher found the office of the *Advertiser*. He stepped up onto the porch and tried the front door—it was open. Walking in, he found what looked like a newspaper office but smelled like a fine restaurant. The heavy odors of fried foods and fresh-baked bread filled his nostrils and made his stomach rumble. Removing his tall, black hat, he held it in his hand as he moved around and inspected the press and other newspaper office equipment. Coals smoldered in a big black stove over near the corner. *This place has a real homey atmosphere*, he thought.

A back door in the long office suddenly opened and a black woman appeared. "Can I help you?" she asked. She held a cloth in her hand and wore an apron; obviously she was cooking in the back.

"Yes," the preacher said. "I need to have something printed. Who might I talk to?"

"Mrs. DeSpain," replied Lita. "But she ain't here. They'll be back from church pretty soon."

"Mind if I wait?" the preacher asked.

"No, make yourself at home," Lita answered and went back into the kitchen.

When Jennifer and the children arrived, their cheeks were flushed from the long walk in the cold. "Oh!" Jennifer said when she saw the tall man waiting in the office. It was like he had instantly appeared out of thin air, his dark form coming forth from the shadows.

"I'm sorry, ma'am," the preacher said. "I was wondering if I might get a little printing done—a man named Jake sent me over."

"Of course," Jennifer said. She turned to the children. "You get cleaned up for dinner." Rushing them away, she turned back to the preacher. "Now, what was it that you needed printed?"

"My itinerary," the preacher said, removing the paper from his pocket and showing it to her.

"I don't normally do this kind of work, but to tell you the truth, things are a little tight around here right now. I think I can have it ready by tomorrow. Looks like you travel a lot. Are you a salesman?"

"In some respects," the preacher smiled. "I'm a preacher, and I'm called just plain Preacher."

Jennifer showed the man a new respect. "We just returned from church. They could use a preacher there. The man talking wasn't much to listen to."

"That smell is delicious," Preacher said. "You must also live here."

"Why yes, yes, we do," Jennifer said, but she noticed the tall man wasn't listening, his mind was on food. "Would you like to join us for Sunday dinner?"

"I certainly would," said the preacher. "And I can pay my way."

"That's not necessary," Jennifer said. "You can wash up in the back. I think Lita has dinner about ready."

At the dinner table, the preacher returned grace in beautiful words. Lita had prepared fried chicken and gravy and fresh corn bread. They all sat at the table; the preacher sat next to Abe. "So, you're a blacksmith?" he asked Abe.

"Yes, sir. I mostly shoe mules."

Nodding, the preacher took another bite of corn bread. "You say you just returned from church—I take it I'm sitting with a Christian family," he observed.

"We're all Christians," Lita bragged. "But Abe here—I don't know what he is. He believes in the Lord all right, but he believes we ain't got much say in the Lord's works."

"Is that right, Abe?" the preacher asked.

"I believe the Lord controls everything," Abe stated. "Whatever happens, the Lord wanted it that way for His own reasons."

"A regular Calvinist," the preacher said, smiling. "That takes a lot of faith, the kind of faith the Lord likes to see."

"Amen!" said Lita. "Dis house needs all the faith it can get!" She gave Jennifer a sly glance.

"Why? Are there problems here?" Preacher asked.

"Well, yes," Jennifer answered. She went on to tell the preacher of the loss of her husband, her plight west, of their hard luck in Black Hawk, and of Jason's injury and dwindled faith.

"I've had my temptations as well, but the Lord saved me in the nick of time. Tell you what," the preacher said. "I feel the Lord has guided me here and after dinner, why don't we go upstairs and pay this Jason a visit. I'll pray for him."

"Wonderful," Jennifer said. "Maybe you can influence him to regain the faith he once knew."

~

After dinner, the preacher and Jennifer went upstairs to visit Jason. He was sitting up in his bed writing; the heat that seeped up through the floor from the new stove made things much more tolerable. Expecting lunch, he was surprised when in walked this tall stranger wearing black. Jennifer came in behind the man. "Hello, Jason," the tall, thin man said in a prominent voice and extended his big, rough hand.

Jason took the man's hand and gave it a slight shake as he looked over to Jennifer, then back to the leather-faced man. "Who are you?" he asked.

"People call me 'Preacher.' Years ago, when this community was no more than a tent town, they called me 'the Bishop of Black Hawk.' I started the first church here, just a tent back then, but now I'm a circuit rider, carrying the Word of God to all of those forgotten little mining towns and new mining camps as well. It's my belief that the church is full of God-fearing people already, so I take it on myself to go where I think I'm needed most, the out-of-the-way places, bars and saloons, the devil's own den."

"So, what are you doing here?"

"I've come to pray for God to heal you," the preacher said quite simply.

Jason couldn't have been more shocked. "Just like that?" he asked mockingly.

"Something like that," the preacher said, his words enforced by his strong faith.

"But I can't even feel my legs," Jason said bitterly.

"Let me pray," Preacher said, placing his rough hand on Jason's forehead. "Lord, I pray You, let this man have feelings in his legs. Restore his lost faith." The preacher paused, his eyes closed and his head bowed in deep prayer. Jennifer stood behind him, her head also bowed.

Jason watched with open eyes as this strange man prayed over him. He wished it could be true, that the Lord would hear this man's prayer and actually make it happen, but he had strong doubts.

"The Lord has great work for you to do," the preacher said, suddenly opening his eyes. "Your great pain is merely a preparation for you. You see, it's been my experience to observe that the Lord hurts those the most that He plans on using the most, so have faith, young man."

Jason remained silent in disbelief, dumbstruck by the intruder.

Turning to Jennifer, the preacher said, "This prayer will be answered, Mrs. DeSpain. I'm sure of it." Then he turned his attention back to Jason. "I'll be back by tomorrow—I'll check in on you to see about your legs."

A disappointment showed in Jason's dark eyes, then he closed them as if to shut out reality and make this man go away.

"Let us go now," the preacher said to Jennifer. "The Lord has work to do."

Downstairs in the front office, Preacher asked, "Do you think you'll have these copies ready by tomorrow?"

"Lord willing," Jennifer said. "I have so much trouble with this ornery press."

"Would you like for me to pray over it also?" the preacher asked with a smile.

"It wouldn't hurt," she laughed, but then her features changed, and she became serious. "Do you think Jason will really have feeling in his legs tomorrow?"

"Nothing is impossible for God," the preacher answered. "Where's your faith?"

"Oh," Jennifer said, placing the back of her hand to her forehead. "I guess it's been tested so much lately that it's getting worn down."

"Ah, the best test of faith," the preacher recalled. "I didn't get where I am overnight. My faith has also been tested—many times."

Jennifer smiled. She was, for the moment, restored. The simple presence of a man of such strong faith had enabled her to see outside of her circumstances. She enjoyed the strength and confidence of the preacher and his bold claims in the world of faith, and she dearly wished his prayers would be answered for Jason's sake.

CHAPTER

10

The Proposition

The clear night sky, frothy with glittering stars, paled with yellow at sunrise, leaving an icy frosting on the town of Black Hawk. Jennifer was already up, sitting at her vanity in her small chilly room, readying for another day. Sitting idly in front of the mirror, she was caught in a trance, staring at her reflection, but she saw nothing. The image of Lance Rivers kept coming to mind. *He's practically unbelievable*, she thought, trying to analyze the generous and becoming man. *He's almost too good to be true. He's smart. He's handsome. He's successful and wealthy. Surely he must have some kind of flaw*. It was difficult to see through him. *Lita thinks he's a blessing—she thinks he's grand*. This worried Jennifer, because she knew she was already attracted to the man, yet a flame still kindled for Jason; but the Jason she loved was not the Jason she now knew. *It seems my life has been filled with circumstances like this—I should know better. Didn't I learn my lesson with my husband, Drake? Or with Charles in Virginia City? They were also handsome and charming. But their desire was easy wealth. It was their passion. Lance is already wealthy and accomplished. He obviously does not have so many of the flaws that plagued the other men in my life*. A growing hunger gnawed at her, a yearning—she had a woman's loneliness.

Jennifer thought she heard something, and then she heard it again. It was moaning, and it was coming from Jason's room, which was adjacent to hers. Quickly, she finished and rushed over. In opening his door, she saw him sitting up in his bed. He had his right leg pulled up and was holding it; a grimace gripped his face.

"Jason! Are you all right? What's wrong?" Jennifer asked as she swiftly moved over to the bed.

"My leg's on fire!" Jason groaned through his teeth. "Get the doctor—something's wrong."

For a second, Jennifer wasn't sure what to do. "Did you take some laudanum?"

"Yes!" Jason snapped. "Get the doctor!"

On that, Jennifer rushed out. She found her coat, bundled up, and made her way downstairs. On her way through the kitchen, she informed Lita, "Jason's having problems. I have to find the doctor." Before Lita could respond, Jennifer was gone.

By the time Doc Moss got to Jason's room, Jason was in pure agony. "Doc! You've got to do something! My leg's on fire!" The searing pain that ripped up Jason's leg had nearly put him in a state of frenzy.

Pulling the covers away, Doc pushed Jason down flat on his back and barked, "Lay still! Let me check something."

Groaning, Jason followed orders while Doc felt the leg and worked it back and forth, bending it at the knee. "This may be good," Doc mumbled as he studied the leg through his thick glasses that made his sorrowful eyes appear unusually large. "Forget the pain. Try to wiggle your toes."

Taking a deep breath, Jason did as he was told, and there was slight movement in the toes. "It's coming back," Doc observed. "You couldn't feel any pain before because that nerve was pinched. The laudanum should help, but you'll have to ride it out. The injured nerve in your back is telling you that your leg hurts—but there's nothing wrong with your leg, it's all in your back." He gathered up his black bag and turned to Jennifer, who stood silent and watched in disbelief. Doc's eyes were red; a slight odor of alcohol lingered about him. He had the look of a whipped old man.

"Doc, yesterday a preacher was here—he said he'd heal Jason with faith, and he prayed over him." She swallowed hard. "It worked."

The doctor didn't seem surprised or amused. He simply nodded. "I've seen it before," he commented, eager to be going.

"But . . . but it's a miracle!" Jennifer said.

"Maybe. Maybe not," Doc retorted. "The human mind is a powerful thing. Watch him closely, make sure he doesn't thrash around. I don't think it's a good idea for him to try to move around too much just yet." Calmly, Doc shuffled out of the room, his mind on a beer.

"Jason, I can't believe it. The preacher prayed for you to get feeling in your legs and you have."

Wrenching and gritting his teeth, Jason's eyes were wet with tears; the pain felt like he was being cooked over a fire. "Pray for feeling? All the feeling I've got is pain, Jennifer! You call that answered prayer?"

"But the doctor said it was good—you could wiggle your toes!"

Turning away from her, Jason had no more to say as he reached for the laudanum.

Standing beside the bed, Jennifer took Jason's hand, but he snatched it away. "Please don't be like that," Jennifer pleaded. Her hair lay flowing over her shoulders, and her eyes were soft and sympathetic.

"Go away!" Jason ordered. "There's nothing you can do!"

Waiting a moment, she finally said, "I'll check on you later." She felt sorry for him, a very disappointed man. But she had faith he'd get better. Quietly, she left the room.

~

After Jennifer explained to the children over breakfast why the doctor had been called, she got them off to school. Once the big stove in the front office was stoked and blazing, she went to work on printing up the preacher's itinerary. *He'll be happy to hear about Jason*, she thought. *I can't wait to tell him*. Maybe she was just imagining it, but for some reason, the press seemed more cooperative as it slipped back and forth easily. She laid out the print and slowly and carefully printed one copy at a time, each emerging from the press in perfect condition. *It's good to know that this machine has the capacity to do well*, she thought, *even if it does mess up often. Sort of like Jason*, she decided as a slight smile turned her lips.

The morning hours passed, and Jennifer stopped once to go back in the kitchen and have a cup of coffee with Lita. "I've never seen such a quick answer to prayer before," she told Lita. "Looks like a miracle to me."

"Dat's all we knew when I was young," Lita said, reflecting on her days of slavery. "Sometimes it worked and sometimes it didn't. Our reverend said it depended on if enough faith was put into it. Abe would say it have to do with God's will."

"There's something very different about this fellow who calls himself 'Preacher.' I can't put my finger on it." She took a sip of coffee. "It's like he has some kind of firsthand connection with God."

"I knew somethin' strange about dat man," Lita said, "when he ate with us. He like an angel. He has a doin' kind of belief. Not like some who got just a talkin' kind of belief."

Jennifer smiled; the thought pleased her, although she'd never knowingly seen an angel. "He'll be by shortly—I'd better go organize the paperwork I have ready for him." She stood and scooted the chair back under the table. She turned to ask Lita if she had ever seen an angel but thought better of it and left the room.

The preacher stood with his hat in his hands in the front office waiting. When Jennifer saw him standing there, at first she was startled. "I'm sorry, Preacher, you frightened me. I didn't hear you come in."

"Pardon me," he said in his usual, stately manner. "Next time I'll make some noise."

An expressive joy flowed over Jennifer's face. "Jason got feeling back in his legs this morning—although it was all pain, he could wiggle his toes. I don't think pain is what he would have prayed for, but I'm happy for him. The doctor said it was a good sign."

"I'm pleased to hear that. How's he doing now?"

"He's sleeping. That laudanum is strong stuff."

"Goes to show you," the preacher said, smiling, "we must be careful what we pray for."

"Yes, I suppose we should," Jennifer agreed. "But how could you be so sure this prayer would be answered at all?"

"My dear," the preacher assured her, "that man has the Lord's attention. I believe God is preparing him for some important work." A knowing smile turned his thin lips. "Besides, all prayers are answered in one way or another."

Gazing into the preacher's piercing and sharp eyes, Jennifer let herself feel the power he held. The power was strong like gravity; it pulled at her from deep within. It was as evident as a guarantee that what he said would come true. "Are you some kind of prophet or something?"

Preacher laughed. "No, I'm merely a humble servant of the Lord." Changing the subject, he asked, "Were you able to get my printing done? I trust you had no trouble with the machine."

"As a matter of fact, it's the first time I've ever run copy on that thing that I didn't have trouble. I can't figure it out."

Still smiling, the preacher reached into his black coat and produced a heavy wallet. "How much do I owe you?"

While Jennifer was calculating, the preacher laid down a hundred dollar note.

"I can't make change for that," Jennifer apologized.

"No change needed," Preacher said.

Taking a deep breath, Jennifer glanced at the bill and back to the preacher. "I can't accept this."

"I represent the church," the preacher said, his voice now strong and convincing. "My congregation is spread out all over these mountains, and this money is from that church. It isn't charity—it's meant to help those in need. That money is from the people that attend my church, no matter where it may be held. You are an investment, and with the power of God, it won't be long before you'll be the one helping instead of receiving. That's the way the church works," he concluded with a smile.

Speechless, Jennifer just stared at him. She'd never known of any kind of preacher that in any way resembled this man. "We are in hard times," she muttered. "I'm not sure what the future holds—I can just hope."

"And hope is a mighty powerful thing," Preacher added. "These copies look fine—on nice and heavy paper, very good. I must be on my way." He turned and made his way for the door, but stopped before he opened it and again faced Jennifer. "Tell the young man upstairs that I'll be back by to check on him. We must prepare him to walk again."

As he walked out, Jennifer called after him, "Thank you—thanks!"

He waved a hand in the air without turning around.

I feel like he's someone extra special, she thought. *I wish I knew more about him*.

~

By afternoon, Jennifer had run some errands and was surprised to see that the few editions she'd left in the local area had all sold. She collected the little bit of money and returned to the office. But now she was faced with putting together another edition and as of yet had almost no news to report and very few advertisements to run. It seemed rather useless; she needed help, someone to be out collecting stories and selling advertising—the job Jason had been doing.

The sun glared down and the afternoon grew warm, the first warm day in some time. Fighting sleepiness, Jennifer sat at her desk and wrote. She had several letters to write and needed to construct some kind of format for the next edition. But it was hard to concentrate; her eyelids were heavy, and her head felt light.

"Mrs. DeSpain, wake up," a man's voice said. At first she thought she was dreaming, and somewhere in that void between sleep and being awake, she lifted her head from the desk and stared sleepy-eyed. What she saw was a dark-haired and handsome man with coal-black eyes; his face was smiling. In a vague sense of consciousness, she mumbled, "Drake?"

"It's me," the man said, lightly shaking her arm, "Lance Rivers."

It took a moment for a slight dizziness to leave Jennifer. Being roused from a deep sleep had caused her to have a lapse of reason. "Oh, excuse me. I must have fallen asleep. I must look a mess."

This was fine with Lance Rivers. Seeing her sleepy-eyed, her face puffy, her lips full, excited him. He was a man who had known many women, but none he could remember had the kind of beauty Jennifer DeSpain had. He had cleverly manipulated his way into her life but was growing impatient. He wanted to be closer to her, to be trusted by her—she was the woman he wanted to give his life to. He knew it the first minute he laid eyes on her. "You look lovely," he said.

Gathering her senses, Jennifer finally realized where she was and who Lance Rivers was. "It's funny," she said. "Sometimes when I fall asleep like that, it's such a deep sleep that I feel like I'm in another time somewhere far away."

"You called me a man's name—you said Drake," Rivers said.

"I did? That's my late husband's name," she said.

"I'm sorry," Rivers said, sensing an emotional lilt in her tone. "You must have loved him very much."

"I was very young." Jennifer had reminded herself of that more than once, now revealing the thought to Rivers. "It was a long time ago."

Rivers nodded. He thought any man who had been married to Jennifer a very fortunate man. "I came by to bring you some money," he said, grabbing his wallet. "The general store in Idaho Springs sold all of your papers in a few hours. They eat up sensational news."

"That's wonderful," Jennifer said, now relaxing a little. It was hard for her not to feel tense around Rivers. There was something that drew her to him, something she didn't yet understand. She feared it was like the fatal attraction a moth had for a flame. *But he has never shown me anything but kindness*, she realized. *He seems to have none of Drake's many faults*.

"I've also brought some news. You might want to print a story about it." Rivers seemed happy to be able to be a part of her world.

"What kind of news?" Jennifer asked.

"Stagecoach robbery. I talked extensively with the passengers who were held up, a lady and three men. But it seems the robbers were after a chest the driver was carrying, a mining company payroll. The robbers made off with all of it."

"This is good news!" Jennifer said, then laughed a healthy laugh.

"I don't mean good news—I mean it's good that you have the news, for I had little to print in the next edition."

"I'm not a reporter, but I took some notes. I can tell you the story best," Rivers said, pulling up a chair to Jennifer's desk.

Jennifer quickly produced pencil and paper and scratched down what Rivers told her. Then she asked questions—some he could answer and some he couldn't. "Don't feel bad—it takes experience to learn what to ask," she said, tickled with the information she had. It was enough for a headline story.

Rivers came around the desk as Jennifer stood; an impulse made him reach for her and pull her to him. She raked his face with her glance; she was critical and yet she was interested. He laid a hand around the back of her neck and pulled her against him. She turned her head away for a moment, until he said, "That's not what you want to do, is it?" She lifted herself slightly and gave him one more heavy, searching look. He lowered his mouth to hers and she drew back, confused.

"You're not afraid, are you?" he asked, his deep, dark eyes holding her in a steady gaze.

Jennifer shook her head, but there was a loose and hopeful expression on her face—and out of his long experience with women, he knew what was happening to her. She was placing him apart from other men and letting herself fall for him.

It took Jennifer a moment to clear her mind. She straightened and backed away, then she shrugged her shoulders and now she was even more pretty—the lines of her face softened, the strain gone from her eyes. "I've been stuck on bad men in the past, and it's difficult for me to understand. I fool myself for a long time, hoping I'm wrong. And they're decent just once in a while—and that keeps me going. Then one day I realize I'm never going to get anything back."

"Why didn't you quit them?" he asked, definitely concerned.

Letting her big eyes wander, she said, "I guess I get lonely, just like anyone else."

"I knew I loved you the first minute I saw you," Rivers said, boldly revealing his inner feelings. "Jennifer, I have so much to offer—I wish you'd give me a chance."

She turned, facing him, still searching. "Lance, I hardly know you. I *am* afraid—afraid of myself. I don't think I could stand another heartbreak."

"I would only give you the very best," Rivers promised. "Please, give me a chance."

Now she turned and took a few steps, putting some distance between Lance Rivers and herself, then slowly turned back to him. "Give it some time, Lance. I have to be certain I know what I'm doing."

"Fair enough," he said, drawing his fine gold watch and checking it. "Then you won't refuse when I ask you out to dinner sometime very soon."

A faint smile was hidden in her expression, but Jennifer responded, a hint of anticipation in her voice. "This all seems a bit fast."

"I'm sorry I've pressured you," he said, sincere in his apology. "But I won't ask to be forgiven, because I've never met a woman like you. I can't help myself."

Color came to Jennifer's face. She was flattered but glad she could control the urge that would have moved her forward. The big, front office had grown small and heavy with the pressure of his presence. She couldn't deny she had feelings for this man and his simple desires. "There's nothing to be forgiven," she said "You've done nothing wrong."

Lance smiled. He knew by the way she responded that she would eventually come over to him, that it would only be a matter of time now. Unfortunately, he knew this time would pass slowly for him. "Well," he said, "I must be going now. Jennifer, I . . ." He waved his hand at the air in front of him, a gesture to suppress his determination.

Coming closer, Jennifer took control with the confident manner in which she held his gaze. "Good-bye, Lance," she said, her voice firm but understanding.

Rivers nodded and moved to the front door. He gave her a quick look over his shoulder as he left, as if he was in a hurry. Jennifer watched him cross in front of the window and then mount his stallion. He rode off at a brisk trot. What was evident was the excitement she felt over something new. The possibilities whirled through her mind faster than she could keep up with them. *I can only pray for divine guidance*, she thought.

~

That evening Grant knocked on Jason's door.

"Come in," Jason called.

Grant came into the room sheepishly. He knew he'd been neglecting Jason, but the truth was he couldn't handle being around Jason the way the man was, bedridden and sickly. It was hard for him to see his good friend knocked down out of life right when he was in his prime and by something as humiliating as a fall from a horse. Yet Grant had heard there was hope, that Jason had moved his toes. "Are you getting better?" Grant asked. "I heard you were in a lot of pain this morning."

"Sit down," Jason said, trying to be friendly, but the pain still pulled at him. He wasn't sure if the pain had subsided or if he'd grown a little more used to it. "I've been wondering when you were going to drop in. You're the only one I can trust to tell me what's going on without sugarcoating everything."

It was easy for Grant to tell that Jason was glad to see him, even if the lines in Jason's face indicated that he was hurting. "Do you think that preacher had anything to do with you getting better?" Grant asked, his curiosity overriding any sense of courtesy.

Jason had to smile. "I don't know what to think," he said. "Honest! That fellow sure seemed strange to me. I thought he was some kind of medicine-show man or pill salesman or something. Just between you and me, that man scares me a little—it's like he can see through me or something."

"I know," Grant said. "When he ate dinner with us, me and Abby were scared to talk."

"Abby and I," Jason corrected.

"Oh," Grant said, his face frowning, "you know what I mean."

"Yeah, I do," Jason agreed. For the moment, the pain wasn't on his mind. "What else has been happening? I hear people coming and going downstairs, and I hear men's voices, but I can't tell what anyone is saying."

Grant's face lit up. "There's this man! And he's rich! He said he was going to let me ride one of his fine horses and you know what? He showed up here with a thoroughbred, and we went for a ride around town! That's the fanciest horse I've ever seen, and I got to ride it!"

"That sounds pretty exciting," Jason said, lifting himself up into more of a sitting position. "Who is this man?"

"Lance Rivers," Grant replied. "He has a horse ranch and raises thoroughbreds."

"What's he doing here?"

"Oh, he runs advertisements in the paper for his horses," Grant said, trying to control the drift of the conversation. The boy knew what Rivers was up to, his motives, and that he liked his mother. Grant certainly didn't want to be the one who revealed this to Jason.

"Is there a stove in the front office now?" Jason questioned. "I noticed it sure got a lot warmer up here, and I could smell the smoke."

"Yeah," Grant said and left it at that.

"Where'd that come from?" Jason asked.

All Grant could do was shrug his shoulders. But Jason knew Grant was a sharp boy, and Jason's suspicion was that Grant didn't want to tell him for some particular reason. Rather than pressure his friend, Jason decided it wasn't important. "I've started a book," he said.

Grant lightened up, relieved. "Really? What about?"

"Oh, it's about my childhood on a plantation and our large family, then how the war tore us apart, about my years in school, and then the adventures out west. I leave out the part about being a drunk." Jason smiled at that.

A smile crept across Grant's face too. It was easy to laugh about now, especially if Jason could laugh about it. "Jason, do you know how to play poker?"

"Sure."

"Think you could teach me?"

"Get the cards, podnuh! I'll skin you alive."

Now excited, Grant jumped up and ran from the room, calling over his shoulder, "I'll be right back!"

Poker proved to be therapeutic for Jason since it kept his mind off of his pain and the tedious boredom that lurked in the small room. Grant, on the other hand, was glad to have someone to talk to, to ask about the things he'd heard from Butch, the kind of things he couldn't ask his mother. In a roundabout way, Jason learned a little more about Lance Rivers, and it troubled him.

CHAPTER

~ 11 ~

Abby's Dissidence

The days of November persisted with the cold promise of a nasty winter ahead. At the breakfast table during the past many weeks, Abby had said very little—there was a shrinking away to her. Her irritable surface remained—in fact, she seemed to take pride in being miserable. It was about all she had left to her, this surface that covered a heartbreak that was tragically felt, a disillusionment that was, in her mind, severe. Abby's role had not changed, that of a fighter with the discomfort she felt around her.

On this particular Saturday morning, Abby sat at the table eating a bowl of oatmeal, while Lita tended her kitchen chores. Grant had left early with Lance Rivers to ride up to a mining claim that Rivers owned and see how the operation was going. Again, Abby felt left out and cast aside. Jennifer was out still trying to establish some kind of regular newspaper route with the local retailers. Abby stabbed at the stiff oatmeal with a big spoon, her young face an expression of anger.

"I wish I was a boy, Lita. They get to do everything! All I get to do is sit around this stupid old building—there's nothing to do here!" She stuck the spoon in what was left of her breakfast and pushed it away.

"You better eat your breakfast," Lita warned. "Got to have something to stick to your ribs to stay warm."

"If I was a boy, I'd be riding up to some gold mine with Grant on a nice horse with that Mr. Rivers," she said, ignoring Lita's advice to finish her breakfast.

"You don't want to be no dirty old boy," Lita said with animation in her voice. "A pretty girl like you—why you'll learn how to tell dem men what to do. Dat's all they want, anyway."

Squirming in her chair, Abby found it easy to complain to Lita. "When I get old enough, I'm going to run away! Then I can do like I want. I already found me somebody to take care of me."

"Oh?" Lita said, a little surprised, turning around to face Abby. "Who's this lucky person?"

"Butch of course!" Abby spouted. "He's the only boy that ever treated me like I was somebody. I reckon I'll have to marry him someday." She let her eyes wander as she imagined a more exciting life. "Butch, he's not afraid of anything, and he knows a lot too, Lita. Did you know he's a good poker player?"

"Who says?" asked Lita, playing along.

"I say!" Abby scorned. "He knows a lot of tricks on how to make money too. We'll never be poor." Then she paused a minute, her mind changing to another subject. "How come we're so poor, Lita? We used to have money back in Virginia City. Now Mother says we can't afford anything I want. She says it might be a while."

"Life is like that," Lita said. "Some times is good and some times is bad. That train robbery set us way back. We just down on our luck right now. It'll change." Lita busied herself greasing the skillets with drippings, then placed them in the oven to preserve the heavy black cured surface.

"If you ask me, I'd say we're about to go under."

"Who told you that?" Lita asked, frowning.

"I heard Grant tell Butch that. He didn't think I heard, but I did." Then she waited a minute, her young eyes watching Lita closely as the woman stirred the coals in the stove. "Lita, what does 'go under' mean?"

"It means 'go out of business,'" Lita answered without looking up. The kitchen was a little smoky from the leaky cook stove. "We ain't goin' out of business," she assured her.

"Well, I'm sick of all of this. I hate that cold and stupid school—it's a waste of time. I'm bored. If I was older, I'd go down to one of those saloons with all the pretty ladies," she said dreamily.

"Oh no, child, no," Lita warned her. "'Those women ain't happy, even if they do laugh. It ain't no life."

No matter what Abby said, she couldn't relieve the resentment she carried. Her vague memories of the loving and kind man she knew as Father often caused her to create memories glorifying this man. She had the idea that if he hadn't been killed everything would be wonderful. It drove her temper out of control, coveting the fathers of other girls. To her, a father was the answer to all of her childhood problems.

"Lita, what was your father like?"

Now Lita stopped, staring at nothing, then she turned to face Abby. "Child, I never knew my pappy. I was only with my mother 'til I was a little younger than you, then they took me away."

Abby knew she couldn't impress Lita with her discontent, because Lita could always better her with an awful story of her own. Abby loved Lita, and the older woman was a good listener, but Lita didn't offer the comfort she was looking for. What she wanted was an ally, somebody who shared her contempt for being so unfortunate. Butch was the only person she had who would agree with her. Since nobody ever seemed to notice her, she figured she'd slip out and find Butch and spend some time with him.

~

Up in his dreary little room Jason scratched away at what he hoped would someday be a complete manuscript. Working on the book was therapeutic. It kept his mind busy and off the pain in his back and legs. He knew how to format a book, something he'd picked up at Harvard. First he made a quick sketch of the ideas he would use, then made this into a simple four-part outline. Then he went back and filled in each part with chapters and outlined each chapter. The only problem was, he didn't have an ending for this book. *I can't end it with me being a bedridden cripple*, he thought, chewing on a pencil. *Maybe I should just go ahead and write what I know, and by the time I get to the end I will have one*. With that, he wrote feverishly, releasing thoughts he'd preserved for years. At first, everything he wrote sounded like a newspaper article. It was a challenge to write differently. But he persisted, rewriting the first chapter again, a chapter about life on a plantation back in a day when things were better.

The door opened and Lita came in doing her daily business of taking care of him. He'd learned not to expose his bitter side around her since the formidable scolding. Besides, without her help, he'd be in a real mess. She never complained and always seemed hopeful. "Dat's good. You ate all your breakfast," she said, piling the dishes to take them away. "You'll be up and around in no time." She gathered up the tray and was leaving the room. "I'll be back to clean you up in a little bit."

"Lita," Jason said, his voice one of concern. "Who's this Lance Rivers fellow?"

Pausing a moment, Lita tried to think of how to explain Lance Rivers without cause for alarm. "He's a nice man. I don't know what we'd done without him."

Well, that was a good answer, Jason thought. *No clues at all*. "What I mean is, is he interested in Jennifer?" That was the only way you could be with Lita, blunt and truthful.

A smile covered Lita's wide face. "I wouldn't blame him if he was," she said, her eyes cheerful. "Miss Jenny's the prettiest woman around." Then, her face changed, a stubborn and determined expression now came. "But don't you worry yourself none about that. You just pray you get better. The Lord has ways of working things out that's right for all us folks."

After Lita had left, Jason found little comfort in her words. He knew she was right, but anxiety plagued him. The problem was that he couldn't even have a normal conversation with Jennifer when she came into his room to visit. Although she seemed to be the same, he knew that he wasn't. His confidence gone, he felt like half a man, an invalid looking at her over a distance of vagueness that had come between them. *What can I possibly say to her? Tell her that I love her?* he chuckled under his breath. *That's ridiculous! How could I ask a beautiful woman like her to love and be with a bedridden invalid for the rest of her life?* He felt the heat of blood running up his neck and into his face, anrgy at his miserable misfortune. As always, thinking of Jennifer and their would-be future was more than he could tolerate.

In defense, he shifted his thoughts to something else—the preacher. Jason still couldn't figure this man out. *What kind of a man is he, anyway?* Jason thought. *A stranger comes in my room and prays over me and feeling comes back in my legs!* Now this was a perplexing and astonishing subject to think about. *I wonder if it really could be true?* Jason thought skeptically. *I wonder if God really does work miracles through prayer? Or is it like Doc thinks, that I'm just healing up like I was meant to all along?* Such ideas overwhelmed Jason's thinking process and sent his thoughts into a tizzy. More questions arose than answers.

Lita returned with a pitcher of warm water, a washbowl, and a towel and rag. Upon Jason's injury, she had immediately elected herself to take care of those responsibilities nobody else dared think about. "Why don't you let me shave dat mess off your face?" Lita asked as she set the items down and prepared to give Jason his towel bath. "You ought to let me cut your hair, too. It's too long."

There was something in Lita that Jason related to—maternal feelings he'd known as a child. He honestly trusted her beyond a shadow of any doubt. "Lita, you act like you've been taking care of me since I was a little boy," he said.

"Lord knows I been takin' care of white folks all my life," Lita said. "Just like the Bible say; be a good servant." She sloshed a rag around in the soapy warm water she'd poured into the washbasin. Jason lifted himself up higher to a full sitting position, his back leaning against the tall headboard.

"I brought some scissors and a razor," Lita said, back to business.

"No, Lita," Jason answered. He didn't want to shave his beard, which was now a little long. And his blond hair had grown even more. "Nobody sees me. What difference does it make?"

"I have to look at you every day!" Lita said steamily. "Don't I count?"

Jason laughed at this energetic and inspiring woman. "I guess you do," he admitted. And for a brief moment, Jason forgot his pain and his misery. Lita's tender attention was something he thirsted for.

Finally, Lita finished and left the room; Jason had escaped the razor for another day. Yet he felt better washed up and cleaned like a fresh shirt—he was ready to get up and go. Then the dismay of being unable to walk struck him, a depression like no other. *I still can't believe such a thing has happened to me*, he thought. *Why me?* The dreariness of that kind of thinking always brought him a dull and lonely hopelessness. But he had a resilience that had enabled him to survive, a way of changing his thoughts that gave him a different perspective. Glancing down at his naked feet as he lay on top of the sheets, he wiggled his toes. He'd gotten better at it and wiggled them until they grew tired. *I will walk again!* he thought determinedly. *But I'll have to be careful how I pray.* He remembered the prayer to get feeling back in his legs and how at first all of the feeling was a fiery pain.

Jason had grown tired of lying in the pitiful little room and wallowing in self-pity. To escape the depression, he was inspired to pick up the pencil and write. *Back to the book*, he thought, gathering up the sheets of paper he'd already written. Glancing over his work, he thought it seemed a little mundane. *I've got to write better than this*, he decided. *This has no feeling. I've got to be in a better frame of mind to write something worthwhile—it's got to come alive!*

~

For Jennifer, it had been a fairly fruitless morning. The sun was out and it was clear and still, but cold. Bundled up in a blue-knitted shawl and wearing a heavy, canvas dress, she shuffled the boardwalks in and out of businesses carrying several of the most recent newspaper editions. Entering the Gilpen Hotel, she quickly moved over to the stove and removed her light gloves and warmed her hands.

An astute clerk noticed her and asked from across the room, "Can I help you with something, ma'am?"

Coming over to the desk, Jennifer laid down her stack of newspapers, each edition only a single page. "Yes," she answered, her pleasant smile showing her white teeth. "I was wondering if I could leave some of my newspapers—maybe your guests would be interested."

The clerk removed a wire-rimmed pair of spectacles from his pocket and slipped them on his pudgy face, a face red and swollen like an overheated pig. His disobedient hair bristled from his scalp, and his jowls wiggled when he spoke, but he was friendly. "You can leave them here," he said, reading over the material, "but I tell you, most of our guests are more interested in events happening around here than advertisements. Or even a good story—like you take the Sunday that the preacher went into a saloon to preach—now that's something!" He wiped a small drip from his pudgy nose and let his plain eyes rest on Jennifer.

"That's amazing," Jennifer said, remembering that Preacher said he gave his sermons in the devil's den.

"Like I said, you can leave your papers here, and I'll collect the money for you, but I wouldn't expect much." The man was kind but truthful.

Leaving a dozen newspapers with him, Jennifer turned to leave, then a thought struck her. "If you ever do need to advertise, I'll be glad to run your ad for you at a bargain rate."

"I'll keep that in mind," the clerk said kindly, then turned back to his business of paperwork.

Back on the street, Jennifer walked along a crowded boardwalk busy with the many sorts of people that inhabited Black Hawk. *He's right*, she thought. *I need somebody out and about to collect the real news—something the people here are interested in reading. If I do it, then who's going to run the office and write and print the columns?* She trudged on, stopping in the hardware store next.

"Can I leave a few newspapers on the counter?" Jennifer asked politely, showing her attractive smile again.

The man she addressed, a balding man wearing an apron, glanced down his long beak at her. "I guess," he answered evenly. He was busy looking at her and not paying attention to the newspaper.

"I'd appreciate it," Jennifer said. "I'll be back by in a few days if you don't mind collecting the money for me."

The man's thin lips smiled slightly, then he picked up a paper and glanced at it. "Advertisements, huh?" He read for a moment, then asked, "What would it cost to run an advertisement? I'm thinking of just running an ad every week, just the hardware company name maybe."

"Oh?" Jennifer said, her mood lifting.

"Yeah, maybe a picture of the building front or something."

"Yes, we can do that." She took a pencil and scribbled down notes on what the man wanted. "I'll be back by and show you some ideas," she said, happy to sell an advertising spot. But when she left, she got to thinking, *Who am I going to get to do a woodcarving for this? I need a picture of the front of his store.*

It seemed like the harder she tried, the more desperate things became. Yet she was determined, carried by her strong faith. *I'll pray about it and something will happen*, she thought, moving down the street again. She worked her way over to Gregory Street and made her way up the hill.

~

Cleverly, Abby sneaked out of the front office door and walked briskly up the street. The imposing odors of Black Hawk seemed to come alive as her heart beat hard with anticipation. She was not accustomed to being alone in public but was stubbornly determined to find Butch. Her search led her up to the corner of Gregory Street and Chase, Butch's favorite hangout. She was overjoyed to see him slouching against the wall of a building smoking a cigarette. He was partially hidden, out of the way of the busy boardwalk. "Butch!" Abby cried, an enthusiasm in her voice.

Turning, Butch caught sight of her, small against the backdrop of some tall wooden business structures and people who hurried by unconcerned. "Hello, Abby," he said coolly. "What brings you out on this fine day?" His smile was genuine, his mood happy.

"I get tired of sitting around that rundown place," she complained, a distaste in her young voice. "I'm not allowed to go anywhere or do anything. So I snuck out."

"Good for you," Butch said as he crushed the smoke under his boot. "I got the morning off—already tended to the horses. Uncle Mike's asleep."

Abby's expression showed displeasure. "All I hear is how broke we are. I'm sick of it. We can't afford anything."

"Money isn't a problem," Butch said wisely. He seemed so full of wisdom and confidence. "If it's money you need, we can get that. It's easy."

"How?" Abby asked, more curious than ever, since money seemed to be the one object that eluded her family.

"Ever heard of panhandling?" Butch asked, while his experienced eyes appraised the street full of traffic and studied the passersby.

"No," Abby answered.

"A sweet young girl like you—why, you'd be better at it than me. All you do is pretend you live on the street and you're starving, then you ask the right people for a handout."

"How do you know which people are the right people?" Abby asked, interested in Butch's idea.

"Nothing to it." He jutted his square chin toward a man that was walking out of a saloon. The man was well dressed and wore a derby hat. He paused to light a cigar. "Take that man standing in front of the saloon," Butch said. "He just won at poker or something, got some liquor in him, and I can tell he's feeling generous by the way he sucks on that cigar. He's in no hurry—our perfect target."

"What do we do?"

"Here," Butch said as he reached over to Abby. "Let me fix you up a little." He mussed her hair and ruffled her coat collar. Then he reached down and rubbed his hand in the muck and smeared a little on Abby's cheek. "Now you look the part," he said. He removed his small-brimmed hat and smashed in the top and flipped up the front quite carefully until the hat's shape was distorted and sad. "Now, you play the part—act like some poor and starving orphan child. Let me see you make an unhappy face."

Trying her best, Abby looked as forlorn as possible. "That's good," Butch said. "Now you come with me and do that. I'll do the talking."

The two made their way down the boardwalk, Butch holding Abby's hand and pulling her along to where the man smoking his cigar stood. Butch tugged at the man's coat. "Hey, mister?"

Turning around, the man glanced down, stodgy at first, his cigar clinched between his teeth. "What is it, young man?" he asked around his cigar.

"Well, me and my sister here, we're hungry. Our pa is a miner and he's been laid up—can't work. We got no money and no food." Butch sounded pitiful, and Abby looked like she'd lost everything in the world.

Removing his cigar from his mouth, the big man sighed, then said, "It's a cryin' shame, all these miners trying to raise a family, then they get hurt and the streets fill with little urchins!"

"I'm so hungry, I could eat a horse!" Abby said unexpectedly, her young and pretty eyes pleading.

The big man smiled and pulled a tall wallet from his vest. He handed Butch a one dollar certificate. "Here," he said. "That's to protect my horse."

"Thank you a whole bunch, mister," Butch said happily. "C'mon, Abby. Let's go get something to eat!"

As the children ran off, Abby turned and yelled, "Thanks, mister!" The man winked back, rolling his cigar in his mouth.

Returning to his hangout, Butch tugged at Abby and pulled her from the boardwalk and out-of-sight. He handed her the money. "See how easy that was?" he asked proudly.

Abby's eyes lit up at the sight of a whole dollar. "I almost laughed," she giggled. "That was easy."

"I do it all the time," Butch boasted. "But I bet you could be better at it than me 'cause you're a poor little girl. You have to remember, got to pick the right ones, 'cause most folks will just brush you off."

Butch and Abby approached five more men, three of whom paid. Their efforts gained them two dollars and fifty cents. "Not bad for a few hours of easy work," Butch claimed. "I think you got the hang of it."

Smiling happily, Abby couldn't believe it. Butch had come

through again and had generously given her the take. She held the money like it was a treasure. "Say, Abby," Butch said. "I got to be going now. Uncle Mike will be waking up soon, and he's going to want me to shag him some breakfast. See you later."

"'Bye, Butch," Abby said, admiring him more than ever. She was beside herself with joy. Once again, Butch had shown her how to manipulate the busy world that at times seemed to want to swallow her. This kindled a fire in her, the kind of fire that burned with ambition. A fast learner, she had the grit to believe she not only could be good at these sorts of games, but could make the people that she swindled like them as well.

On her walk home, Abby spotted a man she thought she could put the soft touch on. She approached him and gave him her practiced routine. Reluctantly, the man reached in his pocket and tossed her a nickel without saying a word and went on his way. Tickled, Abby was ready to move on when she glanced up and saw her mother, who had observed it all from not more than ten feet away.

Shocked and dismayed, Jennifer came quickly over to Abby, studying her disheveled and homely appearance. "Abby—I can't believe it!"

But Abby's stubborn expression and determined will showed on her smug face. She glared at her mother.

Any anger that might have arisen in Jennifer was snuffed by heartbreak. She gently took Abby's hand and moved along, Abby in tow. *Are things so bad that my children are begging on the streets?* she asked herself, a lump in her throat. *Dear God, am I so blind?*

CHAPTER

12

Lonely Holidays

Lance Rivers had been true to his word, persistent until Jennifer consented for a fine evening of dining and entertainment at the Teller House in Central City. After dinner, he helped her into the carriage. The night air stung with a sharp chill. Dressed like a dandy, Rivers came around, boarded, and took the reins, snapping them smartly on the horse's rear. "I'll have you back to warmth in no time," he said as the horse dashed into a smart trot swiftly down the street. It was late, and Jennifer bundled up in her heavy coat, but she felt an inner warmth from a good meal and a play that temporarily took her mind off her troubles.

The street shone a warm glow from behind the frosted windows that lined it. Above, the sky was pitch-black and deep as a bottomless pit. A few people still frequented the streets, but for the most part, the ones with good sense stayed in where it was warm.

Wheeling the small carriage up to the front of the newspaper office, Lance jumped out and tied the horse to a post, then quickly came over and took Jennifer's hand to help her down. "I'm frozen," she said as she hurried up the few steps onto the boardwalk and let herself in.

Once inside, Jennifer tossed a few small logs into the big stove and fanned the dying coals. Soon, flames burst from the wood, sending dancing shadows on the walls behind her. Rivers had done something outside, then came right in, carrying a small bundle.

"Don't bother with the lamp," he said, dragging a couple of chairs up before the open doors to the stove. "Have a seat. It's kind of cozy just like it is." After Jennifer sat down, still wearing her coat, Rivers took the chair right next to her. His glossy black gloves squeaked as he fumbled with the sack and produced a bottle of brandy and two small glasses. "The perfect after-dinner nightcap," he said, holding up a bottle of rare brandy.

Smiling politely, Jennifer said, "Lance, you know I don't drink."

"But this is a special occasion," he said, his influential smile forever present. "I don't know why you can't have just one—it'll warm your bones."

"Thank you, but I'd rather not," she said, the firelight making warm colors on her face.

"Suit yourself then." Rivers poured a glass full of the mahogany color and took a sip. "That's good stuff!" he said, smacking his lips. "Came all the way from Europe."

Jennifer smiled, starting to warm up. She felt lethargic from the fine meal, her eyelids heavy. The winter evening and now the soft firelight made things seem a little dreamy. Lance had been the perfect gentleman, considerate and kind and well-mannered. "I'm sorry I don't have a more comfortable chair to offer," she mumbled. "The office has to double as a sitting room."

"Don't worry about me," Lance boasted. "As long as I'm with you, I don't care if I have to sit in an old, abandoned mine shaft."

The sharp aroma of the brandy on Lance's breath reached Jennifer; it had a fruity fragrance. He seemed somehow invincible, important and powerful, yet humble in his ways. Scooting his chair up close to Jennifer, he put his arm around her and pulled her closer as he held his glass in the other hand. "There's something about a fire," he said, the firelight dancing in his eyes. "It represents the home, the hearth, a kind of security you only find in family. It warms my heart and makes me sleepy to look at it."

Cuddling up to the thick fur on the lapel of Lance's coat, Jennifer closed her eyes for a moment. The stress of the business and being on the edge had taken much out of her, but for the moment, she relaxed, thinking the same things Lance was thinking. She was tired of fighting, tired of worrying, tired of everything. The realm she was in left the world outside, all that remained was Lance and the warm fire. Contentment was a rare emotion that she seldom experienced anymore. "I could go to sleep right here," she murmured.

"Jennifer," Lance whispered, reaching over and pulling her chin up so she could look at him. She opened her big, sleepy eyes and returned his glance. "I must tell you—I'm in love with you."

This caught Jennifer's attention. "But, Lance, you barely know me, and I barely know you. I don't know anything about your background."

Proudly, Rivers took a sip of brandy and said, "I'm from a large family back in Kentucky, a solid Christian family. Thoroughbreds were our livelihood, and we raised the very best. But as it did to so many families and businesses, the war took its toll. I had many sisters and brothers. I lost three brothers to the war, and one sister nobody knows what happened to. Losing the ranch scattered the family. My father died soon afterwards—it was too much for him.

"I raised and supplied horses to the U.S. Cavalry. We had some good blood in our horses, and this made me a living. But aside from all of that, I've always had this vision that I'd find my dream out West. And here I am, and Jennifer, I'm sure you're the dream I've been searching for."

Silently, Jennifer listened. Rivers was the most romantic man she'd ever known and perhaps the most surefooted. It seemed he was a surviver, always able to take care of himself no matter what the circumstances. His qualities were truly attractive.

He paused and casually took a sip of his brandy and swallowed it slowly. "I have plans," he said softly, his dark eyes turning to the lapping flames. He had the look of a man with great vision. "I have to leave town for a while to take care of some very important business, but I'll be back before Christmas. I want you to know I'm doing this for our future. If things go right, we'll be able to live a mighty fine life—mighty fine." He took another sip from the glass.

Too tired to think, Jennifer could only imagine. She didn't

want to think about the problems of courting Lance, only the benefits. Desperation had drained her of any pride, leaving her more lonely and desolate than ever. "I wish it were true. If only it could be so easy."

Lance laughed a little. "You make it sound so difficult—so terrible," he said. "To me, the hard part is *not* being with you, *not* doing anything about it." He squeezed her a little tighter. "If only you knew how much you mean to me!"

"I'm sorry," Jennifer apologized. She realized she was being melodramatic, perhaps overbearing with her worry. Lance had been like a guardian angel to her. Straightening and reaching her arms around his neck, she pulled him over and kissed him—a gentle and meaningful kiss. The kiss ignited a hunger in her, one that let her know how empty her life had been, how lonely she was. Her life appeared as a series of contrasts, during the day fighting the pressure of survival, trying to make something out of nothing, while at night she weakened, the doubt increasing. But now she was wrapped in the comfort of Lance's arms; the kiss was so full of hope. She knew this was what was missing.

Lance knew the price of the game he was playing, but he was willing to fulfill her desires, to fill her needs. He'd been a traveling man for so long that he had neglected the very thing he sought in life, the love of a good woman. To him, this moment was monumental, signifying a time to change, to settle down. When she pulled away, he still felt the warmth of her tender lips on his in this gentle moment of passion. The kiss had said it all. "I'm yours forever," he said quietly. He took the last sip from his glass and bent over and set it on the scuffed wooden floor. Straightening, he turned back to her. "I always knew when the time came I'd be unable to have any resistance. I want to marry you more than I've ever wanted anything. When I return, we'll continue, won't we?"

Staring deeply into his dark eyes, Jennifer studied his face. "I don't know what's right anymore. I only know I can't continue alone for much longer."

Stroking her cheek gently with his finger, he said, "I understand. It's been a long and hard road for the both of us, but I'm glad I found you." Hesitantly, he stood, bringing her up with him. "As much as I hate to leave your company, it's late and I must be going."

"Don't worry, Lance," she said, "I'll be here."

With a major obstacle overcome, Lance Rivers felt a tinge of relief—Jennifer had shown him that she cared. "I'm sure the time will pass slowly until I see you again."

Nodding, Jennifer could only speak with her wanting eyes that said she was vulnerable, susceptible to desires. She backed away, her hand lingering on his lapel. "I'll wait," she said.

Lance Rivers smiled, but then his face filled with repose, a dedication to work he had to do. Turning, he walked into the darker part of the office near the front door and silently slipped out into the cold.

Left standing, Jennifer felt renewed in a way, but sad that she was again alone. There were so many things to consider, like what about Jason? Exhausted, she closed the doors on the stove and went up to bed.

~

Dependable as the sunrise, Abe continued to work hard and long hours. He was indefatigable, up early every morning and returning late every evening, every day of the week. He gave Lita his pay, keeping very little for himself. She did the best she could, buying groceries and a few needed supplies to keep the household going. It wasn't much. His generosity never crossed his mind—he was happy that he was able to help Lita and the rest, glad that someone depended on him. As for work, he'd learned how to sharpen drilling tools to the liking of the Cornish miners, and this brought extra business to the blacksmith shop at Blake's Livery. Mr. Blake couldn't have been happier with Abe's performance. A few days before Thanksgiving, Mr. Blake said, "Abe, you take a few days off for Thanksgiving. You've earned it. I hear there are some wild turkeys down the canyon a ways—go shoot one. Have yourself a good time."

Surprised, the idea sounded good to Abe. "Thank you, Mr. Blake. I reckon I would like to have some turkey—been a long time."

With that, Abe took off, eager to report to Lita with the good news. The day before Thanksgiving, Abe mounted up on Dolly and took off for the woods, heavily supplied with Lita's biscuits and ham hocks. He rode down the mountain, following the creek until it turned off toward Idaho Springs, the place he was told to go to find the turkeys. Riding the busy trail, he followed it until the steep, rock-walled canyon broke into a forest of thick pines.

"Dis look like the spot," Abe muttered as he reined Dolly off the beaten trail. She grunted, carrying Abe up to the area of thickets and breaks. As the sunset reddened the horizon, a slight wind stirred the pines, nipping with the chill of night. Dismounting, Abe pitched camp, building a warm fire. He felt like he was out in the wilderness about as far as a man could be, the call of wild animals surrounding him. There was a time he would have been afraid of the unknown, susceptible to a questionable spiritual world, but now he rested quietly, certain the spirit that was with him was the Holy Spirit.

After a can of beans and warmed biscuits with ham hocks, he rested against a tree, covered with his bedroll. His tough and callused hands lay folded across his broad chest, his old hat pulled down low over his eyes. The temperature dipped low, but he lay comfortable in his many layers of shirts and pants and a worn leather coat, his belly full. The knitted scarf around his neck and ears had been made by Lita, and this simple item warmed him the most.

Abe was a man at peace—happy about life in general. He felt fortunate that in the past months he'd found a spiritual peace in God that had released him from most of his superstitions, and he'd finally found love, something he had wondered if he would ever find. Lita took good care of him, even if she was a little demanding, but he didn't really mind. She was all he could hope for. But then there was that one little problem that troubled him. The bird that had flown in his window back in Virginia City, indicating bad fortune to come, had been something of a wonder, but for all that, he was happy. Hard work and hard times were nothing new. For Jason's misery and Miss Jenny's discontent, he knew of nothing he could do except try and offer some prayer. But if it was the Lord's will, then it was the Lord's will, and nothing he could do would change that. Satisfied with his assumption, he soon fell asleep next to the smoldering embers.

Well before sunup, Abe made a quick tin of coffee and warmed some of the pork. He'd have to get moving and be well hidden before sunrise if he wanted a turkey. Stomping out the fire, he rolled up his things and packed them on Dolly. Leading her quietly through the black thickets, he stepped carefully along, following a deer trail. He came to a clearing with brush all around it, then backtracked and tied Dolly to a tree. Quickly, he removed his big knife and cut brush silently and made a clump of it in front of him. Cradling his double-barrel shotgun, he squatted in the pine needles.

Waiting for first light, Abe knew that the turkeys might fly in, light in the trees, look around, and then light on the ground—but more than likely they'd walk in. Out of his few personal possessions, his gun and his clothes and a few tools, his most prized properties were the small items, one of which was a handmade turkey call an old white-haired slave had given him almost a half-century before. Dawn came and he pulled it out, a small box with a chalk in it. He fiddled with it in the gray half-light and then scratched the chalk, chuckling seductively, like a hen turkey hunting a boyfriend. He stopped, knowing that if a gobbler was around, he'd sounded enough.

Watching closely, all Abe could see were vague forms and shadows as he waited tensely. It was hard not to imagine seeing movement, but then they crept in like a fog entering a small valley. First they weren't there and then they were, looking big as cows. They came out of a little path in single file, the first ones hens, and then some yearling gobblers, then more hens, and finally the chief.

The turkeys fanned out, feeding gently toward him on pine nuts. The big gobbler spread his tail like a fan and let out a gobble that sounded deafening in the early morning silence. He gazed arrogantly around him, daring any turkey in the neighborhood to flap so much as a wattle at one of his wives, and he personally would tear him to pieces. He hustled his gang, coming straight for Abe, who sat patiently, although his heart beat feverishly with anticipation.

From years of experience, Abe knew the old gobbler was a prize, but the meat would be tougher than leather. He slowly poked his shotgun out of a hole in the brush that surrounded him and took aim. A loud *kaboom* invaded the morning silence, then immediately another, sounding like an echo. Turkeys fled for their lives, but two hens remained, their carcasses flopping and flapping, their wings like windmills gone crazy.

Smiling, Abe stood and moved forward. The two hens looked like they weighed around six or seven pounds each, all plump eating. *I reckon Lita will be glad to see this*, Abe thought proudly, the pungent smell of gunpowder filling his nostrils. The hard part was done, and it was the day before Thanksgiving. *It's good to be alive*, Abe thought happily.

~

Jennifer was wrought with dismay and especially disturbed by her financial status. Very little money remained at all, and the paper had been almost a total failure. *Where do I turn?* she thought in the privacy of her small and informal bedroom. What made it worse, it was Thanksgiving Day, but she felt like there was little to be thankful for. Stone-faced, she brushed vigorously at her long hair, as if she held a grudge against reality. Lance Rivers came to mind. In his generosity he'd formed a pact with Grant, leaving her son a fine horse and saddle to take care of until he returned. "Let's see how well you can take care of this horse while I'm gone," he'd said to Grant. "His name is Midnight, one of the finest black stallions I own. There may be something in it for you."

Dazzled with excitement, Grant had taken the responsibility to heart. Without realizing it, he'd slowly become detached from Jennifer, his constant thoughts now centered on the impressive Mr. Rivers. He'd found a role model and did everything he could to imitate the tall, handsome, smiling man.

Feeling helpless, Jennifer realized it was getting harder and harder to reach Grant. *I'm not so sure this is a good thing*, she thought, *but who am I to say anything to Grant? I'm not any better. Lance has me under his spell too!* With that, she got up, now dressed, and left her room. In the small, dark hallway, she passed Jason's closed door. She stopped and stared at it, almost fearful to talk to him. *I wouldn't be afraid unless I thought I was doing something wrong. Maybe I am, but I can't help how I feel about Lance.* Then she rationalized, *I can't avoid Jason forever!* Her courage mustered up, she knocked gently on his door and eased it open. He sat up in the bed with a pile of papers in his lap, the sun giving good light through his window.

"I thought I'd check on you," Jennifer said meekly. "It's Thanksgiving, you know. Happy Thanksgiving."

"Yeah," Jason said, not looking at her for very long when she entered. His eyes fell back to his work. "Happy Thanksgiving to you."

There was a long and uneasy pause. "Well," Jennifer said, trying to sound cheerful. "Looks like you are well into your work. How's it coming?"

"It's coming," Jason said, and gave her sort of a half-smile. He was apprehensive around Jennifer. It hadn't taken him long, picking up the little clues, to realize that she had feelings for another man—a whole man. Not only was he embarrassed by his condition, but now he felt jilted as well. He said no more.

"Abe killed some turkeys," Jennifer said, sensing Jason's resentment. "I'll see to it that you get a nice, hot plate."

Jason nodded without looking up and uttered a barely audible, "Thanks."

Putting on a pleasant smile, Jennifer turned and left, pulling the door closed behind her. Suddenly, she had this feeling in her chest that felt like she was caving in, a miserable and sickening feeling that she was being deceptive. Her fickle romantic ways ladened her with guilt. Each day was growing increasingly more difficult in more ways than one. She held a steady eye on Jason's doorknob, wishing she could just go in and have a heart-to-heart talk with him, but she couldn't. Something else pulled at her.

~

Downstairs, Lita joyfully toiled with a Thanksgiving Day meal, while Abe sat calmly at the table drinking a cup of coffee. It was a special time of year and called for a special touch, as a certain elegance settled over the relaxed scene. Although she didn't have a whole lot to work with, the turkeys were center attraction as they sizzled inside the big cast-iron oven side-by-side. She happily basted them with a special sweet sauce of grease and brown sugar. "Dem sure is some nice birds," she said, delighted with Abe's efforts.

Abe grunted to let her know that he'd heard her. It warmed him to watch Lita happily working in the kitchen, his eyes following her every move. It was a special privilege to be able to sit and watch her work. Usually she didn't like him being in the kitchen while she was cooking.

"You did good to shoot the heads off, 'cause I don't like picking shot out of meat."

Abe grunted again. He didn't really need to say anything.

A big bowl of spoon bread sat ready to go on the stove, and a row of washed sweet potatoes waited, their gnarly shapes looking like twisted tree roots. Lita was going to make a pie out of them.

Turning, Lita surprised Abe with a plate of fatback fried hard—something for him to nibble on. That was good, because all the cooking was making him hungry. "Today," Lita said formally, "I want you to go up and get Mr. Jason and bring him down so he can sit at the table with us when we eat. If he can sit up on the edge of his bed, he can sit at the table."

A frown came over Abe's face. "But suppose he don't want to come."

"Then you pick him up and haul him down like a sack of potatoes," Lita said impatiently.

Rolling his eyes, Abe didn't like the idea of going against Jason's will. But he'd try, because Lita said to. She could see that he was bothered by thoughts of Jason's resistance to such a notion. "You can tell him," she said stubbornly, "if he don't let you tote him down, I'm comin' up with a switch."

Abe then smiled, hiding a deep laughter. The thought of Lita barreling up the narrow steps with a switch in her hand seemed funny.

The door opened and Jennifer came in. Any hint of a smile that might have adorned Lita's and Abe's faces disappeared. There was an aura about Jennifer that hadn't been there before, something shrouded in darkness. "Good morning," Jennifer said stiffly. "Smells mighty good in here, Lita."

"Yes, ma'am," Lita said, too busy for conversation.

Jennifer sensed that she'd walked into a happy atmosphere, only to watch it disappear due to her entrance. This didn't help her disposition any. Finding a cup, she poured coffee and went to the front office. She had been surprised to find her stress so disturbing to others.

When early afternoon rolled around, Abe was sent upstairs to do his chore of fetching Jason. "Yes, sir, that's what she said. Said she was gonna come up here with a switch if you didn't let me tote you down to the table." Abe was a bit put out and a little embarrassed, but he had no choice.

Shaking his head, Jason laughed. The delicious smell of Lita's cooking had been driving him crazy for hours. He certainly wouldn't want to disappoint her. "Well, I guess you'd better get to it then," Jason said, scooting over to the side of the bed. He could sit easily, even wiggle his legs a little. Grabbing a shirt from the corner post, he slipped it on and buttoned it up. "You'll have to help me with my pants," he said to Abe.

In a few minutes, Abe entered the kitchen carrying Jason in his arms like a small child. "Where do you want me to put him?" he asked Lita.

Lita pointed with her spoon to a chair. "Set him down right there, then go holler out back for dem children. I'll get Miss Jenny and we'll be ready to eat."

Lita went into the front office to inform Jennifer that the meal was ready, and Abe stepped onto the back porch to yell for the children, who were brushing the fine horse that Rivers had left for Grant to care for. "You children come on now. Wash up 'cause Miss Lita's got turkey ready."

Scampering inside, Grant and Abby hurried through the motion of washing up without getting very wet, then scrambled for their seats at the table. They were equally surprised to see Jason sitting at the table.

"How'd you get down here?" Abby spouted.

"Abe carried me," Jason said matter-of-factly.

The children laughed hysterically, eager to get to the part of eating turkey. Meat had been a scarcity as of late.

When Jennifer entered, the smiles once again vanished. Everyone knew of the strained relationship between Jennifer and

Jason, a subject no one dared to approach. The meal was a grand success as everyone gorged with a hungry appetite; yet what little conversation there was seemed stilted.

"Good turkey, Lita," Jason complimented.

"Yeah, good turkey," Abby echoed.

"Thank you, Lita—this is a wonderful dinner," Jennifer said, trying to be friendly.

"Best thank the Lord," Lita suggested. "Dat's what this is all about." Then she held her tongue a minute and said, "I guess you can thank Abe, too—he killed the birds."

This broke the ice a little, but after dinner Abe carried Jason back up to his room, and the children went back out to croon over the horse. Abe helped Lita clean up in the kitchen, where Jennifer just felt in the way. "I'll be in the front office," Jennifer said as she left the kitchen. Lita and Abe glanced at each other, speaking with their eyes. The Jennifer they knew had changed; something was different—their attitudes suggested a stifled concern.

Sitting at her desk, Jennifer wished she had something to work on, something pertaining to the newspaper business. The *Advertiser*, like a burst of wind from a threatening storm, at first had gotten off to a promising start but withered into nothing after Jason's accident. Staring blankly into the distance, she realized there was little she could do.

~

The weeks before Christmas had turned the entire town white with a heavy snow that refused to melt or go away. Touched by cabin fever, Jennifer felt more trapped than ever since getting about remained difficult—the streets were a mess with ice and snow and frozen mud. A bitter cold and piercing mountain wind prevented all but the toughest from venturing outside. The newspaper had all but died, the last edition still sitting in a press that refused to print a single copy. The news story was a scanty effort at sensationalism about a bank robbery in Denver where there had been a lengthy shootout and men killed, but others escaped with the money. It really wasn't much of a story, mostly two-day old, secondhand details. *What's the point?* she figured, not caring if the press worked or not.

Jennifer had prayed, again and again, her heart weary with a heavy depression, but nothing changed—it only seemed to grow worse. It had finally come to the point where she could see the end. Without rent payments, they'd soon be evicted and in the hostile environment of the winter streets of a mining town. *If only Lance would return*, she thought miserably. *He's the only hope for us. For whatever it's worth, I can't pretend or play hard to get—I'll have to accept his help*. Without much to do, she grew even more despondent, and the depression made her sad and tired. Sleep became her best friend.

By Christmas Eve, Jennifer idly sat in her chair in the drafty front office waiting for certain despair in the form of the landlord to hand her the final notice. She'd all but given up on Lance Rivers. He had not shown up, and there'd been no word from him. December had been cruel and cold and dark. The days were short, as the sun barely cleared the mountains to the south, then made a quick exit, returning the day to darkness. It seemed this looming darkness closed in around her. The finality of it all was more than she could face. There were no presents for the children and no Christmas spirit to lift her. *It's come right down to the critical end*, she thought dejectedly. *Seems like the more I pray, the worse things get*. Whatever she had held sacred seemed to be fading away. The basics of survival were becoming more and more apparent, things like food and shelter.

Jennifer fell to her knees beside her chair and clasped her hands in front of her face. She wanted to pray, but she was cloaked in darkness, pulled away from her Christian roots. The increasing doubt had become a futility of gloom. *What's the use?* she thought hopelessly. *Why is it that everything I love I lose? Lance hasn't sent any word—probably got scared and flew the coop. Now there's no hope left!*

PART THREE

ROCKY MOUNTAIN FAITH

CHAPTER

~ 13 ~

A Christmas Miracle

Christmas morning came clean and crisp in a rush of wind through the loose old bedroom window. The sun was already up and filled Jennifer's room with a bright and even light. For the moment, she lay still in her bed, the sleepiness from the night before slow to leave. At first, all seemed well, until her thoughts grew clear and reminded her of her desperate situation. *This is going to be a hard day*, she thought miserably. *We're so poor we barely have anything to eat, much less any gifts. I hope the children aren't too upset.* The wind rattled the window again, as if it were hurrying her. Rising from bed, she noticed the faint aroma of something sweet, something like the smell from a bakery.

Quickly, Jennifer got up to get ready. In looking through her dresses, she decided, *Well, it's Christmas Day—at least I can try and look nice*. She selected a heavy cotton blue dress and a white blouse with ruffles. It was one of her nicest dresses and although a bit worn, she knew it was becoming. She carefully made up her face, and the simple effort of trying to look good improved her spirits. *I won't dwell on our misfortunes today*, she thought, *not on Christmas Day!*

Making her way down the thin staircase, Jennifer entered the kitchen. The warm aroma of muffins filled the air, while Lita bustled about, busy fixing a special breakfast. Abe sat at the wooden table, content, listening to Abby tell of her experience in horseback riding with Grant around town. Grant sat next to her, his mouth stuffed with blueberry muffins.

"Merry Christmas," Jennifer said as she sat down at the table. "Something smells mighty good."

Lita turned. "Don't you look nice today, Miss Jenny."

"Thank you, Lita," Jennifer said as she watched Abby excitedly tell Abe what she knew about horseback riding. Abe glanced up at Jennifer and smiled, then returned his attention to Abby.

Setting a tin pan of buttery, steaming-hot muffins on the table in front of Jennifer, Lita showed her white teeth in a big grin. "Abe bought these blueberries special. You try some, Miss Jenny."

Indeed, the muffins were delightful. "These are wonderful," Jennifer said, spilling crumbs in front of her as she took a delicate muffin and bit into it.

In the corner stood a Christmas tree with a few homemade ornaments hanging from it. "That's nice," Jennifer said, noticing the tree. "Where'd that come from?"

"Abe got up early and went out and cut it," Lita answered. "Said he had to ride quite a ways to find a tree."

Abe smiled, pleased that Lita was pleased. As far as he was concerned, this was a good Christmas. Things couldn't be better. He had developed an inner peace he'd never known before, and this was most comforting. "It wasn't no trouble," he said, his eyes grinning.

"I showed the children how to cut some decorations out of paper," Lita bragged.

Abby added, "Yeah, Mother. I made that angel. You see it? The one with the big wings?"

"That's very nice," Jennifer complimented. Deep down she wished she had some gifts for the children.

Unexpectedly, Abe stood and walked out the back door, then immediately returned carrying a weathered box. "Look here what I found," he drawled in his heavy voice as he set the box on the table. "Might be somethin' for y'all."

Removing a plain box, he gave it to Lita. Bashfully, she accepted it and carefully opened it, a framed picture with glass—a picture of Jesus Christ. "Oh, this is wonderful!" she said and rushed over to

Abe. He bent over a little so she could hug his neck. "I'll put it on the wall right over my bed. I know He is looking over me."

"What's this?" Abe said as he removed another package from the worn box. "I believe this is for Miss Abby."

Taking the box, Abby opened it in a panic. A colorful, hand-sewn rag doll fell out. It had long hair made of red yarn and a pie-shaped smiling face with bright button eyes. "I love it!" she exclaimed, hugging the doll tightly.

"Miss Lita made that," Abe said. "She done right good."

"I love it, Lita!" Abby said as she scrambled over to Lita and hugged her tightly.

"Wait a minute," Abe said, while he dug in the box. "Here's something else." He pulled out a box and handed it to Grant, who took the box slowly and inspected it. He seemed to be savoring the moment as he slowly unwrapped it from the brown paper. First there was a jingling sound, then out fell a pair of iron riding spurs. "It takes a good horseman to use dem right," Abe cautioned. "I used one of your boots to make the size right."

Grant's face lit up into a joyous delight. "Wow! Real riding spurs. This is great!" He bent over and buckled them around his boots. "They fit perfect!" he said as he walked about, the spurs jingling with every step. "This is great, Abe! Wow! Thanks!"

"This is for you, Miss Jenny," Abe said, handing Jennifer a paper package. "When Jennifer opened it, she felt the soft warmth of a hand-knitted shawl, a design of bright blue and brilliant white. Draping it over her shoulders, she noticed it matched her dress. "This is lovely." She blinked away a tear.

Lita came over and straightened the shawl, seeking perfection, then stood back to admire it. "You and the shawl make a fine pair."

Admiring the tasteful artwork, Jennifer was touched deeply, almost speechless. "It's beautiful, Lita."

Lita turned to Abe and said, "Go on, get the last present out." Removing it carefully, Abe inspected the package. "Open it," Lita ordered.

A slight smile on his lips, Abe opened the box. The surprise was evident on his expressive face, which was now covered with a big grin. "Bless me," he said joyfully, removing the fine derby hat and placing it on his head. "It fits just right, too!" He smiled even bigger, shifting the hat just so. "Miss Lita, this is mighty fine."

The spirit of giving warmed the group from the inside out, although Jennifer wished she could have been as resourceful and given gifts as well. A touch of sadness in Jennifer was apparent and caught Lita's attention. "Don't you worry none, Miss Jenny. You done more than enough for all of us already. Don't you be getting upset now—everything gonna be all right."

"Yeah, Mother," Grant reassured her. "This is a good Christmas." But he had other things on his mind. "Can I take Abby riding now? We won't go far."

"Yeah," Abby agreed. "We'll ride right around here." The sleek beauty, Midnight, for the time being, was the most important thing to the children.

"Go ahead," Jennifer said, "But be careful."

The children stormed out as Jennifer sat down at the table. "I want you to know," she said, talking to Abe and Lita, "that you're the most wonderful people I've ever known. I don't know how we're going to fare through these times, but God willing, we'll make it. I don't know what I'd do without you."

"Oh, shucks," Abe said, slightly raising his big hand. "We get by, Miss Jenny."

"Don't worry your pretty head none. The Lord gonna take care of us," Lita added.

"I'm sorry," Jennifer admitted. "I guess I've let this get the best of me." She raised her coffee mug and drank a sip. "This has been a very nice Christmas morning."

"Jason's present will be here directly," Lita said.

"Oh? And what is that?" Jennifer asked.

"You'll see, Miss Jenny," Lita answered, holding back a smile.

~

A little later that morning a tall shadow stepped up on the front porch. Jennifer watched through the front window as the dark figure came to the office door. The door opened and in stepped the preacher. He glanced around slowly until he spotted her sitting at her desk, then he walked over, removing his hat and holding it in his long and thin hand. He had the kind of silence that was as effective as speech, and his piercing eyes seemed to be searching her; there was no smile on his lips. "I've come," he said, his voice clear as a bell.

An expression of questioning tightened Jennifer's face. "Yes?" she said, not understanding.

"I've brought something for Jason Stone—a gift if you will."

"Oh," Jennifer said, collecting herself. She had been preparing herself to go up and see Jason, a tough assignment, for the friction between them remained. "I'll take you upstairs," she said, standing.

Up in his room, Jason had enjoyed Lita's blueberry muffins and then, with Lita's help, had washed up. Lying in his bed with his beard and long hair combed, he read over the first chapters of his book and seemed rather pleased. He'd achieved the emotion he wanted in his writing, a work he had found challenging. He glanced away from the manuscript, staring out the window. *Christmas Day*, he thought. *Nothing special!* He wondered if Jennifer would pay him a visit—certainly she would. He wanted to see her but didn't like her seeing him. *A paradox*, he thought apathetically.

The door creaked open and Jennifer stuck her head in. "Jason? May I come in?"

Placing his papers on the small bedside table, Jason pushed his lengthy hair away from his face, exposing his bright, blue eyes. "Sure," he said, a noncommittal tone in his voice.

"I've brought someone—says he has something for you," she said as she came on in. The preacher followed her, still carrying his hat. He stepped in and came over to Jason's bed, a wholesome smile spread across his rugged face. He casually set his black hat on the bentwood chair and removed a Bible from inside his long, black coat.

Watching closely, a blank expression came over Jason's face—this man scared him a little.

"Don't fear," Preacher announced softly. "I've come to pray for you again."

Dumbfounded, Jason found words difficult to come by in

response. He felt slightly nervous as a cool sweat broke over his forehead.

The preacher held his hand over Jason and extended the Bible out in the other hand. He closed his eyes in prayer. "Oh, Lord!" he boomed. "I have come to serve Your will. I pray this man will get up and walk. It's Your mercy and Your grace we seek today—let it be so. In the name of Jesus we pray. Amen." He slowly looked up, a smile on his worn face as he pushed the Bible back inside his heavy coat. "I have faith that God will make you walk again," he said confidently.

Nervously, Jason glanced at Jennifer, who seemed just as surprised as he was. He then wiggled his toes, and of course he could still bend his knees. But walking was an entirely different matter—it was out of the question. His voice slightly shaky, he said, "But I can't walk."

"Faith!" Preacher said. "Where's your faith?"

Jason looked lost. He hadn't expected something so dramatic. Unable to answer, he shrugged his shoulders.

With complete understanding, the preacher held his confident smile. "I've done my job," he announced as he glanced at Jennifer. Then he turned back to Jason. "May this be a day you'll always remember." Picking up his hat, he looked at Jennifer like he could see through her, then he smiled. "Merry Christmas. I'll show myself out," he said, making it difficult for her to leave with him.

After he had left, Jennifer just stood there, looking at Jason idly. She moistened her lips with her tongue. "He just came in," she said apologetically. "He said he had a gift for you and wanted to see you. I didn't know . . ."

"He's a fake!" Jason interrupted, now embarrassed and disgusted. "I can no more walk than a worm." He turned away, humiliated.

Sympathy swept over Jennifer. She was sorry she had brought the man up to see Jason, and now she felt sorry for him, his hopes dashed. There was so much she wanted to say, but the awkward situation made it impossible. "I wish there was something I could do," she said meekly.

"It's not your fault," Jason snapped, now growing irritated. "If

God wanted me to walk, I guess I'd walk. I don't understand why that man had to come here."

With no explanation, Jennifer stood there silently clutching her hands in front of her. A wind whistled at the window, but the room held a warmth that arose from the heat downstairs. Pushing away her mixed emotions, she forced a smile. "Jason, I don't want to see you suffer. Just for today—" She blinked and looked out the window, gathering her emotions. "Just for today, let's make the most of it—it's Christmas."

Jason wasn't comforted by Jennifer's efforts. He picked up the manuscript he'd been working on and studied it. "Just another day," he said bleakly.

Hopelessly disappointed, Jennifer now wrung her hands, her face saddened. Without a word she left the room, leaving Jason to his stubborn discontent.

~

The cold wind increased, rattling the windows and doors as the afternoon passed slowly. Jennifer continued to busy herself at her desk, her mind racing with anticipation—so many thoughts. The children had blown in for lunch and then back out for more riding, completely unruffled by the chilly wind. At one point, Lita had come into the front office to check on Jennifer. Lita seemed gay enough. "I got pies in the oven," she announced gladly. "They'll be ready before long." She turned and headed back to the kitchen.

"Lita," Jennifer said, her voice short. She placed her elbows on the desk and folded her hands in front of her face. "You said something earlier about Jason's gift coming. What were you talking about?"

Turning back to Jennifer, Lita seemed surprised. "Why, I seen him come, Miss Jenny."

"Are you talking about Preacher?"

"Yes, ma'am."

"What kind of gift is that?" Jennifer questioned.

"Didn't he bring a gift from the Lord?" Lita asked.

"He prayed that Jason would walk," Jennifer said solemnly.

Lita smiled knowingly, like she knew some secret, then left.

Am I missing something? Jennifer wondered. *It's like I'm being held in the dark.* She quietly picked up her pencil and again ran over the depressing figures of the newspaper's financial status. It was obvious that her efforts and the newspaper were a miserable failure. There were few options. *A bank isn't about to give us a loan*, she realized. Then her thoughts shifted to her only hope, Lance Rivers. *He hasn't even bothered to send word, and he promised he'd be here*, she thought dejectedly. And time was running out—they'd be evicted within a week. Her faith dwindling, she sat at her desk, practically defeated, dreading the long day.

~

By the time evening came, Lita had joyfully prepared some Christmas specialties: smoked ham, sweet potato pie, and sugar cookies. The ham had been a gift from Mr. Blake, Abe's employer. Darkness came early on the short winter day in a valley surrounded by peaks. The children came in out of the cold, their faces chapped bright red, wearing smiles of anticipation from the aroma of delicacies awaiting them.

Lita called to the front office, where Jennifer had muddled away the afternoon. "Miss Jenny, come on into the kitchen. I got some treats."

Slowly, Jennifer rose from her desk, her mood dark gray. She made her way back to the kitchen wearing a long face. A day full of worry had exhausted her, and she felt like she couldn't deal with any more pretending to be merry because it was Christmas.

Abe sat at the table watching the children relish the sugar cookies like a couple of field mice in a corn bin. He watched Jennifer enter, her shoulders stooped, her worries obvious. Lita caught wind of Jennifer's torment and turned her attention to her. "Why, Miss Jenny, you look fit to be tied. Sit down here and cheer up—all ain't so bad. We got good food, and we all are healthy."

"I'm sorry," Jennifer apologized as she rubbed her forehead. A dull headache distracted her. "We may have to move soon. I'm not sure where we'll go."

"We'll worry about that when the time comes," Lita assured her.

"Dat's right," Abe agreed, hoping to encourage Jennifer. "One thing at a time, dat's all a person can do."

Somehow, this lifted Jennifer. The idea of one thing at a time seemed justified. She had been worrying about everything at once, which only caused a jumbled confusion in her mind. "You're right," she said. "I'm making myself sick over this."

"Here, honey," Lita said, serving Jennifer a slice of pink smoked ham. "You eat that."

Taking a bite, Jennifer didn't realize how hungry she was. The long afternoon in the drab office had taken a lot out of her. It made her feel like crying, but she held her own, thankful for Lita and Abe and their company.

A clumsy bumping sound came from the stairs, and the group in the kitchen turned, astounded to see Jason standing at the kitchen door at the foot of the stairs. He was leaning on the small bentwood chair. He scooted the chair in front of him and took a step, then scratched the chair along the floor and took another step. His face had the look of a child stunned with fear, a wonder remarkable in itself. His arms shook, as did his legs, but he was standing. He had walked out of his room and down the stairs. He was walking!

"Praise the Lord Almighty God!" Lita shouted as she ran over to Jason and took him in her arms. "The Lord has answered our prayers!"

"Praise the Lord!" Abe echoed, immediately taking this sight as evidence of a miracle from God.

Jennifer couldn't have been more surprised or shocked if she'd seen an angel. Her mouth fell open in disbelief. Lita helped Jason over to the table and into a chair. The childlike daze held his face, his eyes sparkling with astonishment. "I walked," he said shakily.

Rushing over to Jason, Jennifer leaned over and hugged him. "It's a miracle, Jason. The preacher brought you a miracle from God." Her eyes glanced upward. "I'm ashamed I ever doubted."

"Let's pray thanks to the Lord Almighty!" Lita said excitedly.

For the first time in a long time, Jason felt true joy. Although the pain in his back and legs was throbbing, it was nothing compared to his elation. He swallowed hard, his teeth showing white through a smile in his beard. "It's a miracle," he uttered, glancing around the room at the surprised faces watching him.

Grant and Abby watched silently, their young faces held in disbelief. "How could you just get up and walk?" Abby inquired.

"I don't know," Jason answered, his voice quivering. "I just did."

"The preacher prayed over him for a miracle, children," Lita informed them. "And now you see how God answers prayers."

Abby wasn't convinced, because none of her prayers to bring her father back were ever answered. But Grant stared at Jason, lost in thought. He felt sure there was an all-powerful God who looked over them, but he'd never seen a real miracle. It would take some thinking for him to figure this one out.

Abe was truly happy for Jason but had mixed feelings. He was sure that God would do what He wanted to do when He wanted to do it, and if that be a miracle, so be it. But somewhere deep within him, he felt a tingle of joy, for the miracle confirmed his belief that there was an active and loving, personal God. "Sure good to have you back, Mr. Jason," he said happily, partially standing, not sure what was the right thing to do.

Waving for Abe to sit down, Jason said, "It's good to be back, Abe. People don't realize what it's like not to be able to walk until they can't. I guess that old preacher really knows something—sure got my attention."

"Just doin' his job," Lita spouted, "and now the Lord done His!"

~

The next few days Jason hobbled around constantly on a set of crutches the doctor had obtained for him, afraid that if he didn't, he might become bedridden again. "I'm going for a hobble," he said, trying to be amusing in spite of the pain.

Noticing the agony that creased the corners of his eyes, Jennifer said, "Are you sure? Do you want some help?" She came across the office, closer to Jason. "I'll be glad to go with you. Let me get my coat."

"I'm all right!" Jason claimed, determined to go on his own. "I need to do this myself. It's been a long time since I've been outside."

Pausing, Jennifer studied Jason. He looked something like an old hermit, with long beard and hair, and hunched over a pair of crutches. But she was glad to see his determination, something that reminded her of the Jason she once knew. "Do be careful!" she insisted.

"Yes, Mother," Jason taunted as he worked his way out the front door. "I'll see if I can find some news."

Watching Jason move slowly past the front window, Jennifer felt an inspiration reminiscent of strength, something she'd been lacking. She began to think a little more positively. *Maybe I can encourage the landlord to give us a little more time—surely it won't hurt to try. Now that Jason is up and about, maybe we've got a chance."*

Not long after Jason had left, a horse and buggy jerked to a stop in front of the office. Jennifer glanced through the window and saw Lance Rivers unloading several boxes. Soon he came to the door and fumbled with the latch because his arms were full. But Jennifer was there and let him in, a fury blazing in her eyes. "Where have you been? You promised me you'd be back before Christmas!"

Smiling, Lance ignored her anger as he came in and set the pile of boxes on the floor. "I got tied up. You know how horse trading can be," he offered as a lame excuse. "But I did remember to get Christmas presents," he said, gesturing at the many boxes.

Unamused, Jennifer resented Lance's irresponsibility. It reminded her of her late husband, Drake, who would come to a home of poverty bearing lavish gifts. Backing away, she glared at him, color filling her face. "If you think you can just come in here with a bunch of presents and buy your way out of trouble, you're sadly mistaken!" she blurted. "Here we are, about to be evicted, and we have no money—what are we going to do with gifts? Anyway, you lied to me!" She turned away, now hurt by his misplaced affections.

Holding his palms out, Lance tried to reason. "I'm truly sorry, Jennifer. I really am. Sometimes I can't control everything. The last thing in the world I want to do is hurt you."

Turning back, Jennifer let her gaze settle on Lance. She noticed he looked a little different, a little pale, like he hadn't slept in days. His usual, overbearing boldness was subdued; he was pleading. In this, she saw him in a different perspective for the first time. "If you really cared for me, like you say you do, I don't think you'd leave me just hanging like you did."

"That wasn't my intention!" he replied, slightly out of control. "What do I have to do to convince you? I said I was sorry."

Catching her off guard, she saw a glimpse of rage in Lance, and this unsettled her. She was beginning to wonder what had happened to the Lance she saw last. "What do you expect of me?" she argued. "You come in here days after Christmas with gifts, like it was nothing. You act like everything is so simple and easy—whatever you say goes. I'm afraid you're only going to cause grief with your presents. Nobody will understand."

"I've got plenty of money!" Lance boasted. "I'll help you with your debts!"

"That's not how it works," Jennifer said uneasily. "There must be some kind of mutual trust. Something has to be established. I need help, but I don't want just your money. Can't you see this?"

Rivers shook his head. He was too tired to reason. What he considered a very minor thing had turned into a crisis. More than anything, he felt unwelcome; his exhaustion made it too hard to think. "I'm sorry," he mumbled as he walked back to the front door. "I need to get some rest. Tell Grant I'll be back by and take him out—show him how to use his present." He opened the door and left before she could respond, leaving her feeling a little guilty but justified.

Just as Jennifer watched Rivers whip the horse into motion, Jason came in. "Who was that?" he asked.

"Oh, him?" Jennifer answered, somewhat put out. "That was Lance Rivers."

Jason's expression showed a cloud of remorse. "So, that was him," he commented bitterly. "What's all this on the floor?"

"Christmas gifts," Jennifer answered. "Lance brought them."

"A little late, isn't he?" Jason said accusingly.

"Yes, yes, I suppose he is," Jennifer sighed, staring out the window, unable to give Rivers any support for his irresponsibility.

CHAPTER

14

Twisted Disharmony

A velvety Chinook wind blew 1876 into Black Hawk and Central City. Miners and glory seekers reveled around the clock, packing the streets, noisily celebrating the New Year. The warmer temperatures brought out the poor souls who had been shut up inside cold cabins and dark mineshafts. Drunken miners yelled and sang and filled the streets in an atmosphere of dancing and joy. For the present, the oppression of a bitter winter had temporarily subsided.

The presents Lance Rivers had left went over well with everyone except Jennifer. Grant was the most excited, finding a new .22 rifle in a long, heavy package. Abby was overcome with excitement as well with a new pink dress, nothing like she'd ever owned. "Look, Mother—it fits!" she bragged as she modeled the dress. Lita discovered a wool coat, and she hadn't even owned a coat before. "That Mr. Rivers!" she had exclaimed. "How'd he know?" And Abe had received a pair of warm winter gloves, something new to him. "I'll be!" he'd said. "Ain't that somethin'?" But Jennifer remained disappointed with Lance, even though her gift was expensive. She had opened a black box to reveal a pearl necklace. "I can't accept this!" she said with despair. "I'll have to return it." Besides Jason, nobody else held any animosity for Lance Rivers, leaving Jennifer feeling outvoted. "We like our gifts!" Abby had protested, speaking for the others. "Just 'cause you don't doesn't mean we have to act like you!"

Jennifer didn't like the turmoil—she decided she'd have to get matters straight with Rivers the next time she saw him.

When Lance came in the office the next morning, he looked rested, yet he was careful when he approached. "I'm sorry about yesterday, Jennifer. I wasn't myself. I thought about you constantly on Christmas, and more than anything I wish I could have been with you."

It was hard for Jennifer to argue. Lance was trying hard to redeem himself. "We have to get a few things sorted out," she said, trying to restrain any emotion from her voice. She reached into her desk and removed the little black case and set it before her. "I can't accept this gift. It wouldn't be right. Not now. If it was mine, I'd be forced to sell it tomorrow."

A desperate concern showed on Lance's face. "I hope you can forgive a fool," he pleaded as he pulled up a chair and sat next to her. "I sometimes tend to overlook the obvious, but this time I've come prepared." He removed his billfold from his vest pocket and opened it. It was stuffed with money. "Here's what I'm prepared to do. I want to make you a loan to get this paper going, not just a little loan, but enough for you to make it work. I don't want you to consider this charity, or my way of buying you, as you put it. I just consider it to be a sound investment."

Turning away, Jennifer didn't know what to say. This was exactly what she'd planned on asking Rivers to do, but that was days before. She swung her glance back to him. "Lance, we have to get some things straight first. I don't want to be indebted to you because of our relationship. Perhaps we can put this in a business trust, strictly to be run through the newspaper. But most of all, I want to be able to trust you, to believe what you tell me, and I think you've jeopardized that."

Rivers nodded. "It's true; I made a mistake. I hate to admit it, but I've never been in love before. You'll have to forgive me. It's not something I'm used to."

Caught by Lance's admission, Jennifer felt a slight relief. She had been consumed by her thoughts, which kept telling her that she was making the same mistakes with the same kind of men over and over. Being overly cautious, she sometimes couldn't find the defining boundaries that kept things in their specific place. Other times, her strong womanly desires made it impossible to determine if there were any boundaries at all. This was one of those precise moments that confused her the most, but she had little choice if she wanted to continue to try and make a successful newspaper out of the *Advertiser*. "There's something delicate in a relationship," she began, trying to explain herself, "but I think it all hinges on being honest with each other, and in order to do that, we have to be truthful. It hurt me deeply when you told me you'd be back before Christmas, and then I didn't even hear from you. But when you showed up late and acted like it wasn't important, well, that's the kind of grief I don't want. Maybe I'm old-fashioned, but that's the only kind of belief I can put faith in."

Reaching for her hand, Rivers took it into his gently. "You've got my word," he promised. "I never realized how serious being in love can be. I can't lose you."

Finally, Jennifer smiled slightly. His understanding meant everything to her.

At a very inopportune moment, Jason entered the office. He quickly saw what was going on. "Am I interrupting something?" he asked, knowing good and well that he was.

Quickly, Jennifer stood and so did Lance. "Jason," Jennifer said, surprised. She took a step toward him, but then stopped, feeling vaguely disrupted. "This is Lance Rivers. Lance, this is Jason Stone, my editor."

Walking over to Jason, Rivers extended his hand. "Good to meet you," he said, curious about Jason's shabby appearance.

"Yeah," Jason said, motioning that he couldn't shake hands because he was holding himself up with his crutches.

Rivers put his hand on Jason's shoulder and said, "Congratulations. Glad to see that you are up and about. I've heard a lot about you."

Forcing a smile, Jason moved away and hobbled slowly toward the front door. His long blondish hair was combed back and curled at his shoulders; his beard hid most of his expression. The pain in his back and legs was stunning and wore him down quickly, but he managed to move along with great concentration. His crutches creaking under his weight as he moved, he said to Rivers, "Yeah, ain't I something!" Consumed by his own thoughts and physical agony, he opened the door and pegged his way through, heavily relying on his crutches.

Curious, Lance turned to Jennifer for an explanation. Seeing this and being mildly embarrassed, she lifted her open hand as if searching for the right words. She found the situation awkward because Jason was her close friend—and then some. "He's not himself. He's in a lot of pain right now. It's hard for him to get around."

Rivers seemed to understand, but before he could speak, Lita banged through the back door, bringing Jennifer a cup of coffee. She spotted Rivers. "Oh, Mr. Rivers! I didn't know you was here. Thank you so much for my new coat. It fits real fine. Let me bring you some fresh coffee." She immediately returned to the kitchen, the old floorboards groaning under her footsteps.

Shaking his head, Rivers turned to Jennifer. "Lita's something else, isn't she?"

"You don't know the half of it," Jennifer responded, a smile evident in her greenish eyes, the kind of eyes that seemed to change color with different lights and different moods. "You seemed to have made a big splash with everyone thanks to your Christmas gifts."

"What about yours?" Lance asked, suddenly serious.

"Oh?" Jennifer still didn't feel right about it. "It's such an expensive gift," she said. "It won't go with any of the old things I own—I'd feel out of place."

Rivers smiled. "Well you just hang on to it for now—it'll be in safe keeping. What about my offer, Jennifer? Here's the money—I want you to accept it for all the *right* reasons."

Taking the stack of bills from Rivers's hand, Jennifer held it for a moment. It gave her both relief and regret at the same time, but it was a gift she had to accept, either that or watch her loved ones be put on the street with nowhere to turn. "Lance," she sighed as she stuck the money in a drawer. "You don't know how much this will help, but still—"

"It's something I want to do," Rivers interrupted. "Don't ever for a minute feel cheapened. I want you to have this in good faith."

He plucked his fine gold watch from his pocket and glanced at it. "Say, where's Grant? I'd like to take him out and show him how to shoot his rifle."

Standing, Jennifer moved from behind her desk. "I'll go get him. He's been a mighty anxious little boy wanting to learn how to shoot."

The ploy had been simple for Rivers: get Grant to like him, and Jennifer would be more inclined to follow. But in the process, Grant's adult mannerisms and his keen observations had impressed Rivers. He was more than just a young boy; he was a responsible young man. Rivers grew especially fond of Grant's adulation and in return offered a mentor's friendship; something like father and son.

Lita returned with the coffee, pleased to serve Lance. He was sitting in a chair next to Jennifer's desk, doodling with a pencil. "This warm spell is nice, isn't it, Lita?"

Turning, Lita rolled her big eyes with affluent praise. "Thank the Lord! Sometimes I think my bottom gonna be froze to that outhouse seat, and somebody gonna have to come pry me off!"

Chuckling, Rivers watched Lita set his coffee before him. Observing her round face closely, he noticed very few lines, making it difficult to determine her age. Yet it was her lively and positive spirit that interested him the most. "I take it you're a God-fearing woman, Lita."

"Oh, yes, sir!" Lita replied, her face grave with admiration for the Lord. "Me and the Lord goes back a long ways." Preparing to leave, she presently stopped to address their guest. "Do you believe in the Lord, Mr. Rivers?"

Leaning back in the small chair, his elbow on the desk and his hand under his chin, Rivers replied smoothly. "Why, of course! I'm a God-fearing man, Lita."

Waiting, Lita was ready to hear more, but Rivers fell into silence. Quick to respond, her expression turned dour as she lectured, "That's a mighty good thing to know, Mr. Rivers. A man without God don't have much of a chance."

Fascinated, Rivers watched her broad back as she left the room. *Amazing faith*, he thought. *I almost envy her*.

Momentarily, Grant came busting into the room, followed by Jennifer. He carried his shiny new rifle, his eyes full of anticipation. "I'm ready!" he shouted, eager to be going. "Why didn't you tell me you were here?"

"Where are your manners?" Jennifer asked, scolding Grant. "Give Mr. Rivers time to drink his coffee."

Standing, Rivers just smiled, his face showing patience. "He's excited to learn how to shoot his new rifle, Jennifer. Don't be so hard on him."

Jennifer had a mother's concerned smile. Deep down she was happy for Grant, happy that he'd found a good friend in Lance Rivers. "Be careful," she advised.

"Don't worry," Rivers said as he followed Grant to the door. "He's in good hands."

As the two mounted their horses and left, Jason watched from the boardwalk down the street. He had a grueling jealousy of Lance Rivers. *That man! There's something about him—how can he be so perfect?* he thought miserably. *He may have Jennifer fooled, but he's no better than that oily lawyer, Charles Fitzgerald, who kept flitting around her in Virginia City. And he can't be any better than her late husband. Why does she seem to be attracted to the same kind of man again and again?*

~

Grant and Lance rode steadily up to a dump littered with piles of debris. The warmth of the sun and brilliant blue sky made for a lazy day. "This place stinks as bad as town," Grant complained.

"Yes, but we have plenty of cans to shoot," Rivers reminded him as he dismounted his fine stallion.

Imitating his new hero, Grant dismounted Midnight and tied him the same way, to the same scrub. He carefully removed his rifle from the leather scabbard and awaited further orders.

Scanning the scene with squinted eyes, Rivers came to a quick conclusion. "Grant, you see that old log? Line up as many bottles side by side as you can find."

Eagerly, Grant leaned his rifle against an old wooden crate and did as he was told. When he'd finished, he came back to stand by Rivers, awaiting his first lesson on how to shoot a rifle.

Rivers twisted his black mustache, thinking, then said, "Grant, a gun is like a woman—it's something you have to treat delicately and with great respect."

Nodding, Grant's eyes remained on Rivers, focused on his every word.

"Always treat a gun as if it were loaded and never point a gun at anything you don't intend on shooting." Bending over, the man picked up Grant's .22 rifle. "This is a single shot H&R .22, a fine gun that will give you many years of service if you take care of it. It breaks in two like a shotgun, like this," and he showed Grant, holding the rifle before him.

The distant banging of the quartz mills floated in on a gentle wind, the kind of wind that reminded Grant of spring. This was a time he knew he would remember, and he cherished every second.

"This front sight on the end of the barrel is called the bead," Rivers said, pointing. "And this rear sight is called a dovetail. You hold the rifle like this," he said, pulling it up to his shoulder. "Squint your left eye and sight down the barrel with your right. Some folks close their left eye, but I advise against it. If you keep it slightly open, it gives you better perspective. Then you place the bead on your target and put the bead right in the slot of the dovetail—all three lined up, the target and the bead sitting in the dovetail. Understand?"

"Yes, sir," Grant said. The truth was, he'd already sighted a hundred things down the barrel. He figured any fool knew that, but he hadn't known about keeping his left eye slightly open.

Handing him the gun, Rivers asked, "Do you know how to load it?"

"Sure," Grant answered as he shoved one of the tiny cartridges into the chamber and snapped the rifle shut.

"Never underestimate a .22," Rivers warned. "It'll kill you just as quickly and just as dead as a larger gun. See if you can hit one of those bottles."

Carefully, Grant placed the rifle up to his shoulder. Taking careful aim, he pulled the trigger. A spray of dust flew up in front of one of the bottles.

"Not bad," Rivers said. "But you pulled the trigger. Never pull the trigger. You gently squeeze the trigger, and the gun should surprise you when it fires. Now, hold a careful aim and try it again."

Reloading, Grant placed the rifle up to his shoulder, remembering everything. The smell of rifle oil and fresh gunpowder emanated from the gun. It was a smell like no other, the kind of smell that reminded him of men and power. He fired again, and this time the bottle spun sideways and off the log.

"Good shot," Rivers said. "You hit it in the side, which made it spin off the other way. The same is true if you hit right under it. That'll send it up into the air."

"Can you do that?" Grant asked.

Taking the rifle, Rivers plucked a tiny cartridge from the box and expertly inserted it into the chamber. He snapped the rifle shut, brought it up to his shoulder, and fired all in one quick motion. The bottle zinged up into the air.

"Wow!" Grant exclaimed. "That was a good shot. Can you do it every time?"

"Almost," Rivers said calmly. "Why don't you practice until you've shot all the bottles off the log."

Eagerly, Grant did as he was told, hitting more than he missed. Rivers watched patiently while Grant plinked the bottles, doing a fine job for a young man with his first gun.

When all the bottles were gone, Rivers said, "Set up some more." While Grant was tending the chore, Rivers continued to speak. "Someday I'll teach you how to shoot a pistol, but first things first. You've got to work your way up." He paused as he searched the snow-spotted mountainside, certain they were the only ones around. "In order to rely on your gun," Rivers continued, "you must practice. A gun is no good to a man that can't use it."

Returning to where Rivers stood, Grant glanced at the line of old bottles that sat on top of the log like a row of tin soldiers. Grant shot them down a few more times, each time setting up a fresh row afterward. It was a long and slow process. Setting up several more, Grant asked, "Why don't you practice?"

Stepping up to address a row of different sized and shaped bottles, Rivers pulled the bottom of his coat away from the pistol he wore on his side. Grant hadn't noticed it before, a short-barreled six-shooter snug in a fine leather holster. Without warning, Rivers drew the pistol and fired five shots rapidly, shattering five bottles into an explosion of sparkling shards. It had been so fast and loud that Grant flinched several times from the concussion of the barking pistol. Frightened from the suddenness of it all, his heart pounded in his chest. The shattered glass tinkled harmlessly to the ground; a heavy cloud of choking smoke engulfed both Grant and Lance. The pistol had quickly been reloaded and returned to its holster. The coat again hid it from view, as if nothing had ever happened.

Slowly, Grant's eyes looked up to meet Rivers's. The look on Grant's face was a look of fear and of respect. Never had he been so shocked in all of his life—what he'd witnessed seemed utterly impossible. He wanted to speak, but a lump in his throat prevented it. Besides, he didn't know what to say.

"That should do it for today," Rivers said, the friendly smile again on his face.

They got to their horses, and Grant snuggled his rifle in the scabbard. He mounted and reined his horse back as Rivers swung over to his side, guiding his mount carefully. "You should clean your gun as soon as you get home," Rivers ordered. "Always clean your gun after you shoot it."

"Yes, sir," Grant said humbly. He was riding back a different boy than he'd ridden out. Now he was more of a man. He could shoot a rifle, but once more, and now even more important, he was a special friend of Lance Rivers.

~

The warm spell was short-lived, and winter came back to nest in the Rocky Mountains around Black Hawk. Clouds bulging with snow lowered themselves into the valleys and painted them white while the sun took a few days off. January was about done, and February looked to hold no promise of relief from the cold.

With great effort Jason stuffed a fat log into the fire and poked at it with his cane to get it square, but the log fought him, trying to roll out of the stove. He swatted it again angrily and mumbled something under his breath.

Glancing up at the disturbance, Jennifer rose from her chair and quickly came over to help him. She grabbed a poker and shoved the log to the back of the fire. "There," she said. "No need to get upset."

But the truth was, Jason was upset—upset with everything. The constant pain in his back that shot down his leg had literally changed his personality. Although he'd graduated from his crutches to a cane, he remained cynical and bitter. His gimpy right leg was almost useless. But the pain was perpetual and relentless, and even though he could bear it at times, it never gave him a break, not a minute of relief, whether he was standing or lying. The tears still came to his eyes when he put his shoes on every morning, as every little move had to be calculated to avoid extra torment. His own hands seemed to work against him, constantly dropping things he'd never dropped before, causing him great agony to have to either bend over or squat down.

But worst of all, Jason had watched Jennifer be manipulated by a man gifted in every way, a generous man eager to share his wealth and his life with her. There had been little Jason could do, a cripple, barely useful. Compared to him, of course that Rivers looked so good. Jason's misery now compounded as he withdrew into his own little world where destiny seemed to be a cruelty all its own. He had begun to realize that his fate was one of failure.

As Jennifer returned to her desk to work, Jason watched her slyly out of the corner of his eye. Although they now worked together producing a limited newspaper, the distance between them had grown vast. There was a friction always present, a wall that separated them, a friendship that had disappeared.

Being acutely sensitive, Jennifer felt Jason's stare burning on her back. She noticed his cross and unintelligible mumbling, his distressed expressions, his short temper, and his quick and insensitive remarks. She was tired of it. Smacking her pencil sharply on her desk, she glanced up at Jason and caught him staring again. "I think it's time we had a talk!" she said abrasively. "I can't go on like this." She stared sharply into Jason's bright blue eyes. "Get over here and sit down!"

Unscathed by her forceful commands, Jason took his sweet time, as if to deliberately let her know that she held no rule over him. He came to the chair beside her desk and plopped down, holding his cane in his hand. "Yes! I think it's time we had a talk!"

Waiting, Jennifer could see that Jason wanted her to talk first. The thought of having a talk had seemed so natural, but now she paused, thinking of where to begin. "Your attitude," she said. "I get the distinct impression that you have something to say."

Making a face like he'd tasted bittersweet candy, it was obvious that he was mocking her. "No kidding! Jennifer? What happened to us? Suddenly, you're a stranger bowled over by some other man. I don't even know you anymore!"

At first, Jennifer found it difficult to reply. "Things change," she said lamely. She shrugged her shoulders as if she were made helpless by circumstances.

But Jason thought he knew what she meant, which was that he was no longer a man but an unattractive cripple unable to support her. He felt a sickening feeling rise and quickly stomped his cane on the floor and jerked himself up to his feet. Now he hobbled in front of her desk. It seemed like everything he wanted to say sounded like self-pity. Finally, he spoke directly to her as she held her eyes on him, watching him closely. "If there was something wrong with Lance Rivers, would you still be so attracted to him? What if he was a cripple—would it matter? Or what if he was poor, what then?"

Taken aback rather suddenly, Jennifer hadn't expected such a blunt question. It was a question she couldn't answer. "I don't judge people, Jason," she said, her features now softening. "I only listen to my heart. I can't seem to help it."

But her answer turned Jason. Instead of arguing, she had been honest, and now he felt sorry for her. *She can't help how she feels!* he thought dejectedly. *Who am I to stand here and judge her?* He was overcome with emotion, the same feeling he had always had for her—he loved her very much. "I'm sorry. This back pain has been most difficult, but losing you has been even harder. Don't you understand? I love you as much as a man can. Yet I have to stand by and watch while another man takes you away." He turned and hobbled a step and then turned back to her. "But I can't blame you," he said painfully. "It's not your fault." He paused, ready to make his statement. "Jennifer, I don't trust Lance Rivers. How could any man be so perfect? I'm afraid he's going to hurt you and your children."

Interpreting this as envy or jealousy, Jennifer tried to comfort him. "Regardless," she said softly, "I think we could be a little more civil with each other, make things somewhat easier on both of us if we're going to try and make this newspaper work. Your injury keeps improving, but your disposition seems to grow worse! I believe we could help each other in a lot of ways."

This wasn't exactly what Jason wanted to hear. "I don't know if I can stay around and watch, Jennifer! There's something terribly wrong with the whole thing."

Looking at Jason, Jennifer felt like she saw the shell of the man she once knew, a man distraught by tragedy, a man totally opposite of Lance. "One thing at a time," she uttered, not realizing she was quoting Abe. "That's all I can do."

Jason made a face as if he understood, and what he clearly understood was that he was being rejected for another man. There was nothing like rejection to deface a man's own judgment of himself. With nothing else to say, he left the office to take one of his strolls.

~

More and more often, Grant would groom Midnight, polish the saddle, and dress up in his best to imitate Lance Rivers, then go for a ride about town. The ride now mainly consisted of parading up and down the streets of Central City where he did his best flaunting, impressing any socialite who might cast an eye his way. He dressed like Lance Rivers in a long coat and similar hat, items he'd managed to convince Rivers he couldn't do without. Of course, Lance had been more than happy to oblige Grant, pleased that the young man wanted to be like him.

A reddish sun squinted through a high layer of golden clouds as Grant trotted his horse up a steep grade. On these afternoon jaunts, the long-legged horse strolled along friskily, while Grant sat on top like a proud king. He was living a dream and would distance himself from the family and poverty he had grown accustomed to back at the newspaper office. Frequently, he convinced himself he was somebody important, part of the local aristocracy, proud heir of the Rivers fortune, an important boy who'd someday be an important man. Naturally, the handsome walnut stock of his new rifle shone from its place under the saddle, a reminder that he was a boy who had power to be reckoned with.

Passing a group of miners' children playing stickball in an alley, Grant quickly turned away. He now sat in a higher place and didn't mix with the likes of them. The children dropped their sticks and rushed closer to see Grant perched high upon the fine horse. A tall and gangly boy wearing heavily patched overalls commented, "He shore got a crook in his nose—look how he holds it up in the air!" The other children laughed and returned to their game. Grant ignored them, simple children with their simple games.

Up ahead, Grant noticed two dance hall girls standing on the boardwalk, taking a break from their usual duties. One was a younger, small girl decked out with colorful feathers, her hair up and her red dress cut low. Her big brown eyes followed him as he came closer. Cutting across the busy street, he quickly spurred the high-spirited horse into a cocky trot, sure to make a lasting impression. In passing the girl, she giggled, and he turned in the saddle to look back at her, a sly smile turning the corners of his youthful lips.

Suddenly the horse stumbled and almost bolted; a woman screamed. Grant had carelessly bumped into a woman carrying a sack of groceries, causing her to spill her package. "You young fool!" she cried. "Watch where you're going!"

Before Grant could apologize, the woman's husband, a big miner with black grit etched in his coarse face, grabbed the reins and held the horse. His wide and powerful hand snatched Grant from the saddle and swiftly down to the ground, shaking him like a dog shakes a rag. "What's a matter with you, boy? You get down there and help pick up them goods!" he ordered, his temper flaring as he flung Grant to the ground.

Hands shaking, Grant scurried along the ground and helped the woman collect her items. "I'm . . . I'm sorry," he uttered weakly.

"What you think you are? Some kind of big shot?" the woman scolded. "You like to run me over!"

The spectacle caused a small group to gather as they laughed at Grant. In his arrogance, he had made a fool of himself, his face now bright red and hot. Once the items were picked up, Grant stood and faced the burly miner. "Here!" the man scoffed, shoving the reins at him. "Why don't you take this over-bred mule and get out of here. Do us all a favor and learn how to ride!"

With his knees shaking so badly he could hardly get his foot in the stirrup, Grant glanced back at the saloon girl, who laughed into her hand. Time approached a standstill, and the pressure of glaring eyes and laughing faces made him feel about as big as a pea. Finally back on his horse, he slithered on down the street, away from the depths of degrading humiliation.

CHAPTER

15

The Ides of March

The sloppy snows of spring fell and drooped over Black Hawk like a wet and heavy mattress. Then the sun brought a little warmth, and the snow melted and washed down the barren mountainside in a muddy sluice until it hit Gregory and Main Streets in a river of mud. In some places, the mud washed into stores and had to be quickly shoveled out and coaxed on down the street.

Eb Waller, a dry goods operator, had the clever idea of erecting a short but strong, board fence around his store to channel the mud on by. What he hadn't counted on was the mud filling the open sewer under the boardwalk and floating up the stench and rot, causing him to have a small lake of sewage around his storefront. He was reluctant to break the fence, which now formed a dam holding the sewage, for fear the flash flood of sludge might get him in trouble with the businesses lined up below him.

The news of the sewer lake was interesting enough that Jason found a pair of miner's waist boots and poled his way along through the mud with his cane. When he came to Eb Waller's store, the strong, putrid odor almost got the best of him, but he managed on closer to where Eb stood. Eb was trying to move the waste over the edge with a shovel and back into an overflowing sewage trough under the boardwalk, but the slimy sediment would have nothing to do with it and simply slid out into the middle of the street.

"Looks like you got a mess here," Jason observed, curious to find a news story.

"Yep," Eb said as he stopped and leaned on the shovel handle in the bright noon sun. He wore long boots and stood almost knee-deep in the souring waste. "I done outsmarted my own self," he said, but he was a man of patience and had confidence that he would figure out what to do with the lake of gray sewage in front of his store. Removing a package of loose tobacco from his coveralls, he fished in it and pulled out some leaves along with a tough stem that resembled a dried-out rat leg. After stuffing the chew into his mouth and getting it situated, he said, "I might just have to bust this fence down."

Reviewing the scene, Jason said, "Looks like it might flow right into Mrs. Kavenaugh's bakery."

"It might," Eb agreed. "Then, it might not. It's hard to tell where sewage will go—seems to always go where you don't want it to."

Carefully, Jason caned his way up onto the boardwalk out of the muck. "So what are you going to do, Eb?"

"I don't rightly know," Eb admitted, and he plunged his way up out of the sewage to join Jason on the higher boardwalk. "You work for that newspaper, don't you?"

"That's right," Jason said, looking at the dull gray soup. It seemed to be moving, as if it were alive and had a mind of its own. "Thought there might be a story here."

One of the boards creaked under the stress, and Eb sloshed down into the sewage to see if he could keep the dam from breaking. Eb was a small man with graying hair; his wrinkled face revealed some concern. Patience made him practical and easygoing; he was a man determined not to get rattled. But when the board busted and the lake emptied, it washed Eb away with it, sweeping him off his feet. He screamed for a second but was silenced by crashing boards and a surge of sewage. The impact of the sludge wave hit Mrs. Kavenaugh's Bakery so hard that it knocked the foundation out of the front and tilted the building toward the street, spilling out its contents. By now there were several victims caught by the instant rush of sewage, all screaming profusely. Mrs. Kavenaugh, a red-haired, rotund woman, came sliding out of the bakery on her belly, screaming bloody murder until she disappeared under the sewage. Before anyone could drown, the gray wash traveled on down the steep grade, leaving Eb, Mrs. Kavenaugh, and several others floundering like fish in a muddy streambed.

Realizing he'd witnessed a catastrophe, Jason smiled at the angry Mrs. Kavenaugh as she flailed at Eb. "You brainless idiot!" she screamed, swatting at Eb, her red hair now gray strings hanging in her face. Confused, it was all Eb could do to protect himself from the woman who outweighed him two to one.

Yet Jason felt a sense of glory, for his news instincts had placed him in the right place at the right time, and in this business, timing was everything. It was somewhat of a personal victory, and for the moment he forgot the pain in his back that was a constant nuisance. Carefully, he stepped around the mess as best he could and made his way back down the hill to the office. He had a story to write.

~

Abe was a man of sound routine, and catastrophes of mudslides or sewer washouts meant nothing to him. Although Jennifer and Jason rejoiced over the number of papers they were able to sell about the infamous sewer break, Abe kept to his regular schedule of working long hours and being timely at Lita's meals. He took his obligations seriously and felt his contributions to the household were important. But spring was coming, and Abe felt he wasn't getting any younger—he'd someday soon have to muster up the courage to talk to Lita about their future.

Early one morning, Abe sat at the kitchen table over a cup of hot coffee strong enough to float nails. This was his favorite time of day, a time when it was just Lita and him. He watched her move about in her predictable manner as she fixed him breakfast. He was a big man and had to have some food if he was going to swing heavy hammers and pound red-hot iron all day long. There was hardly anything he was afraid of, yet he didn't ever know where to start when he wanted to talk to Lita about a more serious life together—he was scared to bring it up.

Finishing up with stuffing his lunch bag, Lita turned to ask, "Do you want some of dat cake with your lunch?"

Instead of answering, Abe was looking at Lita and thinking. He didn't really hear what she asked. Then he snapped out of it. "Oh, I sure do."

Cocking her head to one side, Lita sensed something wasn't quite right. She knew Abe too well. "What's wrong—you actin' funny."

"Oh, it ain't nothin'," Abe said bashfully, shrugging his muscular shoulders. He was a bad actor and even worse at lying.

Coming over to the table, Lita casually slid the chair out and sat in front of him. It was the same thing as if she was fishing and had a nibble, and now she patiently moved in to set the hook. Reaching out, she let her hand touch his big and powerful meaty paw. His hands were huge and strong and callused; the thick, yellow fingernails resembled horse hooves. She softened and asked, "What's the matter? I know somethin' botherin' you."

Batting his heavy eyelids, Abe glanced away but knew he couldn't escape. "Well," he said, his voice deep and hollow-sounding. "I was wonderin' if . . ." Struggling, he couldn't quite manage to spit it out.

But Lita knew what he was trying to say, something she'd been wanting him to say for a long time. However, she didn't want to make it too easy. "Is dis got somethin' to do with you and me?"

Abe nodded but didn't say anything.

Getting closer, Lita had a sparkle in her eyes. Abe could feel the heat from her face. "Isn't there somethin' you want to ask me?"

Rolling his eyes up to look at her face, Abe developed a lump in his throat. His lips moved, but nothing came out.

Relentlessly, Lita moved even closer, her lips almost touching his. "Is this somethin' about marriage?"

"Well, yeah," Abe muttered. His heart was pounding now, and the kitchen seemed awfully hot.

"I can't ask myself for you," Lita said softly, patiently encouraging the big man.

"W-w-well," he stuttered. "I was wonderin' if you would want to marry me? I mean, I know I ain't much, but I sure wish you—"

"Oh, shut up!" Lita interrupted and smothered him with a kiss. Then she put her arms around his head and squeezed him tight and pulled back. "What took you so long to ask me?"

"I was afraid you might say no."

Now happy and smiling, Lita said, "When do you want to get married? Can I get ahold of a preacher and arrange it soon?"

"I'd like that," Abe answered, not only happy but relieved.

"I'll tell folks we'll have a small wedding right here. Dat all right with you?"

Now smiling big enough to show his huge, white teeth, Abe felt a new sensation of courage. "Anything you want, Lita, that's fine with me."

~

Wandering around the boardwalk up on Gregory Street, Jason felt a little envious of the news of Abe and Lita. It was one of those afternoons when you couldn't tell if it was winter or spring, but either way, it was overcast and too cool to be comfortable. His emotions were mixed, as he felt happy for the couple but at the same time felt alone and left out in the cold. "I wish I was announcing my wedding," he mumbled, certain he'd never have a crack at Jennifer again.

Moving slowly, the constant reminder of the pain forever present in his back, evident with each movement, Jason strolled across the muddy street, relying heavily on his cane. He climbed the worn, wooden steps and shuffled down the boardwalk. Coming to the corner of a building, he stopped and leaned against the wall, stroking his long beard. From inside the building, the gaiety of saloon music rang out clearly—it sounded like people having a good time. In front of him, the street remained busy, freighters and mule skinners and mules trying to get a footing in the slick mud. The afternoon was growing late, and he didn't feel like he had anywhere to go.

Most of the folks he observed seemed happy with being busy, but Jason was in one of his moods. *I don't guess I've learned anything about life,* he decided weakly, *and I understand even less!* He watched the traffic die down along with the afternoon light as the sun slipped behind the mountain. It grew cooler as a few people made their way by on the boardwalk, paying him no attention.

"You seem a little down," a clear and unmistakable voice announced from beside Jason.

Startled, Jason flinched, then turned to see Preacher leaning on the wall beside him. "Where'd you come from? I didn't hear you come up," he said.

"I've often been accused of that," the preacher said mildly, shrugging off any importance of surprising Jason. "You look like something's bothering you. Is there anything I can do?"

Letting his head drop, Jason really didn't feel like talking. "I don't know," he muttered. "Just seems like things keep me confused."

"You could be lying on your back up in that bed," the preacher reminded him.

"Yeah, I know," Jason agreed. "I'm glad that's over with, and I thank you, and I thank God and all of that—but there are other things."

Preacher smiled, a relaxed man, his face dark and subtle in the shadows. "You look as if you've lost a loved one."

"In a way, I have," Jason admitted. "I try to be good, do the right thing, and it always seems like I lose in the long run. Seems like the bad people always end up with all the luck, and the good ones suffer. Why is that, Preacher? Why'd God have to create it that way?"

Taking a long glance out and down the street, the preacher took a deep breath. "Creation—that's a big subject. You see, Jason, God's powers have existed without beginning, but all that was possible for Him had not yet been accomplished before creation. Like, how could He have been a father until His children were born? How could He be redeemer until there was someone to redeem? How could He have shown pity until there was someone to pity? Understand, creation would have been impossible if He had completely filled the void by Himself. In order for the world to appear, it was necessary for Him to dim His resplendence. Had He not done this, whatever He created would have been blinded and consumed by His brilliance."

The preacher was poised in a relaxed position leaning against the wall, doing his best to be informative. "You ask what was the purpose of creation? Free will! Man must choose for himself between good and evil. This is why God sent forth man's soul. A father may carry his child, but he wishes the child to learn to walk on its own. God is our Father and we His children and He loves us. He blesses us with His mercy, and if He lets us slip and fall, it is to accustom us to walking alone. Yet when we are in trouble, He lifts us into His holy arms.

"Yes, of course we suffer. As the Bible says, man was born to suffer, but we suffer for a reason. Our souls are purified through what we endure, and then they rise to heaven. And you see, Jason, the wicked may prosper here on earth, but the real torment begins for the unbeliever after death." The preacher stopped; he felt like he was losing Jason's interest.

"Is that supposed to explain how it all works?" Jason asked.

"When you're tired enough, your eyes close by themselves, Jason. Just like someday you'll emerge from the darkness, but only by faith in God."

Making a sour face, Jason knew it was probably pointless to argue with a man as sharp as the preacher. He glanced at the last dying light of the sunset, then said, "What about love, Preacher? What if a man falls madly in love, only to be crushed? Is that part of the plan?"

A broad smile covered the preacher's face. "I take it you're referring to yourself. This woman—do you really love her?"

"Would a cow lick Lot's wife?" Jason fired back.

Chuckling, Preacher said, "Patience is golden, Jason."

Not wanting to hear any more about patience, Jason turned away, ignoring the preacher. *This man has an answer for everything*, he thought irritably. But when he turned back, the man was gone. There was no sign of him on the street in either direction. "Strange fellow," he mumbled.

Day changed to night, and the music came more loudly from the saloon. If anything, the preacher disturbed the troubled waters that ran deep in Jason's soul. *What's the use?* he thought, a little disgusted as he hobbled into the saloon.

~

"Say, Grant, you sure have been quiet lately," Butch said as he dealt the cards. The children were practicing playing poker up in Grant's room after school. Abby was trying to learn not to show her excitement when she got a good hand, and now the matchsticks they used for chips were piling up in front of her. Grant seemed to care less if he won or lost.

"I just don't feel like talking," Grant informed Butch as he picked up his cards. And he didn't. The humiliation he'd suffered up in Central City had scarred him forever. He had realized that he was acting arrogantly and had momentarily lost his concentration. It was such a serious lesson that he redeemed himself by vowing to always remain professional in all of his endeavors from then on. His goal was to be wealthy and successful and well respected, just like Lance Rivers. If that meant being as good with a pistol as Lance Rivers, so be it—he would never suffer such embarrassment again.

"Look, I've got a straight," Abby said joyfully as she tossed her cards onto the bed the children sat on. "You'll have to go get some more matches before long, Grant."

"I'll go get some," Grant said, looking for an excuse to leave the game. It was difficult to concentrate when he was consumed by torment.

Watching Grant leave the room, now Abby could indulge in her favorite private conversation with Butch. "I'll be so good at poker by the time we're older that we can work as a team," she gleamed. "I'll wear pretty dresses, and you can buy me gold necklaces and earrings."

Leaning back on a pillow, Butch smiled, his wide jaw protruding. "Ain't nothing will be too good for you, Abby," he agreed. He liked to see Abby happy. She had a wild fire in her like nobody else he knew—except maybe himself.

"Then maybe we can go to Francisco," Abby said dreamily. "I hear that's where all the ladies get all their fancy stuff."

Butch nodded as he sorted his cards. "That's right," he said, "except I think it's called San Francisco."

"You know what I mean," Abby giggled. "I'll take two cards."

Handily, Butch dealt her the cards and himself three. He ended up with two pair. "All right, Abby, I'll bet you ten matches."

"I'll see your ten," she said, her upper lip stiff, "and I'll raise you ten more." She glared at him, daring him to challenge her.

Searching her face, Butch found no clue to indicate whether she was bluffing or not. "I'll raise you ten more," he said.

"I'll see that and raise you ten more," she quipped.

Studying her face, Butch decided she must have at least three of a kind, since she only drew two cards. "I fold," he said, tossing his cards in.

Quickly, Abby gathered up the matches and added them to her growing pile.

"What'd you have?" Butch asked.

"You have to pay to see, remember?" Abby said shrewdly.

I've created a monster, Butch thought, smiling.

~

Working into the evening, Jennifer looked over a Denver newspaper she had acquired, studying its format. It was a different kind of newspaper from what they printed, yet it was successful. It seemed it dwelled quite a bit on the upper social crust, the wealthy, and the powerful. She was wondering exactly what marketing strategy she should have with the *Advertiser*. Since Jason was able to help, although he was limited, the newspaper was showing signs of hope.

There was some clomping on the front steps, then the door rattled, and Jason came in out of the dark. He didn't seem to notice Jennifer.

"Jason!" Jennifer said. "Look at that mud you tracked in!"

Turning and looking down, Jason saw the huge clumps of wet mud lying on the floor. He opened the door and kicked the mud out with his good leg, then closed the door. He didn't so much as turn toward Jennifer. Walking over to the stove, he moved closer to it, warming up from the chill, his back to Jennifer.

He must be in one of his moods, Jennifer thought. She stood and approached Jason, bringing the newspaper she'd been looking over with her. "Jason, I've been looking at the *Rocky Mountain News*. They certainly seem to cover the social establishment. I was wondering, maybe we should include at least one article about the social events up here in Central City."

"Good idea," Jason said roughly. "You can take notes when Mr. Fancy Pants takes you out to dinner."

"Jason!" Jennifer scolded. "I thought we'd been through this already." But then she caught that odor on him, that reeking aroma of alcohol. Closely studying him for a moment, she noticed he was slightly weaving as he stood in front of the stove. "Jason! What are you doing half drunk!?"

Spinning around, Jason almost lost his balance, but he glared at her, his eyes red. "I ran out of money!" he retorted.

Disgusted with his drunken wit and his condition, Jennifer tossed the newspaper on her desk and left the office, leaving Jason alone. He watched her leave and made a face behind her back. "What does she know?" he mumbled. "What does she care anyway?"

Standing in front of the fire, Jason watched the wood burn. The fire was a consuming beast, something he could relate to. Soon he grew tired and blew out the lamps, closed the doors on the stove, and ambled on up to bed. His back pained him and his head hurt and his heart ached. He was tired of thinking and tired of feeling pain, and for the moment, all he wanted to do was escape.

CHAPTER

~ 16 ~

Wedding Vows

With April came the first signs of spring in the high country, and Lita was beholding to the excitement of matrimony. A fresh morning of clear air and sharp morning sun invaded the open kitchen door. "Oh, Miss Jenny," she said happily, addressing Jennifer, "I got all these plans and so little time."

"Don't worry, we'll get everything taken care of," Jennifer said, trying to calm Lita. "I've already contacted Preacher, and he assures me he'll be able to handle the arrangements. He said not to worry, that Reverend Blackburn is more than happy to let us use his church. And Jake Sandelowski says your dress will be ready shortly, and he's already outfitted Abe. As for the reception, we have all the things we need to bake with—it's just a matter of cooking it when the time comes. Everything is under control."

Rustling the embers in the old stove, Lita turned to face Jennifer. She couldn't seem to get her thoughts organized. She appealed to the younger woman. "I know, Miss Jenny, but I feel like I might fly away. Dis and dat and dis and dat—the whole thing makes me kind of worried. Poor old Abe, why, he don't know what to expect. He just think he supposed to be at the church and say 'I do.' After the wedding, we got to come back here for the reception. Then after that, Abe says for me to have my bag packed—we goin' on a little trip. Miss Jenny,

I don't know nothin' about travelin'—what am I supposed to pack? Then, who gonna take care of y'all?"

It was almost comical watching Lita sort through her worries with her many questions. "I can cook, Lita, and so can Jason. We'll manage while you're gone—you just have a good time and don't worry about us."

Lita shook her head, ruffled from wedding plans. Jennifer studied her as she worked a big white wad of sourdough in a large wooden bowl. Beads of perspiration on her forehead, she had the determination and stamina of a team of oxen and a heart as big as the Rocky Mountains. What made her so special was her humility and selflessness, her deep and unquestionable love. She had lived a life of giving and doing for others, and now, after all the years of patience, she was being rewarded with marriage to one of the finest men Jennifer had ever known. And for a brief moment Jennifer felt elation for Lita, the tender touch of those deep emotions that surround matrimony, the promises of love to keep. Sadly, Jennifer realized that these desires for matrimony burned in her own bosom as well.

Suddenly the press caught Jennifer's attention with its rolling and thumping. Jason was busy printing out copies of the latest edition. "I'd better go help Jason," she said as Lita mumbled something in reply. Leaving the kitchen and entering the front office, Jennifer could see Jason struggling with the ornery press.

"Jason! I can do that!" Jennifer protested, angered by his stubborn bullheadedness. "I told you I'd be back in here in a few minutes!"

Ignoring her, Jason stopped cranking on the machine and made a minute adjustment to one of his wooden blocks crammed into the machine works. Straightening, he grabbed his cane that was hanging on the press and put his weight on it. "Good. Then you crank it," he said, contempt in his voice.

While Jennifer worked the handle on the machine, Jason watched closely, removing each copy as it came off. They worked without exchanging words or glances, an effort that seemed labored. Once enough copies were made, Jason sorted through a small stack and placed them in a backpack that he slipped over his shoulder. "I've got to deliver these," he said. "Be back later."

After he was gone, Jennifer stared at the front door where Jason had exited, as if she might miraculously see answers appear before her. *Why does he have to be so cranky?* she wondered, letting her thoughts run free. *There were times when he was such a good man, a man I could care for, a man I could—* But then she cut off the free-flowing thoughts immediately, as if saving herself from unnecessary grief. She quickly changed to a different frame of mind. *If he wants to be stubborn, then he'll just have to be that way. I've done all I can—it's too hard feeling sorry for him when he's so bitter.* Moving over to her desk, she comforted herself by getting lost in her paperwork.

~

Lance Rivers was always about two steps ahead of everyone else, planning and sometimes scheming. On this refreshing spring day, he rode into Black Hawk to visit Jennifer with the assumption that timing was everything. His plan was well thought out, starting with an invitation. When he entered the *Advertiser's* office, he found her at work at her desk as usual, alone in the office.

"Good afternoon," he announced after he let himself in. "Can't ask for a nicer day. Too bad you have to sit in this stuffy old office and work."

"Yes, it is nice," Jennifer agreed. "I do feel like I have a touch of spring fever."

Coming closer, Rivers smiled, delicate with his words. "That's the way it is here, cooped up all winter until the cabin fever drives a person crazy—then spring is so beautiful you come down with a severe case of spring fever, one right after the other. A person hardly knows what to do. The only cure is to get out and enjoy the mountain air, soak up some sun, and get yourself a little time to relax and enjoy this country."

"That would be nice," Jennifer said, "but the wedding is in a few days, and there's so much to do."

"Anything I can do to help?" Rivers asked, quick to be amiable. "I can get some people to help with the food or something."

"I think everything is taken care of," Jennifer said, reviewing the plans in her mind.

"What about after the wedding? After the reception?" Rivers asked.

"Well, then it's over," Jennifer answered, not sure what Rivers was hinting at. "Abe has plans on taking Lita on a little honeymoon, I think, but that's their secret."

Pulling up a chair and sitting down close to Jennifer, Rivers obviously had something on his mind. "I tell you what," he started, wearing a confident smile. "You've been stuck in here all winter, and things have been hard on you and the children, but now spring is here and the mountains are turning green again. It's the perfect time of year for you to get out—get away from this place and all the headaches. I'd like to invite you to my ranch, and of course, I want you to bring Grant and Abby. I have a big ranch house—plenty of rooms for your privacy. The servants take care of all the cooking and everything. All you have to do is enjoy yourself. Lita and Abe will be gone, nobody here anyway. So, what do you say?"

Jennifer took a deep breath and let her eyes swing around until they landed on Lance. "I'll have to admit, it does sound nice. We haven't been able to enjoy any of this country since we've been here, just stuck in this mining creek with the noisy mills." But then she stopped and pondered, examining the offer. "Oh, I don't know. It might not be the right thing to do, I mean, it might not look right."

"Nonsense!" Rivers insisted. "If you won't do it for yourself, do it for Grant and Abby—think of them. There's so much for them to do at the ranch and more horses than you can count. Jennifer, I've always been a gentleman, and it's my intention to remain so. Give this a chance—get out where you can breathe and think!"

By now Jennifer was almost excited by the prospect of escaping to a fine horse ranch and being waited on for a change, but she didn't show it; her lips were firm. "What about the newspaper? I can't just leave my business."

"Let Jason run the newspaper! We'll only be gone about a week." Rivers's expression changed slightly to one approaching impatience. *Why must women always be so fickle?* he thought. *They want things, and when you offer it to them, then they don't know what they want!* He quickly went back to his pleasant smile, determined to influence her to see it his way. As she watched him, he casually pulled a slim cigar from his vest pocket and made a business of lighting it, taking far too long before he said anything. Now she was watching him eagerly, almost wanting to be convinced. Rivers glanced into nothingness like he was considering a proposition, then brought his attention directly back to her. "I'll have a carriage ready and waiting the morning after the wedding. The ride to the ranch is only about a half-day's ride. There's a lovely green valley we pass through with a sparkling creek running through it under some old cottonwoods—a grand place to stop and have a picnic." He paused as she unknowingly drew nearer, taken in by his description of a place she'd love to see, somewhere away from the mud and the stench and all her problems. This man could provide that for her.

Rivers sensed her weakness and continued, "Of course, there'll be no need to hurry, no schedule to keep, and you'll see rocky gorges like you never dreamed, maybe even some bighorn sheep. And by the time we arrive, my cook, Lilly, will have smoked ribs ready."

To Jennifer this all sounded too good to be true. But a cook named Lilly suddenly sprang at her and a tinge of envy came from nowhere. "Lily?" she said. "I didn't know you had a woman in the house with you. What's she like?"

Rivers smiled contentedly before he explained. By mentioning Lilly, he had aroused a jealousy he felt reasonably sure would surface if Jennifer really cared. "Lilly is the best cook to ever work the range, rode with a few wagon trains that came west, and can cook the best pie you ever tasted." He tugged on his cigar, his eyes twinkling. "Yep, old Percival Lilly has been with me for years—runs the ranch house while I'm gone. Of course, the foreman runs the ranch, but Percival is in charge of the house and feeding all the hands. He's a cantankerous old coot, but a better friend you'll never find."

Jennifer sighed with relief, trying not to show it. She had pictured a woman named Lily living in the same house with Lance, and it didn't sit well with her at all. She was to the point where she'd let Lance cross the vague distance she held between herself and other men—he was growing too close for any misunderstandings or misconceptions. Against her will, a slight smile found its way to her face. "It does sound like fun, but it's so sudden. I wouldn't want to do anything improper."

"Nobody asked you to," Rivers responded. "I'll have a carriage waiting the morning after the wedding. In the meantime, we'll turn our thoughts to Lita. Sound like a bargain?"

Finally relenting, Jennifer agreed to the trip. "Yes," she said. "I'm sure we'll have a wonderful time."

~

The wedding took place on schedule in the Presbyterian Church up on the hill. Reverend Blackburn sat joyfully in the preacher's pew, while Preacher stood tall and lean in front of Abe and Lita. His voice rang through the small church with distinct clarity. More people had shown up than expected, many out of respect for Abe and his skill for drill sharpening; the miners came who admired him and his work. Of course, they looked forward to the reception as well with all of the delicacies. Jennifer sat with Lance on one side, and Grant and Abby on the other. Jason sat two rows back, smoldering. Although he was happy for Abe and Lita, the sight of Rivers with Jennifer nauseated him. The rest of the group included storekeepers and friends whom they'd done business with, and a few unknown faces—hungry souls perhaps looking for a free meal. After all, Jennifer had announced the wedding in the newspaper.

"And do you, Abe Washington, take Lita to be your lawfully wedded wife?" the preacher asked Abe.

"I sure do," Abe answered honestly.

"And you, Lita. Do you take Abe to be your lawfully wedded husband?"

"I do," Lita answered, her eyes watery.

"Place the ring on her finger, Abe," the preacher said.

Abe shuffled through the fancy rented coat, searching one pocket and then another. He wasn't used to having any more than one pocket, and in all the excitement he'd forgotten which pocket he had put the ring in. A minute passed as Abe frantically searched.

By now, Lita had turned her expectant gaze on him; the congregation watched with anticipation. Finally, he felt the little ring deep in the bottom of one of the pockets and fished it out. It was a gold band Abe had made himself, and having to guess at the size, he now worried whether it would fit. He took her hand and tried to fit the ring on, but it was too tight. Lita snatched her hand back and whispered, "Dat's the wrong finger." She helped Abe, who'd now grown nervous and fidgety, and slipped the band onto her ring finger—a nice fit.

"I now pronounce you husband and wife!" the preacher said warmly. "You may kiss the bride," he said to Abe.

Turning, Abe saw all of those people sitting behind him and froze—he'd never kissed but in private. Bashfully, he batted his big eyes and looked to Lita for help. Quickly, Lita reached up around his big neck and pulled him down and gave him a hearty kiss.

A cheer broke out from the congregation as Lita led Abe down the aisle toward the front door. Many of the onlookers abandoned their seats and rushed outside to cheer the two to their rented buggy. "You all tied up now!" one of the coarse miners hollered at Abe. "That's right, Abe!" another jocular voice yelled. "Now you have to get permission to tie your shoes!" But all Abe could do was hold Lita and grin. He didn't hear a word—all he knew was that he was happy.

It seemed like there were more people at the reception than at the wedding. The front office had been cleaned out and things moved for the table and chairs and wedding cake and other goodies. The visitors formed a line out into the warm afternoon sun and on their way in filed past Lita and Abe, wishing them well.

It soon became standing room only as Lita stood behind the small, white cake with a nervous Abe. "Cut the cake," she said impatiently. But Abe's hands were trembling as he took the knife. "Here, give me dat," Lita said as she grabbed the knife and sliced a piece of cake and stuck it in Abe's mouth. He slowly chewed it, then got excited. "Um-umm! Dat sure is good!" The group laughed heartily, then dove into the tables covered with fat hams baked cozily in wood-stoked ranges to a savory completion, while the aroma of apple and berry pies bubbling in the oven back in the kitchen tickled the salivary glands of all present. The jolly miners prompted for a keg of beer, but Lita had said she'd have no drinking at her wedding—they'd have to do that later, somewhere else. It was a joyous feast, the hams provided by a generous Lance Rivers.

With daylight hours dwindling, the reception came to an end as Abe escorted Lita to the waiting buggy under a hail of rice and good cheer. He snapped the reins, and the spirited young horse lurched the buggy into motion. Lita turned and waved to the well-wishers—she was off on her honeymoon.

Turning to Jennifer, Rivers whispered in her ear. "That's a fine picture, a man and a woman being united." There was a wistful kind of hint in his voice.

Glancing at Rivers, Jennifer said, "Yes, yes, it's heartwarming." Her tone acknowledged his hint. The little wedding had been so lovely that they'd both been envious.

~

Late that same night, Jason had gone down into the kitchen to pick at some leftovers, much of which was sitting out on the table. He found a plate, leaned his cane against the table, and sat down for a snack. He was somewhat despondent, sad that Lita was gone, which left a void in the once-cheerful atmosphere of the kitchen. *It's just not the same without Lita here*, he thought, but even more, he worried about Jennifer. He'd heard of her plans to leave in the morning with the children and spend a week with Lance Rivers at what was probably some ridiculously lavish horse ranch. *Rivers doesn't fool me!* he thought angrily. *He'll take her to his ranch and impress her with all his holdings and sweet-talk her into marrying him!* Although Jason couldn't really blame Rivers or Jennifer, he felt left out and alone. He was feeling sorry for himself, ashamed of his fate as he munched on a piece of tender ham. *I guess there's no place left for me*, he thought dejectedly.

Jason heard a rustling movement, and then Jennifer stepped into the kitchen. "Oh, Jason—you startled me." Glancing around, she observed, "Looks like you're having a late snack. I had the same idea, all this good food just sitting here." She had a friendly attitude, as if there were no problems. Much of her anxiety had been lifted due to her anticipation of a short vacation. "You should have plenty to eat while I'm gone—you'll have the whole place to yourself. Maybe you can enjoy a little peace and quiet."

Jason's mood wasn't so friendly. The thought of Jennifer leaving with Rivers grated him. As Jennifer fixed herself a plate, he watched her closely, her flowing movements, her hair up and her face calm. "Jennifer, don't you see what Rivers is doing? He's trying to impress you with his money—taking you to some fancy ranch is all part of his ploy. Don't you see that? Is that what you care about—or do you really care for him?"

Jennifer seemed caught slightly off guard. These were the kind of personal questions she had asked herself and never could arrive at any soul-cleansing, clear answer. "Well, of course I care for him, Jason," she retorted, a bit uneasy. "Money is a nice thing to have—that's no sin, and I don't hold it against him, if that's what you're asking."

Holding strong to his convictions in what Jason considered might be his last personal discussion with Jennifer, he said, "I still think Rivers isn't all he's made out to be. There's something strange about the man. Can't you see that?"

Unconsciously giving the question some thought, Jennifer defended Rivers. "No, I don't see anything like that. He has never shown me and the children anything but kindness. Jason, you shouldn't be so bitter; it makes you think the worst—it even possesses you."

Irritated, Jason ate a few more bites while Jennifer sat down next to him. The silence was a hard pressure in the dim kitchen. Despair beckoned Jason to speak his mind. "Jennifer, what happened to the feelings you used to have for me? I thought we had something real, something that gave me a reason for living. You know I still love you as much as ever."

A color ran across Jennifer's face. This was the showdown she had been avoiding. She glanced away from Jason, searching for the right words, then turned to him. "Jason, what we might have had—I'm sure it was a good thing, and I'm still very fond of you. But you have to understand, things change. Maybe it just wasn't meant to be." She was almost pleading.

"I'm sorry, Jennifer," Jason said coldly, "but I won't be here when you get back. I can't watch Rivers ruin your life."

A little shocked, Jennifer leaned back in her chair, staring at Jason as he ignored her. His statement struck her as a sort of blackmail of her guilt in an effort to persuade her, but she was a more stubborn woman than that. "I wish you wouldn't leave. The newspaper is beginning to show signs of success since you've been up and around again. Why don't you wait, give this some thought?"

Unable to commit, Jason knew he wanted to stay around, but his pride wouldn't allow it. Rather than give her an answer, he finished eating, stood, grabbed his cane, and left the room.

A wave of guilt flowed through Jennifer, causing her to lose her appetite. She sat motionless, her eyes locked into a stare at nothing. There was the fear that Jason might actually leave, which disturbed her, something she hadn't really considered before. It left her feeling empty, for it was something more severe than just losing a close friend. But she couldn't change her plans now, and realizing that, she shifted her thoughts to the trip, something she was determined to enjoy no matter how hard Jason tried to dissuade her.

~

Rivers's ranch was more than Jennifer had expected, an extravagant layout in a plush, green valley nestled up to the spruce and fir trees. The ranch had that cozy, homey look, surrounded by forest-covered mountains that stretched up into the deep, blue sky. It was the kind of place dreams were made of, with the huge log-cabin ranch house spread lazily in the shade with its long front porch and a brick chimney that trickled smoke into the sweet spring air. Several large corrals surrounded a steep-roofed barn, and a long bunkhouse sat a comfortable distance away. Men rambled about, each tending to specific chores, and the sleek, thoroughbred horses gathered in the corners of the corrals with their ears perked. It was nothing short of spectacular as Jennifer took a deep breath and smiled into a pleasant, warm breeze that lifted out of the valley.

"What do you think?" Rivers asked proudly, turning to Jennifer who sat next to him in the open carriage.

Grant had chosen to ride and sat straddled on his horse, awed by the sight, wishing he were a part of what he saw. He had no questions—what he saw was obvious. Abby was standing on the backseat of the carriage, craning her neck to get a better view. "Mother, does all of this belong to Mr. Rivers? It sure is big!"

"It's almost unbelievable," Jennifer replied, answering Rivers. "How much of this is the ranch?" she asked, because she could see for miles.

Waving his arm across the horizon, Rivers boasted, "As far as you can see, that's the brand of Double R, the Rivers Ranch."

"This *is* something!" Jennifer complimented. She felt good; she was relieved of the torments of Black Hawk and felt like she'd escaped into something like a fairy tale. Lance had been true to his word, stopping by a trickling creek where they enjoyed a basket lunch. The entire trip had been nothing short of a sightseeing tour, gorges of beauty and winding, green valleys and waterfalls and streams sparkling in the clear sunlight.

"Let's go," Rivers said, holding his chin out and his head high.

They were greeted on the long veranda by a stooped old man with a gray beard and a bald head. He wore a big smile, his front teeth missing, but his eyes were wild and alive. "How do, Lance. Who might these folks be?"

"Percy, meet Mrs. DeSpain, and these are her children, Grant and Abby."

"By golly—you shore can pick 'em, Lance. Why, if I was any younger, I'd snatch that one away from you!" he said, his sparkling eyes appraising Jennifer. "Yes, sir! She'll shore do!"

As Lance helped Jennifer down, he said, "Percy, unload her things and put them in the guest bedroom. I hope you have something good for supper."

"I always got something good for supper," Percival protested. It's beans and steak as usual." Then he winked at Jennifer. "Of course, that's for the bunkhouse. For you, I got a rack of lamb that's been roasting over the hearth all day—mighty tender it is."

"That sounds delicious," Jennifer replied happily. She couldn't help but admire Percival instantly. He was a bit rustic, but a charming character who looked as if he could have stepped straight out of a story by her friend Samuel Clemens.

"Darling," Rivers said, addressing Jennifer, "I'll show you to your room, and you can freshen up. Then maybe we can have something to eat, and later I want to show you some of the ranch."

Jennifer caught the use of the intimate name and found that it pleased her. Lance then opened the massive front door and showed her in. At first, the den seemed like a dark cavern, but as her eyes adjusted, she could see it was lavishly decorated. It had a man's taste, giant elk and deer horns on the walls, paintings of the frontier, and heavy furniture all under a high, log-beamed ceiling. The huge fireplace glowed with a few embers, and a single lantern filled the room with a warm, yellow hue. A bear rug with a yawning bear's head covered the floor in front of the fireplace, and a very long rifle stretched across the brick wall above the mantel. The den smelled of cigar and wood smoke and leather—a sort of outdoorsman's ambience. Never had Jennifer experienced such opulence in someone's home—not even during her childhood in New Orleans.

"This way," Rivers said, taking Jennifer's hand and leading her through a door and down a long hall. He came to another door, opened it, and showed her in. It was a guest bedroom, the bed being the center attraction with its four large posts and a handmade quilt lying softly over it. The walls were rough-cut cedar, filling the room with a tangy but enriching aroma of the wild outdoors. The furniture, dressers and wardrobe and chairs were of deep walnut. From the windows could be seen the slopes of an evergreen forest. The place was an eyeful, and Jennifer had so far only seen a small portion.

"I don't know what to say, Lance," Jennifer said, unable to control the smile on her face. "This is lovely—so homey."

They could hear the children running up and down the long veranda outside and laughing loudly. Lance listened and smiled. "Sounds like they're already having fun. I need to check with Bob, my foreman, then we'll have dinner after a while. Make yourself at home, darling. Percy's in the kitchen if you need anything."

Without thinking, Jennifer reached out and touched Lance, her hand gently on his chest; her eyes were warm and friendly and seemed to be saying she approved, but her expressive mouth remained silent. Rivers smiled; he knew he had her.

Dinner was a hoot as far as the children were concerned as they laughed at the silly antics and comical expressions of Percival Lilly while he danced around the table serving everyone's particular needs. "More ribs?" he shouted at Abby in surprise. "Why, child, I'm worried you'll wake me up in the middle of the night bah-baaaahh-hhing!" he called, imitating a sheep to perfection.

Giggling, Abby argued good-naturedly, "But it's so sweet, and what's that good smoky taste? I never tasted nothing like this before."

Percival rolled his eyes indicating that anyone with a lick of sense knew the answer to her question. "That there flavoring is from hickory smoke. Hickory is a tree that grows far away from here, and it's hard as a rock." Entertainer and chef, Percival outdid himself when he brought in the pecan pie.

"I haven't seen one of these since I left New Orleans," Jennifer said, the sight of the pie bringing back old memories of the South. "How'd you find pecans up here?"

"My secret!" Percival said as he picked up some dishes and swooshed out of the room.

"Don't let him kid you," Lance said, loving every minute of the dinner. "He has connections down in Ruston, Louisiana. Some close friends of his own a lumber mill."

After the hugely successful dinner, Percival continued to entertain the children while Lance sneaked out the front with Jennifer. A tall, lean man sat on the front porch smoking a cigarette, waiting. A black buggy sat parked, the horse tied to the post.

"Thanks, Bob," Rivers said. He brought Jennifer up beside him. "Jennifer, this is my foreman, Bob Russell."

"Ma'am," the foreman drawled coldly, the lines in his face strict with hardness.

"Hello," Jennifer said, not staring at the man. She had a strong feeling that there was something devious about him, but she brushed away such notions as foolishness.

The orange sunset left long shadows and darkened the sides of mountains as Rivers gently whipped the thoroughbred up a steep and narrow road that wound up above the valley. Once the sun had dropped behind a mountain, the air immediately became chilled. But Lance was prepared as he stopped and draped a comfortable blanket over Jennifer's shoulders. "Right up here around this bend," he said as he drove on.

When Rivers pulled the buggy to a halt, Jennifer could see the entire valley below and the mountain ranges around it. It was a breathtaking view, almost shocking, and certainly baffling. The ranch house was no more than a dot painted on a gentle canvas of varying shades of green. The smell was of high mountain spruce, the air cool and sharp.

"It's something, isn't it?" Rivers said, savoring the sight himself.

Jennifer felt a little light-headed in the thin air, but just the same, she was vastly impressed. "They should call this God's country," she murmured, taken by the view. "It's so high up and so fresh and clean—the mountains and the valleys are so beautiful."

Knowing his timing was perfect, Rivers placed his arm around Jennifer and pulled her close to him. She turned her eyes to him expectantly. "Jennifer, there comes a time in a man's life when he realizes he has to settle down, and there's nothing like the right woman to make him come to that conclusion. My love for you is as big as these mountains. All of this could be yours as well. It's my wish to share it with you and your children. I've never been more serious about anything in my entire life. Jennifer, will you marry me?"

Her heart a rhythm in her chest, Jennifer was completely taken by the events leading up to this special moment and was definitely in love with Lance Rivers. She had anticipated his motives and his question, and had previously given it thorough consideration. Already knowing the answer, she whispered, her lips close to his, her breath warm on his face, "Yes, Mr. Lance Rivers, I'll marry you."

With that, Rivers pulled her closer, almost violently, and kissed Jennifer long and hard, for his thirst for this woman was a powerful and hungry man's thirst. A man who seemingly had everything, yet to whom nothing else mattered any longer, he knew in his heart and in his mind that he had to have her at any cost.

Heated with passion, Jennifer lifted herself to Lance's rough treatment, driven by the long-held and burning desires she could no longer restrain. She had chosen the road she would take and there was no turning back—she would commit completely.

After timeless several minutes, Jennifer gently pulled away and looked closely into Lance's dark eyes. She was sure he meant everything he had said, certain he would hold her in high esteem, and convinced that he would be a good husband—everything that Drake had failed at. She was tired of everything in her life until now, but new promise showed her that things could be good. She felt good about her decision, good about Lance, good that her children would have things she never had, and sure that she could make a life with him. All was well, though deep down, beneath her clear consciousness, was a misty and vague little ghost of doubt.

CHAPTER

~ 17 ~

A Brief Farewell

Jason found staying in the old and drafty building to be lonely, and he slowly grew despondent. *I don't know what she thinks I'm supposed to do!* he thought dejectedly, thinking of Jennifer. *I'm sure that by now Rivers has overwhelmed her with his abundance and has probably talked her into marrying him!* This struck a deep nerve with Jason, one that ran through him like a sickening wave of nausea. His eyes roamed over the empty office in the late afternoon light, a light that weakly illuminated dirty windows and cast heavy shadows. A depressing sight for what was meant to be a newspaper adventure, the place was like a tomb, dusty and silent and forgotten. The heavy, stoic press sat quietly, and the desks and chairs screamed with loneliness. The only sound was the forever present *thud-thud* of the quartz mills in the distance. *God, help me get better so I can walk, only so I'll be able to leave! It's over,* Jason realized as he stood leaning on his cane, saddened by his memories of better times when Lita scurried about and Grant was constantly under his feet with his many questions. He remembered little Abby's voice squealing from the stairs and Jennifer's warm and expressive smile, a smile of contented pleasure. *Amazing how things can change*, he reflected, wishing he had it to do all over so that he might avoid the mistakes that had changed things.

No matter what I think or how I feel, I can't stay, he decided, certain he was making a man's decision—the right decision. Slowly, he made his way through the dark kitchen and up the thin staircase to his meager little room. It was a sad place, a place he'd grown weary of during his bedridden days. Glancing around, he noticed, *I have hardly a thing to show for my life*. Over on the floor he saw a stack of loose papers—his novel, a reminder of another failure. *I wonder how many people have done the same? Started a book with all the ambition in the world, only to watch it dwindle into a stack of forgotten papers*. He leaned over, straining, and picked up his manuscript. Thumbing through it, he discovered he had lost all interest; it was merely a collection of worthless thoughts.

It didn't take long for Jason to pack his things, all neatly stuffed into a few old carpetbags and stacked in the middle of his sagging bed; he had few worldly possessions. *But then there's Dolly, thanks to Abe*, Jason thought as he appraised his worldly assets. *At least I have a way out of this place*. But the fact remained that he hadn't ridden a horse with his bum leg. *If I can just get up and mounted, then I can ride!* he thought stubbornly. Next, he removed his worn, leather billfold and counted his cash. *Not much for a town where prices are high*, he knew, but then again, he had to leave no matter what his financial status. *I think I'll take Dolly for one last look around, then tomorrow morning I'll take off, see if I can find work in Denver*.

Saddling Dolly was more difficult than mounting her, Jason found, but he persisted until he was up and had reined the filly around to head up Gregory Gulch. First, he rode the late-afternoon streets of Black Hawk, perpetually busy with a polyglot of people. Its rough exterior was an exact representation of its inner character. The popular Shoo Fly variety halls with dancing girls and whiskey and gambling overflowed with business, against the wishes of the married women and the upper-class establishment. Further on, in the backdrop of stench from the mills and open sewers that ran under the boardwalks, Jason caught the scent of the smooth and pleasant aroma of Black Hawk Cracker Works, where A. G. Rhoads's soda crackers supplied most of the West's demand for the commodity. Like other industries in Black Hawk, it ran day and night with its two big ovens producing crackers by the barrelful.

Feeling sorry for himself, Jason came to a simple conclusion. *It's only proper that I have a farewell drink to this town*. He wasn't worried about getting drunk since he didn't have enough money, so he rode on, looking for a good place to wet his whistle. In front of the Granite House, he dismounted carefully and removed his cane, which he had stuck under the saddle. His appearance was typical for the day, long hair and long beard, a shabbily dressed man limping on a cane, assumed to be just another miner injured on the job, now forced to scrounge for his subsistence.

"I'll have a beer," Jason said to the bartender.

An astute man, the dark-haired bartender with a pencil mustache waited until he got Jason's money before he poured him a beer.

Taking a good swig of the dark liquid, Jason smacked his lips at the hearty flavor of the amber bock. Turning around, he looked over the place as a new piano player took over for the evening and began with a happy, key-slamming tune. Leaning on his cane and holding his mug of beer, Jason moseyed about the gambling tables, curiously looking on.

"Try your luck?" a roulette wheel operator asked.

Knowing that his good luck had run out, Jason stupidly placed his last large note on the number thirteen, wishing for a miracle. The man spun the wheel, and it ticked loudly until it slowed down and precariously landed on Jason's number. "We have a winner!" the man shouted to make sure that everyone in the place would swamp him in hopes of winning themselves. Counting out a handful of notes, the man paid Jason twenty times what he'd bet.

Quickly, Jason put away the money and exited the saloon, not even finishing his beer. He knew his chances of keeping his winnings were slim unless he left immediately. He'd be tempted to gamble it away, or the girls would be on him, knowing he was loaded, or the pickpockets and thieves would have him targeted. Mounting his horse, Jason quickly kicked Dolly into a trot higher up into Central City. *What a break!* he thought happily as the winnings began to register in his thoughts. That should give me more than enough money to live on for a while. But then he wondered, *God couldn't be in a thing like this—for surely God doesn't help people win at gambling, something the Bible doesn't approve of. Maybe it happened because I'm not much of a godly man anymore—maybe it's the doings of the devil. Regardless, I'm going into one of these fancy establishments and have myself a steak dinner! A man has to have something in his belly if he's got to travel!*

With that, Jason swung Dolly up Eureka Street and stopped in front of the Teller House. He climbed down and limped inside to Ed Lindsey's bar, The Elevator, located on the first floor. Jason knew he could get a prime steak here as he entered, looking around the dimly lit and plushly decorated establishment. The bar was full of well-dressed and well-behaved men, consumed by their conversation and self-assigned importance.

"Can I help you, sir?" a tall man dressed in a funny-looking suit asked.

"I just want something to eat," Jason said, put out by the man's snootiness.

"Sir, I don't know if you realize it, but this establishment caters to the well-to-do. Are you sure you have the funds?"

Reaching in his old coat pocket, Jason removed the wad of bills and flashed them at the disrespectful man who'd greeted him.

"Right this way, sir," the tall man said, his attitude happily adjusted.

But he sat Jason in an out-of-the-way booth, hiding him from the other patrons. *I don't care*, Jason thought. *I just want a good steak*. There had been a time when he would have been offended, but now he seduced himself with thoughts of sorrow and actually found comfort in them.

Soon a quick, little man showed up, eager to take Jason's order. "Kind sir," he started, "the hotel has fresh oysters, prepared to your liking or raw on the half shell. Also, we have mutton, juicy and tender . . ."

"None of that," Jason said, interrupting. "I'll have a thick steak."

"Yes, sir. How would you like that prepared?" the short fellow asked, now a bit fidgety and impatient.

"Over a *far*," Jason replied, acting like he was an uneducated miner.

"I see," the waiter replied, quite certain Jason would never understand the difference between medium and medium-rare. He quickly left, disturbed that he had to wait on the ill-mannered.

Jason could hear a group of men hidden in another high-backed booth behind him—they seemed to be enjoying themselves, merrily toasting and drinking. Jason waved at a girl to bring him a beer, a gesture she didn't seem to appreciate.

While waiting for his dinner, Jason noted that the group of men in the concealed booth behind him were talking in a hushed excitement, then were loudly boisterous. Blessed with acute hearing, Jason tuned in, always suspicious of secretive talk.

A heavy voice said coarsely, "I don't think Grant will run again—all the corruption in Washington now—and how can you sit there and assure me that the legislature will recognize our declaration of statehood?"

There was a pause, then another voice spoke. "I just returned from Washington, Bill—it's a shoe-in! As a state, we have a lot to offer, especially in the form of gold and silver. I've talked with many senators and representatives, and they all agree—keep it under your hat for now, but we're getting ready to become a state. I'm hoping we can do it on July Fourth."

"Boy! Wouldn't that be a hoot!" a different voice said.

"John, I can see it now—Routt for governor! I guarantee you, partner, we'll get you elected governor!"

"Hey, not so fast," a voice said, apparently somebody named John Routt. "Where would I establish my office? We don't have a capital."

There was some laughter, then a man with a mealy voice said, "We have enough votes from the Western Slope—we want our new town of Capital City to be the capital, that's why it's named Capital City—the most beautiful place you ever saw!"

"That's crazy!" came a protest. "That's the most remote place I've ever heard of, over there between Silverton and Lake City. You must be crazy. I think the capital should be located right here, right here in Central City! There's already plans drawn up, a building with a huge gold dome."

"Calm down now, boys," said a smooth voice, obviously the

leader's. "We must be sure we're going to get our statehood before we take all of these other measures into account."

"It's in the bag," a voice of certainty said easily. "But for now, it's important all of this be kept a tight secret. We don't want anything to get ahead of our personal plans in this great state before we're ready for it. So gentlemen, I propose we make a toast and a promise, right here and right now, that this will go no further than this table, at least not until we have all our pawns in place. I'm sure you understand." Then came a confident chuckle.

"Agreed," sounded all of the voices at once, and then there was the clinking of glasses toasting.

Jason's waiter appeared about that time with a sizzling steak and placed the large plate in front of him. "Who are those men?" Jason asked, jerking his thumb in the direction behind him.

The waiter looked insolently at Jason, as if he had a distaste for the men. "Oh them—just a bunch of over-gassed drunks. Most of them represent the Colorado Territorial Legislature. The others are just blowhards, like all politicians. Enjoy your steak." The little man squirmed away.

Starving, Jason attacked his bloody steak, while at the same time trying to piece together all he had overheard. The men who'd been sitting behind him, hidden from view, began piling out. All of them were dressed in fine suits and smoking expensive cigars. As they passed Jason, a few of them gave him a belittling glance, staring down their noses at him, certain he was a grubby, unimportant immigrant unaware of his surroundings or what he might have overheard.

As Jason finished his steak and the important men disappeared, he felt a fire ignite in him, the kind of fire that drives a man to do things far greater than ever expected. *This is the biggest news story I've ever stumbled on!* he thought, his heart beginning to thump in his chest. All of a sudden, he didn't think about Jennifer or his poor disillusions with life any longer. All he could see were bold headlines reading: COLORADO TO DECLARE STATEHOOD IN THE SPIRIT OF '76.

Finishing his dinner quickly, Jason was now filled with energy from the juicy steak. Waving the waiter over, Jason quickly paid him and rose from the table. At that moment, the girl appeared with his beer. Glancing at her, he slapped a coin on her tray and said, "I can't complain about service from the bar, because there isn't any."

Quickly, Jason rushed out as fast as his bum leg would let him and mounted Dolly. He then kicked her into a burst of speed as they raced down the gulch—he had important work to do.

~

Blasting through the office door, Jason quickly hobbled around the room, lighting every single lantern. He then threw some wood in the stove on top of some paper and tossed a match to it. The heat would cut the night chill; he knew he'd be working for hours. He didn't bother writing out the story, but instead, like a professional, he hand-spiked it together using the tiny letters from the small trays, writing the news as he set the type.

The ornery press made printing difficult, but Jason patiently manipulated the machine until he got out at least one readable copy. He sat down to review it, searching for mistakes. It was late in the evening, but he was determined to have a stack of copies ready for the street by morning.

Suddenly there came a tap on the front door, and the preacher stuck his head in. "Anybody here?" he called.

"Over here, Preacher," Jason answered.

"I was passing by—saw a light on," the preacher explained.

"You're just in time. I need some help," Jason said, an excitement in his voice the preacher instantly noticed. "Here," Jason said, handing the preacher the copy he had just proofread.

Taking the newspaper, Jason could see Preacher's dark eyes quickly scanning over the story. "Why, this is big news—this'll turn the entire territory upside-down!"

"I know," Jason replied. "Take your coat off and roll up your sleeves. I need some help to get hundreds of copies printed before the sun comes up."

The preacher looked appalled. "Where is everyone?"

"Don't worry about them. They're all out of town. Let's get to work."

"I'll do what I can," the preacher said eagerly as he removed his long, black coat and his tall hat and laid them in a chair.

The two worked diligently for hours, but the press seemed overly persistent in pressing out smudged copies. Jason was slowly losing his patience. "I can't believe it! I get the best story of my life, and this stupid machine has a mind of its own!"

Deeply concerned, the preacher backed off and stared at the machine. "Looks like a complicated machine, and poor me, I don't have enough mechanical ability to operate a wheelbarrow." But the preacher was thinking; he had something else on his mind. "I have an idea, Jason," he said, picking up his hat and coat and putting them on. "I'll be back just as quick as I can." He left immediately, before Jason could ask him where he was going.

Continuing, adjusting this and that, Jason tried to print more copies but soon discovered he was just wasting ink and paper. If his leg hadn't been game, he would have reared back and kicked the machine, but instead, he settled for throwing a tray of type across the room with a loud crash. "My luck will never change!" he steamed. Going over to Jennifer's desk, he plopped down in the chair. "A last chance to redeem myself—to at least do one good thing before I leave, and now I can't even do that!" Disgruntled and disappointed, he let his head drop on the desk, weary with agony.

Falling into a strange and different kind of sleep, Jason had dreams of confusion until he came to a dream he often had. He was chasing a train, trying to board, but his bad leg wouldn't let him run. The train slowly pulled away from him as he waved and called in desperation. Then, as he watched it disappearing in the distance, Jennifer stepped out onto the back platform of the caboose. She was smiling, waving a scarf in the wind, and blowing him kisses goodbye. He'd try to run, and when he realized he couldn't, he fell to his knees and tried to crawl, scratching and clawing at the ground. It was a hopeless travesty of his life.

A resounding bang brought Jason abruptly out of his sleep. When he raised his head, his eyes squinting, he saw the preacher entering with another man. "Jason! Wake up! I've brought a man that can help us. His name's Hamler. He's been a printer and he's a mechanic. Jason—he knows presses!"

Slowly rising from his chair, Jason's eyes focused on the man. He was of medium height, a stout man who looked irritated but willing to help. He had a shock of straight hair in the middle of his balding forehead, and his face had strong features, his eyes dark and blue and determined. "Let me see this machine," he ordered as he turned around to study the press. "This a fine machine, but where the flywheel?"

"Flywheel?" Jason asked. "What flywheel? It didn't come with a flywheel."

"It not run with hand crank," Hamler said. "It must have momentum to synchronize."

Jason shrugged his shoulders and glared at the man quizzically.

Quickly coming to a decision, Hamler said, "I return," and he hurried out.

Turning to the preacher, Jason looked slightly hopeful but unsure.

"Faith, my good man," Preacher reminded him. "Say, can you fix coffee?"

"Well, sure," Jason replied. "I'll have to get a fire going in the stove in the kitchen."

Once seated, Jason and the preacher watched the flames through an open door in the kitchen stove. The kettle of water sat impatiently on top, slow to come to a boil.

"My mother once said a watched pot never boils," the preacher said good-naturedly.

"Yeah," Jason agreed, not convinced the night would work out.

"This man, Hamler, he's a good man. He's a German, always worked with machines, mostly newspaper machines. Trust me, Jason, if it can be fixed, Hamler can fix it."

Looking up into Preacher's convincing eyes, Jason wanted to believe him.

"Have I ever let you down before?" the preacher asked.

Dropping his head, Jason admitted, "No. No, you haven't."

The preacher sensed a deeper trouble in Jason, something most disturbing. "This woman you love—is it Jennifer?"

"I don't see where that's any of your business," Jason said defensively, then he mellowed in despair. "It doesn't matter now—yes! She's the one."

"But you've given up," the preacher observed.

"It's over, Preacher," Jason said, a small measure of pride now allowing him to hold his head up and his shoulders back. "She's gone with Lance Rivers. I'm sure she'll marry him."

"Then it's not over, Jason," the preacher instructed him. "And never should you give up. Ask God for help. He listens."

Nodding, Jason wanted to believe what he was hearing, but his heartache seemed to take precedence.

The water boiling, Jason stood, leaned over the stove, and poured the water into the waiting coffeepot. Soon the rich aroma filled the small kitchen as Jason poured a small amount of coffee into two tin cups before all of the water had trickled down. The two sipped the hot black liquid in silence, relishing its immediate flavor.

"It's like the whole world all of a sudden turned against me one day," Jason blurted out, confessing a need to discuss his pain.

"We all blunder. We all suffer. We all make mistakes," the preacher comforted. "It's how we handle these problems that's important—but more important than anything is the end result, don't you think?"

Jason had to agree; the end result was the reason for all intelligent efforts.

"Then fear not, my good man," the preacher continued. "You don't know the result, only God does. In the meantime, you'd better give it all you got."

About that time they heard the front door bang open and heavy footsteps enter the building. Jumping up from the table, both men made for the front office.

Hamler had taken a heavy flywheel off a steam engine that ran a sluice box. The machine was in his shop for repairs and waiting for parts, so he simply borrowed the flywheel. "This here ought to do," he said as he worked at removing the crank handle from the press.

Soon he was lifting the flywheel and placing it on the shaft. Then he put the nut back on and screwed it down. Slowly, he spun the wheel and watched the press, then quickly brought the works to a stop. "Looks like somebody mess with the timing. I have to make adjustments." He hunkered down and fidgeted with the mechanical works, as fussy in his meticulous manner as an old woman potting plants.

Feeling a little better about matters, Jason went and got Hamler some coffee, which pleased the man as he took heavy sips from the hot cup. "That's good!" he said, holding the cup with both hands. "One adjustment here, then we spin her through."

In a few minutes, the flywheel was rotating, and the machine was clacking a cadence in rhythm. Hamler oiled a few parts and stood back to admire his success. "*Ja*, you see, it designed to spin fast, and it can make many papers. You spin the flywheel with your hand and that's all."

Jason quickly inserted some papers and inked the type. He rotated the flywheel, and the press spit out uniform, perfect copies almost faster than he could count. "That's incredible!" he shouted, thrilled with the German's work. "Here," he said, reaching for some bills. "Take this—you deserve it."

Humbly taking the money, Hamler smiled. "Many thanks, but I'll need the flywheel back in a few days. It belongs to another machine."

"Can you find me another one?" Jason asked excitedly.

"*Ja*, I think I can," Hamler said, Jason's excitement now contagious among the men. "I go sleep now." He left, rewarded by his success.

Spinning the flywheel, Jason continued to watch in amazement. "All this time," he said to the preacher, "I've been fighting this machine. Then a fellow comes along that knows a little, and all of a sudden everything seems so simple."

"Sounds familiar, doesn't it?" the preacher reminded him. "There's a simple solution for almost everything. Well, I should get some sleep too. You need some help distributing those papers in the morning?"

"Why sure, Preacher—if you don't mind. I'll be here."

"Good night, then," the preacher said. "Never give up," he said over his shoulder as he left and closed the front door behind him.

Steadily, Jason worked, driven by the respect he would gain from the sensational story. Yet his thoughts drifted to Jennifer—he wondered about her, what she might be thinking.

~

It was still dark when the preacher came into the front office of the *Advertiser* and found Jason asleep, sitting with his head on Jennifer's desk. There were four stacks of freshly printed newspapers awaiting their delivery. Coming close to Jason, the preacher reached out and jostled him by shaking his shoulder. Jason lifted his head and looked sleepily at the man, then muttered, "What time is it?"

"We've plenty of time," the preacher said calmly. "What do you say we get something to eat before we get started?"

"Yeah, maybe that's a good idea," Jason said wearily. He was always slow to wake and went out of the office and through the kitchen to the back porch, where he could wash up. The preacher saw there were still coals in the kitchen stove and tossed in a few handfuls of kindling, then laid some stove wood on top of that. It wasn't long before the fire was crackling. When Jason returned, wiping his face and wet hair with a towel, the preacher had already set the kettle of water on top of the stove.

"Looks like it's going to be a lovely spring day. I didn't see a cloud, only a million glittering stars. When it's nice up here in the mountains—it's really nice," the preacher reminisced, just talking for talk's sake.

Jason flipped through the meat cabinet and the pantry and found a slab of pork belly and some eggs. "I'll slice up some bacon and fry some eggs. Sound all right with you?"

"We must have our nourishment. I'm sure we probably won't have another chance to eat for a while. Something tells me this is going to be an exceptionally busy day," the preacher said.

After breakfast, Jason rigged up a pouch for the preacher to carry a load of newspapers in. Jason had his own, a modified version so he could still use his cane. "I don't know what to expect, but we better get going. Guess I'll hit Main Street, and you can work your way up the gulch. When you run out, come back here and get some more, fair enough?"

"At ten cents a copy, we ought to make a killing," the preacher joked. He had no idea how a newspaper could make any real money.

First light was cracking over the mountain as they left the office, each headed in a different direction.

It wasn't long before the newspapers caused a stir, like the earth's trembling before an avalanche. Then it was like the entire mountain came down all at once, people running and shouting in the streets cheering, "Colorado in the Spirit of '76!" Jason was swamped until he ran out of papers and quickly made his way back to the office, where he found it full of folks, the preacher already there calming the disturbed crowd.

The heated mayor of Black Hawk was the first to approach Jason. "Where'd you get a story like this?" he shouted, waving a rolled-up copy in front of Jason's face.

"I have good sources," Jason answered.

"Who?" the mayor cried.

"I don't have to reveal them," Jason said, holding his ground. "But I assure you, the story is true."

The mayor turned and looked at his cohorts. "If this is true, gentlemen, we're going to be big, really BIG!" They all cheered as they piled out while others piled in—all loaded with questions.

"How come you were the first to know?"

"How come the *Register* doesn't have any news of this?"

"I'll take twenty of them papers. Folks up in Nevadaville will want to know about this."

"Do you know John Routt? Is he going to run for governor?"

Then the preacher held up his hands to calm the excitement. "Please, one question at a time. I'm sure Mr. Stone will be glad to answer your questions, but please calm down."

The crowd cooled at the sound of the preacher's voice of powerful persuasion, and Jason answered the simple questions the best he could. This continued for much of the day as the office of the *Advertiser* was the busiest place in town. A representative of the

Register came down and paid a handsome price to run the story for the much larger-scale newspaper. And by the afternoon, two of Denver's biggest newspapers had sent their men up to grab the scoop as well, both paying large sums for rights to the story because their newspapers covered a huge area.

By that evening, the office cleared of people but was littered with cigar butts and tracked with mud; papers were scattered everywhere. Jason glanced around, quite proud of the debris. "This is the way a real newspaper office ought to look after a good day," he mumbled to himself, quite happy. "This is the grandest mess I've ever made!"

Extremely tired, Jason locked up and went upstairs to go to bed. He saw his bags packed and laying in the middle of his bed. He chuckled and thought, *I forgot I was leaving!* Moving his luggage, he fell onto his bed, one thought on his mind; *Lance Rivers couldn't have done what I did today! Jennifer will have to be impressed.* The satisfaction lulled him until he fell into a complete and relaxed sleep.

CHAPTER

18

Homecoming

The flywheel on the old press spun like the wheels of a locomotive as Jason continued printing copy after copy of the *Advertiser's* famed edition. Couriers from surrounding settlements like Georgetown, Idaho Springs, and Nederland came and purchased bundles at a time to take back to their eagerly awaiting readers. At the same time, the locals flooded the office to purchase a copy of the newspaper, which some valued as a souvenir, while others were interested in reading the history-making news for themselves. The magic of print, working like a miracle, seemed to gain the interest of every person in the territory of Colorado.

Jason had printed and sold some 4,000 copies and was still slaving away, printing copies as fast as he could. The preacher had been helpful, borrowing more ink from the *Register*, Central City's well-established newspaper, and bringing it back to Jason, only to take another load of papers to the street where they disappeared as fast as free hotcakes. This was the biggest news since the discovery of gold in Gregory Gulch.

Some remained skeptical, until a reporter from the *Rocky Mountain News* cornered one of the representatives of the Colorado Territorial Legislature. When asked if the story was true, the irritated representative could not deny it, but was quick to accuse his associates of being loose-lipped. Indeed, the premature news had spoiled some of the political and moneymaking schemes that he could not presently attest to.

At the *Advertiser* office, things were anything but despondent and depressing. As Jason worked feverishly, his thoughts were consumed by the attentive chores of printing as many papers as he could. It was almost noon when Butch came in looking for Grant and Abby.

"Howdy, Jason. Looks like you stirred up a hornet's nest with all this about Colorado becoming a state." Butch was casually chewing on a small stalk from a package of loose tobacco. "Uncle Mike says we might have to be hitting the trail before long—says the next thing you know the federal government will be in here with all their stupid laws."

Gathering another bundle of blank paper for the press, Jason turned to acknowledge Butch. "I'm sure things will be different, if that's what you mean, some good and some bad."

"Do you know when Grant and Abby will be back?" Butch asked.

"Sorry, Butch. They didn't tell me much—your guess is as good as mine." Then Jason had an idea and glanced at Butch; he could use a young and able body. "Say, Butch, how'd you like to make some money? I could sure use some help here for a while."

His eyes lighting up at the prospect of money, Butch eagerly jumped at the chance. "You bet! What do you want me to do?"

"You can start by stacking the papers that come out of the machine, then I'll show you how to ink the thing every now and then. It's like feeding wood to a steam engine. It just eats and eats."

Quickly, Butch did as he was told, and the two worked together for hours. Frequently, Jason would have to stop to wait on the customers who had more questions than he'd like. "Just read the paper. Everything I know is in there," he often answered hurriedly, trying to keep an eye on his novice helper. Soon the two had worked out a system where each did his assigned job timed to the slapping of the press. The efficiency of their organized method left small increments of time where Butch found he could talk, something he liked to do.

"Jason? Do you think it's all right for a fellow to change his name?" Butch asked curiously.

"Well, I don't know," Jason answered. "I guess it depends on his reasons."

"Uncle Mike is a swell fellow—took me under wing and taught me everything I know," Butch admitted. "But my father, there was so many of us children, he didn't have time to do anything but work, never showed me nothin'. What I want to do is change my name to be like Uncle Mike's, since he's been more like a father to me."

Actually giving Butch's question some thought, Jason nodded and said, "I don't suppose there's anything wrong with that, you know, if that's the way you feel."

Jutting his heavy jaw out, Butch sort of nodded in agreement, as if he were basing his decision on Jason's advice. He liked discussing this manly thing with Jason, and he liked the fact that Jason treated him with respect.

"By the way, I forgot what your Uncle Mike's last name was," Jason said.

"Cassidy," Butch answered. "I like the way it sounds better than Parker. Butch Cassidy has a nice ring to it, don't you think?"

"Yeah, it sounds decent."

"I told my Uncle Mike that if he'd let me use his name, I'd make it famous," Butch proudly boasted.

"I'm sure you will," Jason chuckled, somehow impressed by the young boy's ambitious qualities.

~

That afternoon, Abe and Lita returned from their honeymoon. Lita was wearing a very large brimmed hat, which she wore smartly tilted at a fashionable angle. It would have kept her dry provided it rained, or at least provided her the shade equivalent of an umbrella. Abe followed her through the front door toting a large amount of heavy luggage. He wore a youthful smile and had a new sparkle in his old eyes. Lita was renewed by a new spirit and loving every minute of it.

"Welcome back, newlyweds," Jason greeted as the two entered. He immediately noticed their good humor, something that showed outwardly like an old coach with a new paint job. "Where'd you go?"

"We been all over," Lita said happily. "Spent some time in Georgetown—and it's a beautiful place. The folks there was so nice to us—made us feel like we was young again."

"Sure was," Abe agreed. He seemed invigorated from the trip rather than tired. He was a new man, one who had persevered and finally found true happiness. And he was aware of his good fortune and was not about to let a moment pass that he didn't enjoy to the fullest. "I'll go get the rest of the things," he said to Lita and went back out.

"What's happening here?" Lita asked, suddenly surprised by what she was seeing. The gloomy and dead office she had left was now a busy mess.

"Big news," Jason said. "Colorado will soon become a state."

"Hallelujah!" Lita cried excitedly. "I know they'll bring some order to this wild and crazy place." She hurried away, excited to be home.

Smiling, Jason got a charge out of Lita and her explosive emotions. He was glad to have her and Abe back, happy to see her round and jolly face. Just knowing that she was in the kitchen gave him a certain sort of satisfaction, a kind of contentment, something akin to security. But then he remembered that he'd soon have to be leaving and he'd have to tell her farewell, something he dreaded.

~

A few more days of hard work continued until the newness of the news subsided. After all was said and done, Jason had printed and sold over 5,000 newspapers, and made a fine profit from selling story rights to other interested newspapers. Not only did the *Advertiser* make money, it made a name for itself, the first newspaper in the territory to report that Colorado was to soon become a state in the centennial summer of the founding of a great nation.

Feeling a sense of pride, Jason reflected some on the little history he knew of Colorado. *Things have come a long way since Coronado first set foot in these mountain ranges in his search for great treasure—which really does exist! And now Colorado will be the richest state in the Union—people will come from all over the world seeking fortune*, he thought with a smile. *And I might have actually played a part in it, reporting this first, making a name for this newspaper.* But then he saddened as he remembered, *It would be a great time if it was just me and Jennifer, like it was when we first arrived here. I'm sure she'll return all enthused and announce she's going to marry Rivers.* He debated, *Should I go ahead and leave before she returns, or wait and see? I just don't understand how people can make the same mistake over and over in their lives. But who knows? Maybe she will have figured out this scoundrel is no good for her, after all.* Then he figured he was a fool for hoping; no doubt Rivers's plans had been successful.

That evening, up in his miserable little room by the light of a flickering lamp, Jason surveyed his situation. He was already packed, had obtained enough money to get him by for a while, and now it was just a matter of leaving. *I'll sleep here tonight—say my good-byes to Lita and Abe in the morning.* Trying to look forward, he had no intentions of leaving a news-making place like Colorado, only he wasn't sure where he might venture. *There are plenty of up-and-coming boomtowns—surely the newspapers there will need somebody with my experience.* He tried to console himself with this knowledge as he fell on the bed, lying on his back with his arms behind his head. He searched the water-stained ceiling for answers, trying to think, but the heartbreak of losing Jennifer throbbed like an abscessed tooth.

Jason's door opened, and Lita came in carrying a tray of homemade cookies and a glass of fresh milk. "I missed my kitchen so much I just had to make somethin'," she said merrily. "These is still hot now, but you . . ." She stopped abruptly as she noticed his things packed and piled in a corner. She stared at them and set the tray down, then glared at Jason. "Where you goin'?"

Feeling like an animal caught in a trap, Jason wasn't ready to tell Lita he was leaving. But he had to say something. "Lita, I have to leave. I don't think I could stand to stay here and work with Jennifer, not if she's going to marry Lance Rivers. It just wouldn't be right, but don't worry—I'll come back and see you from time to time." He gave Lita an impish smile.

"Hush your mouth!" Lita shouted, her eyes bulging. "Have you forgot the miracles the Lord done for you?"

"No," Jason said meekly, "but I don't see what that's got to do with it!"

Lita opened her palm to Jason as she said, "Is Miss Jenny married yet?"

"Well, no," Jason answered. "But I know that's why Rivers took her to his fancy place—to ask her."

Lita placed her hands on her hips and leaned toward Jason, her face in turmoil. "I lose my patience with the likes of your childish ways. I done told you once—the Lord got big plans for you! You'll wake up one mornin' and walk like a new man and throw that cane away! And Miss Jenny, she's a good woman, just a mite confused." Her voice softened now. "Miss Jenny makes mistakes just like we all do, but in the end, the Lord always help her do the right thing. You got to have faith, Mr. Jason, and you know what I'm talkin' about." She paused for a long time, her brown eyes burning a hole in Jason until he had to look away. When she confronted nonsense, she wasn't about to lie back and let it have its way. "Now you promise me," she said, holding her stubby pointing finger out in front of her face, "you promise me you won't leave, not until everything is said and done." Any form of mirth in her had vanished like a fog, now replaced by the fierce and threatening animal known as Lita's scorn.

Shrugging his shoulders, Jason felt like he was a child being scolded by his mother. The problem was, at least with this particular problem, he was right in the middle of it and couldn't see clearly. Worst of all, he wasn't exactly sure what the right thing to do was. His heart begged him to stay, but his pride beckoned for him to leave, and his mind offered little rational thought regarding the matter. He couldn't argue with her for fear she might be right.

Lita was like a windstorm hovering over Jason as he searched for an answer. *Is this what love is good for?* he wondered. *To make fools of men?* Finally, he looked back up to her. "I love Jennifer," he said firmly. "What am I supposed to do?"

"Why, any fool know dat!" Lita said with disgust. "And when you love somebody, you do all you can for dem. You sure don't get up and leave!"

It was all making a little more sense to Jason, and his heart applauded Lita. Pride was losing and had left like a dog with its tail between its legs. "I want to do *something*!" Jason stressed. "I just don't know what to do right now—I can't tell her who to marry or not to marry, Lita."

For a second, Jason thought he noted a motherly smile from Lita, but she was quick with her words. "Then you trust in the Lord—He'll show you what to do," she said calmly, but sternly. "And He'll take care of Miss Jenny, too. Don't think this is all to do with you. Maybe the good Lord is trying to pound some lesson into her too, until she learns from it."

Jason let his eyes roam to the window as he tried to decide. Outside the window was the whole world wide open and waiting for him, but Jennifer wouldn't be in that world. "All right. Maybe I should stay for a while. I don't trust that Rivers anyway. There's something about him, Lita."

Suddenly there was a smile on Lita's face, and her big, brown eyes seemed happy enough. Her entire expression practically glowed in approval. "Dat's good. Now I don't want to hear no more nonsense. Get you a cookie before they get cold." She turned, and her feet scooted across the worn wooden floor and out of the room. The door closed silently behind her, and he could hear her moving away.

Jason tasted a cookie, and it melted in his mouth, a wonderful sugar and vanilla flavor. He felt belittled but enlightened and wiser for it. *How does she do that?* he wondered.

~

Summer-like days were becoming more frequent; cool nights and pleasant days livened the residents of Black Hawk, especially the Cornish men who celebrated any cause with heavy drinking and loud, boisterous laughter. The sloppiness of spring and melting snow and weather that could never make up its mind were soon to be forgotten under clear skies of piercing, brilliant blue. The midday sun was a round, white spot, creating a blinding glare and comforting warmth, never too hot or unbearable.

It was on the middle of a day like this that Jennifer and the children returned, with Lance Rivers driving the open carriage. He wore a fancy vest and was crowned by his shapely black hat, a cheroot protruding from his smiling mouth. He looked every bit the part of the proud and successful family man. Jennifer, on the other hand, wore a long, patterned dress with ruffles on the front and a stylish hat to protect her from the sun. These were obviously new garments, something Rivers had devised, but natural was the pleasant smile she wore on her pretty face. It was the smile of having suffered through undecided nights of dubious torment only to have succeeded by reaching a decision that lifted the burden of stress and uncertainty—a smile that showed self-confidence and the wonder of commitment.

Upon arriving at the office of the *Advertiser*, Jennifer immediately sensed something different, as if a light had been put in the window of a vacant dwelling. First out of the office front door, Lita rushed to them with her arms open to Grant and Abby. "How's my children?" she asked gaily. "Old Lita sure missed y'all!"

When Grant crawled down from his tall thoroughbred and came up on the porch, Lita gave him a bear hug, which he indeed loved though he was a little timid about being hugged in front of everybody. Abby came bounding out of the carriage and was soon in Lita's arms. "We had a great time, Lita," she began, wanting to spill her story. "But I missed you!" Lita squeezed the adoring little girl until Jennifer and Rivers came up on the steps.

Jennifer leaned over Abby and hugged Lita around the neck. "Lita, it's so good to see you again. How was your honeymoon?"

"Oh, child! We had a time!" she bragged, her endearment for Jennifer and the children aglow on her face. "We seen some beautiful country and met some nice folks."

"We did too, Lita," Jennifer added, then a seriousness took precedence over her pleasant smile. She reached over to Rivers, who stood near her on the porch and pulled him closer. His smile was evidence of her news. "Lita, we're going to be married," Jennifer announced, her eyes sparkling.

"Goodness, child!" Lita exclaimed and hugged Jennifer again. "When's y'all's wedding date?"

"We haven't made a date yet," Rivers asserted. "Probably in late July. Depends on how quickly I can make the arrangements." He took a confident pull from his long and thin cigar. "Big arrangements!"

"Oh my," Lita said, translating "big arrangements" into meaning a large and expensive wedding. "Well, y'all come on in—let me fix you something. I know you tired from a long ride."

In the office, hiding behind an open window, Jason overheard everything. He had expected it and was certain of Rivers's scheme, but the reality hit him like a blunt object. He felt sick at his stomach; that old sinking feeling of loss invaded his every emotion. Cringing, he tightened his fist, a sudden anger swelling in him like a fury. But then he heard them coming inside and quickly limped back to the press.

Immediately upon entering the office, Jennifer noticed a difference. The strong smell of fresh ink, the musty smell of machine oil, and literally piles of newspapers stacked and ready for delivery. There was a large and colorful flywheel attached to the press, and the floor hadn't been swept in days. "Jason! What's going on here?" she sniffed.

Jason moved with deliberate slowness as he picked up one of the newspapers announcing the biggest news in years and handed it to her, then turned back to his work, as if she were just another customer seeking information. Jennifer took the newspaper and quickly began to read, her heart picking up tempo as she read. The children had rushed on through and up to their rooms without even noticing Jason. And Lita, sensing an urgency in the moment, took Rivers by the arm and dragged him to the kitchen, leaving Jason and Jennifer alone.

"Why, Jason! This is remarkable! Where'd you get this story? Was it from another newspaper, or is this the first copy? And what's that wheel on the press for?" She soon forgot her announcement and became infatuated with what had been happening in the office.

Remarkably cool, Jason grabbed the ledger book where the *Advertiser* records were kept and hobbled over on his cane and handed it to Jennifer. She briefly scanned the numbers and came to the realization that the newspaper had made more in the week or so that she'd been gone than she'd expected it to make in the first year. "Why, Jason! This is incredible!" She followed Jason over to the press, where he was printing a copy packed with advertisements and what looked like a few stories. "You've turned this business around completely, and in a very short time. Tell me about it."

Coyly, Jason turned and gave her a blank gaze. "Why do you

care, Jennifer? I heard you say you were going to marry Rivers. Do you think he's going to let you run a poor newspaper? Let you stay in this mining hole of a town? Let you stay in this shack of a building?"

Jennifer seemed beside herself with a newfound grief. These were questions she had not yet really considered. What she'd always hoped for was to run her newspaper in a successful fashion, married or not. "This is still my business, Jason! I have an interest in it, and if I want to run it, I will!" she bickered defensively. Her flash of anger surprised her and quickly faded as she drew closer to Jason, who had managed to keep his distance from her until now. "Jason, please don't be this way. I know you're hurt, but we can still work together for now—we can still be friends."

There it is! Jason thought. *The word "friends"! Is she crazy? How can you be friends with a woman you love who's married to another man?* He rolled his eyes in disgust. "Jennifer, I told you how I feel about Rivers. I was going to leave but had a change of heart. If he hurts you or your children in any way, why, I'll—"

"Oh, please don't worry, Jason. He's not that kind of man. All he's shown us is loving affection—he just wants the best for us." She sounded certain enough, she felt. "You know how things are—you might just end up running this paper if I'm not here. Look at the tremendous job you've done, and I wasn't here to help."

"It's not the same, you dumb woman!" Jason shouted, but then he quickly reeled back, offended by his own remark. He glanced up to see the hurt in her eyes. "I didn't mean that, Jennifer, God knows I didn't mean it!"

"I understand," she said softly, not convinced at all that she really did. She could feel Jason's pain and felt sorry for him, but his childish attitude made her angry, and the weariness from the long ride was tugging at her. "Well, I suppose I need to go freshen up. Perhaps you can tell me about the newspaper a little later." With that, she left through the back office door, leaving Jason in a worked-up state of befuddled agitation.

He shook his head dejectedly. *You'd think a scholar from Harvard would know the right words to use!* he thought angrily. *All I did was drive her farther away than ever!*

~

Several days passed, and the tension lightened. Jennifer cleverly worked the details out of Jason about how he had gotten the now-famous story, how he had managed in the office, and in general took care of all of the business affairs. She realized she couldn't have done it any better herself, and she found the heart to compliment the ailing Jason. But the stubborn chip on his shoulder remained.

"We're going now," Jennifer said as she and Lita were leaving. They were off to the dress shop.

Watching them leave, Jason thought, *I guess she's going to see about wedding apparel. I wish she'd open her eyes—she doesn't love Rivers!* This was his way of convincing himself to stay and look out for her, just as Lita had suggested, at least until he saw an end.

About that time, Rivers unsuspectingly stumbled into Jason's world of fanged monsters with whip-like tongues and flaming words of threat, which were as brutal as any pistol-whipping, these monsters with names like bitter anger and astringent remorse—when, in fact, all Rivers did was to step through the front door.

"Hello, Jason. Jennifer around?" Rivers had an easy glide about his walk and a nonchalant attitude.

"She's out," Jason answered coldly.

Rivers seized this moment for something special he'd been waiting for. "Good—good. This gives me a chance to talk to you. I have some ideas and a few propositions for you."

Turning, Jason glared at Rivers as he listened.

"Tell you what, Jason my boy, how'd you like to own this newspaper—and I mean for a cheap price? Sounds like you've done wonders on your own while we were away, not bad for a cripple—of course, I mean nothing personal by that—it's a compliment! Anyway, I don't think Jennifer will be living here that much longer, and I don't think she can make it to work here every day, you know, living out at the ranch and all. But we need a good man like you, somebody we can trust, and I figure the only way that can be worked out is to give you a good chunk of interest in this enterprise, perhaps soon making you sole owner. What do you think?" Rivers smiled, his confidence running high.

"I'll tell you what I think, Rivers!" Jason snapped. "I think you're a shady character, and I think you're hiding something, and I know you can keep your deal and drop dead with it. I wouldn't work for you if it was the last job in the territory." Jason experienced a cool and subtle strength in a surprising flood of courage. "Let me make you a promise, Rivers. If you hurt Jennifer or her children, I'll come after you myself."

The easy attitude with which Rivers had entered was long gone. Normally, he'd slap flies like this away with a quick backhand across the mouth, but something in Jason's eyes prevented him from doing so. Not that the crippled, longhaired man was a physical threat, but there was something in his words that caused Rivers to take it slow and easy. So he tried to reason. "Listen, Jason. I know you're upset, and I know you're very fond of Jennifer. What man wouldn't be? She's an absolute angel. But let me clear this up for you—I only want the best for her and her children, the very best, and believe me, I can offer it."

Totally unconvinced, Jason thrashed out once more. "I don't buy your promises or your fancy ways, Rivers. I say you're hiding something—you're no good!"

For the first time in his life, Rivers was groping for words. Any physical act of violence against a cripple, especially one Jennifer was fond of, would prove completely fruitless. So he relied on his wit, which now let him down. "You're mistaken, Jason. What could I possibly be hiding?" Rivers knew he didn't sound very convincing, so he covered with a fake and friendly smile.

"Just remember what I said, Rivers," Jason said. His words had the ring of iron in them.

Rivers tried to stare down Jason, but realized Jason was too upset to reason with. He turned and left, leaving the door open behind him as he walked down the boardwalk. He stopped and pulled a cigar from inside his vest and lit it as he squinted from the shade of his hat, thinking, *I'll have to take care of that young tough before he causes some real problems*.

PART FOUR

FAITH REVEALED

CHAPTER

~ 19 ~

Anticipation

From a point above Black Hawk on the side of a barren mountain slope, Butch and Grant and Abby were perched like three little birds, observing the busy town below. They sat comfortably in a warm breeze that drifted down the gulch and lifted into the valley below, bringing a pleasant reminder that summer was upon the high country. Expertly, Butch rolled a cigarette and licked the thin paper attentively, absorbed in heavy thought. Abby's attention was on Butch, her smooth young face tanned by her trip to the Rivers Ranch. Grant sat silently on a small boulder, studying the town below, his face shaded by a hat like the one that Rivers wore.

"You know what I think?" Butch muttered, his thoughts carelessly flowing into words as he struck a match and put fire to his smoke. "I think this is going to be the biggest Fourth of July celebration ever. I can feel it in my bones."

"What do they do here for a celebration?" Abby asked. "It seems to me like they celebrate all the time already."

"No, you haven't seen anything like I'm talking about," Butch said knowingly. "You think you see a lot of people on the streets down there, but fact is, most of them are at work in the mines. At any given time, half the men are underground. But when the Fourth comes, almost every one of them will be out on the streets to take part in the contests and eat the good food and celebrate like there ain't no tomorrow."

Grant seemed to suddenly come out of a daydream. "You mean miner contests, like who can drill a hole in a rock the fastest?"

"Yeah, stuff like that," Butch said.

"I've seen that before back in Virginia City," Grant said, reflecting. "They get awfully wild, singing and dancing, and it goes on all night."

"That it does," Butch agreed. "But this year is going to be extra-special—Colorado about to become a state and all. You know, they might have some contests for us too, like I hear there's going to be a blueberry pie eating contest, and you can't use your hands."

Abby burst into laughter at the thought of Butch burying his face in a runny blueberry pie. "You could never win," she giggled. "That big Timmy Blaylock from school could eat more pies than anybody!"

"I don't care!" Butch insisted. "I was just thinking about getting a free pie out of the deal."

"Yeah," Grant said, thinking about it. "We couldn't really lose. I love blueberry pie."

"We had pecan pie at the Rivers Ranch," Abby boasted.

"What's a pecan?" Butch asked.

"It's a nut," Grant answered.

Butch seemed to digest this and store it away, then asked, "What was it like at Rivers Ranch?"

Grant was still under the influence of the grand impression the ranch had made on him. He was more than ever taken by Lance Rivers, the greatest man he had ever known. The marriage announcement had made the hairs on the back of his neck stand up with excitement, the thought that Lance Rivers would be his stepfather and the idea of living on such a fine estate full of thoroughbred horses. It was more than he could fathom, and he now constantly thought of it and of all the possibilities that lay before him. "If I was ever rich," he speculated, "I'd have me a place just like it, a big horse ranch spread out in a green mountain valley with a fancy ranch house and cook and bunkhouse. It's the nicest place I've ever seen."

"Wow," Butch said, trying to imagine. "That Rivers, he's the kind of fella I'd like to be like, although I don't know that I'd ever want to get married."

Quickly, Abby gave Butch a poke in the ribs with her little elbow, causing him to cringe. "You don't know!" she corrected. "I might end up being real pretty, and you might want to marry me then."

"Well," Butch stammered, "you might be right, Abby. Most of these mining town women don't look much different from the men, but in your case I'd have to give it some serious consideration."

Abby seemed satisfied for the time being with Butch's answer, although she wasn't sure what "consideration" meant. Yet she was quick to resolve any over-inflated ideas about smelly horse ranches. "A real lady wouldn't be living on a stinking horse ranch," she said, inviting argument. "The Rivers Ranch is nice, but there's nothing for a lady to do, and it's not busy like town. When I grow up, I might live for a while in Central City staying at places like the Teller House, then I might go to Denver for a while and wear nice clothes and be a real lady. Someday I might even go to Frisco out in Californy."

Nodding, Butch admired Abby's ambitious dreams, but Grant just took a deep breath in disgust. "Abby, you don't know what you're talking about. It takes a lot of money to live like that—where are you going to get all that money?"

"Butch doesn't have any problem getting money!" she stormed. "I might just marry Butch, and we could go everywhere together!"

Grant rolled his eyes and glanced at Butch, who shrugged his shoulders innocently. "I guess it's true," Butch sighed. "Money always has seemed easy to come by. The only problem is—" He dropped his bright eyes and hesitated. "The only problem is, you got to move around, go where the money's at. My Uncle Mike says we might be moving on before long—says this place might be getting a little too civilized."

Stunned, Abby just stared at Butch in disbelief. "You don't mean you're leaving Black Hawk!? You can't leave! What about me?"

Now embarrassed, Butch put on his most honest and convincing face. "Abby, someday I'll find you, and that's a promise."

Throwing her glance up into the mountaintops, a slight breeze lifted Abby's dark hair gently and let it fall back across her face, but she didn't bother to push it away. She was rudely reminded that she had loved her father and he went away forever, and now she had finally found a good friend and he was going to leave also. It left her feeling helpless and weak; even her stormy temper wouldn't rouse to lift her from the gloom.

"Don't worry, Abby," Butch begged. "We won't be going anywhere right away—I'll be around."

This perked Abby up and, as she turned back to Butch, a slight smile shaped her lips. He picked up a rock and tossed it down the steep hill before them. All three watched its tumbling descent quietly for a long time, until it bounced out of sight far below.

~

Lita was bustling about the stove, cleaning up after breakfast, when Jennifer came back to the kitchen for another cup of coffee. Jason was busy up front in the office because the newspaper business had picked up quite a bit since the sensational story. With a proper flywheel now on the press, it worked as smooth as a clock with new works. "It's nice to be busy," Jennifer commented. "Reminds me of the days in Virginia City."

"Yes, ma'am," Lita mumbled, not looking up. There was every hint from her movements that she wanted to talk, and Jennifer quickly picked up on this, so she sat down at the table, ready to listen. "So, how's married life?"

"Miss Jenny," Lita began, setting her rag down that she'd been wiping with and coming over to the table to sit across from Jennifer. "It's a wonderful thing. I reckon the Lord was in it 'cause I never been so happy. It's the first time in my long life that I had a real last name that was mine. The plantation I was raised on belonged to a family named Jackson, and they always said that was my last name. But I knew it wasn't—it was just something they used so they'd know who I belonged to. Abe said he picked his own name after he was freed, so if he picked it, then it's his real name, and now Washington is my real name." A tear flecked her eye, and she quickly wiped it away.

"I'm so happy for you, Lita," Jennifer said, consoling her. "I hope I'm as happy as you after I get married."

This is where Lita wanted the conversation to turn, and she adjusted her posture and addressed Jennifer with a different tone. "Are you sure this Mr. Rivers is the right man?" she asked, knowing full well that Jennifer knew what she meant.

"Well," Jennifer hesitated, "of course I'm sure." She seemed surprised at Lita's prying.

"He's a nice man and all, a gentleman, I suppose," Lita said, her expression showing uncertainty. "But you hardly know him—he's gone all the time."

"He has his horse deals and business to tend to, Lita, and it sometimes takes him away for a while," Jennifer said in weak defense.

Lita wasn't convinced Jennifer remembered what true love was—or knew what true love was, considering the younger woman's past mistakes. "Miss Jenny, when a woman loves a man, it's all she can think about. Yet some folks marries for convenience and some for other reasons, but when it's love, there ain't no doubt. You should know—you told me how it was with your first husband."

Letting her thoughts drift, Jennifer indeed remembered how she had felt about Drake, her fist husband—and it was true, she was obsessed with the emotions of love, but that was long ago. "I was only a young girl then, Lita, and very susceptible to Drake's romancing ways. I think as a woman gets older, she looks for different qualities—has a better sense of judgment."

Shaking her head, Lita disagreed. "I'm a lot older than you, and love still got my goat! If you sure about it, well then, there's nothing I can say. I just want you to be sure, 'cause this Mr. Rivers, why, he could convince anybody to do what he want."

Jennifer reached over the table and let her long fingers rest on Lita's hand. "He's been wonderful to me, and I don't see any reason why we can't have a good life together."

"I hope Mr. Rivers is a God-fearing man," Lita asserted.

"He said he was raised in a Christian home," Jennifer reminded Lita. "I guess anyone can stand a little improvement in their ways."

"I hope so," Lita said, rising from the table. "You better pray to the Lord for guidance, make sure you doing the right thing." She then opened the back door, letting in the blinding sunlight, and stepped outside, leaving Jennifer alone.

Sitting there motionless, Jennifer thought she'd answered all of these questions in her own mind before Lance had even asked for her hand in marriage. Yet a dubious foreboding remained, creating a slight but distressing concern. Lita had been successful in planting a seed of doubt in a garden of vague suspicion.

~

Lance Rivers let it be known publicly that he was getting married, and it would be a grand affair. He wanted the Fourth of July celebrations to be over and not confused with his wedding. "What do you think?" he asked Jennifer as he sat across from her at a dinner table on the patio at the Teller House. It was a warm and pleasant evening; the last of the lingering sunlight had painted the sky a pale violet.

Smiling, Jennifer was persuaded by the romantic atmosphere and looked at Lance with dreamy eyes. "It sounds like you've planned everything. July fifteenth will be a day we can always remember."

Rivers smiled and tipped his glass of expensive sherry, sipping it smoothly. "I want you to be the best-looking bride this county ever laid eyes on, and I told Jake that. I trust you've let him measure you for a fit."

"Oh yes," Jennifer said. "I picked out a dress from a catalog, and he said he'd have it ready in plenty of time."

"He'd better," Rivers said forcefully. "I've already paid him for it." Then he smiled and said, "I trust you're not angry with me for making our announcement in the *Register*. They have connections with the society up here, and I thought it only seemed proper. I wouldn't want you to have to write and run your own announcement in the *Advertiser*."

"Of course I'm not mad," Jennifer said gaily. "We've been busy since Jason's big day, but he's still fuming from our announcement, and I wouldn't want him to have to print anything about it."

Turning serious, Rivers leaned across the table closer to Jennifer. "This Jason concerns me. I'm wondering if he won't cause trouble. He's let it be known that he doesn't like me. He told me so himself."

"Jason's not a troublemaker," Jennifer assured him.

"But there was a time that there was something between you two. Am I correct?" Rivers asked, a thoroughness in his voice.

"Well, yes. I guess there was," Jennifer answered bashfully. "It seems like so long ago. He used to be different, but the accident changed him entirely. He's like a different man. The man before—"

Rivers flashed his hands up as if he didn't want to hear any more. "I'm just making sure," he said, a degree of proclamation in his tone. "I don't want any ghosts from the past interfering with our plans, or jealous suitors, if you can understand."

The talk caused Jennifer to lose some mental balance, for the fondness for Jason remained, and she didn't like any conspiracy against him. "Jason's a good man," she defended. "He's had his troubles."

"I'm sure he has," Rivers agreed, "but I've learned to never underestimate the desperate." There was a force in his gesture that Jennifer didn't care for, as if implying Jason was a threat to her well-being. She regarded Jason as family and was prepared to argue that Lance's worries were unnecessary.

But Rivers spoke first, a grave regret in his eyes. "Jennifer, I know you may find this difficult, but something has come up. I'm going to have to take a trip, but I'll be back to enjoy the Fourth of July celebrations with you. This is a deal I've waited years for, and it involves a large sum of money and many fine horses."

"Oh?" Jennifer uttered, disappointment distorting her face. "Why can't you wait until later?"

"Because I'm not the one setting the date," Rivers huffed, as if there was something that existed that was actually out of his control. "A good friend of mine from Kentucky will be bringing a load of horses to Nebraska. This has been in the works for some time."

"Well," Jennifer sighed, disheartened, "if you must go, then you must go." It was apparent that these trips did little to comfort her, and Rivers recognized her grief.

"But let me say this," he continued. "After we're married, these trips will be far and few in between. I'll have a large enough herd to breed my own string of thoroughbreds, and anyone who wants to buy them will have to come here. And if I must take a trip—you're welcome to come."

This did little to comfort Jennifer. Big talk about big deals had kept her first husband away most of the time; something she couldn't bear. But Lance assured her that things would be different, and she attempted to replace her worried expression with a smile. "I'm sure you won't want to miss the Fourth! I doubt there'll be a sober man in town."

Rivers chuckled, thinking she was probably right. But there would be good food and goodwill and dances and balls and on and on too. It was an event of good cheer that nobody would want to miss. "I'll be leaving in the morning," he said, now feeling a little better about his untimely departure. "If there are any wedding-arrangement problems, you see to them just as you want because I want you to be happy. Order the finest of everything—money is not an issue. This will be the best day of our lives!" He toasted the air with his wineglass and tilted it until it drained. When he set it down on the table, he said intimately, "Jennifer, you're looking at the happiest man in the world!"

Ordinarily, Jennifer never experienced emotions overwhelming enough to cause her to lose control, but for a brief moment she felt a joy that unsettled her. It was as if she'd been wishfully looking into a dreamworld and all of a sudden found herself living in that very world. Briefly, she thought she could see happiness and goodness just a breath away, promises of her life to come.

Rivers took advantage of her instant frailty and came around the table and, lifting her, took her in his arms and buried her in a long and passionate kiss. Other patrons stopped their conversation to witness the disrespectful exhibition, but Jennifer didn't care—she was lost in a dream. Lance Rivers certainly didn't care what anybody else thought.

~

The few weeks edged by slowly for Jennifer as she thoroughly attended every wedding arrangement until all was settled. Her dress was a beautiful piece of work tailored for the wealthy; its long, flowing trailer of silk and a soft veil of lace gave it an angelic appearance. The cake would be a five-decked construction of white icing decorations, with a bridal scene at the very top. The invitations had been endless, for the list Rivers left with Jennifer included every well-to-do person in the territory, but she'd printed the invitations by herself on fine paper and eventually got them all mailed. Jason had been silent with remorse, and she hadn't had the heart to ask him for help with her wedding preparations.

Central City and Black Hawk had been busy with their own preparations. The Fourth of July was by far the biggest event of the year, and banners were strung from building to building and draped over the hurried streets. The weathered gray boards and tints of dusty brown took on the American colors of red, white, and blue as streamers and flags rippled in the mountain breeze. Outdoor stands were erected for contests and bands and tasteful delights of all sorts. More people poured into the settlement than could be imagined, sleeping wherever they could find a place to relax, while children ran wild and unattended.

There was a spirit in the air of immense anticipation, which flowed like an electrical current. It was July 3, 1876, the centennial year of a country built on freedom, and the Territory of Colorado had every reason to believe that she would soon become a state of this great country. In essence, the party had already begun; the bars, saloons, and dance halls were overflowing and carrying their festivities into the streets.

But Jennifer didn't feel like celebrating. There'd been no word from Lance, and he had promised to be back in time to enjoy the holiday with her. It became apparent that his routine of extended trips that left her unknowing and uncertain were continuing. Frightening memories of Drake and his lengthy absences left her depressed. Nothing good had come of his absences, which eventually left her a widow. Moping around, she tried to let the newspaper office keep her busy, but her mind remained on Lance. Jason simply ignored her, put out by her plans to marry a man he considered too shady.

Finally, ground down by worry until an anger arose, Jennifer sought Lita to talk to. She found her out back of the building, hanging wet clothes in the warm sunshine. Lita knew right away that Jennifer needed help, just like she knew when a child needed comforting. The slight wind ruffled Jennifer's dress as she came toward Lita, her arms folded across her chest and a betrayed expression on her face.

"Sit right down there on dat old milk stool," Lita said, happy to be of service. "What's worrying you, child?"—as if she didn't know.

"What does he think he's doing? I must not be very important to him if he can't come back when he says he will! Wouldn't surprise me if he didn't even show up for his own wedding!" Jennifer found it easy to vent her anger with Lita, who patiently listened and always seemed to have the right answers.

With strong hands, Lita forced the wooden pegs over the heavy denim she hung out to dry. The wet clothes had the fragrant and clean smell of store-bought soap. The clothesline wasn't very high, so she could reach it, and when she hung Abe's long overalls, she had to drape them over to the next cord. "You just angry," Lita said into the bright daylight. The sun was so severely clear in the mountain sky that the rays seemed almost piercing. "Mr. Rivers, he must be an important man to have to worry with business at a time like this. Most folks won't be doin' no business tomorrow—they'll be having fun instead."

"Why does he do this to me?" Jennifer asked, deflated. She had begun to feel sorry for herself and wanted Lita to assure her that things would be all right.

"What's most important in a man's mind—dat be what he take care of first," Lita said, a statement she knew for a fact.

Truth was often enlightening and sometimes unpleasant. But as Jennifer thought about what Lita had said, she realized it was certain. Just like long ago, she knew her husband, Drake, loved her dearly. But his interests carried him far away and kept him for lengthy periods. *It's happening again*, she thought miserably. *And we're not even married yet*. She swelled with self-pity and gave Lita a forlorn glance. "What should I do, Lita?" she asked sorrowfully.

There was no doubt in Lita's mind as to what Jennifer should do.

She clamped the last wooden peg on one of Grant's white shirts and came over closer to the younger woman. She leaned over to her, her eyes lifted in a kind of spiritual faith. "Miss Jenny, you better go and get on your knees and pray to God about this with all your might."

Glancing up, Jennifer squinted into the light and saw Lita's face as a shadow. "Yes, I will. But you know, now that I think about it, I don't think Abe would ever leave you like that and let you worry."

"Heavens no, honey," Lita assured her. "Abe wouldn't do that."

"And," Jennifer continued, the thoughts tormenting her, "Jason wouldn't do that to me either."

"No, ma'am. He wouldn't," Lita confirmed.

Standing slowly, Jennifer glanced around the mountainsides that surrounded Black Hawk as if she'd suddenly become aware. There was a slow understanding taking place, and she realized she hadn't even prayed yet, but a prayer was already being answered. "I am the light," an inner voice echoed. A strange sort of comfort eased her anxiety; she had the feeling that her eyes were being opened, as if she had suffered through some kind of blindness. After all this time, she realized that there was just a fine line between dreams and memories.

Lita watched closely as Jennifer moved softly across the packed dirt toward the back door. She had more than a notion that something spiritual had just happened, that Jennifer had been made to see. Lita experienced a simple joy that lit her face into a glorious smile. She knew the Lord had been at work right before her very eyes.

Finishing the afternoon in the office with the disheartened Jason, Jennifer had a quick dinner, listened to the children tell of their exciting plans for the holiday, then slipped off to bed early with the excuse that she was very tired. But up in her room she sat near the window and watched the Chinese-made fireworks flashing in the sky. The smell of black powder hung in the air, with little white clouds drifting above the streets. The Cornish miners had joined in singing their frolicking songs with great heartiness. Almost every lamp in town glittered in the increasing darkness. It was a time of joy and celebration.

Yet Jennifer felt left out, deliberately forgotten. *How can he be so insensitive?* she wondered. Part of her wanted to simply disappear, never to be seen again. Another side fanned the flames of anger, provoking her to take a stand and be heard. *Maybe there is a logical explanation for him being late—something out of his control*, she reasoned. *He might even show up this evening*, she wished silently but realized her vanity was stoking her saddened heart.

Without giving another thought to her dwindling hopes, she folded her hands and bowed her head in prayer. "Dear God," she whispered, "I don't have any idea what's happening, nor what I've gotten myself into. I'd rather be a good servant more than anything. Please help, show me what I should do. In Christ's name," she prayed, "Amen."

After she blew out the lantern, Jennifer crawled into bed. The fireworks continued their irregular explosions, sounding like gunshots, while the flashes flickered on her wall like lightning. A small shard of rage stung her, letting its presence be known, but confined itself within the realm of rationality. *I will not condone being neglected and alone and forgotten*, she thought determinedly.

CHAPTER

20

The Fourth

Morning started with a bang as a group of riders thundered down the street, firing their guns in the air. Startled, Jennifer sat straight up in bed, alarmed at the gunfire, then remembered it was the Fourth of July. From her bed, she could see the extreme blueness of the sky as a cool morning breeze filled the room. For once, the stamp mills were silent, and the air seemed clean and fresh. It was a day of celebration, but she couldn't help but wonder about Lance and their plans.

Rising from bed, Jennifer readied herself, questions remaining unanswered in her mind. She was mostly wondering about the future, wondering if she was really making the right decision. Surely Lance had been tied up with his business dealings, something that rather disgusted her. But stubbornness pulled her forward—she was determined to have a good time and set her worries aside, if nothing else, for the sake of the children.

~

Downstairs, Lita whirled about the kitchen, dressed in a colorful print dress. She wore a white apron over her red dress with white trim, careful to keep the dress spotless, her hair pulled back neatly in a bun. Humming a cheerful tune over the sizzling sausages that fried in a skillet, she made quick work of preparing breakfast.

The thumping of a cane from the stairway announced Jason before he entered. "Good morning, Lita," he said stoically as he crossed the room to the coffeepot. Lita noticed he was dressed a little nicer than usual and had brushed his beard and long hair, something of a change for him. He was obviously in a hurry.

"Mornin', Mr. Jason," Lita replied, her eyes searching him for clues. "Where you off to in such a rush?"

"I've got plans," Jason answered quickly as he sat down at the table. "Big day in town, you know."

"Oh, I know all right!" Lita said as she fixed Jason a plate of scrambled eggs and sausages. "Abe gonna try his luck at one of the contests—I can't wait." She brought Jason's steaming plate over to the table and set it before him, a curiosity in her expression. "What kind of plans you got? We all gonna go down to the parade and later watch the contests."

"I'll be around," was all Jason said.

Lita knew when she was being cut off too quickly, but her nature didn't allow for any such nonsense. "You ain't gonna spend no time with Miss Jenny and the children? They be out havin' fun today, too."

"I'll be around," Jason answered impatiently, resisting Lita's prying.

Sensing Jason's discord, Lita reminded him, "Never saw a man dat was happy with himself once he give up. And I know you got the stuff that makes you special. All you need is a little faith, 'cause like I been telling you, the Lord got big plans for you." She stood with her hands on her hips as he tried to eat.

"What is this, a sermon?" Jason protested. "All I wanted was breakfast!" A slight anger raised the tone of his voice as he glanced up at Lita. Her face now took on an appearance of subtle patience, but the forcefulness remained.

"I just worry about you, dat's all," she said sternly. "If you don't never do nothin' else, just promise me you'll never give up! Don't never give up!"

Turning, Jason stopped eating for a moment as he studied Lita, her big brown eyes locked in on him. "Lita," he said softly, "I'm just a man—and a cripple at that. I've done all I can do, and now I can't change what's going on around me. It's very simple."

"It is simple!" Lita scorned. "Your faith is weak. Things happen and things change!" She turned and moved to tend the stove as she continued talking. "You won't be a cripple forever—then what'll be your excuse?"

Jason didn't like arguing with Lita because she somehow always seemed to make more sense than he could debate with. "Thanks for the breakfast, Lita." Leaving his plate unfinished, he stood with the aid of his cane and went to the door that led to the front office. Stopping before he exited, he mumbled, "As for the sermon . . ." But he thought better of what he wanted to say and simply left.

Shaking her head, Lita knew all too well that Jason was at a turning point where he might go either way, a life of misery or a life of promise. She was quick to offer a little prayer for his benefit as she wiped off the table.

The racket of stomping feet grew louder as the children stormed down the stairs and into the kitchen, anxious and excited. "I hope breakfast is ready so we can hurry up and eat!" Abby called as she raced into the kitchen past Lita.

Grant was quick to get to the table as well. "I told you it was ready, Abby!" he scolded. "I could smell those sausages all the way up in my room."

"Yes, it's ready," Lita confirmed as she prepared their plates. She didn't want to show it, but she was about as excited as the children.

When Abe came in, he wore a new pair of blue-suspender overalls and a wide smile to match. "I'm hungry," he growled like a bear, teasing Abby who giggled at his antics.

"You better eat good. You'll need all your strength swingin' that big hammer," Lita said encouragingly. She couldn't wait to see Abe compete in the miner contests of strength, speed, and power.

"Do you think you can win?" Grant asked with his mouth full.

"I sure hope so," Abe replied. "Lita might be disappointed if I don't."

"You hush!" Lita scolded with a faint smile. It was true, she wanted her big man to do well, but he didn't *have* to win.

"Some of those hard rock miners are pretty good at driving a drill," Grant reminded Abe.

"I know," Abe responded, now hungrily digging in to his plate piled high.

"What? You don't think he can do it?" Abby argued. "I bet he could smash the whole rock in two with one blow!"

"What are you fussing about?" Jennifer asked Abby as she entered. "You sound like a bunch of magpies carrying on down here."

"Don't you look nice!" Lita complimented as she studied Jennifer's dress. The newspaperwoman wore a light and flowing indigo cotton dress and a pleasant smile. A red and white scarf around her neck looked smartly patriotic.

"Thank you, Lita." Jennifer fixed a cup of coffee and stood watching the gang fill up on breakfast at the table. "There's going to be a lot going on, and I want you children to stay close to me, you hear?"

"Yes, ma'am," Grant and Abby chimed together.

"Lita, I'll help you carry the pies to the pie-eating stand. I think they'll be having that first, won't they?"

"Afternoon," Lita answered. "There's so many things goin' on, it'll be hard to keep up with everything."

Turning, Jennifer glanced around and then peeked into the front office, then looked back at Lita. "Have you seen Jason?"

Rolling her eyes away, Lita answered, "Yes, ma'am. I'm afraid he's already ate and gone."

A subtle displeasure flashed in Jennifer's face. She was of the mind that Jason would be present, since Rivers hadn't shown up, and maybe have fun with her and the children for the holiday. But then again, she realized she always took Jason for granted, having grown used to his loyalty. He was like a member of the family, always present through bad times and good times. A wave of sadness touched her momentarily as she regretted that he wouldn't be spending the day with them.

~

Festivities in Black Hawk and Central City got off to a roaring start first thing in the morning. By 10:00 A.M. the streets were bristling with citizens dressed in their finest attire, packed a half dozen deep on the boardwalks. Red, white, and blue banners draped over every roof and rail, while hundreds of people were garbed in the same colors. The soft summer breeze drifted down the gulch carrying the first notes of a parade march, while onlookers stood on their tiptoes to get a glimpse of the high-stepping color guard. The crowd broke into loud cheers with the thrill of drums and horns and tunes from the miner's guardsmen while they proudly marched by. By the end of the parade, the watchers moved to hear the day's speakers from a high stand looming over the townsmen. The oratory was for the Spirit of '76 and promises of statehood from glassy-eyed politicians, eager to stir the emotions. The townsfolk cheered until they were hoarse and slapped each other on the back in congratulation. The celebration had begun.

After picnic lunches of fried chicken and clabbered cheese, the excitement escalated in expectation of the afternoon's contests. Saloons had arranged makeshift bars consisting of a wide board stretched across two kegs in front of their businesses in order to view the spectacle on the streets, while the dance hall girls added to the gaiety in their colorful dresses and long-feathered plumes and overpowering fragrance.

Sitting in a chair in front of one of the saloons, Jason held a frothy draw of amber ale as he watched the frenzy in the crowded streets. He looked at the crowd, then back at his beer. There was something going on in his mind and in his heart, an inner battle of sorts. It boiled down to two choices—he could either resort to drowning his heartaches in alcohol and become numb to the world, or he could get up, find Jennifer and the children, and join in the fun. Feeling sorry for himself had become the business of the day for so long that he hardly knew any other way. But something tugged at him; perhaps it had to do with Lita's breakfast talk about faith.

Carefully, Jason took a light sip from the tart brew and made a face. For some reason unknown, the drink didn't taste right. Perhaps it was his inner way of rebelling, a last savage instinct for survival. *I suppose there are basically two kinds of people*, he thought. *There's those who are weak and give up, then there are those who always keep trying no matter what the odds*. He dwelt on this for some time, then looked at the heavy glass of beer and set it down. Slowly, he reached for his cane hooked on the back of his chair and came to his feet.

"You're not leaving, are you, honey?" a sweet-talking saloon girl called from a few feet away. "Beer's on the house today."

"Thanks," Jason said and smiled as he limped toward the few steps that led down into the crowded street.

~

Big Abe pushed his way through the throng of people with Lita in tow, and Lita held Jennifer's hand as she pulled her along, while Grant and Abby clutched Jennifer's dress, tagging along behind her. Their small train squirreled and weaved, fighting the mass of festivity. "I can't see anything!" Abby screamed from behind, angered by being crushed by the crowd. Abe heard her complaint and turned around, facing the women and Grant. He handed Lita his derby hat. "Here, Miss Abby," he said as he lifted Abby into his huge arms and then set her up on his wide shoulder. She towered a good six feet above the ground, high enough to see everything. A wide and excited smile crossed her pretty young face as she clutched his gray head with her little hands. Abe turned and continued leading everyone else.

The next big event was the fireman's footrace. Taking a position on a high boardwalk, Jennifer and company watched eagerly as eight spans of firemen struggled in their harnesses to pull each hose cart in a race against time. The lively crowd cheered them on as their faces grimaced in pain and their legs became like rubber, fighting the weight that held them back. "C'mon, Benjamin!" a small Cornish woman yelled through her cupped hands. "Let that mule in you come out!"

Straining and groaning at the end of the finish line, the exhausted firemen fell in a heap, gasping for air. At the same time, a pistol was fired in the air to start another group into a panicked frenzy of muscle strain and sweat against the ticking seconds of the time clock. Onlookers screamed at the firemen as they raced by, encouraging them to use every last ounce of strength. When the last hose cart passed Jennifer, Lita, Abe, and the children, the crowd broke into heavy applause and cheers for the hearty firemen. Soon after, the winners were announced and rewarded with a shower of beer. Hearty laughter broke out as all the firemen congratulated each other and tipped the bottoms of their pint-sized mugs in the air, celebrating.

"We got to get on down the street," Lita said, tugging at Abe's arm. "They'll be starting the drilling contest soon."

Abe's face lightened up. "You're right—let's get goin'." Still carrying Abby on his shoulder, Abe led the way, again pulling everyone behind him until they came to the roped-off pavilion, where brawny miners warmed up for the test of speed and skill at drilling through solid rock.

"Here, Miss Abby," Abe said as he gently set her down next to Lita. "I got to go now. You be sure and pull for me."

"Don't worry. I know you'll win!" Abby said excitedly, her eyes sparkling with merriment.

Abe stepped over the rope and went up on the huge platform and talked to the judge for a moment, then went and took his place near a huge boulder of granite. He picked up the hammer and warmed up a bit, swinging it in the air. Glancing around, Abe expected his drill-turner to show up at any minute, a fellow he'd practiced with named Sam Sloop. Slowly, the crowd grew, pushing Lita, Jennifer, and the children tighter into the rope. Most of the murmur was concerning bets on the different drill teams.

Each team consisted of two men, the hammer man and the drill-turner. The drills by regulation were seven-eighths of an inch in diameter and varied in length. Each drill had a star-shaped bit on the end, and each drill team had its own secret prescription for sharpening these steel tools to take the biggest bite out of hard rock. The drill-turner squatted down by the slab of Gunnison granite, cut six feet thick and flat on the top, holding the drill erect and straight, rotating it between each slam of the hammer. The hammerman's job was to land as many powerful blows on the small end of the drill stem as possible in the given fifteen minutes. Sometime during the interval, the hammerman and drill-turner would swap positions, giving the exhausted hammer-wielder a chance to catch his wind. A winner was announced after measurements were taken to see which team had drilled the deepest hole. A grave danger awaited each drill-turner, for a missed blow with an eight-pound sledgehammer could have devastating effects on his exposed hands.

Each mining camp in the gulch had its own champion, and hundreds of gold dollars backed these men. Townsmen wagered with each other, betting everything from gold to mules to wagons, for this competition was the grand event of the day. Jennifer watched nervously as Abe warmed up, practicing swinging his sledge. The crowd pushed from behind even tighter. "Where's Abe's partner?" Jennifer asked Lita.

"I don't know, Miss Jenny. He should have been here by now."

Abe glanced around nervously, his eyes searching the crowd for Sam. Most of the other drill teams were ready as the judge waited for the crowd to build to peak excitement before starting the contest. The pushing and shoving for position to watch the contest became almost unbearable when Jennifer felt a hand tightly clutch her arm. She turned and unexpectedly saw Jason standing next to her, smiling through his beard. "Can't miss this one," he said.

A surprised look held Jennifer's face, but secretly she was glad Jason had decided to join them in the festivities. "Yes," she answered, not quite sure what was the appropriate thing to say. "In all these years in mining towns, I've never watched a drilling contest before."

"I'm sure you won't be disappointed," Jason said with certainty. He nervously fidgeted with his beard. "Though sometimes these contests can get a bit gory."

"Oh?" Jennifer answered. "How's that?"

Lita had noticed Jason, but continued to watch Abe, who scanned the crowd with a worried look on his face. His partner was yet to show. Grant and Abby held tightly to the rope in front of Jennifer and Lita, not giving up their good spectator positions.

"I'm here, Abe!" a swaggering man yelled as he came up the back of the platform to join Abe. It was Sam Sloop, and he was already drunk as a skunk. "We'll tear them up, by golly!"

The disheartened expression that swept Abe's face practically silenced the crowd. Rushing over, the tall judge grabbed Sam by the arm and swung him around, almost causing him to fall down in his drunkenness. "Sam! You've had too many! I'm afraid I have to disqualify you from this contest! It's too dangerous to let you compete like this, friend! " He then pushed a protesting Sam into the waiting arms of some other men, who helped him off the platform. Noticing the disappointment in Abe's face, the judge turned and held his hands up to the crowd to silence them. "It looks like our blacksmith is without a drill-turner. Could I have a volunteer?"

The hush that fell over the onlookers quickly went into a heavy murmur, everyone voicing an opinion, but no volunteers raised their hands. "Why, that man's a blacksmith—he ain't no hammer man!" one miner observed, a word of caution for anyone who might volunteer the safety of his hands. "Yeah, but he's an expert with a hammer, and I hear tell he has a secret for sharpening drill bits that's the best in the gulch!" another burly miner replied. "But he's old!" another argued. "Yeah, but look at the arms on that rascal—he's strong as a mule." "He'll never last!" came the voice of another.

Lita turned, looking back at Jason and Jennifer, her eyes wet with tears. She was heartbroken at Abe's disappointment. Jennifer clutched Jason's arm with both her hands in an icy grip. "Jason! Can't you do something? Talk one of these miners into helping Abe."

Glancing around, Jason could see most of the miners were men of heavy experience; there was nothing he could tell them about mining or a drilling contest. "Jennifer, I can't convince these men to get up there. Why, only a fool would do something like that!" Half-shrugging his shoulders, he noticed that Lita was staring at him. "What?"

"You get up there, Mr. Jason! I know you can do it!"

Jason felt Jennifer's fingernails bite into his arm as her grip increased. He turned to see her green eyes penetrating his own, the kind of look she hadn't given him since the days when there was promise between them. This look, for a moment, took Jason away as he felt his heart skip a beat. Out of habit, he opened his mouth to say something, but nothing came out—it seemed her grip and steady stare had paralyzed him.

"Mr. Jason!" Lita said impatiently as she poked at him. "Get up there and help Abe!"

As if rudely awakened from a dream, Jason turned back to Lita. "Are you crazy?" he said. "Can't you see I'm a cripple—all I'll do is embarrass Abe. I've never even held a drill bit, much less turned one under a hammer, and there isn't any way I could swing the sledge. Abe would have to hammer the entire fifteen minutes!"

"Where's your faith? Ain't I told you the Lord is with you, Mr. Jason?" Lita pleaded, as dead serious as she'd ever been.

Exasperated, Jason turned back to Jennifer for help but found a want in her eyes that no man could deny.

Up on the platform, the judge had been patient for Abe's sake. He again asked the crowd for a volunteer, and there were no responses. Sorrowfully, he looked back at Abe. There was no need to say anything, since a man couldn't compete alone. Slowly, Abe set the hammer down and began walking around the slab to leave the platform.

Suddenly the crowd burst into a cheer and then roaring laughter. Jason gimpily climbed the steps up to the platform using his cane. The drilling contestants were just as surprised and couldn't hold their laughter. "A cripple!" one of them called mockingly, and the laughter became contagious. Even the judge couldn't refrain from a big smile that creased his face. "Are you sure you know what you're doing?" he asked Jason as he reached the platform.

Giving the judge an icy-cold stare, Jason replied, "Of course not!"

"Then God be with you," the judge said and looked to Abe for approval. "You have a volunteer. Will this man do?"

Abe was the only person who wasn't smiling or laughing. His expression was one that challenged any man to question him. "This is the bravest man in the gulch," he said in his deep voice. Quickly, a silence fell over the other miners, as well as the eager audience. Abe went back to his position, rolled down his suspenders, and removed his shirt. The sun shone brightly from straight above, out of a cloudless, piercing blue sky. A warm breeze drifted down from Castro Hill as anticipation grew. Abe's huge chest muscles cast dark shadows on his brown skin as he spat on his callused hands and picked up the sledge. He gave Jason a quick glance, a look of confidence and determination.

If only Jason felt the same way, he'd have felt a lot better. Fear swept through him, almost turning his stomach upside-down. *I'm a complete fool!* he thought hopelessly as he removed a light jacket and squatted down near the slab of rock. The tool lay before him, a long steel rod that had grown hot in the sun. He picked it up, the black steel burning his soft hands. *Well, I'm committed now,* he decided as he held the rod erect and over a mark on the granite. Taking one last look at the crowd, he immediately spotted Jennifer near the front, her eyes on him. These were appraising eyes, eyes that sent many messages from a lovely face full of hope. He felt a newfound strength and cast his glance up to Abe, who had the kind of determination like that found in one of the locomotives fighting its way uphill. Jason nodded, indicating that he was as ready as he could get, his cane lying on the boards beside him.

Sensing that peak anticipation had been reached, the judge readied the timekeeper. There were six drill teams on the huge platform, mostly robust Cornishmen from generations of hard-rock mining families. Stripped to their waists, their muscles bulged and flexed in the noonday sun. All had grown serious, ready for the competition and, they hoped, the 500 dollar prize money for first place. For such a large crowd, not even a whisper could be heard. All bets had been placed, and the moment had arrived.

With hammers raised high in the air, the hammer men watched the timekeeper as he stared at a huge gold pocket watch. The timekeeper nodded his head, and the array of sledge hammers broke the silence with ringing, piercing blows. The first blow shocked Jason so tragically that he forgot to rotate the drill, a stinging pain ringing through his hands and arms and down his back. The slam of the hammer sent fiery sparks and rock particles biting into his face and exposed arms. Then there was another blow every bit as forceful as the first, reminding him of the trip hammers in the stamp mills. "Rotate the bit!" Abe shouted hoarsely, bringing the hammer down again in an ear-ringing clang. Nervously, Jason tried to concentrate on his work, trying to hold the bit erect as he rotated it. He was nervous and frightened. He tasted the granite grit between his clenched teeth and felt it stinging his eyes. One miss of the sledge would cost him a hand. But something strange happened—he found a power deep within him, a strength to concentrate on the job at hand as Abe's rhythm picked up pace. The hole was deepening, aiding him in holding the bit erect and straight. Behind each team was a man with a water hose that wet the hole and flushed out the drill cuttings. A vapor of wet dust hovered in Jason's face, hampering his vision.

Down and up the hammers went, increasing in frequency until they reached sixty-eight times a minute, then seventy, and seventy-two, until they reached seventy-five times a minute. The audience broke into wild cheers, each rooting and screaming for their team as sweat covered the glossy, muscular hammer men. The pain in Jason's back had increased to numbness as he spent every ounce of his energy concentrating on rotating the bit in time with Abe's powerful sledge. Towering over Jason, Abe grunted behind each blow, sweat pouring from his balding forehead and trailing down his face in streams and raining before him. His glistening muscles rippled in the sunlight as his massive frame swung its weight into each mighty blow.

Lita screamed for her man, and Jennifer found herself caught up in the excitement as well. Unknowingly, she raised her fist and shook it in the air, calling at the top of her lungs, encouraging Jason, the man who appeared so small compared to the rest of the muscular miners. The children were lost in the ecstasy of the competition, hanging over the rope, their screams lost in the roar of the crowd.

The team next to Abe and Jason was from the Casey mines, a hardened pair of experienced Cornish miners deemed certain to win. With increasing power, the hammer man pounded with the force of a steam-driven rock crusher. His hammer raised quickly and came crashing down with a deafening ring again and again, until once it came down and there was no ring, only a muffled thud. Suddenly the hammer poised in midair and the crowd groaned, knowing what had happened. The drill-turner flinched, for a second out of his head, then quickly gained composure and glanced up at his towering partner. "Bring the hammer down! Bring it down!" Again the hammerman fell into a rhythm of blows as the hand that held the bit looked as if it was red with paint. Men cheered and women cried, but the bloody hands held and turned the bit. The blood ran down into the hole and mixed with the water, each blow splattering water, blood, and mud over the nearby onlookers. Soon the splashing out of the hole was thick and red.

With all his might, Jason tried to concentrate, but blood was splattering all over him and into his eyes. He dared not turn loose of the drill for fear the same thing could happen to him. He couldn't possibly wipe his eyes. He tried to blink it away, but it was impossible. There was no time to pray, but he yearned for an inner strength, something to sustain him through this longest fifteen minutes of his life. As if by miracle, he suddenly gained control with a new confidence—the fear had finally left him. The pain in his back had turned numb—it was all coming together and for a moment, he found himself a full man again.

Abe was beginning to slump after each blow, exhaustion quickly coming over him. Jason knew that in growing tired, Abe's accuracy would be questionable. Words came out of Jason's mouth, surprising himself. "Come on, Abe! You can do it! Reach down, get that extra bit. You can do it!"

This helpful encouragement seemed to snap Abe out of his slump as again he erected himself and swung the hammer with all his might. The blows came steady and fast, hard and true. Each ring of the bit now chimed musically to Jason. In a brief fifteen minutes, he'd overcome something that had been holding him back for a long time.

Old Abe had reached deep and given every ounce of strength he had. His throat burned like fire as he gasped for air. Just about when he thought his lungs were close to bursting and his arm muscles screamed for mercy, the timekeeper called, "Time!"

Leaning on his hammer, Abe was deaf to the cheering crowd, his heart pounding in his ears, and the ringing in his head almost made him collapse. Hands still shaking, Jason lifted the long bit out of a deep hole in the rock. He tried to stand, but his back had grown numb. It took him several minutes to straighten, using the drill bit as a cane. He looked at Abe and threw a hand on his round and sweaty shoulder. "Good job, Abe!"

Abe nodded, still slumped and leaning on his hammer handle. "I knowed you could do it, Mr. Jason!" Abe gasped between breaths. "I knowed you could do it!"

When the judge got down to the end where Jason and Abe stood tiredly, the platform resembled a slaughtering block because of the injured Cornishman. He pronounced the Cornishmen's drill hole evenly round and measured it while the onlookers had grown quiet—it was the deepest hole so far, reaching some thirty-five inches. Then he stepped over in front of Abe and Jason and did the same, measuring the hole in the rock before him. After careful scrutiny, the judge stood and announced, "We have a winner! Thirty-six-and-a-half inches! Congratulations to the blacksmith and his helper!"

The excitement escalated into a frenzied disbelief; a blacksmith and a cripple had won the drilling contest. Abe threw his big arm over Jason's shoulders, a wide smile covering his face. "We did it, partner!" Abe said, still panting.

Jason was beside himself, all problems forgotten. After getting paid in gold coins, Jason and Abe shook hands with the other miners, then left the platform. Lita immediately took Abe in her arms and gave the big, sweaty man a huge hug. As Jason descended the steps behind Abe, Jennifer's natural reaction was to do the same as she'd seen Lita do, hugging Jason, forgetting all else, including that he was a bloody mess. After the hug, she stood back and looked at him, his face glowing with pride. "You were great!" she said happily. "We need to get you back and get you cleaned up. You're a mess."

Glancing down, Jason saw he was sweaty and splattered with blood. "Yeah," he laughed. "Turning that drill bit is hard work!"

"It's brave work!" Abe said, overhearing them.

"Well, you two deserve something special," Lita said, all smiles. "We gonna get you cleaned up, then take you to eat some pies!"

~

The rest of the afternoon was a hoot. Jason and Abe had certainly worked up an appetite and made hogs of themselves at the adult pie-eating contest. Abe had summed it up best, saying, "It sure was good!" The children were even more spirited in their pie-eating contest, trying to eat without hands around their contagious laughter, while Butch was the comedian, getting pie all over himself. But as Abby had predicted, the big fifth-grader in their school, Big Timmy Blaylock, set a new record for pie eating by consuming four and a half pies in only fifteen minutes.

The sun lazily made its way toward the peaks in the west as the day cooled down and the sky darkened to a deep turquoise. Jennifer, Jason, Lita, and Abe walked home along the boardwalk in the lazy, late afternoon light. "I'm tired and I'm full," Abe announced sleepily.

"You done good today," Lita said. She pulled Abe closer as they moved slowly along.

The children tagged along behind, Butch causing Abby and Grant to laugh as he made fun of the pie-eating contest. As Jason and Jennifer came to some steps down off the boardwalk, Jason used his free hand to hold her elbow and help her down the few steps. But as they moved along, he didn't remove his hand. To be able to touch her made him feel very good.

Jennifer also did not mention his hand as it held her arm and helped her along the way. His touch was warm and brought back some old feelings she had ignored for so long. She treated it as if it wasn't a big thing, just the courtesy of a man helping a woman along in the darkening evening. But somewhere in the vagueness that surrounded her reasoning, she found great comfort.

CHAPTER

21

A Dream Comes True

The day had been a booming success as far as Jason was concerned. While preparing for bed, he could hear the partying outside that continued on into the night hours. Unbuttoning his shirt, he hobbled over to the open window, leaned on the edge, and peered out. Somebody had built a bonfire down the street, and a crowd gathered around it, dancing to the tune of a fiddle. Smiling, he turned away from the window and limped over to the small chair. He removed his shirt, then sat down to take off his shoes. In bending over, he noticed the small of his back was completely numb. *Must've been the drilling contest*, he thought. *That was quite a strain!* But when he stood to remove his pants, the heavy weight in the front pocket caused him to lose all thought of pain. The gold coins made a heavy, clinking sound. They meant much more than their dollar value, for they represented a quest he had conquered. The event had caused him to overcome a bitterness that had been like a lengthy illness.

Crawling into bed, Jason put his hands behind his head and sat in the flickering lamplight, staring at the open window. Although he was physically tired, he wasn't sleepy. Too many things kept his thoughts flurrying, all thoughts eventually reaching the focal point—Jennifer. *She was so beautiful today*, he thought. *It was kind of like the old days when we were together. She actually hugged me after the contest—and then she didn't mind when I held her arm on the walk home.*

These thoughts gave him a lifting feeling, until he could feel that queasy tingle in his stomach, the kind of sensation that sparkled with hope.

Abruptly, Jason's thoughts shifted direction. *Lance Rivers! What kind of man is he? Who does he think he is?* His blood rushed, making him feel hot in the face. *I guess Rivers thinks he's got control over her now—he thinks he can just run over her. He must think he's something to ignore her on a big day like today!* But secretly Jason was glad Rivers had made an error, since it gave Jason a chance to have the most enjoyable day he could remember for a long time.

Yet Jason knew his love for Jennifer was an undying flame. *Who am I kidding when I talk about leaving?* he thought miserably. *Even if she does marry that shyster, she still might need me. As little as he stays around, how's he going to look after her?* Jason detested Rivers and hated himself for it. *I've never let hate overcome me like this before!* he thought, disturbed by his own sort of self-betrayal.

Jason lifted the glass chimney and blew out the lamp. For a moment, the room reeked with the smell of warm oil. Lying awake in the darkness, he couldn't stop or even control his thoughts as they surrounded every aspect of Jennifer. He couldn't help but wonder, *Was she really attracted to me today? She certainly acted like it, just like old times.* This is where he wanted his thoughts to stop, but he kept rerunning the scenes of Jennifer's face, her approving hug, and her green eyes as he mentally constructed a portrait of this romantically mysterious woman he loved. "God, if You could only help!" he muttered; the thoughts circled in his head until he fell into a heavy sleep.

When Jason awoke, there was only the slightest hint that a new day lay just over the mountain; a pinkish tint played with the darkness. But he was barely awake as he lay thinking in the bed. He had had a dream like no other, a dream so real and lifelike that he had to be sure it was only a dream. Remaining very still, he scanned the room and surveyed his surroundings. The transition from this dream to reality had to be slow and cautious, since he really didn't want to leave such a peaceful place as this dream had taken him to.

As Jason's mind came around, he realized that the dream had been something special, for it had awakened a new spirit in him.

What had happened was nothing more than an average day in Black Hawk, but what wasn't average was Jason. He had been given a gift in this dream—a gift of vision. He noticed a light, or a sort of glow in every single individual. It wasn't a regular light, like sunlight, but something more like a living light, a light of warmth and humility. Everywhere he went, he noticed everyone glowed with this rich light, and in looking down, he found it emanated from him as well.

Slowly, as the fog cleared and Jason came to his senses, he was able to scrutinize the dream more clearly. *What was that light I was so attracted to? It made every single person entirely beautiful. There was no animosity, no lust, no loathing, no greed. The light was as if it were pure joy.* Thinking harder, he tried to recall a single word that best described the light. After a moment, there was no denying it. *Love, that's it!* he decided. But he needed more. Why had this dream made him feel so wonderful?

Rising from the bed, Jason walked over to the window and looked out. The street was littered with debris from the day and night before. The fire he had seen down the street still smoldered, a trickle of white smoke in the day's first light. The day thus far was still; not even the mills had cranked up yet. Turning, Jason went to put on his pants and noticed the cane hanging on the corner of the chair.

A sudden shock caused Jason to get so lightheaded that he almost lost his balance. In total disbelief, he glanced down at his own pale legs, which seemed stretched a long way to the floor. His back felt tired, but there was no pain. Scared to move and stunned by this new discovery, he just stood there waiting for something to happen. Nothing did. Skeptical but curious, he took a step, and then another, until he came to the faded mirror on the wall. He glanced at his bearded face to make sure it was still himself that he was looking at. Twisting a little and testing, no pain signals caused him to jump. Amazed by this, Jason pulled on his pants, then thought, *The real test—putting on my shoes*. That was always the most painful part of the day. Slowly, he bent over while sitting in the chair and put his shoes on effortlessly. "Incredible!" he said out loud.

Always trying to figure things out, Jason had the idea that his back had been jolted or shaken from the contest and that whatever had happened had put it back in line. But it wasn't a question he would dwell on long, because a new excitement intensified and motivated him to get moving. The back pain being gone and the ability to get around easily were practically a miracle, but the phenomenon of the dream and it having happened at the same time was too much. The joy he felt was so uplifting that he couldn't wait to get out on the street—he had a use for some of the prize money.

~

Sneaking out of the building undetected was easy at such an early hour. Jason casually made his way down the quiet and empty streets until he came to Polk's Barbershop. *Everyone must be sleeping it off*, he thought with some amusement. Casually, he sat on the bench in front of the shop and watched a new day come into being. Sleepily, the town slowly came to life. First, he saw a woman up on the hill hanging clothes on a clothesline behind her house. Then he saw a man on a horse cross an empty intersection a block away. A few miners walked together silently to work, obviously guarding sensitive ears and other problems caused by hangovers. Before long, a few freighters rolled by on squeaky wheels, the drivers like stone in their seats. The smell of the morning was mountain air laced with breakfast as smoke began drifting from stovepipes nearby. Completely relaxed, Jason had never felt more at ease or more peaceful.

"What brings you out so early?" a recognizable voice asked from beside Jason as a tall-framed man sat down beside him.

Turning, for once Jason was glad to see the preacher. "A vision," Jason answered. "Fancy, how you always manage to show up at the right time."

Also relaxing, the preacher laid his arm on the back of the bench and crossed his long legs. Jason noticed that he wore long and pointed black shoes, shoes that were well worn. Raising his eyebrows as if to question, Preacher asked, "Why is this the right time?"

"It's strange. I woke up from a miracle dream and walked over to my window, no more crippling back pain. I don't pretend to understand how my back got well all of a sudden, but I really can't understand the dream, not at all. It was a life-changing dream," Jason said earnestly.

"Please tell me about it," the preacher said.

After Jason had explained the dream as best he could, then described the light as love, he noticed a big smile on the preacher's face. "What is it?" Jason questioned, knowing the preacher had the answer. "What does it mean?"

"What happened to you, my friend, is, I feel, indeed a miracle from God. Let me explain. You see, every now and then, with His perfect timing, God gives us a slight glimpse of Himself, or a slight glimpse of heaven, if you will. It's to let us know what He's really like, what heaven's really like. This glow you called love—you were seeing a little bit of God, and it is true, He can show in every one of us. After all, He created us. It's my guess He wanted you to see this before He set you on your feet again. I still believe you are to be envied, for it certainly appears that God has big plans for you." Preacher seemed rather proud of his explanation. He felt sure of it. He then moved his eyes back down the street, noticing how the town had come alive within a few minutes.

Jason studied the profile of the preacher's face, a face of serenity. He noticed a similarity in the preacher to his very own patient father. His father had taken him on his knee as a boy and answered his simple, childhood questions. Now it seemed like the preacher was doing the same thing, answering childlike questions. Only now Jason wasn't so impatient with the preacher; he liked the answers he heard. He believed him. Even now, he was growing interested in what people said about God having something in mind for him. The recent events had lifted him above his problems so that he had a better and more understanding view of them, the ability to see a bigger picture rather than just focus on some tiny thing at a point in time. "I guess it's taken me awhile to come around," he muttered, half-thinking out loud.

"I always knew you would," Preacher boasted, slapping a hand on Jason's leg as he uncrossed his own in preparation to stand. "I never had any doubts." The preacher stood and stretched, then looked back down at Jason. "Waiting for the barber?" he asked.

"Yeah. A new man, you know. I feel like looking the part, thought I might get cleaned up a little."

Preacher nodded, then moseyed on down the boardwalk.

~

After his shave and haircut, Jason walked out into the morning sun, another mild summer day of bright sunlight in Black Hawk. If the mountains hadn't been in the way, he felt like he might be able to see for hundreds of miles. Walking on down the boardwalk, he headed for Jake Sandelowski's. It was time for some new clothes.

A little bell hanging from the shop door tinkled as Jason entered. It was a shop that spoke heavily of England, with British chairs and mirrors. A pipe tobacco smell and the unmistakable odor of new cloth irritated his eyes. On display were women's dresses in one window, and the attire took up most of the front of the long and narrow building. A man's suit was on display, the kind a dandy would wear, but this wasn't what he was interested in.

A rustling came from the back, and Jake appeared, walking quickly. He had a cordial salesman's smile and extended his hand. "Good morning, sir. How can I help you today?" Then Jake stopped and studied Jason, his manner momentarily set back. "Have we met? You look familiar."

"Stop it, Jake. It's me, Jason Stone."

Jake's mouth fell open. "Why, you've changed! You got all that hair cut off, and, and where's your cane? Just yesterday I saw you at the drilling contest and you . . ." His words trailed off in his dismay. He stared at Jason speechless, then his face lit up. He raised a finger before his face. "Oh, I see. A new man! And you need new clothes!"

"Now you got it," Jason said, smiling. "But I don't want any of that fancy dude stuff, just some decent clothes like you might see a businessman wearing."

"I've got just the thing," Jake said, leading Jason to the rear of the store. He was a young man and full of life, excited to be of service. "A young bachelor like yourself, let me show you what the ladies prefer—take it from me, I know from experience."

Jason knew of Jake's womanizing ways, but he let him make his suggestions. It wasn't long before the two made a compromise, Jason picking the toned-down versions of Jake's men's wear. Trying on a handsome brown suit and white shirt did the trick for Jason. The light vest had a snug and comfortable fit. "I'll wear this," he said. "You might just burn these," he added, referring to his old ragged clothes he'd taken off.

Jake laughed. Jason was acting a bit strange. He could no longer resist asking. "What happened to the cane? I thought you were crippled from a horse-riding accident. Did you experience a miracle or something?"

"Something like that," Jason replied. "I'll take these other two suits and these shirts and these pants. I like both pairs of shoes. I'll take them too."

"Certainly," Jake said as he professionally wrapped the garments. Undoubtedly, he was tickled with a fine sale so early in the day. "This should do. You'll have the womenfolk turning their heads now."

The first thought that came to Jason's mind when he left the store was turning Jennifer's head. She'd be surprised to see him on this particular morning, and he couldn't wait.

~

Carrying his packages, Jason was careful where he stepped in his new and squeaky black leather shoes. He couldn't resist smiling because he felt as good as he looked. Even the lilac water the barber had splashed on him had livened his mood. For once he felt whole again and was ready to take on whatever came his way with a new enthusiasm. As for Jennifer and her plans of marriage, well, so be it; it still didn't stop the way he felt about her and the way he was sure he'd always feel about her. He'd learned that anything could happen, and hope had become a real and intense brightness in his future.

The midmorning quickly warmed the chill from the air, the buildings facing south, bright in sunshine. Jason hurried along, eager to get back to the newspaper office. Ironically, he did pass a few women on the boardwalk and noticed that their eyes quickly ran up and down his frame, only to lock in on him for an instant too long. He smiled politely and continued on his way, a brisk canter to his step.

When Jason got to the office, he eased the front door open and stepped in. Searching the shadows, he saw Jennifer sitting at her desk with a cup of coffee, reading some newsprint. He set the boxes down and walked toward her desk. She had looked up when he entered, but it hadn't actually registered with her what she was seeing. After he set the boxes down and walked toward her, she realized that the stranger was Jason.

"Oh!" Jennifer uttered unconsciously, taking great care to set her cup of coffee down easily without jostling it. Dismayed, her eyes remained on Jason, her face an expression of total surprise. She'd almost forgotten what he looked like. The beard and long hair had hidden his now revealing and smiling face. Plus, he was dressed quite differently in a finely tailored brown suit and—there was something else. "Why, Jason! I didn't recognize you." She stood as he came nearer. "You look so different! You're walking!"

Spreading his hands, palms up, Jason held his wide smile. "I'm a new man, Jennifer. Something happened last night, something difficult to explain. When I woke up, there was no back pain, and I could walk normally again. I honestly believe that it was nothing short of a miracle from God."

The events of the day before had given Jennifer disturbing thoughts. What she had witnessed was part of the old Jason, the brave and unselfish man she had once known. Just watching him up on the platform with Abe had moved something deep within her, an old passion she thought she had laid to rest. Moving slowly, she came from around her big desk, her nimble, long fingers searching for loose strands of hair and shoving them nervously back into place. "This is wonderful!" She made a move to hug him but stopped halfway with her arms extended, then realized how ridiculous she was acting and went ahead and gave him a big hug anyway. "This is wonderful," she repeated.

Jennifer's fragrance stirred Jason as he put his arms around her. But maintaining his goodwill, he pulled back as his eyes searched her face. "Something much more has happened to me than just being cured physically. It's hard to explain."

The old light was in Jason's eyes, Jennifer noticed. It was the kind of light that exposed his love of life, a light she had missed seeing for so terribly long. Enamored, she said, "I can see that much more has happened. You're all cleaned up, new clothes and all. You must feel wonderful."

Glancing down at his attire, Jason nodded. "Oh this, yeah, well it was an afterthought. I had plenty of money from the contest, and I felt like a new man, so I sort of cleaned up. But that wasn't exactly what I was talking about. What I meant was, well," he paused, savoring the private moment with the woman he loved, "I had this dream, Jennifer." His face suddenly grew serious. "It was so vivid—I thought it was real! I could see this light in everybody, and it was a good light. In a way, I thought maybe I'd died and gone to heaven. But it changed me—it changed the way I see people now. I kind of understand."

A curious look gave slight expression to Jennifer's smooth face. She did sense something extremely different about Jason, as if he'd had some kind of life-changing experience. The man before her was quite handsome, but more than that attracted her as she tried to will away unwanted feelings. Her lips trembled slightly; her face was too close to his for comfort as she turned aside and moved a safer distance away. Now embarrassed, she felt her own secret passions had become clearly evident.

It was true, Jason could see that he'd disturbed her. "Perhaps we should talk," he suggested, his voice friendly and calm.

Turning back to him, Jennifer's eyes were filled with thoughts, while her mind arranged a way to say them. She took a breath first, then said with a vague force in her tone, "Jason, I know what we used to have, but things changed." She paused, casting her eyes down, then looked back at him almost apologetically. "And now it appears things have changed again," she said sadly. Standing near her desk, her hand reached down and her fingers lightly touched the desktop, then did a slow waltz as she spoke. "I'll always care for you, but you must realize I'm engaged to another. We shouldn't play with this thing. It's much too powerful and too dangerous."

Jason knew exactly what she was talking about. He too felt the great urges that were difficult to control. Moving forward, he came close again, and judging by the shock in her face, he felt like he was invading the very privacy she had just warned him about. He reached out and grabbed her arms just below the shoulder, as if holding her steady so that she might understand him. "Jennifer, listen closely, then I won't ever bother you like this again. I could never bear to see you hurt. All I want is to see you happy. That's how much I love you! If I can't make you happy, then maybe Rivers can, and if he can, then I'll be all right. I no longer have any animosity for Rivers. He's just a man, just like me, and he finds you irresistible, just like I do. I can't condemn a man for that." Jason stopped and looked hard at her. He saw fear in her eyes. "I don't mean to scare you. I'm a man of my word. All I want to do is help, anything I can do. Does this make sense to you?"

Now thoroughly confused and in an emotional whirlwind, Jennifer had to sit down. Releasing his grip, Jason followed her around the desk as she found her chair and retreated to it. A heavy weight seemed to snuff out the glow that made her sparkle. "Oh, Jason. I'm so worried. Where is he? What's he doing? How can he do this?" She raised her eyes, pleading for help.

Shrugging his shoulders, Jason smiled. "It's probably nothing, Jennifer. I imagine he's wrapped up in a horse deal, and trying to get the horses moved can be a problem. A group of thoroughbreds can be worth a tidy sum. I'm sure he has to look after his investment. It may have cost him a few extra days, something you probably shouldn't take personally."

This made Jennifer feel better since she had needed someone to talk to. But what was hard to understand was that Jason's feelings had changed drastically. "Jason, how come you no longer hate Lance?" she asked innocently, now feeling a little easier with him.

"Like I said, I had this dream. I see Rivers now as a man and nothing more. He has feelings and desires just like us, and like us, he makes mistakes. Everybody does. I'm sure the last thing in the world he'd want to do is hurt or disappoint you." Jason was leaning on the desk, over her now, his pleasant and convincing way of putting things easing her worries.

Her hand moved across the desktop and came to rest on top of Jason's. "I've had nobody I could really talk to about all of this. You have been so close for so long, always looking after me, and you never fail to surprise me. I thought I'd lost you to misfortune, but you always manage to do something to get my attention. I sometimes wonder if I know what I'm doing."

It was a question for the heart. Jason asked, "Do you love him?"

Jennifer looked Jason in the eye as long as she could, but she had to turn away to answer. "Yes. He's so kind and decent, and he makes me feel like I'm the only one in the world for him. He makes me feel like I'm somebody special." She said all of this dreamily, but added with a sour note, "Of course, he has to be around in order to make me feel this way."

"You are somebody special, Jennifer," Jason assured her. "Never let anybody convince you differently."

Glancing up again at Jason, she had the look of a scared little girl on her face, a little girl that needed to be told again and again that things were going to be all right. "You're so kind and unselfish about all of this. Jason, please forgive me. I know I've hurt you."

Smiling, Jason nodded, as if he was agreeing with a joke that had been played on him. "It was my own fault, Jennifer. Don't blame yourself. If I hadn't been so self-centered and bitter. . . ." He stopped, thinking about it. "Never mind all that. You did as you saw a need to, and I, well, I'm just a human being and I'm still around. Maybe I can make up for some of the grief I've caused you and your family."

The conversation had run its rough course, and now Jennifer felt like she'd let the great burden go. Again, she and Jason were quickly becoming close friends who could talk openly. Her voice softened, now somewhat wistful. "So, now that you're well, I take it you won't be leaving like you said you were."

"No way," Jason said, shifting his weight and standing erect. "You've got this big wedding, and I understand it's going to be quite an affair, imported champagne and all. I hope I'm invited, sounds like a wonderful opportunity to get falling down drunk." There was a twinkle in his eye.

"Oh, Jason!" Jennifer scolded. She'd been taken in before she realized that he was teasing her. A natural smile appeared. "Will you really come to the wedding?"

"Of course," Jason answered. "The best friend I've ever had in my life is getting married—I wouldn't miss it for the world!"

CHAPTER

22

In the Middle of the Night

Lita had spent most of the day helping Clara Brown with her clothes-washing business. Like Lita, Clara was a deeply religious woman, a black woman freed from slavery in Kentucky, who worked tirelessly to earn money to bring her scattered family to freedom in the West. When Lita met this remarkable woman, who most called Aunt Clara, a friendship was immediate.

"When we come here to the mountains," Lita said, bent over a washboard, her heavy fingers scrubbing a pair of miner's coveralls, "the first thing that happen to us was a man robbed us on the train, took all we had. It was mighty rough on us dis past winter, no money and all—but the Lord done took care of us."

Clara smiled; she was older than Lita but steady in her determination. "When I got here, I didn't have nothin' either. All I seen was dirty miners and I said to myself, 'Self, you ought to go in the clothes washin' business 'cause ain't none of these men got nothin' clean to wear.' So here I am. The Lord took good care of me."

None of Clara's hardship stories were beyond Lita, for she'd seen it all too in her days of slavery as she watched her family split up, never to be seen again. But the horror stories weren't out of bitterness but were more of a method of camaraderie. Now that both led lives remarkably improved over the old days, they began to spend more and more time together.

As the lazy summer day rolled into late afternoon, Lita said, "I reckon I better get home and cook up somethin'. I got a bunch of hungry mouths to feed."

Clara stopped her work and checked the time of day by the angle of the light. "All right then, I got to do the same."

Gathering up her few things and placing them in a bag she slung over her shoulder, Lita began her walk home. The walk home was easy, all downhill, down Gregory Gulch to Black Hawk. She'd come to know most of the regular townsfolk, and on the walk home she caught several compliments about that blacksmith husband of hers and his ability to accurately swing a sledge.

"Hello, Lita," a big man named Durfee said, tipping his hat. A stocky Cornishman, he'd competed in the rock-drilling contest. A large draft beer in his hand, he was obviously feeling pretty good, even a little wobbly as he showed his teeth in a big grin. "You tell that old Abe that I'll get him next year when it comes time for the rock-drilling contest. Who'd ever thought a blacksmith could swing a hammer like that?"

"That's all he do all day!" Lita remarked, pointing out the obvious. Then she smiled, for she had to brag a little. "You better grow some bigger muscles then," she advised

"That'd be good advice," Durfee agreed, holding up one of his huge and bulky arms to suggest they were little things. "I'm lookin' a might puny."

They both laughed as Lita went on her way. It was a good feeling to be known and liked in the summer mining community, a place where most of the working folks were happy immigrants. Glancing out at the dusty street, she saw a big freighter creak by, four black mules grunting against gravity as they climbed the hill. Then she noticed a young boy riding a pig, the switch in his hand a constant reminder of who was boss. She thought this a strange sight, since the pig was wearing a saddle.

Back at home in the kitchen, Lita prepared dinner, humming a tune under her breath. It wouldn't be long before everyone appeared, expecting something good to eat. Within the hour she had thick pork chops grilled in a skillet, a loaf of sourdough bread piping hot out of the oven, and a pot of tasty beans. And just like clockwork, Abe came in from the back porch where he had just washed up.

"Somethin' sure smells good," he said, smiling at Lita. "I'm hungry."

"You always hungry," Lita reminded him.

Grant and Abby rushed in and found their seats at the table. The summer days kept them outdoors, where they played and worked up an appetite.

"Take your hat off," Lita told Grant, and quickly he removed his hat.

"What we having for dinner, Lita?" Abby asked.

"Pork chops, child," Lita answered as she fixed the plates and set them on the table.

"Oh goody," Abby said. "I like pork chops. Is that what smells so good?"

"I reckon it's the sourdough," Lita said.

Lita was so busy that when she turned around with a plate in her hand, she almost bumped into Jason. She hadn't heard him come in, and when she looked up and saw him, she almost dropped what she was holding. The look on her face was utter disbelief. Jason smiled as the others froze, speechless.

"Maybe I should have warned you," Jason said pleasantly.

"Goodness!" Lita exclaimed, quickly setting the dinner plate in front of Abby. She turned back to Jason and threw her arms around him and gave him a big hug. "I told you so—I told you so! The Lord done did a miracle!" She backed away and examined the man before her. "Here you is like you used to be, all cleaned up and healthy and well. This is a grand moment. Praise the Lord!"

"Amen!" Jason added, actually proud to be back from the world of pain and bitterness he had disliked so much.

"Where'd you get those clothes?" Abby questioned, forever outspoken.

"I bought them with my share of the money Abe won in the contest," Jason said as he took a seat at the table. He reached over and gave Abe a pat on the arm. "I can thank him for that."

"I couldn't have done it by myself," Abe said honestly. He looked closely at Jason, as if an old friend had returned after a long departure. In Abe's mind, all happened for a reason, all was part of God's plan, but he was happy to see Jason revived. "Good to see you over that spell," he complimented.

"Yeah, you're good-looking again," Abby giggled.

But Grant kept his face down as he ate. He felt ashamed, because he had given up on Jason a long time ago, and their friendship had suffered greatly. In a way, he even felt like a traitor, since he held great admiration for Lance Rivers and he knew that Jason didn't like Rivers. Now that his old friend was back, he couldn't find any words that were appropriate.

Jennifer came in and instantly sensed the happiness of this little gathering, something of a gentle current drifting in the air. It was a peaceful setting, the afternoon sun throwing a long, soft light through the open back door. The aroma was homey and enticing. Jason's remarkable recovery had struck on a clear blue day and, without warning, had steadied their spiritual beliefs.

"What do you think, Lita?" Jennifer asked, insinuating Jason.

"Why, Miss Jenny, it's just like I said. God made him well and now he's walkin'." She sat down along with Jennifer so that all were now seated at the table. "He's lookin' good too!" she added.

Jennifer caught the subtle hint and it was true, Jason had never looked better. She found his presence slightly unsettling; her heart struck her chest gently; her breaths were short.

"Mr. Jason, would you like to give thanks?" Lita asked.

"I certainly would," Jason answered as they all bowed their heads. "Dear Father, we thank You for this fine food and this wonderful group of people, but more than that, I'd like to give thanks not just for the healing of my back, but for the healing of my soul, for I've seen the light. Amen."

For an instant, Jennifer was stirred so deeply that she thought she might lose control. There had been something in Jason's voice that disturbed her, something that aroused her emotions, a vague regret. But she quickly regained her composure and put on a face that was convincing enough, the kind of face that hid inner feelings.

~

That evening Jason stood at his window before bed, his eyes clearing from the lantern light as he watched the last dying light make the night sharper. The smooth, rounded mountains stood out softly in shallow perspective, and a deep purple essence hung on their outlines. In the far distance, the black, arrow-headed spruce cut into the sky. The summer evening was as soft as a gentle embrace, the kind that made him feel renewed and alive. *I've made it this far—I've got to look forward*, he thought. Deep down, he knew that it was hope that drove him, and he was glad. Within him was the knowledge that his nature had changed, and in this, he found peace. Well-contented, he retired, finding it easy to drift off to sleep.

The sounds of the mills and people in the street faded as the night grew darker, edging toward the early hours of morning. A sweet and cool pine smell moved down the slopes and refreshed the town. It moved down the streets and whispered through windows, invisible and penetrating, casting a spell over those who slept.

Lita heard it first, a thumping—something was moving downstairs. Abe laid beside her in a deep sleep, his breathing deep and regular. She quickly plugged him with her elbow, causing him to stir, then whispered, "Abe! Abe! Wake up. Somebody downstairs!"

"What?" Abe groaned.

Quickly rising from the bed, Lita found her housecoat in the dark. "C'mon Abe, somebody down there."

"All right," he mumbled as he struggled to crawl out of the bed. He fumbled in the dark to find his overalls, until Lita struck a match and lit the lantern.

Together, they silently crept down the stairs, Abe holding the lantern out so they could see the way. Then came the sound again, a muffled knock at the back door of the kitchen. Coming to the door, Abe held the lantern high and Lita called, "Who's there?"

"It's me," answered a ragged and tired voice.

Lita looked at Abe, extreme worry on her face, then unlatched the door. The lantern light caught the pale and drawn face of Lance Rivers, who slumped against the doorjamb. "Help," he said weakly, then fell through the door and collapsed facedown. Crouching over him, Lita and Abe could see the back of his coat was saturated with blood, a small hole in the center of his back.

"Quick," Lita said. "Get them lanterns lit in here and let's get some water boiling. This man's hurt bad!"

Abe did as he was told, and Lita grabbed a towel. Down on her knees, she rolled a moaning Rivers out of his coat; the back of his white shirt was brimming in a scarlet red.

"He been shot, Abe!" Lita said after a quick examination. "You better go see if you can find Doc Moss."

"Oh, Lord, help us," Abe said, leaning over to look for himself. "I'll hurry. He looks like he bleedin' to death."

Suddenly panicked, Lita dabbed at the bloody hole with a towel and then laid it on Rivers's back to soak up some of the blood. She quickly got up and scurried upstairs, calling out loud, "Miss Jenny! Miss Jenny! Come quick!"

In an instant, the entire household was awake and down in the kitchen. Upon seeing all the blood, Jennifer lost her head. "Oh please, somebody do something! Jason!" she said fearfully, turning to him.

Jason was as shocked as everyone else but managed a suggestion. "Let's get him off the floor—we can take him up and put him in my bed."

Grant and Abby stood in their pajamas, watching silently in horror. "Grant, you take your sister back upstairs and take care of her," Jason ordered.

"Yes, sir," Grant mumbled, half-terrified from all the blood. He had a problem bringing the scene into reality, not understanding how a man as great as Rivers could be in such a dilemma.

Rivers was semiconscious, but at least aware of where he was. "Jennifer," he moaned pathetically.

"Lance, what happened?" Jennifer asked, her eyes already wet with tears.

But Rivers was in no condition to answer questions. He groaned wearily as the three did their best to get him upstairs. Once in Jason's bed, Rivers's face twisted in agony as they rolled him over on his stomach.

"Abe gone to get the doctor, Miss Jenny," Lita said.

Coming to her senses now, Jennifer wanted to do all she could to help. "Well, let's get him out of these bloody clothes and at least get him cleaned up," she said with urgency.

Working as a team, the three worked diligently, having Rivers cleaned up by the time Abe led Doc Moss into the room.

Doc Moss hadn't been in bed long when Abe had awakened him. He'd had a fair night of cards and, in turn, drank his share of beer. Fortunately, he was a little drunk, which was a lot better than being hung over. Doc scanned the room and the people in it, then from behind his thick glasses, his eyes went down to where Rivers lay on the bed. A puckered bullet hole leaked blood into the towel beside it. Removing his coat, Doc rolled up his sleeves and then opened his bag. "This may not be pretty," he said solemnly. "I'll have to probe around to see if I can find the bullet. He'll be in a lot of pain."

Jennifer stared at Doc dumbfounded, as did Lita and Jason, as if they were waiting to be told what to do. Abe already had the good sense to leave. Doc simply stared back at the searching eyes impatiently. "Well!" he shouted. "Go on out. You don't need to see this. Lita, you stay here, I might need an extra pair of hands."

Jason led a frightened Jennifer out of the room and pulled the door closed behind him before he spoke. "Come on downstairs. I'll make a pot of coffee. I have a feeling we won't be getting any more sleep for a while."

Down in the kitchen, Jason sat across the table from Jennifer. She slumped, her face in her hands, distraught over a cup of untouched coffee. Every now and then they could hear Rivers scream in agony, and each time, Jennifer shuddered. Feeling helpless, Jason reached across the table and let his hand rest on her shoulder. She felt frail and cold.

"Don't worry," Jason comforted. "I'm sure Doc will do all he can."

"How could this happen?" Jennifer wailed. Obviously, she was upset and beside herself. Fear and disappointment tormented her troubled mind. She felt lonely and shut out and very weak. All she could picture was Rivers's pale and sunken face. The face she had seen didn't even look like the man she knew.

"A man shot in the back," Jason tried to explain. "I'm thinking he was probably ambushed."

Jennifer couldn't hold back any longer and began to sob. Standing, Jason quickly came around to hold her while she cried it out. The hours seemed like days as they waited impatiently for the doctor's conclusions. Outside, the night was aging toward dawn, and a fresh morning wind stirred the smell of the mills. A train whistle announced the coming of a new day as the light of day slowly cast an orange tint upon the windows, then brightened into a clear light. Abe came into the kitchen, silently patted the coffeepot to see how hot it was before he poured himself a cup, and joined Jason and Jennifer at the table. The two eyed Abe expectantly.

"They still in there," Abe said, which was all he knew.

Soon there was a rustling, and Lita showed her tired face, perspiration on her forehead. She looked bewildered and tired. She carried a mess of blood-soaked and wet towels in a washbasin and set them on the counter. Jennifer jumped to her feet and confronted Lita. "How is he, Lita?"

"The doctor right behind me," she offered wearily.

Doc Moss came in, stooped from the night's long work. His face looked old and worried. Jennifer quickly addressed him, "Well?" she demanded.

"Pour me some coffee and sit down over here," Doc ordered impatiently. The old man sat at the table and waited for her to put his coffee in front of him. When he got it, he turned all of his attention to the metal cup, carefully stirring in a spoon of sugar. He then removed his glasses and rubbed his tired eyes. Jennifer sat at the table, leaning forward on her elbows, hopeful. Jason sat erect, now alert and eager for the news as well.

Replacing his heavy spectacles, Doc shook his head, as if disgusted. "He's a strong man. Most men would be dead by now." He squinted, reluctant to continue. "I've seen just about every kind of bullet wound you could imagine. I was a surgeon in the war—I've seen it all. What I'm trying to say is that this is not good. He's lost a lot of blood, and it's weakened his condition considerably. The bullet entered his back, and it's too close to his heart for me to try and remove. He's bleeding internally." Doc stopped and shook his head again.

"What are you saying, Doctor?" Jennifer questioned urgently. "Isn't he going to be all right?"

Doc sat silently, as if he didn't hear the question. There was no indication that he was going to respond, when all of a sudden he said, "I'm afraid not."

Jason sat nervously fidgeting with his fingertips as he watched Jennifer's heart sink. Hope was a pleading cry in her expression. "But there is something you can do, isn't there?"

"Any attempt to get that bullet out of there will kill him for sure," Doc Moss said. He again took a sip of the tar-black coffee as he suffered as the bearer of bad news. "He's conscious, and I've given him a good dose of laudanum to ease the pain." Doc turned his eyes to Jennifer, eyes that were old and wise and knowing. "Jennifer, I'm not going to lie to you—he might make it through the day, but that's about it. I'm sorry."

Horrified, Jennifer froze in disbelief as she stared at the old man. Lita stood off to the side, silently watching. Abe kept his head down, afraid to see what this news was doing to Jennifer. Jason felt the pain she was suffering. The doctor got slowly to his feet and picked up his black bag. "I left the laudanum at his bedside, in case he grows too uncomfortable." The exhausted man shuffled on out the back door, the bright light a strain on his eyes.

Nobody had moved yet when Jennifer placed her hands on the table and pushed herself to her feet. "There's always the chance of a miracle," she said, glancing at Jason to indicate he was literally walking proof. "I'm going up to see him." She bravely held her shoulders back and left the kitchen.

Abe raised his head and looked at Lita, then at Jason, wonder in his brown eyes. Lita knew the doctor had made a correct diagnosis, since she had been in there and had seen it all with her own eyes. Jason drummed his fingers on the table, a genuinely sincere but helpless look on his face. Silence hung heavy in the room, the promise of the new day having already been destroyed.

~

Silently opening the door, Jennifer let herself into the room where Lance Rivers lay dying. She slipped over to his bedside and pulled up the little bentwood chair and sat down. His big hand lay beside him and she took it into hers, softly caressing it. Rivers's eyes opened slowly, and he turned his head slightly. The sunlight filled the little room, a morning light that came in with the sounds of the day. She tightened her grip, pulling his hand closer to her chest.

"Jennifer," Lance whispered. His expression lightened, replacing the lost and lonely look it had held previously. "I was worried I'd never see you again."

Her heart pounding in her chest, Jennifer felt the desperation, a definite sadness in her smile, one that she probably wasn't aware of. Many things raced through her mind, but for the moment, she was content to be close to him.

"I'm finished, aren't I?" Rivers mumbled. His eyes were sunken and his cheeks hollow, his lips dry and cracked.

A flashback for a moment revealed the face of Drake DeSpain in Jennifer's mind. She was rudely reminded of having been through this once before, watching her loved one slowly die from a bullet wound. The memory was as painful as the present, as she once again felt like the loving, helpless observer.

Rivers watched her closely, sensing the urgency in her eyes, the deep suffering she experienced. He managed to give her hand a little squeeze, a painful but faint smile on his dry lips. "For what it's worth, I love you more than ever," he uttered. "I'm sorry all this had to happen."

If she hadn't have already cried it all out of her system, Jennifer knew this would have been a good moment to fall apart. But she held on, wanting to make the most of the time at hand. "And I love you, too," she answered with all the sincerity she could muster. "Lance, what happened? How could something like this happen?"

Rivers turned away, his mind complex with her question. "I got shot in the back. There's no defense for that—I don't even know who did it."

"Were you robbed?" Jennifer asked, her voice soft and low.

Again Rivers seemed perplexed by her questioning, as if he wanted to tell her more, yet something prevented it. "No," he mumbled, now growing tired quickly. He closed his eyes, the weariness and the laudanum placing him somewhere in between sleep and reality.

Patiently, Jennifer sat the morning away, spending most of her time looking at her sleeping fiancé. His breathing was heavy and raspy and irregular. *I can stay by his side. At least I can do that for as long as it takes*, she thought sadly. *He's a good man. I wonder why anybody would shoot a good man. Dear God, none of this makes any sense to me. I pray that You help him! Give me some answers. Show me how to handle all of this.* Her own weariness pulled her down into a low and depressing mood, but at least she'd be there during his waking moments.

Downstairs, Jason felt useless. He wanted so much to do something to help—anything. The children hung inquisitively close underfoot, asking questions that couldn't be answered. His thoughts were with Jennifer, but he'd feel like a fool if he interrupted her at a private moment like this. He couldn't possibly barge in that room with her and Rivers, although he was curious. *What's she doing up there?* he wondered. *She's been in there for hours.* It was one of those things where he knew he'd have to be patient and wait. In the meantime, he did honestly feel sorry for Rivers, and he did this easily by putting himself in Rivers's shoes. *What if it was me? All ready to marry the most wonderful woman in the world and get shot in the back and know that I'm going to die. Why, that's absolutely worse than just losing your life. You lose the loved one you were prepared to share your life with, having never tasted that experience.*

His many thoughts provoked Jason to take a walk. He stirred the morning dust with his new shoes as he moved along, his mind muddied by the confusing mental process of searching for understanding. In the middle of the night, all of their lives had been changed by unexplained trouble at the back door. And now there would be much suffering.

CHAPTER

~ 23 ~

Confession

The news of Rivers being shot traveled quickly. Grant and Abby sat on the front porch of the office as the curious gathered and asked the children all sorts of questions.

"Mr. Rivers is shot in the back, in a bad way—that's all I know," Grant had said again and again. He was quickly growing irritated.

Butch came running, finding his friends bored with folks that loitered out front. "Let's go," Butch said, waving his arm. Grant and Abby followed like pet geese as Butch led them to an alley down the way. "Tell me the story," he demanded.

"There ain't nothin' to tell," Abby said, frowning. "Mr. Rivers came to the back door in the middle of the night, and when me and Grant got down to the kitchen, he was lying in a puddle of blood. They said he was shot in the back."

Butch's eyes grew wide with excitement. "I bet Rivers was in a shootout of some kind. I bet he got some of the bad guys."

Disturbed about his future being ruined, Grant couldn't find much glory in seeing his friend Rivers shot and now supposedly dying. "It don't matter," Grant cut in, half-angry. "Now he's going to die, and there won't be no horse ranch or nothing. He was going to teach me all about his operation, but I don't guess it's gonna happen now."

"You don't know!" Abby argued. "Anything can happen."

"That's right," Butch agreed. "He ain't dead yet, is he?"

"I don't think so, or we'd hear about it," Abby figured. "I don't guess Mother will be getting married for a while, at least until he gets better or something."

Still soured, Grant could only see loss. "He better get well!" he said with some force behind it.

"So, do you think it was a bushwhack or a shootout?" Butch persisted. He liked the idea best that Rivers had been in a glorious gunfight.

"Who knows?" Grant answered, offended. He rearranged his hat, the one Rivers had gotten for him that resembled the one the horse rancher wore. For Grant, the whole mess was a sad affair, destroying his grand visions of wealth and success. On top of it all, he really liked Rivers and viewed him as a hero.

"I seen a fella shot once," Butch bragged. "It was a bloody mess."

"This was a mess too," Abby said, recalling Rivers on the kitchen floor. "But it was scary. I didn't know somebody could have so much blood in them."

Still, Butch found glamour in the event, although he didn't approve of shooting people, not unless they really deserved it. "C'mon, let's get on back in case something happens. Wouldn't want to miss anything."

Racing along, the children ran back to the newspaper office where small groups huddled outside, whispering speculations and wondering if Rivers was going to pull through. Oddly enough, no betting had started yet as to how long Rivers would live.

~

For most of the morning and part of the afternoon Rivers lay unconscious with a fever. Jennifer sat tirelessly wiping his head with a damp rag, whispering encouragement. She couldn't take her eyes off of the physically rugged, handsome man who had depths of feeling. He had been mumbling in his sleep, fighting for his life. He came to, slowly opening his eyes and taking in all of Jennifer with a forlorn look.

"Jennifer," he said in a raspy voice. "There's something I want you to do."

"Oh, Lance," Jennifer said, almost pleading, eager to fulfill his desires. "Anything I can do, I will."

"Get a lawyer up here," Rivers said, and then coughed. He was trying to put some force in his voice, but it simply wouldn't come.

"What for?" Jennifer asked. "A lawyer can't help."

Rivers blinked, as if the words he wanted to say were the most difficult he'd ever spoken. "Let's not pretend. I don't have much longer." He swung a deliberate glance back at her. "I don't have a will. I want to leave you everything."

Stunned, Jennifer brought her face closer to his. "But you can make it, Lance. I know you can."

"Then do it as a precaution," he said, his eyes glaring and glossy.

For a moment, Jennifer just sat there, unable to move. The finality of death was a vague vision she never could comprehend until long after such an event was over. But she got up and went to the door, where she stopped and looked back at Lance. The once powerful, big man already resembled a corpse, his frame appearing thin and his face hollow. It was a pitiful sight, the kind she knew she'd never forget. She left to find somebody to go fetch a lawyer.

It wasn't an hour later that Jason appeared with a young lawyer in tow. He knocked gently and then entered the room. The small room reeked of death. "This is William Smith. He's an attorney."

Smith was a small man with little, round spectacles and a carpetbag in his hand. He seemed a bit nervous. "I understand you want to make a will," he said, looking at Jennifer.

"No, you fool!" Rivers spat rudely. "Does she look like the one who's dying?"

Smith had thought Rivers was asleep because his eyes were closed, but when Rivers spoke, the little man had jumped. "Yes, sir," Smith said, digging in his bag and producing pencil and paper. "And how would you like for this to read?"

"Everything!" Rivers said impatiently. The pain twisted his face when he spoke. "I want to leave her all of my earthly holdings."

The lawyer scribbled on his paper as Jason turned to leave. "Wait," Smith said. "I need an outside party as a witness."

Jason glanced at Jennifer, and she gave him an expression that said she wanted him to stay, that she needed his support.

After a few minutes, Smith looked to Rivers. "Are you strong enough to sign this?" he asked, his voice shaky.

Rivers held up a weak hand to accept the pencil and paper but couldn't quite manage it. "Help me, Jennifer," he groaned.

Assisting Rivers with the paper, Jennifer helped guide his hand as he signed his name. Then Jason jotted down his name as a witness. Smith stood, eager to leave. "I'll have this drawn up nicely with copies immediately. I'll bring it back for your approval, Mr. Rivers."

"You just make it good," Rivers said. "I'll be dead by the time you get done."

"Lance," Jennifer warned, noting the fury in his tone as the little lawyer rushed out. "Please be calm."

"Give me the laudanum," Rivers said, looking over toward the bottle. "This pain is unbearable."

Jason watched as Jennifer administered the drug to Rivers and then helped him wash down the bitter taste with a glass of water. He found Rivers suddenly pitiful; the man with all the big plans was now a dying shell with nothing. He didn't know whom he felt sorrier for, Jennifer or Lance. Feeling uncomfortable, Jason slipped out of the room, leaving the two alone.

~

Jennifer had skipped dinner; the exhaustion had drained her. She had left Rivers's side for a while to go freshen up, to escape momentarily from the death that lurked in the room like a heavy fog. A thousand thoughts fought for a place in her mind, each bearing its own discord, all working together like an army bearing her to certain defeat. There were the memories, the good ones with their sweet little tingle of happiness, and these brought about sorrow and despair, while the undesirable memories, such as remembering Drake on his dying bed, were reminders of the longsuffering that the death of a loved one could bring. There was no way to shut these thoughts out as they gathered like clouds of a storm; she prepared for the inevitable.

When Jennifer returned to Rivers's room, the last of the day shone in the window. She went to light the lamp and found Lance staring into nothing, his eyes wide open and unmoving. Her heart skipped a beat as she froze, searching for some detection of life.

"I'm not dead yet," Rivers muttered.

Jennifer sighed with relief. "The pain, how is it?"

"I don't feel any pain anymore, Jennifer," Rivers said, as if he were disappointed. "I'm certain it's near the end."

The restrained fury in his words had reached into her and set off a wild and running imagination. She had only heard one man speak like this before, Drake DeSpain, her late husband, as he had laid on his deathbed. Rivers's words, like Drake's, had reached a violent depth of expressiveness.

"There are some things I've got to set straight before I die," Rivers said as he turned to look at Jennifer. His words were slow and deliberate. "It's what a man sees—and what a man feels. How can I say it, Jennifer? Is it the spring wind after a hard winter? A fire in the night? Something in a woman's eyes or her lips or the turn of her body? Or something to make him kill if he has to?"

Coming close to his side, Jennifer placed a gentle hand on the side of his face. "Lance, would you like to pray?"

A sympathetic smile faintly curled his thin lips. "Pray? Not hardly. I'm not ready to pray. I have to make a confession before I could think of praying."

"A confession?" Jennifer questioned, a lightness in her voice

"Yes—it's only fair. It's something I have to do." He stopped and rested, taking a few shallow breaths, then said, "I fell in love with you instantly the very first time I laid eyes on you—on the train."

A quizzical look held Jennifer's face in a kind of suspense. She didn't recall ever seeing him on a train. "But we didn't meet on a train." She thought that perhaps Lance was delirious.

"Yes, I kissed you—after I robbed you."

Shock set Jennifer back. A sudden anger cut the wires of reason and raised her instinct of fear. Then there was a raw, primal fighting that pushed her on. Reaction came soon afterward, disbelief at first, dismay; then the fatigue of betrayal pulled at the lines of her face. "You're the Kissing Bandit?" she muttered faintly.

"That was only a gag for the most part, but I meant it when I kissed you." Rivers watched her closely; he could see the news was tearing her apart. "No, I'm not a kissing bandit. I'm a bank robber and a highwayman, a ruthless no-good thief."

Jennifer fought her emotions and desperately searched for a reasonable conclusion, an excuse to make this not true. "But you're a successful horse rancher—I saw your ranch and all of those thoroughbreds, the ranch hands . . ." Her voice died off as she started putting clues together from the past.

"How do you think I bought all those things?" Rivers asked. "And my outfit at the ranch, why, they're nothing more than an outlaw gang, what's left of them. Most of them were killed in this last robbery attempt; the same one that's going to kill me."

A mixture of hate and regret pulled at Jennifer as she sat frozen in a state of dismal melancholy. "What happened?" she asked weakly.

"I wanted out," Rivers said. "I figured since we were getting married, I needed to pull one last big job, then I'd send the gang on their way. We tried to hit the Bank of Denver, but something went wrong. They were waiting for us. I think I'm the only one that escaped, but a bullet caught me. Now it's over." The lamplight was kind to her face as he noticed it go to grave wonder. He saw the situation without illusion. He had spent the active years of his life dealing with hard men, trading on their fears and weaknesses, matching their sly and hidden trickeries, avoiding their traps and setting his own, with always the stark knowledge in his head that someday the game, for him, would go fatally wrong. There were times, as now, when the lonely knowledge knocked down his guard. He'd wished for peace and personal happiness, knowing it would never really come to him. This was his present feeling, and she could see it in the dying flame in his eyes.

Jennifer was doing her best to be brave, but it was difficult. "That day the bank was robbed here, when you came to my office, then helped the sheriff, was that you? Did you rob the bank?"

He nodded weakly.

"How could you do this to me?" Jennifer sobbed, now breaking down. "You ruined our lives by robbing my life savings, then came along and bailed me out with my own money like you're some kind of hero. You trapped me and tricked me when I was so desperate that I had nowhere else to turn. I thought you were a Christian, raised in a Christian home, but you're nothing but a horrible deception!"

"Christian home!" Rivers mocked. "Jennifer, I never had a real home. All that about Kentucky was a lie. I was abandoned by my mother and placed in a Christian orphanage in New York City. It was a nightmare in deprivation, and although I studied the Bible," he paused to gasp for breath before continuing, "and knew about God, I always blamed Him for my situation. I fought Him, Jennifer—I thought I could do it on my own. I didn't want His help."

"You talk about God like He was real. You must believe in Him," Jennifer said bitterly.

"Of course I do," Rivers said. "I've read the Bible many times, and I guess I understand most of it, but where was God for that poor child that was me? I fought, Jennifer, and I fought hard. A man makes his own ways if he wants to survive, and I chose my own road. I didn't have time for God just like He didn't have time for me. Now I'm reaping the reward for sin, which is death, but I don't dare cry. Maybe you'd like to know; there's mighty few people I admire. Most have a price or a weakness. But I admire you, and I've loved you as much as I know how to."

The impact of the entire story had made its mark, and now Jennifer accepted it. The hurt and the pain would remain for a long time, but whatever had happened was done and no matter how bad it was, it was over. A simple compassion filled her as she saw before her a pitiful and sad dying man, a man who'd played the game and lost. As drained and wrung out as she now felt, she could only think of one thing. "It's not too late, Lance. God is a forgiving and loving God. You must ask Him to forgive you—accept Him into your life before it's too late."

Rivers tried to smile. "You amaze me," he said in wonder. "You're nothing but good, and now we have the good trying to save the bad."

"Pray with me, Lance," Jennifer pleaded, taking his hand.

"How about you, Jennifer? Can you forgive me?"

She bit her bottom lip and closed her eyes. The agony of the straightforward question put her on the spot. She knew God was forgiving and loving—but could she do the same? It was one of those things she might do in time, but for the present she resented all Rivers had put her through, and she hated the kind of man he really was. "I'll pray for God's help, Lance. This is all such a shock to me. You've robbed me, deceived me, taken advantage of me." She paused, holding back the pressure of tears. "God will forgive you, Lance. I'm only hopelessly human. I'll get over it in time."

The hardness had left Rivers's face as he, for the first time, saw death very near, a concept most uninvited. It was a moment that might bring any man to be humble, and Rivers had indeed known about Christ early in his sad life. "I remember the children in the orphanage praying together. It was comforting, Jennifer, for we had nothing else. But still, children died. Our faith didn't save us. I only wish I could've been different. I'm sorry I didn't accept the Good Book and its ways." He seemed to be lost somewhere in a memory, then uttered, "I don't see how a man like me could ever make things right with God."

Rivers looked at Jennifer and saw tears in her eyes. "It's funny. I thought I was really something. I really did. And now I can see that I was nothing, absolutely nothing."

"But God loves all of us, and He loves you," Jennifer said. "Christ didn't suffer and die on the cross for nothing. He did it for sinners, for us."

Rivers smiled. He knew the story well. It haunted him, running from God and living a life of evil. "Jennifer, let me settle with my own Maker." He closed his eyes, a grimace on his face. He knew his time was short. "There's something else I have to do, Jennifer. You have to get Grant in here. I've misled him terribly. I've got to tell him the truth."

Hesitating, Jennifer gave it some thought. Her natural instinct was to hide the horrible truth from everyone, but then she knew that wasn't the right way. She'd never be able to survive behind a lie. She knew the truth would hurt Grant, but it was something that had to be done. "I'll go find him," she mumbled, standing. Disappointment was obvious in her face.

When Jennifer came back with Grant, he looked timid and shy, scared of death and scared of the dark form that barely resembled the Lance Rivers he had known before. He couldn't bear looking at the man in his present condition, which distorted the grand perception of the person he so dearly admired.

"Come closer, Grant," Rivers said, lifting a weak hand.

Cautiously, Grant approached, fearful of catching something horrible that he couldn't detect.

"Son, I know you think I'm somebody special, and it's my own fault for I've misled you." Rivers took a painful breath and continued, slightly lifting his head. "Don't be like me, Grant. I'm no good. I've led you on and lied to you. I'm nothing but a lousy bank robber. I was the masked man that held your mother up on the train. And now I got shot in a holdup, and I'm paying the price." Rivers leaned back on his pillow, his strength quickly draining.

At first, Grant didn't understand what he was hearing, or he didn't want to hear it, the story being such a far-flung impossibility. *Not Rivers!* he thought. *Anybody else, but not Rivers!* But then it registered, squashing him like a heavy boulder as Grant felt a flood of hot blood heat up his neck and cheeks. Never had he been so taken in by anyone. He was angry and felt like a fool. Unable to stand another second in the presence of this liar, Grant scrambled from the room, slamming the door behind him. He went straight to the hat rack and pulled down the hat he wore that was like Rivers's and stomped it flat on the dirty floor. A few moments later, he stormed out into the darkness of the evening.

~

That night, as Jennifer sat next to Lance, exhaustion pushed her into sleep. But something woke her in the small hours of morning just before dawn. A soft but chilly breeze stirred the curtains in the window as the lamp flame flickered and almost went out. She glanced at Lance. He lay still, his mouth open, his expression frozen in surprise. There was no mistaking—he was dead. She stood over him and stared, hopeful that she was wrong but knowing better. The great man that had plundered into her life like a conquering nomad and had captured her heart now lay dead before her, a pathetic scare-crow-like figure—Lance Rivers was gone forever. Although his confession sickened her, feelings ran deep for this man she had planned to marry. She felt that beneath the contrived actions, there was some goodness in him, for she had often felt it. She lifted the sheet over his face, her eyes tearful, but she didn't cry. "Farewell, Lance," she whispered. "I pray you 'made things right,' as you put it."

It was almost too sad to cry about, but it left her feeling empty and hungry for some form of security she could rely on. It was a time she sought God for comfort, but harsh reality had a way of being impossibly persistent. She got up to leave, having no idea what she was to do next.

Lying in her bed, Jennifer couldn't sleep. She felt whipped down like the grass under a heavy thunderstorm. If there was anything she wanted, it was to be comforted by a friend, somebody understanding—like Jason. Yet how could he ever forgive her for being so naive and foolish? Since Rivers occupied his room, he had gone over to the Gilpen Hotel and checked in. *What am I going to do with everything Lance left me?* she wondered. *It's all stolen*.

Finally, first light colored the window curtains a pale orange. Jennifer gave up on trying to get any rest and got up. She knew there were arrangements to be made, and she knew she'd have to contact the town marshal and tell him everything. It would be a hectic day.

Doing the best she could, Jennifer tried to freshen up, but the dark circles under her eyes couldn't deny the way she felt. Shuffling downstairs, she found Jason, Lita, and Abe drooping over their coffee cups as they sat at the table in silence. They all raised their eyes to her expectantly.

Jennifer stopped and mumbled to the floor, "He's dead."

Rising slowly, Jason came over to her and took her in his arms. "We'll do all we can to help, Jennifer, promise. Don't worry about a thing."

Abe stood up and placed his hat on his head. "I'll go get the undertaker, Miss Jenny." He patted Lita on the shoulder with his big hand as he left, her face weary with worry.

"There's something I must tell you," Jennifer said in a low and shaky voice, pulling away from Jason, a faraway look in her tired eyes. "Rivers made a confession before he died. He said he was a bandit, the same that robbed us on the train." Her shoulders slumped.

Jason and Lita stared at Jennifer silently, unable to comment. The moment held the room suspended in time, the truth taking a moment to sink in. Lita said, "I never would've thought dat! May God have pity on him." There was a distant anger in her voice, one that expressed her hurt feelings.

For Jason, it was a matter of a number of unknowns adding up; his intuitions about Rivers had been correct. There had been something definitely shady about the man, and now it made sense. But foremost, he was worried about Jennifer. "I'm sorry," he said sincerely.

He's probably thinking "I told you so," Jennifer thought. But then she looked into Jason's comforting eyes and saw no animosity, only care and concern. She stepped forward into his arms as he held her in the dim, kitchen light. No words were needed. It was a time of mourning.

Lita shook her head in disbelief. She had, until now, considered herself an expert in judging people, but Rivers had fooled her entirely. It would take a while for her to get things settled in her own mind.

~

The town marshal sat in a chair next to Jennifer's desk taking in the whole story without a single change of expression on his long face. His hat sat in its usual place, far back on his head to reveal the shock of stiff, black hair above his forehead. Jason watched as Jennifer told her revealing story. The marshal licked his lips under his walrus mustache, then stuck a finger rudely in his ear and twisted it, as if he had a deep inner itch.

"Well, I don't know Miz DeSpain. Maybe he was what he said he was, but there ain't no proof. And as for the will and all them things he left you, why, the law can't say where he got them." He stopped and thought it over a little longer, reviewing basics, which seemed to strain him slightly. "Nope. I can't take that property unless you just want to outright donate it to the city. It's up to you—there's no legal action I can take."

Turning to Jason, Jennifer looked for answers. Jason spoke first. "Thanks, Marshal. We felt it was only right to report what we knew. At least you can rest easy knowing that he won't commit any more crimes."

"That much is certain," the marshal said as he got up to leave. He strutted toward the door, still turning over the information in his mind, and stopped and turned. "You know, I'd have never thought it of Rivers. He just didn't seem like that kind of fella—all smart and educated and all."

"He fooled everybody," Jennifer added.

As the marshal left, Jennifer turned to Jason. "I can't keep all of that stolen property," she admitted firmly. "What am I going to do?"

"You should keep what's yours," Jason advised. "After all, it *was* your money he took. As for the rest of it, what about donating it to a church?"

Saddened, Jennifer turned away. "You know how the churches are here, with congregations of maybe ten or fifteen people. How many would it help by donating to such a small group?"

A light came on in Jason's eyes. "I know," he said positively. "Preacher could put it to the best use—he's all over. He knows who needs help."

Jennifer seemed to brighten up at this prospect. "You're right, he *is* all over. His church is all the people in many places. He would know where the money was needed the most."

"So be it then," Jason said. "We'll make some kind of arrangement with him, see how he wants to handle this."

Silence crept between them. There was one piece of touchy business left. "The funeral. It's in two hours."

"I know," Jennifer answered. "It wouldn't seem right if I didn't go."

"Then I'll take you," Jason offered politely, "if you'd like."

"Yes," Jennifer sighed. "I'd like that very much."

CHAPTER

24

Statehood

Truly, Jennifer and her clan felt the lingering pain of being betrayed by Lance Rivers, except for Jason, who had all along been suspicious of the domineering man. The funeral had been brief, and attendance was low as the rumors took root and began stirring the towns of Black Hawk and Central City. Some of the talk placed Jennifer in a precarious situation, where doubt and distrust matured into fabricated stories, insinuating she aided a fugitive of justice. The household at the newspaper office quickly discovered the brutal discord of rising mistrust, the injustice of the innocent being accused.

In her room, Jennifer folded the expensive wedding dress and laid it softly in a trunk. She had the good sense to be thankful that the wedding hadn't taken place, but her heart saddened at the thought. *It's like I'm cursed when it comes to matrimony. These ambitious men I get mixed up with, only to be left heartbroken.* Like an abandoned ship floating in an empty sea of crushed romantic dreams, she felt distant and alone.

Outside, Grant stood on a stool beside Midnight, by the small makeshift stable, the glossy coat of the thoroughbred shining under the curry brush he worked in his hand. No matter how he tossed the thoughts around in his head, they always came back to the same thing—he'd been made a fool of. His trust had been broken into fine and irreparable pieces. Although he wanted nothing to do with anything of Rivers's, he loved Midnight, a horse he considered he'd earned with a very painful payment.

When Jason approached, Grant lowered his eyes to the ground as he kept working the brush. Jason was another matter, a good friend he'd jilted in favor of the glory Rivers brought. *I let Jason down*, he thought, the memories painful to recall. *I ignored my best friend when he needed me the most—and all because I thought I was some kind of big shot, hanging around with Rivers and all. Life isn't fair! Why didn't God show me the way? Why didn't He help me?* Grant's face held a frown as he worked the horse's black coat. He couldn't bring himself to look at Jason, who now stood close by.

"Midnight's looking mighty nice," Jason noted, the horse turning his head at his name.

Sneaking a quick glance at Jason, Grant couldn't help but notice how decent he looked, his respectable clothes and clean-shaven face, his hair short and well-groomed. This was the old friend he knew, the one he'd loved. "Yeah," Grant mumbled, too embarrassed to say anything more.

"I was thinking," Jason continued, "maybe I could saddle up Dolly and we could take a ride—maybe go up to Nevadaville and see the new mining works they got up there."

Grant's hand arrested the currycomb on the horse's broad rump. "I dunno," he muttered. "I don't much feel like riding."

"I can't think of a better way for two men to have a little talk than while riding. Might be a good time to get a few things off our chests."

This had some appeal to Grant. Inside, he was about to burst. There was always the chance Jason would listen to him, maybe even forgive him and help him through his bewildering crises. "I guess we can," he said softly as he stepped down off the stool and went over to the tack shed to get his saddle.

Gathering up Dolly, Jason put her bridle on and saddled her up.

Riding up Gregory Gulch and through Central City, huge, puffy clouds of white and gray cast a cool shade. It was a pleasant summer afternoon, the streets bustling with the day's business. Grant hadn't said a word as Jason kicked Dolly up beside the young man on his tall, black steed. "You want to talk about it, Grant?"

"What's to talk about? I'm an idiot," Grant said sharply.

"I'd know about that," Jason confided. "You're just an amateur. I've been an idiot plenty of times. As a matter of fact, I'm an expert at it. I could probably give you lessons."

Grant threw Jason a sly look to see if he was being made fun of and decided Jason was being serious, making fun of his own ridiculous mistakes. They cut their horses off of Main and up the hill toward Nevadaville. Soon they were alone on the mountainside, speckled in sunlight that streaked through the cottony clouds. "Are you mad?" Grant asked.

"Of course not," Jason replied. He smiled a little. "What happened to you could happen to anybody. Why, look at Lita and your mother; they were fooled by Rivers too. Don't blame yourself, Grant. All you can do is learn from it—life has to go on."

"But I sort of ignored you, and you were my friend." Grant glanced over at Jason to see what his reaction was, but Jason was looking ahead. "I wasn't there for you like a friend ought to be," he said meekly.

Jason cocked his head and turned his attention to Grant. "Don't worry about it. I was being a hard case, only thinking of myself, wallowing in self-pity and, in general, mad at the world. I don't blame you. I wouldn't have had anything to do with me either."

For the first time, Grant smiled. Jason had a likable way of getting under his skin. "You mean we can be good friends again?"

"Why sure!" Jason said happily. "Everybody makes mistakes. You made a mistake; I made a mistake. Let's forget it. Forgiving is the way of real men, Grant."

Now Grant was wearing a smile he couldn't restrain. "You seem so different, like you're happy about life. Is it because Rivers is dead?" Grant asked, a little fearful of prying.

"Not hardly," Jason replied, a bit more serious now. "You see, the change that came over me happened before Rivers returned. Aside from healing up and being able to walk again, you might say I saw the light."

Giving this some thought, Grant had to ask, "By seeing the light, you mean something about God?"

"Absolutely! God showed me the light, and it was wonderful. I see everything differently now. It's kind of like I can see the spirit in people, and believe me, no one is bad all on their own. That comes from somewhere else."

Digesting this, Grant rode on as Midnight grunted up the steep grade. He liked the words Jason spoke. "Do you think you could teach me how to see the light?"

"I can surely help," Jason offered gladly. "It's something we can work on together."

"I want to do that," Grant said.

"That's a deal, good friend!" Jason said as he leaned over and extended his hand. They shook on it, two friends together again.

~

Afternoon drifted into evening, the mountain atmosphere like a sedative. Lita made a quick and easy dinner of some fresh vegetables she had purchased from a vendor on the street. There was corn so sweet that she served it boiled, a refreshing delight right off the cob. She had tomatoes too, red and vibrant and tangy. A pile of sliced roast beef sat beside the vegetables, and a fat loaf of bread rested on a wood platter next to a large knife for slicing. "Now," she said, talking to herself, "if anyone hungry, they got the fixins."

About that time, Jason and Grant came in, both beaming with the afternoon's success but hungry from the ride.

"What's to eat?" Grant asked. He was getting to the age where hunger was perpetual.

"It's on the table," Lita said, pointing a finger. "Tonight everyone helps themselves."

"Say, would you look at that!" Jason said excitedly. "Where'd you get those fresh vegetables?"

"I keep my eyes open, that's how!" Lita teased.

"Abe's not in yet?" Jason asked, noticing the place was kind of quiet. He peeked through the door and saw the front office was dark and empty.

"He done ate and gone back to work," Lita said, disappointment in her tone. "Since y'all won dat drillin' contest, he been working day and night sharpening everybody's drill bits."

By now, Grant had his plate fixed and sat down at the table. Jason wasn't far behind. Lita was about ready to leave when Jason asked, "Seen Jennifer around?"

Lita saddened at the question. "She not feelin' well, Mr. Jason. She done gone on up to her room."

Lita left, and Jason and Grant ate dinner together, talking about innocent and pleasurable things that friends talk about. "Are you still working on your book?" Grant asked, his mouth full.

"No, I haven't worked on it for a long time, but you can bet the ranch that I'm ready to get back to it," Jason admitted happily. "The book may not sell out west, but I bet it gets some attention back east."

"How can you get started again?" Grant questioned, definitely curious, since writing was one of his premium interests.

"I don't know. I just do it. I think all book writers have their spells, but a sincere writer never quits trying."

Grant liked this advice as he warmed up to Jason more and more. "I'm really sorry about what happened, Jason. Now I know how much I missed you."

"I missed you too, Grant," Jason said, happy that matters were resolved. "We'll get caught up on things, I promise."

Grant believed this and looked forward to again learning from his true friend, Jason Stone.

~

Dark came late on this summer evening as the clouds cleared out, giving way to a deep, violet-blue sky. Up in his room, Jason dug out his old manuscript and began reading through it. The old ideas slowly returned as he made notes, working on the remaining plot of the novel. It was mostly written—but a great deal of work remained. The light from the window faded, and he fired up his lamp. Time became nonexistent when writing was the chore—hours flew by. Catching himself, he realized it was getting late, the noise from the street dying down to a low pitch. Setting his work aside, he thought of Jennifer. *I wonder how she's doing? Maybe I should check on her.* Quickly rising, he went to her door and knocked gently. There was no answer. Carefully, he turned the knob and peeked in. The room sat idle and empty in the darkness.

~

Jennifer had sat in a chair at the window watching the day wane. Depression had brought a terrible blackness that surrounded her like a heavy blanket. The humiliation of her terrible experience was now taking its toll—a lost lover, betrayal, and now the people of the town eyeing her with a mounting pressure. Part of her wished she'd grabbed Lance Rivers and shaken him violently until she'd shaken some sense into him. The other side of her felt sorry for him, sorry for herself and lost promises. The small room grew darker and darker and closed in on her—it was getting late. Grabbing a shawl, she threw it over her shoulders and left, her thoughts idle and forlorn.

Out on the streets, the crisp and cool mountain air chilled Jennifer's cheeks as she moved slowly along. Red-eyed men full of drink watched her warily, thinking a woman out at a time like this had but one purpose. Yet she had no idea of the danger that lurked nearby; the banging music and laughter pouring out of the saloons drowned out the catcalls aimed at her. Well into the night she strolled aimlessly, overcome with despair. The night had a quality of memory as her mind went wearily among the days of the past, and every event was colored a dull gray. She wandered on past the Gilpen Hotel, unsure of any destination. Ahead, she could hear the locomotives hissing and steaming in their stalls at the station, the mammoth iron creatures forever ready for another day of mule-like work.

Wandering on, she found herself in front of the gingerbread house some called the Lace House. It was a decorative affair where the carpenters had brought a storybook look from their native country. The carved woodwork covered every eave and roofline. It stood proud and tall over the street. To her, it represented everything a family dwelling could—a husband, a wife, and cheerful children. Its warm and cozy cottage-like face lifted above her, and the stars twinkled in the moonless sky, silhouetting its gables as she gazed up at it.

There was something in the scene that made her even sadder; the life she'd wished for had eluded her.

Memories reeled her through her past, a past void of the complete family she had wanted with all her heart. It became suddenly and rudely apparent that what she had wanted the most in life had never really existed at all. It was a simple desire: a man who loved her, was true to her, and respected and took care of her. *Is that so much to ask?* she wondered, her heart sinking. All she wanted now was to find some answers. If she could, she would have cried it all out, but for some reason, the tears wouldn't come. Although she thought she had loved Rivers, he had hurt her beyond anything she could have ever imagined. It was hard to cry for a man who'd misled her and lied to her, a man who had led a life of evil under a veil of respect. Staring at the Lace House made her wish she had it to do over again, its lonely presence before her a wistful cause for shame.

A shuffling in the shadows caught Jennifer's attention. Fear came instantly to her, an instinct that told her to run. Quickly, she moved along, but she could feel she was being followed. The saddened despair was replaced by a heart-thumping fright. Heavy footsteps behind her grew closer. Now she was rushing frantically, trying to place her steps in the darkness. The presence behind her was like some sort of evil, seeking her out like a predator seeks its prey. Suddenly the boardwalk ended in blackness. A misplaced foot threw her off balance. Unable to see the ground coming up at her, she misjudged and crashed into it abruptly. The shock of the fall temporarily stunned her as she came to her knees, slightly dazed, dirt on her face and hands.

"Ah, a lady in need," a husky voice said.

Glancing up into the pitch, Jennifer saw a big, black shadow lurking over her. His face was dark and bearded, a whiskey bottle swinging loosely in one hand. In a quick and powerful movement, he reached over and snatched her up like a weightless rag doll. Pulling her close to him, he whispered in a foul, whiskey breath, "How about you and me, dearie? I could use some sweet company tonight."

"Let go of me!" Jennifer screamed, fighting to get loose.

The burly miner was strong as an ox and had no intention of

releasing her. "Don't worry, honey," he laughed as he dragged her along. "I won't hurt you none."

"Let the lady go!" a voice demanded out of the dark.

Startled by the interruption, the miner turned to address the stranger. He held Jennifer like a captured rabbit. The man confronting him, he could see, was dressed like a dandy, his face a dark threat in the shadows—a mere silhouette. Disgruntled, he growled, "Find your own. This'n here's mine."

"Let her go or I'll drop you dead where you stand!"

These were the kind of words this miner had heard before. Coming from the well-dressed man, he knew the sound of a man confident with his gun, and he'd seen bigger and tougher men than himself lying bleeding to death on a barroom floor because they had doubted. He wasn't so drunk that he figured the woman was worth dying over. "Take her!" he barked as he shoved Jennifer at the shadow. "But I tell you, this ain't right." He turned and staggered off, glad to get off so easy. Those fancy dressers weren't only experts with cards but usually deadly with a gun, something he sincerely respected.

The hand that clasped Jennifer's shoulder had a warm and comfortable grip. The shadow pulled her to him. "Jason!" she cried, hugging him tightly.

"Jennifer, I was worried about you," he said softly in her ear, his face against hers.

Now she was shivering with fear, grateful to God that Jason had come along. She didn't want to think of what might have happened had he not. It had been silly and childish to go wandering off like that in the middle of the night, drowning in self-pity. "Jason," she cried again, more softly, burying her head on his shoulder. "Hold me close."

Having held his emotions for a great while, he hugged Jennifer with every bit of feeling he had. This woman he loved dearly, and he would never let her go again. *This time things will be different!* he thought stubbornly. He reached for a handkerchief and gently wiped her face, an endearment in his touch.

Confidently, he turned and walked Jennifer home, her head on his shoulder, his arm around her neck. She was dazed and dismayed, confused by all that had happened. However, their needs for the moment were mutual. A warm and tender understanding offered the security they both had been searching for.

Passing the light that spilled from the windows onto the boardwalk, Jennifer gathered herself, steady in Jason's arms. "How'd you turn that wicked man away so easily? Do you have a gun?"

"No," Jason answered as they moved along through the nightlife that frequented the streets.

"But . . ." she muttered.

"I wasn't afraid," Jason interrupted. "I'd do anything to protect you."

These words comforted Jennifer as she snuggled up closer in his arms. A tingle of wonder enlivened her. The old spark, no matter how she had tried to douse it, had never left. What she had questioned became obvious now as the spark became a flame and warmed her throughout.

~

When morning came, Jason found Jennifer sitting in the kitchen over a cup of coffee, talking with Lita. Their conversation stopped abruptly as he entered, both pairs of eyes following him over to the cupboard where he found his stained coffee cup. They still weren't quite used to his sharp appearance, his shaven face and trimmed hair, his newly found attitude of happiness and understanding. Both Jennifer and Lita watched Jason closely, as if expecting some words of great wisdom.

"Mornin'," Jason mumbled and pulled out a chair. "You two seem mighty quiet."

"Naw. Miss Jenny was just telling me about last night," Lita said, her voice full of wonder. "It's a good thing you come along. How'd you know where to find her?"

Jason shrugged his shoulders as he sipped the hot coffee from the metal cup. "I don't really know. It was sort of like Somebody was showing me the way. I'm thinking God had something to do with it."

"You know He did!" Lita rebuked, certain. "How can you doubt such a thing? Why, look at yourself, your body healed, you all cleaned up and lookin' mighty fine, and most of all—your soul's been healed. You just like a brand-new man, and God done all this for you!"

Smiling timidly, Jason nodded in agreement and then glanced at Jennifer. Her eyes had settled on him but seemed to be looking through him entirely, as if she were lost in thought. "Jennifer," he said, "are you feeling better this morning?"

Snapping out of her trance, Jennifer was caught off guard. "Oh, yes—I'm fine." In reality, she was beside herself, lost in grief and embarrassed over the matter with Lance Rivers, embarrassed over her irresponsible act the night before. The events of the past few days were settling in; the realization that Rivers was dead and gone had finally hit her. But most of all, she felt sorry for herself, having been made a fool of, and now the town stared at her with accusing eyes. "Everybody thinks I'm a crook because Rivers was," she mumbled with a trembling sorrow in her voice.

"After all you been through?" Lita retorted. Her patience grew short. "The Lord pulled you through every time! Why are you giving up on Him now? There's always a way!"

Jennifer glanced up, wanting to hope, wishing Lita was right.

Speaking up, Jason said, "Why, sure there is! You need to print an editorial—you could call it 'The Lance Rivers Story.' Tell everything you know and be truthful about it. As for the inheritance, tell the people what you plan on doing with it, how you want to get it back to the people. I bet we'll sell a lot of newspapers."

Brightening at the suggestion, Jennifer asked, "Do you really think it will work? Do you think people will believe me?"

"Sure they will," Lita assured her. "Everybody believes what's in the paper."

"Well? What are we waiting for? Let's get to work," Jason said, standing and waiting for Jennifer.

"You two!" Jennifer said, now smiling. Her features had changed. She lifted her face, now appearing fresher. "How would I ever get along without you?"

~

With an angel-like face, Abby watched from an upstairs window as all sorts of people flocked to the office below to buy a newspaper. *Everybody wants to know about the secrets of Lance Rivers*, she thought bitterly. *He's dead now—what difference does it make? Why can't they be happy with that?* Somehow, the rebellious side of her secretly admired Rivers. In her mind, he was something of a hero, a master of deception, a man who had elevated himself to wealth and fortune. He'd been a man above hurt and pain. *If only he hadn't been so unlucky*, she thought.

Down below on the street, she caught a glimpse of Grant talking to Butch. She noticed something wrong in the way Butch held himself, his shoulders slumping, his hands in his pockets as he stared at the ground where he made marks with the toe of his boot. Quickly, she left her perch at the window and ran downstairs.

Outside, Abby strolled up to Butch and Grant as if she had only happened by. Butch glanced up at her sheepishly, then let his eyes wander off to the mountainside.

"What's wrong?" Abby asked.

Grant smirked and then looked to Butch, waiting for him to answer. When he didn't, Grant said, "Butch has to leave, Abby."

A hot flush rushed over Abby's face. She wasn't sure what emotion she was feeling, but it soon turned into anger. "Why do you have to go?" she stormed.

"Uncle Mike says we've worn out our welcome here," Butch replied.

"But where will you go?" Abby asked, desperation in her young voice.

"Oh, I dunno. Maybe Abilene, maybe Tombstone. Uncle Mike ain't sure yet," Butch replied, his tone quickly becoming apologetic.

Coming closer, Abby stared under the brim of Butch's hat, into the shadow of his face. "You can't leave—not now!" she insisted. "You're the best friend I've got!"

"I'm sorry, Abby," Butch said meekly. Then he lightened up a little. "Abby, I promise I'll find you again. I will! I'll get rich and famous, and I'll come get you!"

By now Abby's young face had grown intense, her dark blue eyes reflecting the hurt that she felt inside. She wanted to thrash out at Butch for having gained her affections—now only to leave her. She wanted to cling to him so that he couldn't escape. The tangle of fear and loss pushed her near that edge she'd been to before. First her father and then Rivers and now Butch. It seemed like every time she grew close to a man, he left her forever. Life was nothing more than a series of disappointments and heartbreaks. Her eyes grew wet, and she turned and broke into a run back to the newspaper office.

Butch's glance followed Abby until she disappeared. "I guess she don't like good-byes," he murmured.

Grant didn't either. He admired Butch's street smarts and his spunk. "When you leavin'?"

"In the mornin', I reckon," Butch said, feeling a little clumsy at telling one of his best friends farewell.

"Well, I guess I'll be seein' you around," Grant said as he extended his hand for a shake.

Taking the hand offered him, Butch gave it a limp shake and then pulled back. "Yeah, I'll be seeing you around." He turned and shuffled half-heartedly on down the street, slumped under a heavy burden.

Grant watched Butch go until his friend rounded the corner and was out of sight. The feeling he had was like his stomach was an empty cavern with ghostly echoes that ached with pain. This new experience of losing a friend was something he didn't care for.

~

"I want everything in this will to go to the preacher," Jennifer said, "except for the money he stole from us. That part is rightfully ours."

William Smith looked at Jennifer through his small, round, and thick spectacles. His eyes were so magnified by the glasses that he resembled someone looking through a fishbowl. "Yes, Mrs. DeSpain," he acknowledged, and quickly jotted something down on his pad.

Jason smiled, proud of Jennifer for what she was doing. The church she'd picked to donate the ill-gained property to was the church of the itinerant preacher. "How's it feel to be rich?" Jason asked, looking over at the preacher.

"It feels wonderful," the preacher said. "I've always thanked God for being rich. As for all this property, well, I'm sure the needy will be thankful for all the help I'll now be able to give them in the way of food and goods." His face was long, drawn, and well-tanned, like old leather, yet a delight sparkled in his wise eyes.

A deep sense of satisfaction came over Jennifer as she smiled at the preacher. "I suppose you'll sell the ranch and horses and all of the other holdings."

"Certainly," the preacher answered as he looked over the list of property items. A slight smile touched his lips as he read something on the list. "Except for this," he said. "You'll have to keep this particular item."

"What?" Jennifer asked curiously, unable to imagine what he was talking about.

"This gold mine that Rivers owned. I can't be any part of trying to sell that," the preacher said with a hint of laughter in his voice. "Every miner in town knows the Wild Horse Mine never produced a thing. The miners used to laugh behind Rivers's back the way he poured money into that useless hole. No, I can't be a part of trying to unload that. I doubt you could pay anyone to take it."

Shrugging her shoulders, Jennifer looked to Jason for advice.

"Oh well," Jason said. "Every man has to have his dream. I guess it won't hurt anybody if it just sits there."

After the meeting, Smith left with his instructions to get the matter transferred into a legal document. Jennifer offered a warm farewell to the preacher as Jason followed the tall man outside, where they stopped on the front porch.

"That's a fair chunk of fortune you have to divvy out, Preacher," Jason commented into the afternoon light.

"Yes, it is. But if you've seen what I've seen—the starving, those without shelter, people freezing, young children sick from neglect, then you'd know what a great help this is," the preacher admitted gravely.

"Strange how all these things work out," Jason said, thinking out loud.

"In your case as well, I noticed," the preacher said, laying a hand on Jason's shoulder. "You were a stubborn soul, but a little faith can go a long ways. It appears God has shown you His blessings."

"Indeed," Jason admitted.

"And the woman, Jennifer—?"

A glimmer of hope appeared in Jason's eye as he looked at his friend, anticipation accompanied by a shy smile. "I've got a ways to go yet, but I have a hunch there's a chance."

"Keep your faith, my good man," the preacher said, slapping Jason on the back. "Keep your faith."

Warming up to this encouragement, Jason took a moment to let it sink in. Then a quizzical expression revealed a thought he had. "Preacher, I was wondering, who are you? Do you have a real name?"

"A name?" the preacher mused. "Let's see, I've been called all sorts of things, some not so good. Most folks refer to me as the Snowshoe Itinerant."

"No, I mean do you have a given Christian name?" Jason asked the bull-throated old preacher.

"Yes, of course. John Lewis Dyer."

"Well, Reverend Dyer, you've certainly had a positive influence on my life. I want to thank you," Jason said, reaching to shake the preacher's hand.

"My pleasure, and positively a pleasure for the Lord," Dyer said, taking Jason's hand and clasping it with both of his. "The Lord has great plans for you, Mr. Stone—never believe any different!"

"I won't, " Jason said.

The preacher left, his tall figure visible for some time on the street as Jason watched him depart. *That's some man!* he thought. *If only everyone could be a little more like him!*

~

The August 1, 1876 headlines of the *Advertiser* read: THE CENTENNIAL STATE—STATEHOOD FOR COLORADO!!!

The late afternoon was typical for midsummer, warm and quickly cooler as the sun dropped behind the muscular mountains, leaving a brilliant copper reflection on the flat-bottomed clouds. Jason and Jennifer had closed up shop for the day and sat on an old bench on the front porch. Red, white, and blue bunting was strung from every corner of every building in sight with banners that shouted the Spirit of '76, all in celebration of statehood. Tired from having printed and sold hundreds of newspapers that day, Jason and Jennifer leaned their weary backs against a rough and weather-grayed wall.

"Looks like we're in for another all-night celebration," Jason said, gazing down the street where a crowd gathered through a dusty haze for a street dance. "And now there's a governor's election. I suppose John Routt will win. Big celebrations—kind of like Independence Day."

"There's something different about it," Jennifer observed. "Not just a July Fourth party, but something strangely exciting, like it's something more from the heart."

Turning to Jennifer, Jason caught her attention and gazed into her eyes for a long moment. Confidently, he placed his arm around her neck and pulled her close. "It's all from the heart, Jennifer. That's what it's all about."

Suddenly Jennifer was overcome with a warm passion, a feeling she'd known once before with Jason. "Everyone has been so nice to me since I explained what happened in the editorial. But, Jason—the change in you has been the most astounding of all," she said softly. "I'm not talking about your appearance, but something much deeper."

"I've seen the light, Jennifer," Jason said calmly. "It made a different man of me. I think it's the Holy Spirit—it's a kind of inner wisdom, one that brings peace of mind and generosity of the heart."

"I'm sorry, Jason, about everything. I must seem quite the fool," Jennifer said, her voice sincere.

"Don't blame yourself," Jason said. "I was a terrible character to have to get along with. Circumstances gave us a severe challenge, but in the end, as I'm so often reminded by our close friends, it's the results that are important." He paused a moment, then added, "Jennifer, we can never be strangers again."

Something in what Jason had just said, something in his eyes, caused Jennifer to reflect on the past year—its dangers and desperation, the terrible mistake she had almost made, the companionship with Jason she'd almost lost. "Hard times have bonded us—seems we've been through it all," Jennifer agreed, reflecting on the past year. "If it hadn't been for Lita, I might have lost faith, but hers never wavered, like a guiding star in a desolate darkness."

"You weren't alone. There were plenty of times I almost gave up," Jason agreed, thinking back. "Lita and the preacher both had a lot of patience with me, and now I understand what they were trying to tell me—that faith and hope are the things that carry us." But then he turned his attention to the present. "Now I have one important thing remaining."

"Oh?" Jennifer questioned.

Pulling her closer, Jason kissed Jennifer on the lips with all the passion he could muster. It was the kind of kiss that meant everything in the world to him, a kiss where he did all he could to show how much he loved her.

At first, the surprise display of passion frightened Jennifer, but when she felt the kind of meaning it had, caution vanished like a windswept vapor. Like a phantom from the past, the kiss awakened her, bringing a distant dream to reality. It was a good and wholesome feeling; a current tingled her nerves—it was a moment of escape into a wonderful place full of good and giving things. By the time Jason pulled away, any fear she might have had was long gone. She said, "That was wonderful."

Jason smiled and held her tightly, comfortable in their relaxed position. "My love for you is the strongest thing I've ever known. And, Jennifer, I'll always love you and always take care of you—if you'll let me. That's a promise," he said boldly.

The corners of Jennifer's mouth turned up pleasingly as she held a certain deep and inviting look in her eyes. "That's a wonderful promise," she said, squeezing him a little tighter. She put her head down on his chest, and a small fountain of joy seemed to bubble up inside her. He was warm and he was real—and he loved her. That was enough!

She was used to reading other people's stories. Now she was writing them—and adding a new chapter of her own.

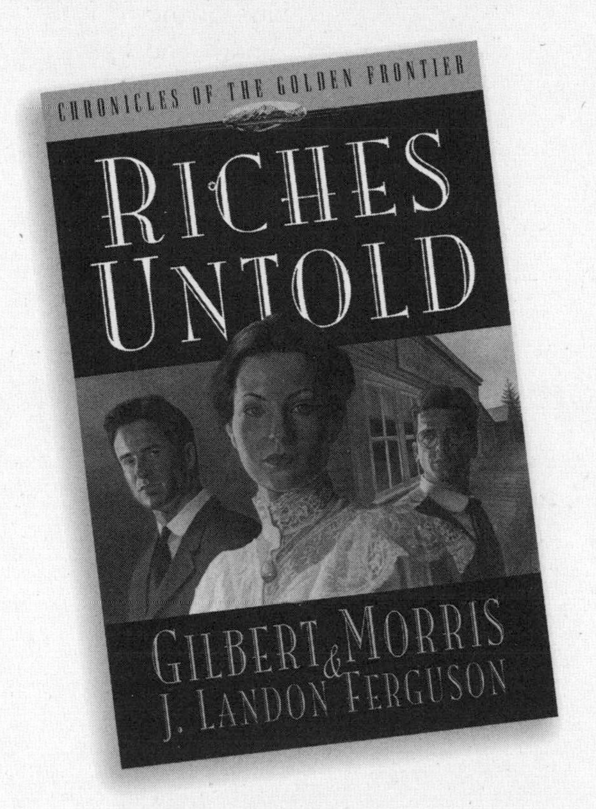

It doesn't take long for young Jennifer DeSpain to realize that marriage is nothing like the romance novels she secretly reads. When tragedy strikes, she boldly moves to a Nevada boomtown to run a newspaper, determined to make it a success despite its significant problems and, with the help of some colorful friends, to make a difference in the lives of the miners.

Life couldn't be better. She finds romance, purpose and success in Virginia City, Nevada. But what Jennifer doesn't yet realize is that she could have so much more—if only she could see the love that is standing before her.

BOOK 1 IN THE CHRONICLES OF THE GOLDEN WEST